Our Desperate Hour

Our Desperate Hour

Novels of the Great War

John F. Andrews

46 North Publications, llc

 Formatted with Vellum

From a Marine Father to his sons and their comrades.

Semper Fidelis.

Foreword

This is a novel, not a history book. It is a work of love; an ode to Marines and to all the Americans who fought in World War One, their "docs", and their families.

Map of France
Location of The Battle Front in May, 1918

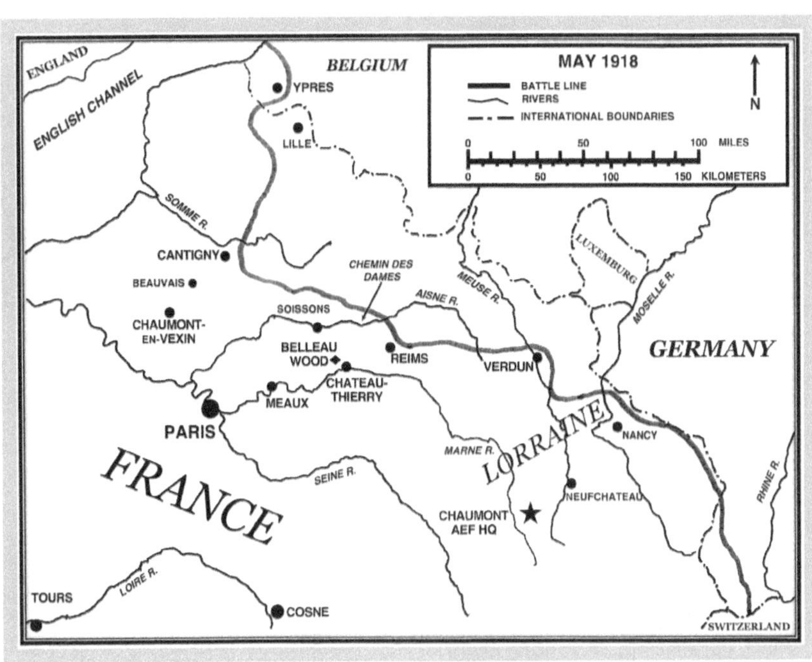

Chapter One
Major Albert "Ab" Johnson, US Army Reserve

Paris, France
Thursday, May 30, 1918

The army lied to me. And I think it's about to get worse.

My old friend Ira Cunningham—now Major Cunningham, US Army Reserve—charges toward me with a scowl that tells me my arrival is unwelcome. His fists are clenched. I overpay the cabbie who brought me from the train station to get him out of my hair.

Ira stops two feet from me. I face him and narrow my eyes. Do I extend a hand or duck?

"We've gotta talk." Ira glances back at the building behind him. "Now. Not here."

I snatch my luggage and double-time it to keep up as he leads me into a café two doors down. Empty sidewalk tables and paper tape criss-crossing the windows to prevent them from becoming shrapnel flash a warning. The war is near.

Wary faces glare at us when we enter. The waiter frowns as he takes an order. The chef, wearing an immaculate white double-breasted chef's coat, apron, and striped trousers, hustles us to a window table away from the other patrons. I order two coffees, black, since Ira's French is embarrassing.

Ira's eyes don't stop moving. He's winding up.

Before Ira can say anything, the waiter sets two china cups of strong-smelling coffee in front of us.

My hearing goes haywire.

A thunderous explosion blasts the air from my chest.

Then—nothing.

Chapter Two
Major Ab Johnson

Pain pounds like a spear stuck between my nose and the back of my skull. Blood floods my throat. I'm choking and cough out a mouthful. The only smell is blood. Muffled shouts and screams barely make it through my ringing ears. The world is black. I try to open my eyes, but they're caked with something—sand, dust?

Where am I?

How did I get here?

What's all the yelling? I can't make out the words.

My head is trapped. I can't move. Something solid pushes my face into a flat, hard surface.

My arms and legs pulse with an electric current.

Each beat of my heart sends a new jolt through my head. Each shot of pain stops coherent thought.

It means I'm alive. But where?

The weight pushing my head down disappears. Hands grab under my arms and yank me up. I hazard a blink. No luck. I reach up to rub the dirt from my eyes. One touch to my nose launches another lance through my skull. I try blinking, but the world's a blur.

"Ab, can you stand? We gotta get out!" That's Ira's voice, as though he's shouting through a pillow.

I reach up and try to brush off my eyes without touching my nose. I blink. The blur is less, but none of this makes sense.

We're in a room. Ceiling collapsed. My face was pinned to a table in a pool of blood, coffee, and plaster dust. There are chairs, fractured coffee cups. I glance to my side and see two unmoving legs wearing striped trousers protruding from beneath a collapsed ceiling beam. The chef.

The café. Having coffee. With Ira.

"Get out!" Ira shouts.

A woman moans, clutching a screaming child. A man limps away from his table, holding a napkin to his bleeding head.

I grab a napkin and brush the dust off my eyes and then place it ever so gingerly beneath my nose. A gob of blood chokes me, and I spit it out. Ira pulls me through the shattered doorway toward an intact building stoop.

"We should go back, help the others," I shout above the ringing in my ears.

"All you'll do is bleed on them. Come on."

"What was that?" My hearing is returning, but my ears still ring.

Ira leads, as we pick our way over debris and shattered glass. My brain's never felt this way—thoughts dull, slow, uncertain. Ira pulls a chair over to the stoop leading into an intact building and guides me into it. It looks like a Parisian café chair. I glance back and see toppled chairs and tables in front of the former café now buried in debris. How the hell did we get out of there?

Things are making a little more sense. I blink and take in the surroundings. The buildings along the street—Paris. To my right, where we were, is a rubble pile with the remnants of walls around a smoldering crater in the center. Stones, bricks, plaster, and glass extend onto the street. A chunk of blasted wall crushed the roof of a cab. The cabbie's beret sits on a head turned at an unsurvivable angle.

I tip my head back. Everything spins.

Bile mixes with the blood in my throat, my brain too numb to be anything more than a bystander. I spit out another mouthful of blood. It's as if I'm watching through a dusty looking glass.

"Close your eyes. Let me clean up your face," Ira shouts, his voice now clearer.

I hold the napkin under my nose while Ira wipes off my face. I try squeezing the nose to staunch the bleeding. A shot of pain stops me.

Ira's face is in front of me, inspecting me with a frown. I've seen that expression before. Where? Chicago. When one of our friends, a fellow reporter, was tortured by the Mob and dumped, barely alive, in front of the Tribune Tower.

Okay. I'm Ab Johnson and this is Ira Cunningham, and we're in Paris. Got that much. The way he's looking at me tells me I look like hell.

I can see better now. I'm hurt, a building has blown up, Ira's in an army uniform—a major. I blink.

Uniformed army soldiers and officers erupt from the building to my left like bats from a cave. One small man in a navy uniform shoots past into the rubble to stand by a man cradling a young girl in his arms. I know that officer but can't remember his name. A scarlet stain surrounding a void on the center of the girl's pink-and-white-striped pinafore brings bile into my throat. A little girl torn apart by shrapnel, held by a man who must be her father.

"Trudy, here!" Ira shouts.

What's she doing here? Ira's daughter, Trudy, cute as ever, petite, porcelain skin and black hair, wearing an Army Nursing Corps uniform and cap. She inspects my face and takes over holding the napkin to my nose.

The navy officer stoops down and touches the child's neck while saying something to the distraught father, shakes his head, and shouts, "She's dead." His name's Arthur. A navy surgeon. Where did I meet him? The man holding the girl pleads in French and grabs Arthur's left leg. Arthur jerks his leg free. "She's dead—there's nothing I can do," he shouts. The father continues to beg for help as Arthur rushes away.

A woman I recognize—Alice Simmons—picks her way through the rubble with an army captain. Taller than most of the men around her, slender, with auburn hair in a loose bun, Alice is Trudy's best friend from Minneapolis. A journalist with an RN. My son Jack's friend from college. They kneel next to a woman whose right arm is a mangled mess, blood spurting. A colonel joins them and squeezes the woman's arm with both hands.

Arthur rushes over, shoves the colonel away, and grabs the arm above the elbow. The colonel nearly trips as he staggers back, his face red with rage. The captain gives Alice his belt. Alice encircles the arm with it and pulls it tight, speaking with Arthur, nodding. The captain uses a short board to support the shattered wrist.

There's a little less fuzz in my ringing ears. I blink. I must look terrible—I see it in Trudy's eyes. She's been Jack's chum since childhood.

Jack. *Jack.* That's who I need to find. But he's not here. With the goddamned Marines—somewhere. This isn't the place I'll find him. But how do I know that?

I lean back in the chair, Trudy holding the napkin to my nose. Ira steadies me with a hand on each shoulder. I'm a bystander. One of the wounded. A casualty before I can even report for duty. Useless.

My fog is clearing a little.

Bells clang, engines roar, and hoofbeats echo as emergency vehicles approach. A horse-drawn fire engine pulls to a stop. The crew pulls a hose as they wade through debris toward the smoking center of the ruin. A motor ambulance screeches to a halt, followed by two more. One crew takes away the man still holding the child, pleading, crying. Another crew loads the woman onto a stretcher and hurries her away, followed by Alice. Arthur—what the devil is his last name?—and a captain approach. It seems to take Arthur a moment before recognition dawns on his face. "Let me look at you, Major Johnson."

Trudy eases the napkin away from my nose. Arthur and the captain inspect my face, telling me to blink, move my eyes, open and close my mouth. "Nose is broken," Arthur says. "You'll have to get to a hospital."

I once watched a doctor *fix* the broken nose of a union leader who had been roughed up by mine goons back home in Butte, Montana. I want no part of that. "I'm sure I'll be okay. Just need a washcloth and some aspirin." I try to pop my ears—sound is still muffled.

"No. It has to be fixed. That's an order," Arthur says.

"Lieutenant, I'm not sure you can order a major anything other than a drink at the officers' club," I say.

"But I can," a voice next to us says—the colonel Arthur shoved away from the woman. "Local hospitals'll be jammed." The colonel turns to the captain. "Take him to the American Hospital in Neuilly." The colonel glares at Arthur. "Lieutenant, Junior Grade, do you make a habit of interfering with fellow physicians in the middle of life-threatening events? *Never* do that again." Arthur's face is red; I'm guessing it's more in anger than embarrassment.

The captain returns. Ira and Trudy help me to an idling Dodge staff car. I keep the napkin to my face to catch the blood. My head feels full as I bend down to get into the rear seat.

Ira slides in next to me. "What would Helen say if she could see you now?"

Chapter Three
Major Ab Johnson

What would Helen say? I'd get an earful from the woman I love, wife, mother of a son I belittled at the wrong moment. "She'd repeat her parting comments to me at the train station. That I'm an idiot and that I better get my head out of my keister, pronto." The driver grinds the gears and pulls away from the curb. "She told me that no son should go into war without the full support of his father. I tried to explain my reasoning about Jack's mistake when he joined the Marines, for the hundredth time, but she'd hear none of it."

"Some of your comments about the Marine Corps were bad, Ab," Ira says.

"Well, I'm not wrong, in my opinion," I say. "But I should have kept my mouth shut. At least Helen and I agree on that."

Jack, why the hell did you have to go and join the Marines?

It's coming back to me. I'm in the army, again. Left Butte, Montana —home, work, Helen—and rode on a troop ship to France. I was supposed to go to a safe job in Tours. Helen demanded that I find Jack, to reconcile before it's too late. That should have been easy from there. Then new orders sent me here. I fumble at my inside coat pocket. The orders are still there next to my France roadmap. I can feel the lump of my wallet in my back pocket.

I glance down at myself. My army uniform is peppered with white powder streaked with blood. I'll need to change it before reporting to duty.

Where's my luggage?

Oh, yeah. I got out of the cab in front of the American headquarters building. Ira came up to me, saying there was something important he had to talk about. I carried my suitcase and garment bag into the café and set them down next to our table.

Then the explosion.

"Some welcome, Uncle Ab," Trudy says.

I'm not her uncle, but she's called me that since she was a kid.

"Ira, does this have something to do with what you needed to talk with me about?" I ask.

"Part of it, old friend," Ira says. "And by the way, powdered with flour, you do look old."

"Go to hell," I mutter. He looks like a snowman, covered with flour and plaster dust. "Is it safe to talk here?"

"I know Private Haskins, who's driving," Ira says. "He's in the necessary loops. I want everyone in this car to not repeat what we say."

"Uncle Ab, what's the last thing you remember?" Trudy asks.

"Train station, getting the Paris edition of the *Times*, reading it while waiting in the cab line. Seeing that navy surgeon, Arthur Beck, butt in front of me. Beck's luggage. I remember that. Italian leather, soft as butter, tan. The *Times* reported the fighting is to the north, well away from here."

"Ab, you know better than to believe everything you read in the papers." Ira chuckles.

That coming from a man who was an associate editor of the *Minneapolis Star* before we rejoined the service. Two newspaper editors in our mid-forties hoping to have one last wild moment before dotage droops our chins. The army promised Ira a position in the press office. They guaranteed me a liaison position with the Services of Supply headquarters in Tours, a good hundred and fifty miles south of here.

Idiots. Ira and me.

Naïve idiots.

We were a couple of well-meaning, patriotic suckers who volunteered to rejoin the army at an age when we should have known better. My old man warned me when I joined the first time, after college—never volunteer. He meant it with some irony, but he was right. We're an army family—Grandpap, Dad, me, my younger son, Oscar. But Jack bucked tradition and joined the damned Marines. The last time I saw him was at Quantico. The day I should have been filled with pride while pinning the brass bars on his shoulders. But I had to blab. To tell Jack that the Marines are a bunch of peacocks who look good in a parade but have never won a war. That his grandfather would roll over in his grave. Dad and I never respected the Marine Corps. Well, they are peacocks. I told him he should request a transfer to the army. I could pull a few strings. Okay, maybe I was a little over the top, but now he's headed here. I have to find him, reconcile somehow. I can't have him going into battle with those words ringing in his ears. Helen made that clear. "What the hell's going on here?" I ask. "I thought Paris was safe."

"As any mirror will now attest, Paris is unsafe," Ira says. "I'm pretty sure that was a welcome present from the Kaiser's Paris Gun."

"I haven't seen anything about that in the papers," I say.

"Ah, now you know what I've been doing since I got here," Ira says.

"Okay, tell me what I need to know."

"The French put a moron named Duchene in charge of their Sixth Army. He's the brother of someone important. The Sixth defended the Chemin des Dames area, northeast of here. It was supposed to be an impregnable fortress in a quiet zone. Well, to coin a new word, the Germans pregged it. Colonel Nolan, the head of our intelligence section, personally warned them that the Germans would attack there. Duchene was insulted that an American presumed to have intelligence. It turned out that *le general* was the one lacking that, in both senses of the word. The Germans cut through the French faster than Sherman through Georgia. Over thirty miles in the past week. They're somewhere northeast of here, depending on their progress yesterday. They could be here in as little as a week."

"A week?" I ask. "Are you sure?"

"Could be two if they stop to sample the wine. A few exhausted French units are trying to delay the inevitable. They have no reserves left. Don't tell the Germans, but there's nothing but staffers between Meaux and Paris."

"What can we do?"

"Not much. We only have four divisions ready to fight. None of them are anywhere near here. The First is fighting at Cantigny, and the Second is moving up to reinforce them. The Third is far to the south, and I'm not sure where the Fourth is. Perhaps in Lorraine? The rest are in various stages of training. They'd be nothing more than range targets against seasoned Germans. Hell, the Germans have a hundred divisions on the western front. The French aren't telling, but word has it that ten to twenty German divisions are in this offensive. Imagine—twenty seasoned German divisions against a few thousand staffers running around protecting their asses."

Ira's words lie on me like a shroud.

Chapter Four
Lieutenant (junior grade) Arthur Beck, US Navy Medical Corps

It takes a good five minutes to scrub the blood off my hands in the first-floor men's room after they let us back into the building. I'd gotten as far as Lieutenant Colonel Tuttle's office and no sooner set my suitcases down than the explosion forced us to evacuate. I take off my coat and shake out the dust. Damn it, I got some blood on my sleeve. Probably from that man with the dead girl. Couldn't he see my job was to tend to the living?

The rush to get here this morning was a waste. Jumped the cab queue at the train station, paid the greedy bastard a fiver to push it so I'd be here for my eight o'clock meeting with this fellow, Tuttle. Why route me here? I volunteered to come to France to work with George Crile's surgical research center—which is not in Paris. I need to get there.

Now I stand here, my uniform soiled and bloodied, my spare in the suitcase. I'm a sight. And off to a great start. These people don't know what they're doing, if the medical care I saw outside the building is any indication. No emergency equipment, not even a simple tourniquet or dressing. Of course, I managed to tee off that colonel when I got him out of the way so I could properly compress that woman's brachial artery. Hell, for all I know he's a psychiatrist. Heat of the moment.

I head up one flight to Tuttle's office. The clerk and two other men sweep up dust that coats the furniture and floor. "As I said before, I'm Lieutenant Junior Grade Beck. I have—had—an eight o'clock with Lieutenant Colonel Tuttle."

The clerk blows dust off an appointment book, opens it, and frowns. "Sorry, sir. You've been bumped to 1100."

"Why wasn't I told?" The audacity. Bumped?

"A colonel and a general wanted him in a meeting. They outrank you. And they're army, sir. You'll have to wait. Officers' men's room is down the hall. With respect, sir, you look like you need to clean up. Shower there, too, if you want, sir. Have faith—the hot on full gets lukewarm after five minutes." He looks at my bags and smiles. "Nice luggage, sir. Navy issue?"

They're custom-made Italian leather, from Milan. Not that this ignoramus would know the difference.

I take my suitcases to the officers' restroom, where I shower in the tepid water, shave, and put on my clean uniform. By the time I get back to Tuttle's anteroom, the clerk and his fellows have the place in order, though still dusty. I wipe off a guest chair with my handkerchief, sit, and try to focus on my upcoming meeting.

I slip one of my medical books out of a suitcase, take a deep breath, and open it to George Crile's chapter on contaminated wounds. I want to make sure I phrase things like George would when I meet Tuttle. But the words are little more than smudges of ink. The force of the explosion still echoes with each beat of my heart.

Two army officers enter, talking about the Paris Gun. Oh no. The colonel I pushed out of the way to save that woman with the hand trauma. He's in his forties, fit-looking, with a trim mustache and short light-brown hair. The other has silver oak leaves on his shoulders—a lieutenant colonel. Tuttle? He's about five-ten, similar build as the colonel, around forty, with dark brown hair and a thin, long face. I set the textbook down.

The colonel stops and stares at me for a moment and then walks into the office. I'm in the doghouse if he's in charge. He wasn't doing a bad job, but who in their right mind wouldn't want the best surgeon in the area to take charge?

"Anything in my office damaged in the blast?" the lieutenant colonel asks.

"No, sir," the clerk says. "The papers on your desk were scattered, but I got 'em back in order. Lot of dust, but the boys and I cleaned her up pretty much. Cleaning crew'll have to do the rest tonight."

"Good work," the lieutenant colonel says.

I clear my throat. "I'm Doctor Arthur Beck. I have an appointment with Lieutenant Colonel Tuttle. I assume that's you?"

He appraises me with an impatient scowl and turns to the clerk. "Get that new major down here toot sweet. What's his name?"

"Johnson, sir."

"If I may," I say. "Major Johnson was injured in the explosion. They took him to the American Hospital to fix his broken nose. He may not be available yet, but I am."

"This place is going to hell. Sit, Lieutenant. I'll deal with you later." He glances down. "Nice suitcases. Italian?" Tuttle walks into the office and shuts the door.

This is not a good start.

Chapter Five
Major Ab Johnson

Dull pain pulses between the front and back of my head like a pendulum as the morphine wears off on my ride back to headquarters. Ira took off as I waited at the hospital, and Trudy stayed behind while I argued with the doctors, who wanted to keep me for observation. I have to report for duty. And find my suitcase and garment bag. Where did they go in the chaos?

The only thing about the building that says "American" is the flag above the entry door, which is up a stoop. In America, we'd call the entry "second floor," but in Paris it's the first. The building where Ira and I attempted to have coffee is a jumble of debris with a trickle of smoke rising in the center like a simmering volcano. The fire brigade and others are picking through the remains of the once handsome building. Three blankets tied at both ends lie near the former café—corpses awaiting removal.

I could have been one of them. Ira, too. Less than a degree of windage and an untold number of Americans could be lying there.

I mosey over to the ruins and ask a fireman if my bags are inside. He goes into the café and comes out shaking his head. "It's a mess in there, sir. But I don't see any luggage."

Stolen, I suppose. This *is* Paris.

I'm stiff as I walk up the steps to enter the American headquarters building. A corporal sits at a reception desk in the lobby, where American soldiers scurry back and forth along with suited men who I assume are reporters. I approach the corporal.

"Help you, sir?" The corporal asks.

I hand him my orders. He reads them and snaps his fingers. A private hustles over like a glorified bellboy.

"Take Major Johnson to his new office, three-thirty-seven."

"My suitcase and garment bag were in the café in the building that blew up. I checked, and they're missing."

"I'll alert lost and found, sir," the corporal says. "No guarantees. It is Paris."

"Any place I can get new uniforms?"

"There's a supply depot way on the south side of town," the corporal says. "I can put in a requisition if you give me your size." He chuckles. "You know, too-large, large, mediumish, and too-small. Nothing tailored like that navy uniform I saw earlier. Sheesh, and his suitcases? Musta cost more than I make in a year."

"Order me large of everything and I'll hope for the best. Two sets." I follow the private up two flights of stairs and along a well-lit hallway with white walls and a terrazzo floor. The smell of three kinds of tobacco smoke permeates the humid, still air. The transoms above the doors we pass are wide open, I suppose in the hope of some air movement. Hope is cheap.

The private opens a green wooden door to a room with no transom, extending a hand. What the hell? He must have worked at the Ritz before joining the army. "Your new digs, Major." He hustles off before I can complain. At least he didn't demand a tip.

The windowless room must have been a broom closet. It's maybe six feet square, filled with a battered wooden desk and an elderly desk chair. A two-drawer filing cabinet is jammed between the desk and the far wall, if I can use the word "far" figuratively. Holes in the walls speak of previous shelves. I'm not certain the desk chair would pass a safety inspection. The flaking dark gray paint and bare ceiling bulb support my assumption it was a closet. If this is how they treat their majors, I'd hate to see what the lieutenants and NCOs work in.

I take a deep sigh, survey my new kingdom, and test the chair with my hand.

Is this a joke? I didn't expect a palace, but a janitor's closet?

The chair threatens to collapse as I slump into it and think about the events leading up to this moment.

I came over on the SS *Caserta* and landed at the port of St. Nazaire, where most of our troop ships dock. No sooner did my boots kiss my ancestral French soil than a private handed me orders directing me here. For what? The orders didn't say. The outfit is G-4-B, sanitary train. I'm clean—well, not now—but not sanitary and don't know much about trains. I have a bad feeling about this. I'd been promised that position in Tours when I signed my contract.

Sucker.

Idiot.

Me.

Should have known better. This is the army, after all.

So I head to the men's room to see what I can do to improve my appearance. Once there, I stand before a mirror, inspecting a visage that reminds me of a prize fighter who should have retired. One way past his prime. My hair needs a cut, the dust adding more salt to my brown pepper. Blue eyes seem more prominent when surrounded by raccoon-eye bruises. My nose sports a new bandage, packing protruding from each nostril above a fat upper lip. I shake out my coat one more time. Ira got most of the flour dust out of it while the doctors worked on my nose, but it's still filthy. The bloodstain on the front is the worst part. If I try to wash it off, it'll look like I dove into a pool. If I don't, they might call a medic to see if I have a chest wound. It's a lousy idea to report to a new post in a uniform that looks like I've just left a battle. I hope they forgive me.

A private rocks from foot to foot as I near my office. "Sir, um, you're Major Johnson, right?" I nod. "Lieutenant Colonel Tuttle wanted you in his office a while ago."

I follow the private. We pass Beck, pacing the hall outside Tuttle's office. He's hatless, wavy black hair neatly trimmed and face clean-shaven. His sharp, angular features are more striking than handsome. *Intense*—that's the word for the fellow. Beck glances at me, his face drawn in frustration. He's in immaculate navy blues that must be custom-tailored. About five and a half feet and probably no more than a hundred twenty-five pounds in his shoes. Must be early thirties. And here I am, forty-six, a good six inches taller but at least sixty pounds heavier. Wish I could say it's all muscle, but who am I kidding? I should have asked for an extra-large uniform.

"Thanks for the help earlier," I say.

"Hope they gave you something for the pain."

"Codeine pills. Said aspirin might worsen the bleeding," I say.

"I agree," Beck says. "Meeting with Tuttle?"

"On my way now."

"Remind him that I'm still waiting for my audience with him. He's made me wait an hour. My patience is running thin."

"Oh-kay." I shake my head. *Audience?* I recall several conversations with Arthur during our Atlantic crossing and was disappointed at how little he knew about the military. I figure the naval officer training program has been shortened in the rush to get doctors into uniform. Makes me think of Jack and his comrades being rushed through Marine officer training. I sigh.

As I enter the office, a colonel and a lieutenant colonel stand with their backs to me, looking out a window, one pointing at something in the distance. I assume the lieutenant colonel is Tuttle. The bird colonel is the one who sent me to the hospital. I stand at attention, suck in my gut, and salute. "Johnson, Major Albert, reporting for duty, sir."

"That navy lieutenant told us you were injured." Tuttle faces me, brow knitted.

I tell them about the morning's activities.

"I hope that isn't your only uniform," the bird colonel says.

"Sorry, sir," I say. "Someone stole my luggage after the explosion."

"Okay, we'll give you a pass for now, but you don't want to show up anywhere except a battle in that uniform, Major," the colonel says.

"For what it's worth, I asked the corporal at the front desk to order me a couple new ones. He didn't say when they'll get here. I'm sorry, but I'm stuck with this one until then."

"Major, you look like crap," Tuttle says. "Were you knocked out?"

"Yeah," I say. "But I had to report and get to work."

"Mind a little fuzzy?" Tuttle asks.

"Yeah, that too," I say. "But it's getting better." Well, that's a lie. My ears still ring, and I'm having a hard time hearing the colonel, who's soft-spoken. And my brain is still at least half-full of cotton. Other than that, and my nose, I'm in top shape. It's bad when you start lying to yourself. Worse if you believe your lies.

"I was stuck in a meeting with our French counterpart and his minions all morning. Missed the excitement here." Tuttle picks up a pipe from his ashtray. He pulls on it twice to revive it and lets out a stream of smoke. "Oh, for Christ's sake, sit down before you collapse. Want me to send for a cold pack?"

"Yes, thank you, sir."

"You're one of the oldest majors around." Tuttle frowns at my personnel file. "Forty-six. Hell, you're older than either of us. How many times did they pass you over for promotion? Should I worry about your competence?"

Before I can answer, the colonel holds out a hand. Tuttle passes him the file. The colonel lets out a slow breath. "Unimpressive record. Commissioned after college. Journalism major? Trained in the Quartermaster Corps, served at the War Department for a year and a half, then the Paris embassy staff, then out. Montana National Guard two years later, out in '14. Why the hell did you rejoin?"

My pulse jackhammers the middle of my face. I wipe sweat from my brow. "I've been asking myself that since St. Nazaire. Patriotism. And, I suppose, the desire to make a difference. I do know supply and French. I was one of the main translators when I worked at the embassy. My mother's side is French. I've spoken it since childhood. I understand the language and people as well as any American can, I suppose. They guaranteed me a post in Tours, on the Services of Supply headquarters staff."

"Well, that's another lie the army told you," Tuttle says. "I hope your French is better than your predecessor's. What kind of work did you do before you rejoined our blessed army?"

"I'm a journalist. Got a job with the *Chicago Tribune* after the army, then Associated Press, Paris bureau for two years. Moved to Butte, Montana, where I still live. Crime beat. Worked my way up to associate editor at the *Butte Miner*."

"Butte?" Tuttle frowns. "Isn't that a hundred miles beyond the edge of the earth?"

"Great place to be a reporter—plenty of crime, corruption, and shenanigans. Great fishing and hunting."

"You're old enough to have sons in the service."

"Yes, sir. Oscar's twenty-one, a second lieutenant at Fort Knox. Jack's twenty-four, a Marine second lieutenant."

"That's too bad," Tuttle says. "I mean about Jack." He takes a pull on his pipe, as though considering his next words. "Don't mention that he's a Marine to our army brethren. Touchy subject around here."

"Marines handle drunken sailors while the army wins wars," the colonel says.

Almost my exact words to Jack. A pang of anger surprises me. It's one thing to say it myself, but to hear someone else cut down Jack's unit . . . I struggle to keep my face neutral.

Tuttle takes another puff and blows a smoke ring. "Oh, I assume you've guessed that I'm Tuttle. First name's Arnold. Our boss here is Colonel Sanford Wadhams. If we keep you, I'll need to know what to call you. Al? Albert? Bert?"

"Ab, sir."

"That'll set you apart from the other ten thousand Johnsons," Wadhams says. "What do you know about medical supply?"

"Not much. But a crate's a crate. Ammo or bandages, same process."

"Know the difference between Liston and Thomas splints?" Wadhams stares daggers into my eyes.

"No." I look away.

"Sinclair skate? Jones splint?" Tuttle narrows his eyes.

"Sorry, sirs. I am a fast study." Though my mind is moving at a snail's pace right now.

"Great. I didn't want anyone who knew their job." Tuttle's face flushes. "Look, if you order a hundred crates of Thomas splints without specifying arm versus leg, and all we get that month are arm splints, it matters. A lot. It's as bad as supplying a regiment carrying Springfield rifles with British .303 rounds." Tuttle gazes out the window. "After we got rid of that fool who thought he spoke French, we needed a supply jockey who could, so here you are. Shit. We're running out of time." Tuttle shrugs at Wadhams with a hopeless expression.

Wadhams glares at me and hands the file back to Tuttle. "All things medical and sanitary fall under G-4-B, from the surgeon general to the privates digging latrines." He stands and walks to the window. Tuttle studies my file while Wadhams continues. "The priority on shipping has been troops, bullets, and guns. Medical is short of *everything*."

Tuttle closes my personnel file with a snap. "Along the way, you'll hear the term *sanitary train* to describe what we do. Don't let the name fool you—it's neither sanitary nor a choo-choo."

"Sirs, I'm sorry they didn't send you someone with medical experience," I say. "That's not my fault, however. I volunteered to come here to do liaison work in Tours, where a crate really is a crate. Can you give me a thumbnail sketch of what I need to know?" A sinking feeling worms through my chest.

"Okay, but it's a big thumb," Tuttle says. "We're a temporary branch office. Our headquarters is in Chaumont, and our zone of operations will be in the Lorraine region when we have enough divisions ready to fight. Our temporary assignment is to coordinate the medical support for the Second Division. They're about to join the First in a fight around Cantigny, north of here. I've heard it called a *warm-up* before they get into anything big. After that, they move to Lorraine, where we're building our base hospitals. Forward of the base hospitals will be the evacuation hospitals and then the field hospitals and then the ambulance dressing stations. Those are as close to the front as we can safely drive our few ambulances."

"Few?" I ask.

"Shipping priorities, like I said." Tuttle takes a puff on his pipe. "Your new job is to liaise with our French counterparts. Some are great —I have a lot of respect for the French medical community. Some of their military medical folks are . . . well, arrogant dunderheads."

"I got to know a few of the officers with the Eighth Evacuation Hospital," I say. "They came over on the SS *Caserta* with me last week."

Tuttle gazes out the window. "Each division is supposed to have four evac hospitals. We only have two for the four divisions ready to fight. We don't have one fully functional base hospital."

"What about the Paris hospitals?"

"Off limits. The French don't want American casualties here. Pershing doesn't like the congestion and the distance from Lorraine."

"A friend of mine in intelligence told me the fighting is getting closer." I point at my nose.

"Intelligence doesn't share much with us," Tuttle says. "However, my eyes tell me the French government is fleeing Paris like rats from a sinking ship. You met the Paris Gun up close. Things will become interesting around here very soon."

"I understand that the Second Division is half Marine," I say.

"Yeah. I wish that wasn't the case, but we're so desperate for infantry that we'll take what we can get—for now. Again, I caution you, don't sound too friendly toward the navy or the Marines."

I chuckle.

"What?"

"Lieutenant Beck is waiting for his *audience* with you. He was the only navy medical officer on the transport ship I came over on, so he stuck out like my nose does now. He talked as though he was God's gift to medicine. One of the doctors in Evac 8 knew him in Chicago, where he earned the nickname *Hot Shot*. Had the worst case of seasickness on board. A couple of the army doctors offered to hydrate him rectally."

"I plan to insert my boot in that part of his anatomy," Wadhams says.

Chapter Six
Lieutenant (junior grade) Arthur Beck

It's almost two-damned-o'clock, and my stomach is grumbling. These clowns have made me wait for three hours. Nobody makes me wait like this. Nobody.

The only friendly face I've encountered while I paced in the hall was Ab Johnson. I glance at my watch again and rub the back of my neck, working out a kink. What's so important that I have to wait? Are they doing this on purpose? This is ridiculous. Don't they know who I am?

Tuttle's clerk finally summons me. Tuttle's office is large, though not expansive, with a well-worn oak desk and an empty leather desk chair. The full colonel sits in one of the two wooden guest chairs, his back to me. Ab Johnson stands as the clerk hands him a cold pack. Ab is half a head taller than me, heavyset in a way that seems to be on the overweight side of vigorous. His graying dark brown hair is longer than most of the other officers. Before the injury, his face reminded me of some of the cops and reporters I've met—strong jawed, blunt, neither handsome nor off-putting. The bruises forming around his eyes make their sky blue almost luminous. Ab nods toward Tuttle, who stands at the window.

I snap to attention with a click of my heels and salute. "Beck, Lieutenant Junior Grade Arthur, reporting for duty, sir." My cousin, Hans

Ochs, had drummed one military fact into me—when in doubt, click your heels and salute. Hans was a lieutenant in the German Army when I lived with his family during my two years in Frankfurt. Hans had brimmed with military zeal, assigned to an elite unit. I gaze at the wall behind the deck.

Tuttle moves from the window and walks behind me, as though inspecting me. I remain rigid, holding the salute. The man makes a full circle, stands in front of me, and waves a hand near his forehead. Not a German salute. "Nice uniform. At least the navy knows how to do one thing right."

"Lieutenant Beck," the colonel says. "The only reason I don't personally ship you back to the States in a rowboat is that we're desperate for surgeons. You allegedly are one."

Allegedly? My face is hot. Does he know who he's talking to? I'd like to give him a piece of my mind, but better not. He could be the head of this whole program—a chief of service sort of thing. I need to be careful.

I let my right hand down, not sure if I should assume the pose of *at ease* or *attention*. The second would be right in the German army, but here? The navy skipped all of this for the doctors it was rushing through at Great Lakes Naval Station.

An explosion rescues me.

It seems to be at least a few blocks away. The other three rush to the window and lean out, leaving me like an abandoned bride. A shudder ripples through my gut as I remember this morning's experience.

"That's the fourth today," Tuttle says. "Sounds like it hit to the north."

The colonel and Ab return to their seats. Tuttle sits behind the desk, opens a file, and peruses it. The office feels airless despite the open window. A horse-drawn wagon careens past on the avenue, its bell clanging, men shouting in French—probably a fire engine.

"Lieutenant, I don't normally handle personnel matters for the navy, but your egg is now in my basket," Tuttle says. "You were supposed to join your regiment a week ago, and they're rather put out about your failure to report for duty."

"I—"

The colonel looks up and shakes his head. "No excuses. Repeat after me. *No excuse, sir.*"

My jaw tightens. This isn't my fault. I'm a surgeon, for God's sake, not the moron who wrote the orders. Tuttle circles his right hand in a *come-on* motion.

"No excuse, sir."

"Good. Now, what's the reason for your late arrival?"

"It's not my fault. I arrived in St. Nazaire on the twenty-third and reported to the personnel office. They made me wait there until yesterday due to the low priority of my orders."

"Sir," the colonel says with a sharp edge. "I don't know what they taught you, but you end sentences to a superior officer with the word *sir*. Get used to using it."

"Sir."

"Navy teach you to salute like that?" The colonel turns in his chair and his eyes lock on mine.

My heart won't slow down—this is like the first time I presented a case at grand rounds as a student. The colonel's eyes are fixed on mine. How can he stare this long without blinking? It's not my fault. Sweat trickles along my right temple. "No . . . sir." I need to shift the conversation somewhere—anywhere—else.

"Don't click your heels like that again unless the Kaiser wins." The colonel sighs. "I know we're rushing officers in, but did the navy teach you anything about the customs of the service?"

"No . . . sir."

"I'm Colonel Wadhams, by the way. I have the privilege of commanding this unit, and now you. Has the navy improved their uniform standards?"

"Sir, the uniforms in my size didn't fit very well. My tailor made it." My heart will not slow. I take a deep breath and ease it out.

"Just one problem." Wadhams looks at Ab, who shrugs. "Everyone seconded to the AEF is supposed to wear an army uniform. You could get by with that in the ports, or at a navy hospital, but not where you're going."

"Where do I get one . . . sir?"

"The quartermaster of the unit you report to," Ab says, intoning as though he has a bad cold.

Tuttle reads from the file before him. "Impressive resume, Lieutenant. Bachelor's and master's degrees in bacteriology from the University of Chicago. Several years of research and multiple publications, then med school at Rush." He pauses and reads. "Internship and surgical training at Cook County Hospital. Now on staff at Cook with an assistant professorship at Rush."

"When did you join the navy?" Wadhams asks.

"Five months ago. They needed an urgent faculty replacement at Naval Station Great Lakes."

"That where some fool taught you that German salute?" Wadhams's eyes bore into me.

"No, not that." I need to keep the years I lived with Hans's family in Frankfurt, Germany, under the carpet. It was a great opportunity at the time, doing research with Dr. Paul Ehrlich, one of the top microbiologists in the world. But Ehrlich supports the Kaiser's war with Germanic passion. And Hans is now in the Kaiser's army. Damn it—I joined the navy to shed the stain of being German-American. My academic career will suffer if there's any question about my loyalty.

"Why are you here in France?"

"George Crile recruited me to work in his research unit here. They wanted to include a navy surgeon."

"*Major* Crile." Wadhams frowns. "Get used to using rank rather than the first names of your superiors, Lieutenant."

"Your navy has seen fit to transfer you to the Fifth Regiment medical staff," Tuttle says.

"The Fifth Regiment? Is that a different research unit?"

"Sir. Use that more."

"But I had a deal."

"Sir," Wadhams says.

"Sir." I'd understand them treating me like this if I were a medical student—hell, it's the way I treated the students all the time. But I'm not a student, I'm the best surgeon in this room.

Tuttle frowns. "Our section is responsible for the Second Division sanitary train. You do know what a division is, don't you, Lieutenant?"

"No . . .sir. Well, I know it's a big unit, but no detail. They taught us a little about ships. Uh, sir."

Tuttle crosses his arms against his chest. "I'm feeling like a tutor for a couple of idiots." He sighs. "Okay. Our divisions have twenty-seven thousand troops, with two infantry brigades and support elements. The Third and Fourth Brigades are the infantry components of the Second Division. The Third Brigade is army, the Fourth is the only Marine unit in my army. Each brigade has two regiments. The Fourth Brigade of Marines is composed of the Fifth and Sixth Marine Regiments. A bell in your head starting to ring, Lieutenant? Navy doctors and corpsmen take care of the Marines. That's where you come in."

"How many hospitals do we have?"

"None," Wadhams says. "All the hospitals are *army*, staffed by *army* medical. Navy doctors run the regimental and battalion aid stations for *your* Marines. The only surgery you'll do is hemorrhage control. Stabilize the patient and ship him to us—we do the fancy stuff."

That's a ridiculous waste of my time. "Any GP can do that. I'm a fully trained surgeon. Look, there's been a big mistake. George—I mean, Major Crile—is expecting me. All of this other business, including this meeting, is making me late. I have important research to begin there. Sirs."

Wadhams bores his eyes into me. "You're with the Fifth Marine Regiment. You want a transfer, take it up with them."

Distant thunder draws my eyes to the window. I blink, trying to focus, unsure what else to say. These people are nuts. My orders are screwed up. They can fix it, but won't.

Tuttle goes to the window. Wadhams joins him and points. "That hit farther away. Do you think they have more than one of those guns?"

The bells, motors, and hooves of emergency vehicles grow louder outside. Wadhams faces me. "Lieutenant, the following is not my role, but out of a sense of *collegial* courtesy . . ." He sighs. "How many navy uniforms did you see as you wandered around this building over the past few hours?"

"None."

"Good," Wadhams says. "The American Expeditionary Forces are under the command of the United States Army. The army isn't a bit happy to have a Marine brigade in France. That is a *gentlemanly under-statement*, mind you. The Marines and your navy colleagues are not welcome here. You're under army command now. We don't intend to include the navy in our medical system beyond *your* care of *your* Marines. Lieutenant, when the history of this war is written, navy medical will get nothing more than a footnote. The Marines won't even get that if General Pershing and the Second Division commander, Major General Bundy, have their way."

More emergency vehicles clatter and clang outside as my disbelief grows with Wadhams's words.

"Major Johnson and I are driving up to meet with the Second Division medical staff in the morning," Tuttle says. "My clerk will assign you an overnight billet. Report here at 0500 hours with your gear. You'll ride with us, then we'll hand you off to them. Dismissed."

I look at the other officers. Ab Johnson says, "That means go to the waiting room, talk with the fellow at the desk there, and he'll tell you where to spend the night. Be back at the front door before 5:00 a.m."

My face is on fire as I tear the lodging chit from the clerk's hand, pick up my suitcases, and storm out the door. I won't stand for this.

Chapter Seven
Private Carl Larsen, US Marine Corps

Chaumont-en-Vexin, France
Friday, May 31, 1918

The breeze feels good as I close my eyes, thinking about the run we're about to go on. Hope the wind keeps up, since the day's already getting hot and humid. But hope is as fickle as a Minnesota spring.

I walk to an open-sided mess tent with a dozen standing-height plank tables. Four Marines chide a homely private who looks as though he walked from the backwoods straight into a uniform after a bad cut and shave. Marines in the tent watch, several smiling at the ribbing taking place, others wearing expressions of disgust. Sure, hazing is part of enlisted life, but there are limits.

The Marine being kidded is the one I came here in search of, Private Hiram Stoops. Hiram is rumored to be the best runner among the litter-bearers of the Third Battalion, Sixth Marine Regiment—the 3/6. I'm part of a small running group that started training together in Quantico. We have a run scheduled later in the afternoon, and our leader, Lieutenant Overton, wants to see if Hiram is as good as his reputation.

"Have you ever heard anything more ignorant than that?" Private

Worthington speaks with an exaggerated East Coast blue-blood accent I know to be fake. The others laugh while Hiram struggles with a word.

"Um, sir, I—I'm sorry. I'm not so good with my letters," Hiram stammers.

"Hey bub, let the guy finish his food," a Marine says.

Worthington and his friends bunch fists and glare at the Marine. "Shut the fuck up if you value your nose." No East Coast accent.

This is teeing me off. I take a deep breath. Not yet. Stay calm.

"And ugly. That's the other thing. An ignoramus with a face only a donkey could love. Where do you hail from again, Stoops?" Worthington continues as the others laugh.

"I'm from Osakis. That's in Minnesota, don't you know, sir."

"And your mother, is she as butt-ugly as you?" Private O'Brien asks with a fake upper-crust Bostonian accent.

"And where the hell is Osakis, Minnesota?" Worthington asks.

These mugs are getting on my nerves. I'm from Minnesota too.

"For that matter, where is Minnesota? It's west of Wyoming, isn't it? Or is that Iowa? I can't keep all those Podunk places straight," a man from Brooklyn named Thackery says.

"Um, well, sirs, I'm not so good on maps, neither."

"Are you accusing me of being an incompetent cartographer?" Thackery's face reddens.

I keep quiet. Let's see if Hiram will stand up for himself. I'm getting steamed enough to deck at least one of these bozos if they keep it up. For now . . . *Hold your peace, Marine,* as my colonel would say.

"Why, old chap, it's a good thing you didn't matriculate at Princeton," Worthington says. "We'd eat you alive."

"What's that, sir?" Hiram asks. The others laugh.

Well, I interviewed there last year and was accepted. This bullshit is knee deep.

Hiram's a black-haired fellow, a shade under six feet tall, with the thin, wiry body of a runner. His weak-chinned face wears an expression of hurt innocence with a feral look—in the sense of a doe, not a wolf. These bastards put Hiram up to reading an article about jurisprudence from *The Wall Street Journal*. Hiram's face reddens as his tormentors chortle.

"Enroll. You matriculate when you *enroll* at university. Any fool knows that. For example, Stoops, I matriculated at Princeton a year and a half ago. Private Owens on your right matriculated at Yale, Thackery at Columbia, and Mr. O'Brien at Harvard. We're from a place called the East Coast; you might have heard of it? The sun deigns to shine on us before she bestows her remaining rays on the masses that live in . . . what did you call it? Okra?"

Hiram picks at his food, his blush not fading.

Yale? Another lie. Another place that accepted my application. Where Overton was going to school before he joined the Marines. These guys are digging a deep hole.

"Cat got your tongue, boy?" Thackery asks.

"The chap is rather stupid, methinks," O'Brien says.

"Ha, that's good, old boy. Stupid Stoops," Worthington spits out.

I've had enough of this bullshit. "How'd you all end up here as privates?"

"When our fair nation calls, members of my class have a patriotic obligation to serve," Worthington intones. "That and the fact that military service will look good on my résumé when I run for office."

"We allowed patriotic duty to interrupt our studies prior to graduation, thus our status among the ranks of you plebeians," Thackery says.

"Please don't call me Stupid Stoops," Hiram says. "The bullies back home called me that, and I don't like it, know what I mean, sir?" The lilt of his central Minnesota accent is in stark contrast to the East Coast boys.

"Hiram, I'm Carl Larsen." I extend my hand across the table.

"Nice to meet you, sir." Hiram's palm is calloused and rough. Farm boy for sure.

"You're interrupting us," Worthington says.

I face Worthington. "I don't give a shit. You may think your blood is blue, but it'll run red like the rest of us *plebeians* when a bullet hits."

"And what's your excuse for consuming our air?" Thackery asks.

"Hiram, looks like you're done with chow. Let's go. There's something I want to talk about with you, okay?"

"I asked you a question. I expect an answer, boy," Thackery says.

I take a breath and speak in my own blue-blood accent. "Sorry, old chum. I saw your lips moving, but the only thing issuing forth was fecal." I pause for effect and to allow him to ponder the meaning of the last word. "Thackery? The closest you got to Columbia was in a streetcar. Owens has probably never been to Connecticut. Worthington dropped out of *high school*, didn't you, old bean?" I change back to a normal Minnesota accent. "Hiram, none of these guys are in college anywhere. They're ribbing you." I motion to Hiram. "Come on. Some of us here aren't assholes, dontchaknow?"

Worthington and Thackery block the exit. Both are built like heavyweights. Anger clouds Worthington's face as he bunches his fists. "Not so fast, *Little Colonel*. Your boss ain't here to hide behind."

I stand a foot from Worthington, who all the guys refer to with the name "Worthless". "What happened to the accent?"

Thackery clears his throat. "Um, the old man is headed this way. Better skedaddle."

Worthington glares into my eyes. "This ain't over, fucker."

Chapter Eight
Private Carl Larsen

After getting my running gear, I jog to the spot near the mule corral where our running group agreed to meet. Our leader, Lieutenant Overton, had been a track star at Yale before he signed up for the Corps. He invited men to the group based on running ability, not rank. I had been an all-state distance runner in Minnesota. Most of the others in the group have taken advantage of our day off, but Hank Lenert and Frank Welty are coming with us today.

The afternoon heat lingers. The distant crackle of rifles at the range mixes with the hoots and catcalls from the nearby corral as a group of men toss hay from a cart. A whiff of mule passes my way. A strange tension has lingered in headquarters all day, but I don't know why. Maybe Overton knows something.

The noise from the rifle range tugs at me. I enlisted to be a rifleman. After infantry training at Quantico, they handed me a wrench and a tin of boot polish and made me Colonel Albertus Catlin's orderly. A fucking orderly. You gotta be kidding, I thought. Someone must have pulled strings—probably my old man. My expert rifleman's qualification disappeared in a puff of Cadillac exhaust.

One thing boot camp taught me is that life's not fair. So I shouted, "Aye, aye, sir," and became the best Cadillac mechanic in the USMC.

I threw myself into it, taking care of the colonel's gear, running things to the laundry, shining boots, brewing coffee. His Cadillac touring car purrs like a kitten. The rank barrier relaxes when we're alone on the road and the colonel treats me more like a student than a private. He lectures about military organization, strategy, and tactics while I drive. I've learned a lot as the fly on the wall in meetings. If I decide to join back up after college, I'll have a leg up on the other officer candidates.

"Hey," Hiram calls out as he jogs up.

"Hay's in the field," I say. "Ready for a run?"

"Youbetcha."

Hiram looks like he just came out of a farm field. He's wearing a green undershirt, shorts over his muscular legs, and well-oiled hobnail combat boots. He's a good twenty pounds shy of my one-eighty and looks as if he's descended from Appalachian refugees. Back home, people kidded me about looking like I'd just got off the boat from Stockholm.

"Let's limber up first, then." I hit the deck to stretch my legs. I point at Hiram's boots. "Dontcha have sneakers?"

"Never had any of them fancy running shoes, you see. These boots? Best I ever wore. Whatcha doing, sir?"

"Stuff I learned in track to stretch my legs and loosen up the tendons. I'll show you a few things." I continue my routine, instructing Hiram in each step. "You only call officers *sir*. Dontcha remember that from boot camp?"

"Sure. But I have a hard time not calling everyone that."

"So, what were those guys doing to you back there in the mess tent?"

"Well, so, anyways, one of them, Mr. Worthington, claimed I couldn't read. I said I could so, and they handed me that paper. They put money on it and made me try to read. Well, I don't know where they found somethin' with so many big words, you know. I can figure out some things in the papers, but I never saw no words such as those."

"You know what toasts me about it? They set you up. I can't stand it when people do that. I've seen enough of that at home."

"How'dya know they were joshin' me about where they went to school?"

"I'm the colonel's orderly. I know things. I've dealt with horses' patoots like them my whole life. In fact, the ones back in Minnesota were born a couple of shelves higher in life than those bums. I'll introduce you to a real Yale man in a couple of minutes. How far'd you get in school?"

"Well, you see, I got partway through the third grade when Dad died that winter, and so that's how it was. Ma needed me and the others to work the fields and take care of the animals. My two brothers got our meat. Sis did the indoor work and milkin'. I worked the garden and fields. They got further in school, my sister and brothers did, so they taught me my numbers and letters. But I never got good at reading and writing. How 'bout you?"

"Dad grew up on a farm north of St. Cloud, not all that far from Osakis. I spent my summers there as a kid. But Dad went to college and into business. He's an executive at the Minneapolis Heat Regulator Company. They make thermostats."

"What's those?"

"Things that regulate furnaces."

"Huh. We used wood."

"Anyhow, so I grew up in a Minneapolis suburb called Edina. Since we didn't have a high school, Dad sent me to Shattuck Military Academy. It's in Faribault, south of Minneapolis. Good school. I learned how to deal with pricks like Worthington and his friends there, and a lot about the military too. That and my dad's connections are probably the reasons I ended up as Colonel Catlin's orderly." I stand and stretch my arms, looking toward headquarters. Our other running partners jog toward us in the distance. "Oh, and the fact that I can fix Caddys. That's the kind of car my old man drives. Now mind you, I like working for the colonel, but I joined to fight with a rifle, not a wrench."

"What's a Caddy?"

"A Cadillac. It's the car they issue to the colonels and generals. Top shelf. Learned how to make 'em hum by working on my old man's."

I drop to my stomach and start push-ups. Hiram does the same. As I reach fifty, something hard drives my face into the ground. Worthington's voice snarls, "Who's the asshole now?"

His boot is on my neck.

I can't breathe.

This is not going well. I try to push up from the ground to get some air.

The pressure lets up enough for me to breathe. I gasp for breath and glance over at Hiram, pinned to the ground by Thackery's boot.

My arms tense, ready to deck the bastard when I get the chance.

"You interrupted our session so rudely, we thought it might be good to continue our conversation in a more . . . private place," Worthington says.

"How's it feel to be the *Little Colonel* now? Don't have the big boys to cover your ass, do you?" Thackery chortles.

"Fucking orderly. How can you call yourself a Marine?" Worthington hisses.

Hiram has that look again—the deer. I spit out a few blades of grass. "Whatcha want?" Two pairs of hands grab under my arms, yanking me to my feet. Four against one, but I'm thinking about how to take them all down. Thackery keeps Hiram facedown with a boot on the neck.

Worthington strides in front of me, winds up, and slugs me in the belly. Owens and O'Brien tighten their grip to keep me from doubling over. Sweat stings my eyes, air gone from my lungs, unable to take a breath. A hundred feet away, our other running partners sprint toward us. Lieutenant Overton's face contorts with fury as he nears.

"What the hell is going on here?" Overton shouts.

Thackery takes his boot off Hiram's neck as Owens and O'Brien let go of my arms. I bend down, and the wind finally returns. I take two deep breaths. "Mr. Worthington . . . and his friends . . . were in the process of . . . beating the tar out of me. I don't know . . . what they have in store for Hiram . . . sir."

"Sir?" The color drains from Thackery's face.

Overton wears shorts, a blue T-shirt with a large white *Y* on the front, and well-used sneakers. He looks straight out of the Ivy League—tall, sandy hair, blue eyes—a sorority girl's dreamboat.

"Lieutenant Overton, these are Privates Worthington, Thackery,

Owens, and O'Brien." I wipe sweat from my eyes and notice Hiram stand at attention and salute. The others stand with sullen versions of attention. My breathing calms.

"You all right?" Overton asks.

"Fine, sir." That's a lie. Man, my gut hurts. But I have a way to making these guys hurt worse. I give Worthington a wink. "And ready for a run when you are, sir. Twenty miles today?"

Worthington's face pales.

Overton stands, appraising the situation. After a long minute, he says, "Carl, these fine Marines should join us. Private Worthington, since you seem to be the squad leader here, identify your unit."

"Supply, sir."

Overton scowls. "I bet your CO would agree that a little PT might be just the thing right about now. Help clear your heads a bit. Carl— you lead. I'll take the rear to make sure these chowhounds don't drop out. Take it easy for the first quarter mile. Is this Stoops?"

"Yes, sir."

"We've heard you're a good runner," Overton says. "Always run in combat boots?"

"No. Well, you see, sir, back home I went barefoot in the summer and put on whatever shoes I had the rest of the time."

"This is Private Lenert and Pharmacist's Mate Second Class Welty," Lieutenant Overton says. "Lenert's a runner with 3/5 and Welty's a corpsman with Twentieth Company. Good runners. Now that that's done, let's go, Carl."

I lead the group onto a rutted dirt track. Hedges and low stone walls separate the road from the farm fields. The verdant, rolling countryside looks like eastern Minnesota, near the Wisconsin border. Spring flowers are in full glory, and winter wheat shimmers on green stems in the late afternoon sun. Unlike Minnesota, weeds and poppies dot the forlorn fields, as though the farmers have abandoned them. I hear heavy feet and loud breathing in my wake. Makes me smile.

I kick it up a notch. Our course is about eight miles according to the odometer of the colonel's Caddy. After a mile, Overton calls out for me to halt. Our four companions aren't in top shape. Worthington and Owens double over, puking, while the other two gasp for air.

Overton stands next to me, out of earshot of the others. "We'll have these laggards stick with us for about two more miles, then we'll shake loose for a proper run. That'll give me time to find their first sergeant and arrange an appropriate reception for them."

After three miles, I resume my usual pace and relax into rhythm.

A staff car speeds toward us when we're about two miles shy of camp. It skids to a stop in a swirl of dust. "Carl, get in—colonel needs you back on the double. We got big trouble."

Chapter Nine
Private Carl Larsen

We reach headquarters. I jump out before the car comes to a halt and rush into the building to find Colonel Catlin. "Sir, what do you need me to do?"

"Gas up the car, then pack and load our gear. Wash up if you have time. Orders are for us to head out soon."

"Where are we going, sir?"

"Frankly, son, I have no idea. Troop trucks are supposed to arrive at 1800 hours. I have men going all over kingdom come rounding up our unit. As best I can tell, we've been handed over to the French and aren't heading north. Rumor has it that the Germans have broken through to the east and are barreling toward Paris."

Pandemonium sweeps the camp as I accompany Colonel Catlin on his rounds. Platoons of sea bags—our version of the army duffel—are stacked for shipment to our next destination, wherever that is. We pause to watch Sergeant Stecker organize his platoon, his voice raspy from shouting. Mules whinny and clomp, hauling wagons laden with equipment toward the railhead several miles away. My uniform sticks under my arms, still hot from our run.

The colonel voices doubt about the sanity of the jackass who cut our orders. The only reason the division can move at all is the fact that most of the men were packed and ready to march north to Cantigny tomorrow. Major General Bundy had given the division today off, and troops are now scattered around the local villages, with a few officers going as far away as Paris. The stragglers won't make it back until morning.

At six-four, Colonel Catlin towers over most of the men as we walk among the troops. Being next to him always makes me stand at my tallest version of six-one. Catlin urges sergeants on and pats the backs of lieutenants organizing their platoons. As units coalesce, Catlin inspects "his lads," as he likes to call us. Some of the privates and corporals sneer at me after Catlin is past them.

I'm used to those fools.

A motorcycle speeds toward us from the west and skids to a dusty stop as we inspect Lieutenant Grant's platoon. A French captain works his way out of the sidecar and hobbles over. He salutes the colonel and hands him a slip of paper. Catlin dismisses the man and reads. "The French now say the troop trucks will be here at 2200 hours. Lieutenant Grant, your men can stand down. If you can find any hot chow, grab it. Assemble at 2130 hours in case the French are early." The colonel gives Grant a wink, and both laugh while I do my best to keep a stony face.

We shouldn't have rushed.

Troop trucks, which the Frenchies call *camions*, finally rumble in around 0400 and continue to arrive over the next four hours. Marines cough and bitch in the dust raised by the trucks as a red sun rises in the east. These nasty trucks have four wooden bench seats in the back that form an *I*. The top of the *I* faces forward. The bottom faces the tailgate. The long axis is a two-sided bench seat facing the sides. Solid rubber tires beneath a suspension without springs guarantee spine-crushing jolts with every pothole and bump. The canvas covers protecting riders from the sun funnel throat-choking road dust through the troop compartment. They must have been designed in Stuttgart to demoralize the occupants and bruise their asses so bad they won't be able to fight. But they beat marching with a full load on a hot day.

Makes me feel pretty good about driving the Caddy.

Colonel Catlin circulates among the Sixth Regiment troops while they clamber into the camions. The privates grumble about many things, but not the colonel. He's one of the few senior officers in the division with combat experience. He commanded the Marine detachment aboard the USS *Maine* when she blew up in Havana Harbor and was awarded the Medal of Honor after the battle at Veracruz, Mexico, in 1914. No slouch, my colonel.

Word is that the colonel's boss, Brigadier General Harbord, headed for the division's destination hours ago. *Where* is the big question. I try to wheedle info from the camion drivers, but none of them speak English. My high school French is useless with them. One of the Marines says his driver comes from a town that sounds like *Way*, and another from *Sighgone*. I know world geography, but have no idea where those towns are. Somewhere in Asia.

I follow as the colonel approaches his battalion commanders, who snap to attention. Catlin waves them off, saying, "Don't know where we're headed yet. Suspect it will be around Meaux." I smile as the colonel pronounces the word *Mow* instead of *Meeuu*. I spent some time working with him on his French words. My French teacher at Shattuck harped on one point: Even if you can't form a complete sentence, pronounce the words properly. "Overheard a private say we're headed there, and frankly, they're at least as well informed as I. A French officer in the lead car is our guide. The French are so worried about security that they won't tell me anything. I must look like a spy." The others laugh.

"Colonel, the men are getting mighty hungry," Major Sibley says.

"I know." Catlin shrugs. "Heck, my stomach's grumbling too."

"I'll tell them they can eat some of their dry rations."

"Sounds fine," Catlin says. "Oh, and one more thing. I don't want anyone standing at attention or saluting from now on. The Germans have good snipers. That's an order."

The men snap to attention, salute, and shout, "Aye, aye, sir."

The colonel laughs. "Save your salutes for the Frenchman who orchestrated this circus."

I smile.

We're finally getting into the fight.

Chapter Ten
Lieutenant (junior grade) Arthur Beck

From Paris to Chaumont-en-Vexin
May 31 to June 1, 1918

Those bastards set me up in a small, seedy hotel for the night. After a meal that proves that not all Frenchmen can cook, I read a medical text, hoping to calm down after the events of the day. Memories of my arrival, the explosion, and my meeting with Tuttle distract me. They treated me like an intern. I try to sort out my anger. Three more shells from the Paris Gun this evening are exclamation points punctuating a gnawing fear in my gut. I didn't sign up for this. They promised me the position at George's—Major Crile's—surgical unit. An academic unit well back from the front.

After turning the lights out, I lie awake searching for solutions, but I don't know enough about the military to come up with a plan. I finally abandon all hope for sleep and take a long soak in the bathtub of the shared bathroom down the hall. The water is tepid.

I pack my suitcases and find the reception desk empty at four in the morning. I drop my key on the desk and lug my gear the four blocks to G-4-B HQ. Paris sulks, its night-cloaked streets devoid of lamplight. I jiggle the handle of the locked front door. Birds chirp, heedless of the war in the predawn. Light flickers through cracks in the curtains of a few upper-floor windows. A hint of wood smoke lingers in the air. I sit on the bottom step of the stoop and wait as dawn lightens the eastern sky.

A staff car pulls up at quarter to five. The driver loads my suitcases, offering admiring comments about the fine leather. At five, Lieutenant Colonel Tuttle and Ab Johnson emerge through the front door.

The nerve. They probably knew I was down here the whole time.

"Glad to see you showed up on time, Lieutenant." Tuttle's tone is sarcastic.

"Yes, sir. Thank you, sir." I want to say that they kept me waiting for forty-five minutes.

Johnson is wearing the same soiled and bloodied uniform as yesterday. Doesn't he have a change of clothes?

They put me in the front seat of the Packard while Tuttle and Johnson ride in the back, cradling steaming mugs of aromatic coffee that make my stomach groan. Paris goes by while we drive. A cop—I wonder if they call them cops here—and a clutch of three young women in drab clothing stand on one corner. We pass a train station coming to life— black coal smoke drifting skyward from locomotive stacks, steam spewing from the pistons, and porters loading luggage while travelers board cars. A whistle shrieks.

Tuttle stares out his window, his jaw muscles tight, expression angry. Am I the source? Or is it Johnson, whose nose angles to the left and sports gauze plugs in each nostril? He resembles a raccoon that collided face-first with a car. I gaze at the passing city, not sure how to break the ice.

An explosion behind us startles me.

I turn and look through the rear window. Smoke rises amid a dust cloud about three blocks away. Something hard smacks the roof and the driver guns it, swerving around falling debris.

A body flashes from above and bounces twice as it hits the sidewalk.

Jesus Christ! I blink.

Tuttle laughs. "I thought I'd seen everything." He points to the body.

"Should we stop?" I ask.

"It's a mannequin in a tuxedo. The shell must have hit a men's store."

Thank God. I thought it was raining corpses.

Bells of distant emergency vehicles clang, and the few pedestrians on the sidewalks scatter. My pulse quickens, and my right leg bounces in a restless rhythm. I sit on my hands to still them.

"Lieutenant, do you know anything about what you're getting into?" Tuttle asks.

"No, sir."

"Know much about the Marines?"

"No, sir."

"Nice to know the navy is doing such a fine job of educating their officers." Tuttle opens a briefcase, pulls out a folder. "Colonel Wadhams is a forgiving man, but you managed to displace several senior French officers to ascend to the top of his list of least favorite people. Impressive accomplishment, Lieutenant." He opens a folder and reads.

My face is hot, neck tense. The audacity of these men is astounding.

I try to calm down as we pass through a succession of suburbs where crews of older men remove street signs. A young boy wearing a beret and a striped shirt waves at us. Two women carrying shopping bags stare at us, their faces devoid of emotion. The day heats up, and more pedestrians appear as the miles go by. They seem like a blur as I ruminate over the past day's events. Johnson and Tuttle read documents in silence, so I settle back and try to come up with some way to not make an ass of myself at the next destination.

Tuttle shoves a folder back into his briefcase. "Why the navy?"

"I debated army versus navy. My father's experience in the army during the Civil War wasn't good."

"What happened to your father?"

The blood-curdling nighttime screams terrified me as a child. Outbursts of anger, raging at trivia, and moments of catatonia made me avoid bringing friends into our home. "He joined the Union Army two years after he and his parents emigrated from Germany, sir. The Illinois Regiment."

"Quick route to citizenship."

"Right. He fought in a couple of battles before he was captured. He refused to tell us about it. My mother let the name of the prison camp drop once. Anderson-something-or-other. The psychiatrist said he was a coward, mentally weak." The psychiatrist also told me it runs in families. The matter has troubled me for years. I don't want to end up like my father.

"Andersonville was an inhuman nightmare." Tuttle's voice is tight with emotion.

"With that in mind, the navy sounded good to me, sir." I gaze out the window. Tuttle understood more about Fred Beck in one sentence than I have in my thirty-four years.

"In the army, we call that a tactical error."

"What, sir?" I drum my fingers on my right knee.

"Joining the navy." A moment later, Tuttle returns to his reading.

After another hour, we approach a dust cloud that resembles a fog bank. The driver inches the car forward to an intersection where a troop truck chugs across. Our driver honks and speeds into traffic. Dust stings my eyes, and I begin to cough. The car jolts to the left. The driver of the truck we cut off curses in a foreign tongue.

I blink twice to clear my eyes. We're traveling in the opposite direction of a truck convoy driven by Asian men. The troops riding in the trucks wear American army uniforms.

"If this is like every other column I've seen, they'll come to a stop," Tuttle says. "When that happens, pull up to the nearest staff car."

We bump along for ten minutes and catch up to another staff car heading in the same direction, fading in and out of sight amid the dust. We pass scattered clusters of French civilians waving American and French flags, shouting, "*Bonne chance,*" and "*Vive les Américains!*"

The column staggers to a halt. Our driver picks up speed to catch up with the other car, then stops behind it. Tuttle and Johnson slide out. I do the same, not sure what else to do. I brush dust off my shoulders and don my hat. An officer hops out of an ambulance and strides toward the car in front of us, a Cadillac touring sedan with the top down. The approaching officer salutes, and one of the men in the car shouts, "Who are you?"

"Major Evans, General Pershing. Adjutant, Sixth Marines."

"Major, what the hell's going on here?"

"We received orders from the French to move out last night, sirs." Major Evans's eyes seem to dance between the two officers in the Cadillac. I can only make out the backs of their heads, but Evans called one of them General Pershing.

"George," General Pershing says, "when I gave Foch permission to use the Second Division, didn't I tell him I wanted to know where they'd be sent and when?"

"Yes, General, you did."

The general turns to Evans. "Where are you going?"

"Not sure, General. Maybe Meaux? It appears that information is above my pay grade."

"That's General Pershing?" I whisper to Johnson.

"Yes."

"I mean to have a word with him. He can fix my problem." I square my shoulders and take a step in the direction of the Cadillac.

With my second step, a hand clamps on my wrist and yanks me back. "That would be the biggest mistake in your short career," Johnson says.

"Why?" I try to pull my hand back, but Johnson's grip holds.

"Trust me."

Tuttle glares at me. Johnson continues to hold as we listen to the exchange between Evans and General Pershing. Why won't they let me talk with Pershing? He can do my transfer. When you want something done, talk to the guy in charge, right?

"Well, it sure as hell isn't above mine," General Pershing says, "and they didn't have the courtesy to let me know about this. Colonel Marshall and I were on our way to inspect your division before its departure for Cantigny." Pershing turns to Marshall. "George, we need to get back to Chaumont. I have some ears and fingers to bend." The Cadillac turns around and takes off in a whirl of dust.

"Major Evans, I'm Tuttle, Medical Corps. I'm supposed to meet the division medical staff. Know where they are?"

"I've got Lieutenant Boone here, sir, but the rest are scattered about in no particular order, I'm afraid. Our departure was very . . . French, if you catch my meaning."

"We'd better get back to Paris." Tuttle nods toward me. "This extraordinary young surgeon is assigned to the Fifth Marines."

"Hop in that Dodge staff car over there." Evans points. "You can bring only one suitcase. We're traveling light."

What the hell kind of outfit is this? I can't bring my things? My soiled spare dress blues are with my underwear, socks, and books in one, and the rest of my uniforms are in the other. All bespoke—custom tailored. Damn. I'll take the one with the books. "How will my other one get to me later?"

"The army will take care of that, Lieutenant." Tuttle smirks. "Besides, you'll need to get an army uniform when the quartermaster catches up with your column. Leave one with us."

Evans turns to Johnson. "What happened to you?"

"Caught in a building collapse next to headquarters. Paris Gun. Broke my nose, and then someone stole my luggage."

"Huh. Make it more colorful if you plan to tell it to Marines, though they'll like your uniform. Kinda salty, as we say." Evans looks me up and down. "On the other hand, Lieutenant, don't expect to keep that uniform so clean. You're about to go into the shit with the Marines."

Chapter Eleven

Hospital Apprentice, Second Class (Medical Corpsman) Lyle McCormack, US Navy Medical Corps

The Dodge's engine dies with a jolt as I brake to a stop. Dagnabit, I hate clutches. I've driven the truck on the Martin farm a few times, but I never got the hang of it. I push in the clutch and grind the engine back to life, happy I don't have to get out and crank it like our Ford ambulances. I haven't gotten past second gear since we left Chaumont-en-Vexin hours ago—fine by me, since shifting involves the damned clutch. Lieutenant Orlando Petty and Lieutenant Junior Grade Weeden Osborne ride in the back seat. At least they don't give me crap about the clutch, but I'm pretty sure I saw some rolling eyes in the rearview mirror. Road dust chokes the life out of conversation when we're moving, but the two officers in the back seat talk during the delays.

I may be a greenie, but I'm downright salty compared to the navy officer moseying toward us with Major Evans. His spotless navy blues and leather suitcase are so out of place that I'm not the only one staring at him. Where'd he find such a snappy uniform? Everyone in the brigade —Marine and navy—now wears army olive drab by order of General Pershing himself. Marines still wear their Eagle, Globe, and Anchor collar pins, though. I get out, knowing I'd better take care of his suitcase.

"Don't scratch it." The lieutenant hands me the fanciest suitcase I've ever touched. The padded handle oozes luxury.

I glance at him and turn to carry the suitcases to our Dodge. My face must look like a beet. Napoleon Beck. Hot Shot. Miss Minnie Martin's nephew—the one who had been too important to come for visits during the time I lived and worked on the Martin family farm.

Beck had filled in for a sick instructor in the last week of my bacteriology course back at Great Lakes. He seemed smart enough but had the disposition of a donkey with a burr up its ass. I settle back behind the wheel and let the car idle. Beck gets in the front next to me and turns to the back seat. This is awkward. I flex my hands on the wheel. My left little finger aches today, as it often does, a nagging memento of my life before Miss Minnie took this orphan in.

"I'm Doctor Arthur Beck. There's been a terrible mistake here. I was supposed to report to Major Crile's research unit, but some fool hijacked me and sent me here instead. I need to confer with the top man here to arrange a transfer. Are you him?"

"I'm Lieutenant Orlando Petty." Petty's face is rigid. "I'm the assistant regimental surgeon. Our boss is Lieutenant Commander Paul Dessez. He's the man you're looking for."

"Where will I find him?" Arthur gazes back along the long line of vehicles, as if trying to find the next staff car.

"No idea." Petty's voice has an edge. "But we're steamed at you."

"Why?"

"Sir. Use that word. You were supposed to be here five days ago. The skipper had to put me on sickbay duty in your place. This jolly fellow is Lieutenant JG Weeden Osborne. He may be a dentist, and the same rank as you, but he's senior to you based on time in grade."

"I hear you're a Cook County hot shot," Osborne laughs.

I peek over as Beck's face colors.

"You're lucky we're so shorthanded," Petty says. "The skipper'll probably let this one pass."

"It's not my fault. A series of incompetent fools delayed me."

"Sir."

"Sir." Beck's face flushes.

Osborne whistles. "Sure lives up to his reputation." He smiles and looks at me with a shrug. Petty doesn't seem to be amused.

Osborne's breezy manner makes me smile. He is a few inches shorter than my six feet, slender, handsome, sandy-haired, with a quick, rosy-cheeked smile. Everyone calls our other passenger, Lieutenant Orlando Petty, "the professor," which is what he was before he joined. Why a guy in his forties would do this puzzles me. Petty wears owlish round spectacles on a narrow face that rarely smiles. He's thin, about the same height as Osborne.

"You'll meet our boss soon enough," Petty says. "Until then, you're with us."

"So, let me get this straight," Beck says. "This is the Fifth Regiment?" He reaches into a coat pocket and hands Petty his orders.

Petty reads the orders. "More or less."

Beck looks confused.

"I'm in the Fifth," Petty says. "McCormack—the driver—and Osborne are in the Sixth Regiment."

"So, Beck, why here?" Osborne asks. "You look like the sort of chap who should be rubbing elbows with the brass back in Washington."

"What do you mean?"

"Well, your luggage cost more than my yearly upkeep at Allendale. And your uniform is clearly not out of the same crate as mine. I assume your silver spoon is packed in an engraved rosewood case—"

Petty cuts Osborne off. "Run through your training, Beck."

I keep my eyes forward, waiting for the column to move while Arthur rattles on about his training and awards. The name Allendale caught my ear. The county welfare worker had talked of sending me to the Allendale Farm orphanage before the Martins took me in. Osborne must be an orphan too. The Dodge idles while the officers talk. Since our departure after 0600 hours, the column has never moved at more than five miles per hour between stops. This far back, nobody knows where we're headed other than eastward.

"I know Allendale. You an orphan?" Beck asks.

Osborne's lightness vanishes as I glance in the rearview. "My parents and brothers died of diphtheria just after my fifth birthday." Osborne seems to compose himself with a sigh. Petty looks at Osborne with a concerned expression. Beck must have made the same connection as me, but the way he asked the question brings me back to that thought about the donkey with a burr.

"Left my sister and me," Osborne says. "After high school, I got a slot at Northwestern. Stayed there for my dental degree. Did charity work on the north side of Chicago for a while, but I knew I had a different path, which led to the navy. The navy is now my family."

"Know anything about the Marines, Beck?" Petty asks.

"First to fight. Famous band. Snappy uniforms. Sir."

"Stow the sarcasm. They're very proud of that uniform."

"You do know that where the Marines go, so goes navy medical, right?" Osborne asks.

"I guess I knew that," Arthur says. "I just didn't imagine it would be me, sirs."

"Get used to it, Hot Shot. *We serve them*," Petty says.

I stifle a laugh. *Hot Shot.*

"We have some education to provide," Osborne says. "Where shall I start? Know about divisions, brigades, and that sort of mumbo jumbo?"

"I had that lesson. They didn't get below the regiment, though."

"Okay," Osborne says. "Marines identify themselves by their unit. The First Battalion of the Fifth Regiment is known as 1/5, but just to keep *hot shots* on their toes, they sometimes call it the First of the Fifth. The Second of the Fifth is 2/5, the Third is 3/5, and so forth. Each battalion has four companies that are numbered in a way to confuse the enemy or the US Army, whichever is more threatening to the future of the Marine Corps at the moment."

"Where do we fit in?" Beck asks.

"We work at the regimental and battalion aid stations. The rest are run by corpsmen like McCormack here."

The engines of camions rev. I glance into the rearview—Petty simmers in the back while Osborne smiles as though on a grand adventure.

"Tuttle told me we have no hospitals. He's pulling my leg, right? Sir."

"No," Petty says.

"Surgical facilities?"

"None."

"Anesthetics?"

"No. We do have some morphine, though."

"Then what's the logic of sending me here? It's a waste to send a fully qualified surgeon to a place where he can't do surgery. This is the stuff of general practice. I might as well dig latrines."

"Don't tempt me," Petty growls.

Chapter Twelve
Medical Corpsman Lyle McCormack

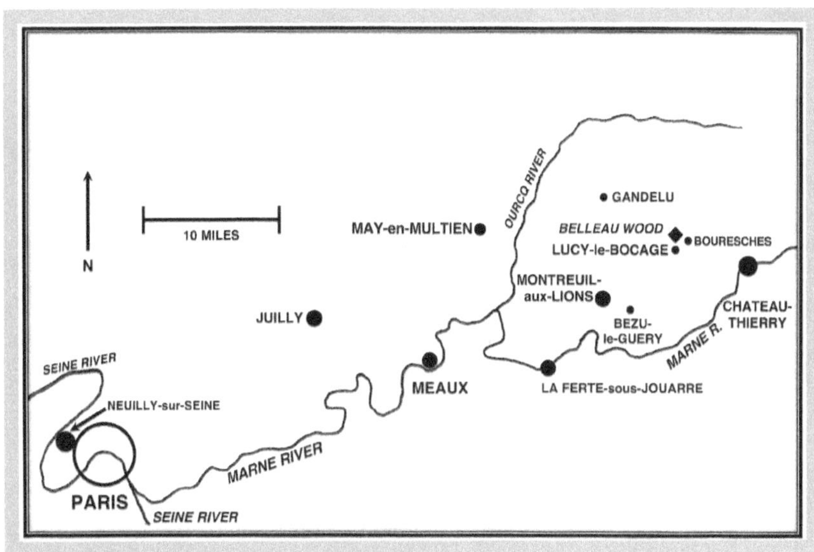

On the Road to May-en-Multien

It's been two hours since we picked up Napoleon Beck. My butt is sore. Nose, eyes, and lungs clogged with the dust from a hundred camions and cars in front of us. The camion in front jerks to a stop.

I kill the engine—again.

Dagnabit.

Marines from the Ninety-Sixth Company hop off the truck, bitching about the seats, the bumps, and the fucking Frogs, as they call our wonderful French hosts. Marines line up at the side of the road to relieve themselves while others light cigarettes, milling in the shade of the trees on the far side of the ditch. I've worked with the Ninety-Sixth on and off for the past two months. Gunnery Sergeant Fred Stockham took me under his wing. Stockham does that for the greenies, the new guys. The Gunny, like me, is an orphan. I get out and walk over to Stockham, who looks at me while lighting a hand-rolled cigarette.

"Stop and start, stop and start," Gunny says. "I'd think with all the stops you'd get the hang of that fucking clutch, McCormack." Stockham gives me the gimlet eye of an old hand. The Gunny stands taller than most, lanky, muscular, with brown hair and eyes on a face that changes from stern to friendly in a blink.

I shrug. "Drove my first car a month ago."

"Damned dust is going to choke me to death."

"If that cigarette don't first, eh?" I say.

Stockham laughs, pats me on the shoulder, and gestures toward my passengers. "Who's the greenie?"

"New doc."

"And the others?"

"Lieutenant Petty's a battalion surgeon—works with 2/5 or 3/5, I'm not sure. The other's our new jawbreaker, Lieutenant Osborne. Grew up in an orphanage on the Illinois-Wisconsin border called Allendale Farm. They thought about sending me there."

"Introduce me."

I mosey over to the car and catch Osborne's attention. "Sir, there's someone I'd like you to meet, if you have a moment." Osborne climbs out and follows me across the road. "Lieutenant Osborne, this is Gunny Stockham."

The two shake hands, and Stockham says, "McCormack tells me you were at Allendale."

"It opened a few months before my parents died. I grew up there."

"After my folks died, I bounced from one well-meaning family to another," Stockham says. "Finally, the street, sleeping in boxes. Some do-gooder got me into the Home of the Friendless in Detroit. Great name. Fit my sorry ass. They did me good. I hung out at the firehouse nearby. Couple of the firemen made me their mascot after a carriage ran over their dog. When I got old enough, I joined them. The USMC came later."

"How'd you know about Allendale?" Osborne asks me.

"They talked about sending me there at one time."

The camion horn honks with a rumble of its engine. Stockham says, "Lieutenant, whenever you have a chance, think about my boys in the Fourth Platoon, Ninety-Sixth. Plenty of teeth to work on. We'll leave the door unlocked for you." He yells at his men to mount up and jumps on board. Osborne and I jog back to the Dodge, and I get her running again, promising myself to master the danged clutch.

I got a feeling the clutch will be the least of my problems soon enough.

Chapter Thirteen
Lieutenant (junior grade) Arthur Beck

Osborne and the driver leave to talk with a fellow wearing a few stripes. "I've been thinking about our last conversation," I say to Petty. He remains silent. "I just don't see where my background will be useful here," I continue. "I have so much to offer at the right level."

"You want to bestow your brilliance for all to admire at the highest level, professor?"

"Well, I—"

Petty's huff cuts me off.

"Using the Beck criterion, I should be the head of the metabolism section at a base hospital," Petty says. "Hell, I'm a full professor, tenured, assistant head of division at Jefferson. Sure, we're not the high and mighty University of Chicago, but—"

"I didn't realize . . ."

"You don't know a thing about me, and you presume to suggest you're somehow better, higher—I don't know what. Why'd you join the navy?"

"Probably the same reason most of us did. It's a great position for a surgeon. To innovate, experiment, and have the type of case mix you'd spend a career to collect. The volume will allow us to shorten the research cycle time by years. Don't you see that?"

"War is opportunity."

"Essentially."

Petty glares at me. "I'm here to make a difference in a way a professor of metabolism never can at home. I can research diabetes or pituitary disease all I want, but I can't do much to treat people with those disorders. It's exciting to have thyroid extract, and I can't tell you the thrill I feel when I start someone on iodine therapy for their goiter." He pauses. "I'm here to serve these guys. You don't understand the privation those men in the truck ahead of us go through, the risks and sacrifices they make for us. I'm honored to be in their company."

"But I think—"

"Beck, you're with the Fifth. It's your sow's ear. Make the best of it."

The camion in front moves forward while Osborne and the driver, whose name I forgot, hop back in.

The Dodge jerks forward and stalls.

After skirting north of Paris, the road curves southward. We begin to pass refugees about two hours later, a trickle at first. Over the next hour, the exodus becomes a river. The people resemble charity cases I've taken care of at Cook County. Children trudge along in resigned silence behind haggard mothers and grandmothers. One looks on the edge of starvation, cheeks hollow, skin pale, clothes a size too big. A young woman pushes a baby carriage filled with clothes, pots, and dishes. A child, who can't be more than five, struggles to keep up with her. An old man guides an ox pulling a cart stacked to an improbable height with household goods, topped with a mattress. The animals pulling carts and wagons look as though they're done in, old enough to be put out to pasture or taken to the glue factory. Two ducks, a chicken, and a rabbit swing in cages dangling from a wagon pulled by a swaybacked horse. To my left, an old couple drives five cows. An elderly man wearing a dusty brown beret pulls a mangy goat by a rope.

I never thought about the effect of war on the civilians. Sure, they're suffering, but it's not my fault. I didn't start this war.

The column halts about two hours later. Marines jump off the trucks, stretch backs and legs, and complain. The camions drive off, leaving us in the middle of a rolling wheat field surrounded by woods.

My gut tightens as distant thunder creeps under my skin after the camion noise fades away. I don't have to ask about the noise—even I know it's artillery. I'm tired, hot, thirsty. My throat is raw, and I don't have a canteen. The last drops of the water the driver brought were gone an hour ago. Petty wanders off and returns with two canteens, neither of which he offers to me. This is bullshit. I've done nothing to provoke these idiots. I treated interns with more respect.

Another officer walks toward us carrying a package. "What have we here? Didn't see a ship pull in, Orlando."

"Commander, this is our truant, *Professor* Beck."

"I guess I won't get to shoot him for desertion, then."

"No. You'll just have to decide what to do with our new Chicago *hot shot*," Petty says.

"Here, split this up." The officer hands the box to Petty. "I'm Lieutenant Commander Dessez, and you're in my doghouse, Lieutenant."

This is not my fault. Why can't they understand that? "Commander, there's been a terrible mistake. I—"

Chapter Fourteen
Private Carl Larsen

The good cheer of my fellow Marines despite the hardship of the dust and camions makes me smile. They're hungry and thirsty and grousing. My last hot coffee was twenty-seven hours ago, not that I'm counting. But we're finally going to take it to the Heinies. We roll into Meaux after 2030 hours. The only civilians are old men and refugees. There is a smattering of French soldiers in tattered uniforms among the refugees. A buddy in Quantico told me that the French nicknamed their troops *les poilus*, which means *hairy ones*. French enlisted men used to wear bushy beards and mustaches. Then came German gas attacks. The name stuck even after they shaved the beards to wear their wear gas masks.

The *poilus* we pass are not the proud warriors who trained us a few months ago in Lorraine. They're not marching and have no unit cohesion. They're scattered as if fleeing the enemy. Their blank stares and stiff movements are those of men who have seen too much, done too much, and can no longer think—automatons on a trek to a destination that no longer matters as long as it's away from the front.

As we enter central Meaux, I ask where French headquarters is, drop the colonel off, and hunt down a parking spot along the narrow street. Camions, staff cars, and motorcycles crowd the roads, with honking and yelling in three languages at intersections. Here, the French army soldiers and officers wear the well-pressed uniforms of headquarters staff. The sort of fellows who've never been in a trench.

My shoulder muscles tense at the sound of distant artillery that is now obvious away from the noisy camions. The face of a French major scurrying between buildings is stressed. He pulls on his smoke with a knitted brow and evasive eyes.

Colonel Catlin storms out of headquarters an hour later. He plops in the rear seat and opens his briefcase. "Carl, get me out of this jam and find a spot to look over this map for a minute. Those fools wasted my time with a briefing that was so classified they told me nothing in many words."

The streetlamps are dark and curtains drawn—blackout conditions —as dusk settles over Meaux. I drive the car to the east side of town and stop under a bridge. "Sir, can I use headlights?"

"No, son. We're on a complete blackout. The Boche fly at night and shoot at anything lit up. Pull the top up." I get out and pull the canvas top over and secure it. The colonel flips on a flashlight and shines it on a small map. "We're supposed to head northeast, out of town, along this route." He shows me the map. "We're going somewhere near Gandelu, see that?"

First gear whines as we creep along the Gandelu road for an hour. I blink on my headlights every few minutes as night deepens. Even the colonel agrees to their use. Out of the darkness, a voice commands us to halt.

My pulse quickens—I hadn't seen the man.

A Marine corporal demands our identity and destination.

"I'm Colonel Catlin, CO of the Sixth Regiment."

"Sorry, sir. I've been waiting for you—they told me you'd come this way. Germans captured Gandelu a few hours ago. I'm ordered to direct all traffic away from there. Take a right here, head to the next intersection, then turn east."

I check my compass, then turn south as directed. I say a silent *thank you* to my father for the boot camp graduation gift—a radium-dial Radia compass. I check it at the next intersection and head east. A half-moon eases its head above the horizon, and I feel more comfortable without headlights. After an hour of ruts and potholes, an army corporal stops us. Seems like someone knows more about where we're going than we do. He hands the colonel a slip of paper.

Catlin uses his flashlight to read the handwritten orders. He huffs. "Carl, now we need to go to Montreuil-aux-Lions. Let's find it on the map and hope the Boche haven't taken it by the time we get there. This is driving me nuts. Whoever is running this show is a . . ."

I'd like to finish that sentence for my boss, who's too diplomatic to call them morons.

Chapter Fifteen
Lieutenant (junior grade) Arthur Beck

Vicinity of May-en-Multien

The driver parks the staff car in a field for the night. Men trudge by, complaining about the march, the road, the lack of food, and the Frogs. I need a new angle, a rationale to convince Lieutenant Commander Dessez to transfer me to Crile's unit. The *sirs* haven't accomplished anything, though I'll keep it up for now. I think my persistence on the matter is making me sound like something I can't stand—a whiner.

My nerves tingle with the mutter of artillery. Something primal distracts my thoughts. The eastern sky flickers as though from lightning, but I'm pretty sure it's artillery explosions. I stretch my neck to relieve a kink, to no avail.

The murmur of conversation dies down as sleep overtakes the exhausted men nearby. I'm surrounded by a jumble of Marines from so many units it makes my head spin. Dessez comes by and tells me to follow him. We join Lieutenant Colonel Wise, who commands 2/5, and Major Berry, the 3/5 CO, conferring nearby. All the while, I'm struggling to figure out a plan to convince Dessez to authorize my transfer.

"Any idea where we go next?" Dessez asks.

"That's what Berry and I were talking about," Lieutenant Colonel Wise says. "All we know right now is that we're supposed to wait here for further orders. How are we fixed medically?"

"Order your men to not sprain their ankles," Dessez says.

A car approaches. I squint to make it out, finally seeing the outline of a staff car emerge along the road. The car stops and a voice calls out, "Is Colonel Wise there?"

"Yes."

"Good. It's Preston Brown. I've been looking for you."

I follow Dessez to the car. Nothing better to do. "Who is this Brown fellow?" I ask.

"Colonel Brown is the division chief of staff," Dessez says. "Don't get on his bad side."

"We're now attached to General Duchene's French Sixth Army," Brown says. "We're ordered to deploy south of the Paris-to-Metz road. Don't take that seriously. Frankly, Duchene's been driving me nuts all day. He's issued three sets of contradictory orders. I'm convinced he isn't finished. Did my best to keep them from sending you hither and yon. Had to get away from him. I was afraid I'd put a bullet though his head if I stayed any longer." The senior officers laugh.

I join the laughter to be one of the team. I have no idea what Colonel Brown is talking about. This sounds like an unplanned emergency operation by a medical student pretending to be a surgeon.

"So here's what's up," Brown continues. "The Germans have broken the back of the French. They cut through the Chemin des Dames area north of here as though the French weren't even there. A machine gun unit from our Third Division is holding them off along the south bank of the Marne in a place called Château-Thierry. By the skin of their teeth. We're moving into the area northwest of them, on their left. Be ready to dig in as soon as you arrive."

"So," Wise says, "you're saying we take hungry, exhausted men who haven't slept and march them—how far is it? And go into the line immediately?"

"Like I said before—"

"No wonder French casualties are so high," one of the captains in the group says.

"On the good side, I'm told the French are going to be in front of us for a while. I'm afraid the best they can do is to delay the Germans. General Degoutte—who's a good man, by the way—is the French commander directly over us. He's promised to buy us as much time as possible. He knows our men are tired. His are worse off."

Brown sets a satchel on the hood of the car, pulls out several papers, and lays them out. "I want you to move out at 0430 hours. That'll give the troops a few hours of shut-eye. March them to Montreuil-aux-Lions. We're setting up division HQ there. That's fourteen miles from here. Love to get you camions, but they've all disappeared. We'll have further orders for you by the time you arrive. Any questions?"

"Where the hell is this Montreuil?" Wise asks.

"I'll show you." Brown turns to his driver. "Hit the headlights." The sudden dazzle blinds me. The others crowd around a map, talking and pointing.

An odd buzzing sound overhead catches my ear.

Brown shouts at his driver to douse the lights and stuffs the papers into his case. "Get out of here." Brown scrambles into the car and slams the door behind him.

The car engine revs, then the rear wheels tear at the turf in a quick turn, spraying dirt on me. The others run away, leaving me confused. I stare at the sky, still blinded by the headlights. I've heard noise like this before, but where?

Then it occurs to me—an airplane. Coming this way. I've seen a few of them back in Chicago, a novelty.

The buzz grows louder.

I struggle to see it in the night sky.

Flickering lights.

Staccato banging.

I cock my head, trying to understand.

Someone grabs my shoulder and slams me into the ground.

Dirt showers me.

Rapid blows as strong as a sledgehammer, faster than I can count, pound inches to my left.

My heart races, mind confused.

Are those bullets?

Chapter Sixteen
Lieutenant (junior grade) Arthur Beck

Vicinity of May-en-Multien

Dirt rains on me as the soil a foot to my left erupts before I can comprehend it.

A blinding flash.

The air blasts out of my lungs.

My ears scream.

High-pitched, mind-numbing ringing floods my ears.

I lie shaking, unable to think.

A hand slaps my shoulder, and a faraway voice yells, "Get up, Hot Shot, got work to do."

Petty. He'd be dead if he were on my left side.

My legs tremble as I stand, struggling to stay upright, hands on my knees. I gasp for air. An electric current hums through me—my hands shake, mind muddled. After catching my breath, I stagger toward the vague outline of men standing near our staff car—Petty is talking with Dessez and Osborne. I can't make it out over the ringing in my ears.

"What the hell was that?" I ask, though I know. That airplane tried to kill us. Kill me.

"Your first taste of war, Hot Shot," Dessez shouts. " German plane strafed us. Your ears are haywire because he dropped a bomb. Mine are too. Come on, we need to check our men."

I follow, trying to pop my ears, hands tingling, brain far away.

How would my father have reacted to this? I imagine him curled up in cowardice.

I'm stronger and better than that.

Who am I kidding? I'm shaking.

Motionless lumps surround me in the vague moonlit field. How could one bomb kill so many? Corpsmen go from one body to the next, giving no aid. They're all dead.

Dessez and Petty check men lying nearby while I stand, unable to do anything but shake.

One corpsman laughs, and then another.

Has madness descended on them? Laughing at the dead, leaving the bodies where they lie. Two chuckling corpsmen walk over—our driver, who I now know is named Lyle McCormack, and another. McCormack. The name is vaguely familiar, but I know I haven't met him before today—or was it yesterday?

"Status?" Dessez is cool on the outside, but he seems short of breath.

Lyle turns to us. "They're fine, sir. Must be exhausted to sleep through that, eh?"

The nearest body moves. "What the fuck was that?" he asks.

Another rolls over. "Fucking Hun plane. Dropped a bomb in your sleep, fuckhead."

"Let's check that group back there." Dessez makes his way toward a cluster of men.

As we near, one of them says, "Pipe down, Cooke. You want Herman to come back and finish the job?"

"One of you hurt?" Dessez asks.

"Yes, sir. Our captain said he wanted to see at least one Kraut before the war's over. Then sure enough, that plane shows up. Lieutenant Cooke got his in the hinder."

"All right. Lieutenant Junior Grade Beck at my side is the new hot shot from Chicago who'll show us how it's done. Welty, assist. Lyle, pull a blanket over and give us a little light. I don't want Hot Shot to do a rectal unless he means to."

Lyle and another corpsman tent a woolen blanket over Lieutenant Cooke. Then the corpsman named Welty flicks on a flashlight. Cooke points to his posterior. The bloodstained edges of a rip in the seat of his trousers shine in the light. Cooke loosens his belt and pulls the trousers down, revealing a shallow grazing wound along his left buttock. It doesn't need stitches. "Get me gloves."

"They're packed. Learn to live without," Dessez says.

"Alcohol for my hands?"

"Got a hip flask?"

"What do we have to clean the wound?" I ask.

"Show and tell, Welty," Dessez orders.

The corpsman wets one side of a cotton ball with iodine and paints the wound, touching it only with the wet side of the puff. "Here you go, sir," Welty says as he hands me the iodine bottle and another cotton ball.

My hands shake like fall leaves on a windy Chicago day. This isn't me. I try to steady them. No success. Now they're really going to have a field day at my expense. Damn it.

I dab the wound. "Move the light over there a bit." I nod in a direction that will let me see the wound better.

Some hot shot I am.

This is my closest encounter with my own mortality. My dad used to shake like this after loud noises. Is that my future? I force myself to concentrate, but the memory of bullets smacking the ground inches from my head won't let go. I can't settle my hands down. "Hand me a small dressing."

"Small, like his ass," a man says, and others laugh.

"Or his brain," another says.

"Shut up," Lieutenant Cooke says. "I'm seriously wounded here."

"This doesn't look bad enough to send you off for some cute nurse to swoon over," Dessez says.

"You'll put me in for my wound stripe, won't you, Captain?" Cooke asks.

"Sure, as long as you quit bitching," the captain, whose name I don't know yet, says. "Doc, how soon can my lieutenant return to duty?"

I apply a dressing to the wound and turn a questioning look to Dessez.

"As soon as Hot Shot sutures up the lieutenant's trousers. We'll keep an eye on it and re-do the dressing later this morning. Oh, and Welty? Hit him with a dose of anti-tetanic serum after you pull out silk and a needle for Hot Shot. I want to see how the hell a fully qualified surgeon sutures with shaky hands. If he does okay on Cooke's britches, maybe I'll let him do it on human skin."

My neck tightens at the words.

Welty helps me thread the needle. My hand tremor causes my face to warm more. I take a deep breath, then repair the rip in Cooke's trousers, all the while struggling to keep calm. I wouldn't make an intern do this. But I wouldn't let an intern this shaky touch a patient with a sharp object.

And I did make more than one medical student suture up ripped clothing at Cook County.

As we walk away from the others, Dessez says, "Good thing Cooke's wound was minor. I hope you're steadier with a scalpel, Hot Shot. I expected a lot more from a Cook County wunderkind."

"Nobody ever tried to kill me before." A hot shot with shaky hands. Wunderkind? Hell, the surgical program at Cook is one of the best in the nation. Someone from Chicago is behind this *Hot Shot* business. But who? Damned right I'm a hot shot. I know they called me that behind my back at Cook County. "Napoleon" too. I worked my keister off while they made up names for me.

"Get used to it." Dessez's words interrupt my thoughts. "It's nothing personal, mind you. It's war. I need surgeons who can keep their heads *and* hands in the game."

I take a deep breath. Calm down, damn it. This is their game—I need to learn their rules. "Where is the equipment I'd need to take care of Lieutenant Cooke if he'd been seriously wounded?"

"Come." Dessez walks to a nearby ambulance, opens the back flap, and clicks on a flashlight. A jumble of boxes fills the back compartment. "Well, here's your ambulance and supplies. If that bomb had killed Petty and me, you'd have been on your own. How long do you think it would take to unload this thing?"

"Ten or fifteen minutes. In a pinch? Maybe five with help."

"Know where things are stowed in there?"

"No, sir."

"So you dump the supplies, find what you need with a flashlight you hope doesn't invite another round of strafing. Then you load your casualty on the floor after you stabilize him and drive off without headlights. Where do you go?"

"Honestly, sir, I have no idea."

"Show me your compass."

"I don't have one."

Dessez clicks off the flashlight. I hear him fumbling around in the medical bag slung over his shoulder. "Here." Dessez crouches over and clicks the flashlight, revealing a compass. He douses the light, then stands, pointing toward his left. "There's west. You'd drive roughly that way, maybe a bit south. Meaux is out there somewhere. There's probably a hospital, but I don't know where it is. Beyond that, there's Paris. I don't know where or how far. Somebody in Meaux must know. None of us have maps."

"Cooke's lucky."

"We were all lucky," Dessez says. "Tomorrow, Marines go into the line of fire. We don't have enough of anything—not one dressing station, aid station, or a hospital between us and Paris. Hell, we don't have a tent to pitch and no safe water. And I'm stuck with a shaky-handed hot shot. Shit."

I step to the side as my eyes and mouth water, and descend into a spasm of dry heaves.

Chapter Seventeen
Private Carl Larsen

Saturday, June 1, 1918

Driving the colonel's car in the dark has been an exercise in hope and prayer. Colonel Catlin finally tells me to park for fear of running over Marines asleep on the ground. I lean back after killing the engine, and sleep overtakes me.

A sorry sight emerges in the lightening dawn after my full bladder awakens me. Some Marines are awake, smoking, munching hardtack and salt pork. The grinding noise of a hopeful private sharpening his bayonet draws my eyes. Others still sleep, scattered around the fields. Four ambulances are parked helter-skelter, some drivers sleeping behind the wheel. I get out of the car to stretch my cramped legs and take a leak. The colonel stirs in the back seat when I return.

Hardtack with a warm canteen of chlorinated water would have started us out on the wrong foot any other day, but excitement surges through me. We're heading toward the sound of cannons rumbling far to the east. My fingers itch for my chance to grab a rifle and take it to the Heinies.

I drive the colonel to Montreuil-aux-Lions. The town's a mob scene of Marines and soldiers. A sergeant shouts over the din of truck engines and motorcycles ahead of us. We locate most of 2/6 amid the jumble. Colonel Catlin and Major Holcomb, the CO of 2/6, order the lieutenants and NCOs to find the stragglers and ready the battalion to move out.

The Sixth Machine Gun Battalion rolls in on camions. The officer in charge of supply and transport must have bent a few regulations and fingers to get them here. Otherwise, they would have had to march the seventy-five miles from our old camp. The gunners carry Springfield rifles—their machine guns are in a mule train plodding along days behind us.

Seventeen camions carrying dry field rations arrive midmorning. Brigadier General Harbord, the Fourth Brigade CO, rides up in his Caddy. He speaks with Colonel Catlin, then orders the men to dump the rations on the side of the road and grab what they can. Harbord helps unload. He stands about my height, but he's bigger, a fit man in his fifties with a strong, square jaw. Like most of the privates, it grated on me that the brigade commander was an army general with no combat experience. But a general who gets his hands dirty can't be all bad.

Harbord orders Marines to board the trucks that brought the rations. The French officer in charge argues with him in broken English. A French captain walks over and parleys in French for a minute. The other officer shrugs. The French captain speaks with Harbord, who points toward Colonel Catlin. The man walks over and extends a hand. "Forgive me for not saluting, Colonel. I am Captain Jean Tribot-Laspierre, the French Sixth Army liaison officer to the Fourth Brigade. General Harbord suggested I spend some time with you."

General Harbord gets into his staff car and dons the sort of helmet Frenchies wear. They call it an Adrian helmet—he's the only American I've seen wear one. I bet he does it to show camaraderie with the Frenchies. Not a bad idea in my book. He leads the caravan of camions forward. Major Holcomb, Tribot-Laspierre, and Catlin ride in the back seat while I drive at the rear of the column.

The truck ahead stops, and men hop down, shouldering their packs. Tribot-Laspierre tells us the place is called Ferme de Paris, which is

Americanized on the spot to Paris Farm. The general drives off after ordering the camions to stay.

Battle noise fills the air—thumps from artillery batteries to the east, nearby explosions, machine gun bursts echoing along with the crackle of rifle fire. Airplanes buzz high above as a dogfight plays out—the planes are too high to make out the markings, but the triplane is winning—a Heinie. I wipe a bead of sweat from my brow and hustle over to help a group stacking wooden ammo crates. Catlin and Holcomb point Marines to their new positions. Marines I trained with in boot camp double-time it away, gear jangling, rifles bouncing, bayonets flickering in the sunlight, leaving me with an empty chest. The private I beat for the highest shooting score at boot camp winks and teases me by making a motion with his right hand as if tightening a wrench.

I keep the Cadillac idling while Colonel Catlin orders the camion drivers to return to Montreuil to pick up supplies and stray Marines. Captain Tribot-Laspierre argues with the lieutenant in charge of the camions and proves that not all Frenchie officers have their heads up their asses. Catlin and Tribot-Laspierre ride in the back while I drive and lead the camion column back to Montreuil.

We no sooner arrive in Montreuil than the missing battalions of the Sixth Regiment wander in. The men of 1/6 gather rations and ammo while four camions beat a hasty retreat. Someone must have warned them about Tribot-Laspierre and Catlin. Nearby, Major Sibley, the CO of 3/6, and his officers confer around an old road map. The colonel orders the battalion commanders to have their men collect two days of rations from the roadside pile. I smile and pitch in as Catlin encourages his lads with infectious bravado, helping privates grab their pound of hardtack, a slab of bacon, and a couple ounces of coffee each.

Catlin orders the First Battalion to load onto the camions he still controls. The Third Battalion is stuck hoofing it since they're going to a reserve position behind the other battalions. I drive Catlin and Tribot-Laspierre, leading the camions to a hamlet named Lucy-le-Bocage.

The Sixth Regiment post of command, the PC, moves three times that day, but Catlin and I spend little time at any of them. Lieutenant Colonel Harry Lee, the second-in-command, works with the signal corps to get phone lines into the PCs. The final PC of the day is at a place called Maison Blanche Farm.

Several hours later, I follow Catlin, Lee, and Tribot-Laspierre as they inspect the thin line of Marine riflemen—one man deep, each digging foxholes six feet apart. Colonel Lee frets over the lack of solid intelligence about what we face. Catlin cracks a wry grin when he asks if Lee means "intelligence" in both senses of the word. Tribot-Laspierre says nothing. This ribbon of Marines is all that stands between the retreating French troops, an unknown number of experienced Heinie divisions, and Paris.

I may be a lowly private, but the odds are obvious. Tribot-Laspierre told us that the French are doing a delaying action in the hope the Heinies will pause to regroup before marching to Paris and give us time to organize. One officer quips that a battle plan based on the hope an opponent won't attack is as bad as no plan at all. But that hope is all we have.

Marines scramble to dig individual fighting holes. Catlin stops, gazing across the wheat field between us and a looming forest. The private nearest us uses a bayonet to chip into dense earth. He scoops the loosened soil into his mess kit and dumps it in front of his hole. "Bet you wish you'd brought your shovel from Verdun," Catlin says.

The private jabs the bayonet into the ground without looking back. "Bet your fucking ass. I hated those fucking shovels. But I'd give anything to have one of the fuckers now. Dirt's like a fucking rock."

"Well, at least your mess kit's getting some use. Mine sure isn't," Catlin replies. The private continues to stab the soil, cursing. Two privates digging adjacent holes stop and watch. "What are you calling these things—the holes, I mean?" Catlin asks.

"Some of the guys are calling 'em foxholes. I'm calling it my fucking grave. The fuckers that sent us here intend to bury us in 'em."

The private in the next hole coughs. The digger glances over at his buddy, who points at the colonel. "Oh, uh . . . sorry, sir. I didn't realize . . ." He begins to stand.

"Don't salute hereabouts, especially to me, son."

An artillery shell explodes in the field about a hundred yards to our front. Soil fragments pelt our helmets. "Best deepen your fucking grave. Might fucking save your life," Catlin says. I smile as the colonel walks back to Lucy. No secret why the men love him.

Heinie artillery picks up, as though saying, *we know you're there*. I check my gas mask as we enter the village of Lucy-le-Bocage. Signal corps men rush in and out of a temporary PC in one of the stone buildings next to a French PC. An American ambulance idles behind another building, the smell of its exhaust melding with the aroma of manure. A young corpsman scurries back and forth, lugging boxes from the ambulance to an aid station. I explore Lucy while Catlin and Tribot-Laspierre go into the French PC.

The buildings in Lucy are sturdy stone-and-mortar constructions with red roofs—some metal, most tile—spared from the shelling so far. A nexus of several roads creates an island in the village center with a large covered well on one side. The rest of the town lines the roads radiating outward. Most of the houses have gardens inside rock walls that separate small yards.

I wander to the eastern edge of Lucy. The Marine line faces east across fields of fully headed green wheat waving in the breeze. Blood-red poppies dot the field. To my right, the wheat ends at the top of a shallow ravine formed by a dry creek called Ru Gobert. We'd walked along it during the inspection. The privates dubbed it Gob Gully, and God help any Marine taking exception to the privates on place names. A dirt road runs along the south side of Gob Gully to the village of Bouresches. A trickle of French soldiers shuffle along the Lucy-to-Bouresches road. Teams of French litter-bearers carry men with bloody dressings, setting their loads down every hundred yards or so. The poor bastards wear ragged uniforms, many without rifles. Defeat and fatigue etch the gaunt face of the one nearest me. He looks into my eyes. I say, "*Merci.*" The man nods and limps toward the aid station. They may have been beaten, but they bought us a precious commodity—time.

Lucy stands on a slope at the southwestern corner of an undulating north-south valley. Men from 1/6 scrape foxholes in front of a road heading north along the valley. Saint Martin Wood stands behind them, forming the western edge of the valley. The terrain north of Lucy slopes uphill for a couple hundred yards, then disappears as it goes downhill.

The forest to our front curves like the inside of a kidney, wrapping around toward the north with a commanding view of the valley. I don't understand why we don't set up our positions inside the woods. It'll provide great cover, unlike these open fields.

The name of the eastern woods in French is Bois de Belleau.

Belleau Wood.

Chapter Eighteen
Major Ab Johnson

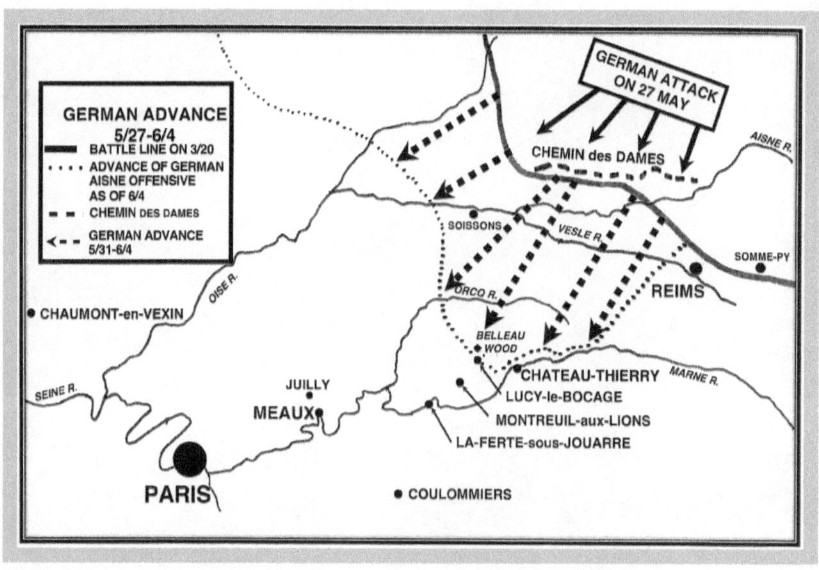

Paris

The names of splints, dressings, and medical kits swim in my head. Fear of ordering the wrong supplies throbs with the heartbeat in my nose. The concussive veil that hung over me has cleared. Tuttle and I returned to Paris well after dark last night. The night staff didn't know anything about a new uniform for me. Major Evans said I looked "salty". I like that, but staff work demands I look squared away.

After a few hours of shut-eye, I return to headquarters. Staffers stare at me—the nose and the filthy uniform. Okay, from now on I'll think of it as "salty". The day staff tells me that replacement has still not arrived. Rumors and contradictory fragments of information fill the halls and break room. The fact that General Pershing didn't know about the movement of the Second Division disturbs me. It confirms Pershing's fear that American troops will no sooner put boots on the ground than they will be tossed into the melee willy-nilly by our allies like cannon fodder. Sons like Jack, all of them. I haven't been able to figure out if Jack's in France yet. The personnel department is in Chaumont, not Paris. They didn't pick up when I tried to phone them earlier.

Tuttle and I meet with Colonel Wadhams in Tuttle's office, each with steaming mugs of strong coffee. "Major, you have to do something about that uniform," Wadhams says. "We have things to do and people to meet, and you're an embarrassment."

"Sorry, sir," I say. "I have two on the way. The corporal at the front desk says they will be here later today or tomorrow."

"What do we know so far?" Wadhams asks Tuttle.

"Information's spotty. The French are in what they call *la soupe* out east of here. The Germans have penetrated as far as the Marne, about thirty miles in from the original front. The French Sixth Army is in disarray. Elements of our Third Division hold a bridgehead in Château-Thierry. The Second Division is forming a defensive line somewhere east of Meaux. The word I have is not encouraging. It may be too little, too late."

"Medical assets?"

"One ambulance company with two dozen Fords," Tuttle says. "Their only medical supplies are those they could stuff into the ambulances. I talked with the man in charge of Fourth Brigade transport. The French proved themselves to be as true to their word as a professional lady's promise about not having the clap. Well, he was a little more colorful than that, but you get the idea. We're on our own. Medical supplies, food, kitchens, and machine guns are being carried on animal-drawn wagons. It'll take them days to reach the division."

"Hospitals?" Wadhams asks.

"None."

"None?"

"Yes, sir," Tuttle says. "Evac Hospital 8 is somewhere in Lorraine. I haven't been able to get through to anyone who can turn them around. Evac 7 is at sea. The division's medical supply depot is a hundred miles south of here."

"So if anyone's hurt, he's SOL." Wadhams sighs. He walks to the window and seems to look at the traffic outside. "The French promised me they'd take care of our casualties when we went into the line at Cantigny. One of the first things you two need to do is meet with them and find out if that's still the case."

"I'm heading there at 0900," Tuttle says. "They told me the Paris surgical chief wouldn't be in before then."

"Think of what we'll need if the French can't deliver," Wadhams says. "I trust them as far as I would that madam's word. By the way, Johnson, all Parisian prostitutes fester with gonorrhea. One hundred percent."

Tuttle and I arrive at Paris District Medical Headquarters at 0824 hours. At 1015 we're shown into the office of a colonel wearing a spotless uniform with medical pins. Our rank difference worries me. The French are more rigid in their hierarchy than us. The colonel sips a cup of coffee while reading a report as we stand. After a long minute, he lifts eyes flaming with contempt. He motions for us to sit, opens an ornate onyx box atop his desk, and pulls out a cigarette. He holds the cigarette out.

My ancestors lopped off a king's head to stop this sort of crap.

Tuttle raises an eyebrow at me as if to say, *don't aggravate our hosts.*

The Frenchman inside me bristles.

Okay, I'll play nice.

I pull a lighter out of my pocket and light the idiot's cigarette. The colonel puffs, gazing at the ceiling, his long, bent Gallic nose in profile. It's easy to imagine a mob of my Parisian cousins chasing the bastard with axes and torches to the guillotine. I stifle a smile.

"You Americans have inferior uniform standards," the colonel says. "In our army you would be subject to a disciplinary action for wearing such filthy clothes."

"My apologies, sir," I say in French. "I was caught in one of the Paris Gun explosions, and my other uniforms were lost in the event. I have new ones on the way." I hope. This is getting embarrassing.

"Thank you for seeing us, Colonel," Tuttle says. "Major Johnson and I are organizing the sanitary train for the AEF Second Division. The division was supposed to go into the line in Cantigny. In that sector, your sanitary train was going to take care of everything above the regimental level. Now that they've moved to the Château-Thierry area, we need to confirm if that's still the case."

The colonel takes a slow drag on his cigarette and aims a stream of smoke at me. He speaks in accented English. "The situation is not good. Not good at all. We have thrown new divisions into this fight. Several have not been heard from again. Nothing—not a word. What we do know is that the only thing rosy is . . . how you say . . . the smiles on Boches' faces. We have lost so much ground . . ." He sips his coffee. "Our hospitals are lost—forty-five thousand beds in all. The supplies, personnel, equipment, ambulances—we assume all are captured."

"That's a staggering loss, Colonel," Tuttle says.

"*Oui.* The only hospitals in that sector are in Meaux. They are beyond capacity. We are evacuating those who are stable to hospitals west of Paris. Our hospital trains are . . . allocated, you might say. You cannot situate your hospitals near Meaux. The roads are too congested. The Boches have advanced so quickly that we assume it will be lost in perhaps four days. They will be at the gates of Paris within a week, two at the most. You are on your own."

"All our medical assets are in Lorraine."

"You'll need to get busy, then. I'm not sure what I can offer you other than my best wishes. I am trying to find hospitals and doctors for my own men, and they are my highest priority."

"Certainly," Tuttle says. "We must do everything we can to provide for our men."

"I am to understand that they are to hold off the Boches at all costs. You must understand that there should be few for the hospitals if they do fight to their deaths as ordered."

I hadn't heard that. *At all costs?* Does this idiot really think Americans would fight to the last man for the likes of him? My pulse throbs, muscles tense at that lunacy.

"We will not go into battle without aid stations and hospitals," Tuttle says.

"Perhaps you need to understand who is in command . . . *Lieutenant* Colonel."

Tuttle shows no reaction and presses on. "There are some things you can help us with. They won't take much effort—mostly clearances from your high command. We need to find facilities in that sector to use as hospitals. We have no base hospitals in this region. Do you think you can prevail on your chain of command to allow us to use the American Red Cross Paris hospitals? Until this time, they have forbidden us from doing so."

"If your troops are defeated, all those hospital beds, the staff and equipment, and the men occupying them will become prisoners of war."

"We don't think that will happen," I say.

The colonel's face flushes red. He leans forward, eyes hot with rage, and shouts in French. "The arrogance! You Americans think you are so . . . brilliant, so . . . strong. You think you know everything." He pounds his fist on the desk. "We are *so* much more experienced. Ours were seasoned troops, unlike yours. You are but children. And General Duchene is in command in this sector, not your fellow Pershing."

I've had it with the pompous prick. I use my calmest voice, in French. "We have to plan on the assumption our men will hold. To do otherwise is foolhardy, Colonel. Why else would Marshal Foch send us?"

I hold the colonel's gaze and wait. The colonel stares at me for nearly a minute, sighs, looks down, and snuffs out the butt end of his cigarette in a cut-crystal ashtray. He teases another out of his box, holds it out for

me to light. I don't move. He finally looks at Tuttle. "I will see what I can do, but don't hold high expectations. Part of the, how you say? Resistance . . . to Paris hospitals is your own high command. You will not be allowed to place any hospitals in Meaux or to the east of there for the reasons I have just explained. Don't ask me again." He pauses and shrugs. "I will talk with my staff about Paris. You will have to speak with yours. *Bonne chance.*"

I struggle to cool my temper by watching Paris drift by on the ride back to headquarters. Tuttle is quiet. His eyes dart from side to side, his jaw muscles tensing as though having a conversation. Tuttle says, "Well, *that* was interesting. Makes me wonder if our real enemy speaks German."

"The loss of forty-five thousand beds is devastating," I say. "That is, if we can take him at his word. Of course, he could be exaggerating to garner sympathy. But I get the feeling that our allies tend to minimize their losses when they talk with us. I'm still new at this—what does that mean in terms of personnel?"

The lines around Tuttle's eyes harden. "It would cripple us. Figure at least one nurse for every fifty patients and one physician for every hundred. And then there's the equipment, supplies, and support staff. Well, you can do the math." Tuttle looks out the window, and his face seems to relax. "By the way, you did well back there. Maybe you'll turn out to be of some use after all. Your French is a lot better than mine. You also stood your ground."

"Thank you, sir," I say. Is Tuttle softening an inch?

"You kept your cool back there. I wanted to shoot him."

"Good thing you don't carry a gun, Colonel. In my reporting days, I learned that whether it's a miner or a Copper King, people don't like to be confronted with truths they can't accept. I'm afraid we have an ally that can be counted on for little aside from bureaucratic petulance."

Chapter Nineteen
Major Ab Johnson

Paris

My lack of medical knowledge matters less than I first feared. That doesn't make me feel any better, though. I spent so much time in the past year angry at Jack and his foolish decision to join the Marines that I never stopped to think of myself as a Marine father. The realization that I am that father hit like a bolt of lightning after dealing with that French colonel.

The French are not going to honor the promise they made to General Pershing, the promise to provide medical support for the men —Marines and soldiers—about to go into battle to save Paris. They lied. The French part of me seethes. The father in me wants to go into the high command planning rooms and smash a few noses. No wonder the militaries of the world censor all the news coming out of this war.

We're on our own with inadequate everything. Months of recent plans that included French support have evaporated like morning mist. And it feels as though this now all depends on me—that I am, somehow, the lynchpin.

I may be one of the few officers here working with a sense of parental responsibility. The men fighting this war are not chess pieces.

They are flesh and blood sons, husbands, fathers. If the idiots leading these countries, especially the royal ones, ever thought that way, this war would have never happened.

So with nothing but French best wishes, we have to set up a medical system under their large noses without them knowing it. I'm not alone —I know Wadhams and Tuttle will support me on the Paris end. I need to figure out who I can work with closer to the fight itself.

Right now, we have twenty-seven thousand men rushing to battle with twenty-four little Ford ambulances and only the medical supplies the docs can stuff in them. No hospitals, no hospital trains, and a French order that we not set up hospitals here, there, or anywhere. The doughboys in the Second Division are all Jacks to me now. Army soldier or Marine, that doesn't matter anymore. They are Americans—that's all that matters to me.

Someone ran a phone line into my tiny office. I hold a cold pack on my nose between calls. That keeps the throbbing at a reasonable level. I can't afford to take the codeine pills they gave me at the hospital, and I'm not willing to take a chance on aspirin yet for fear of bleeding.

I'll start with what I can do here from my office.

Operational security would dictate that everything I'm about to do should be done face-to-face, not on the phone. The Jacks I'm responsible for won't wait the week or two that would take me, so I'll be cagey in what I say, and lift the phone.

I call the French rail regulator to expedite transport of the medical gear stalled in Chaumont-en-Vexin. The Frenchman whines about the complexity of the system, the higher priority of other shipments, and a dozen other lame excuses. I manage to get a word in edge-ways, reminding the officer of the imminent threat to Paris and that the lack of medical support makes effective action untenable. The man doesn't budge. I hang up, cursing the Frenchmen who ordered troops to the front with no concern about what happened to them after they arrived. The French Army mutiny last year now makes perfect sense to me.

Next, I call the American Red Cross—ARC—headquarters. I need to hear an American voice. American Red Cross Military Hospital Number One—ARCMH-1, where they fixed my nose—is full of French casualties. Trudy's hospital. Oh, God, how is Trudy doing? I haven't talked with her since the explosion. Unlike the French, the operator puts me right through to the hospital director. After introducing myself, I tell him I need to find hospitals capable of taking care of our men.

"We certainly could," the director says, "if a few things fall into place."

"Like what?"

"So far we've been taking care of French casualties. Let's just say we'll have room in the next day or so. Give us a full day to tidy up, and we'll be in business."

"That sounds promising," I say. "It seems like there's a 'but' in what you're saying."

"We'll need to get permission from the French to do this. I can talk to them. You'll have to get permission from the AEF to bring American casualties here. They've refused so far."

"Anything else?" I hate to ask.

"Well, let's say, everything. We'll need American doctors, nurses, staff, and tents to expand."

"Okay," I say. "I'll work on the AEF and those other things if you get the French to budge."

It takes me a half hour to get a phone connection to AEF HQ in Chaumont. I think about the confusion French place names cause for Americans. The Second Division was in Chaumont-en-Vexin, which is about fifty miles northwest of Paris. The Chaumont where the AEF is headquartered is over a hundred and fifty miles southeast of Paris. I wait and wait while a private tries to find the staff officer I need. My bladder is full by the time I get the right major on the phone, so I don't mince words. I tell him he needs to get Pershing's approval to use the Paris Red Cross hospitals if he expects to have medical care for his troops.

The private who had ushered me to my office when I arrived knocks on my doorframe. "Gotcher duds here, sir. Hope they fit."

Finally.

He hands me a box and I go to the restroom to change. There are two uniforms with shirts and ties folded in the box with an officer's cap on top. The cap is tight—a hair too small. I slip out of my soiled uniform and put on the trousers. I can barely button them. The shirt goes on next. The creases worry me, and it's snug, but that won't show. The tunic buttons barely close. I suck in my gut. When I relax, a button zings across the room.

Damn it. Am I that fat? I mean, sure, I am fatter than I want to be, but this uniform is size large.

So what's going to look worse? My old uniform that fits but looks like a horse dragged me through a flour mill, or one I can't button? I keep the new one on, leaving the tunic open, fold my old one, and carry it all down to the front desk.

The corporal at the desk gives me a quick head-to-toe glance and holds up one finger. He reaches under his desk and pulls out a garment bag. "Had a feelin' that you were a tad optimistic on your size estimate, sir. Got a couple extra-larges pressed and ready to go for you."

The man keeps a straight face but must be laughing inside. I would if I were him.

"There's a place two blocks away where you can get alterations." The corporal writes an address on a memo pad. "I'm betting these new ones will be a smidge large on you, sir. We can send your old one to the laundry and hope for the best."

I take the new uniforms to the lavatory. The corporal's right, they fit like sacks, but at least the buttons don't burst. I take my old uniform back to the corporal in one of the boxes, and then get back to work. The next call is to the Red Cross headquarters to look at other hospital options. It turns out that while America debated entering the war, the American Red Cross was busy doing its job over here. They tell me there are four hundred beds in ARCMH-2, seventy-five in ARCMH-3, and five hundred in ARCMH-5. The closest hospital to the new front under American Red Cross control is in a small town called Juilly, twelve miles northwest of Meaux. That French colonel didn't mention this. The 220-bed hospital is too far from the front, but it's the only facility around that area that the French haven't taken over. It is, technically, not in Meaux and is northwest, not east of town. I call the hospital director and explain the situation. He clears us to use it if the French don't object, and I find staff and supplies. The Red Cross is better prepared for this war than the US Army Medical Department.

I finally take a deep breath and put in a call to the French Sixth

Army chief surgeon, Médecin Inspecteur General Lasnet. After going through two lieutenants, I speak to him in French. "*Bonjour*, General. I am calling on behalf of Colonel Wadhams. He requested I call to follow up on inquiries about the placement of American army hospitals to support AEF operations in the Château-Thierry sector."

"A mere colonel deigns to have a *major* call me? On his behalf? *He* does not have sufficient rank to talk with me; *you* certainly don't."

"I call on behalf of AEF Medical since I speak French."

"Not very well, I may add, *Major*. Do you have a cold? State your business."

"There's an American Red Cross hospital in Juilly. We need an evacuation hospital for our forces and propose to use that. Colonel Wadhams thought I should check with you first." I listen as papers rustle in the background. Lasnet speaks in a muted voice, probably with a hand over the receiver, asking someone why the French hadn't taken it over. My gut tightens in anger. Lasnet must not have known about the hospital. I just screwed up. How can I fix this?

"You see, *Major*, we have lost all our hospitals in this sector in the past week. *We* need everything available for *our* casualties."

"And ours?"

"Not my concern. Remember, they are ordered to hold off the Boches at *all costs*."

There's that idea again. Even French soldiers won't do that. I may be an idiot, but I'm not a fool.

We argue in French for another twenty minutes, negotiating potential locations for our other division hospitals. In the end, Lasnet insists that no hospitals will be approved within twenty-five miles of the front. The distance is absurd. Hell, the location of the front is unclear. I finally browbeat the man to allow us to locate triage in a town named Bezu-le-Guery, five miles back from a town called Lucy-le-Bocage. When Lasnet takes a breath, I say, "If we use Bezu for field hospital triage, then we need to set up a field hospital reasonably close. There's a small Catholic hospital in La Ferte-sous-Jouarre. Perhaps if I spoke with the nuns there?"

"*Non*. You will not. I forbid it."

I have a road map I bought when I worked for the Associated Press in Paris open as we argue, pencil in hand, circling sites and options. I might as well try to convince Lasnet that the best wine in the world is brewed in the Bronx. "All of which brings me back to Juilly. It's not near the front, not in Meaux, and is the only hospital short of Paris available for our use. If you insist, I'll ask General Pershing to talk with Marshal Foch to get his clearance . . ."

"I will consider it and speak with my superiors. I forbid you from calling yours."

That's as close to a *yes* as I'm going to get. I better do something to keep Lasnet from commandeering the Juilly hospital. I need to get out of this cubbyhole and grab some java, but I put in a call to arrange armed guards to protect the hospital in Juilly. Not to guard it from the Germans, but from our French allies. This could end my career, but I have the feeling everything I do from now on carries that risk.

The next thing is to get the uniform alterations on the one extra-large I'm not wearing. The man tells me he'll have it done in two hours. Fast for Paris, but I figure there aren't very many customers coming in for tailoring this week, given the German advance.

After getting back to the office, I stop by the coffee room. I'm tired of answering questions about my bruised face, going from bronc busting to running with the bulls in Pamplona to barroom brawls with the navy. The last one works the best and gets me in the right mood for what's coming. Back in my office, I think about Jack, our times in the Montana mountains, fishing, camping. My favorite photo of him—one of the things lost with my luggage—is of a towheaded Jack at age seven holding his first catch, a small rainbow trout from Rock Creek Lake. The photo and that time are imprinted on my memory as if it were yesterday.

My next actions could end my career, but Jack's Marines depend on me. I call the Red Cross director and tell him we have the green light to use the hospital in Juilly. The director tells me he has already ordered the hospital to take over an adjacent school building and to order supplies from a Red Cross depot to the south. So far, so good.

It's a funny thing about career suicide. They can only fire you once, no matter how many toes you stomp on. So I stomp. What is the phrase? Better to beg for forgiveness than . . .

I call the quartermaster section and order them to send tents to ARCMH-1 and the hospital in Juilly. I work through the noon hour with growing urgency. Since lunch is a French sacrament, I work the American end of the problem. At around three, I telegraph a medical unit in the west of France and order them to send all of their available operating teams to Juilly. The only ones available are two navy teams at a coastal hospital.

I've never really thought about the dark side of inter-service rivalry. I remember what Colonel Wadhams told Arthur Beck about the army doing all the "fancy stuff" in medical care. The colonel may not like me sending navy surgeons to Juilly, but so be it.

The idiot I used to be thought the Marines were useless. That idiot has not been proven wrong yet, but my son is about to go into battle with them. I'll be damned if I'll let him or any of his fellow Marines die for a lack of medical care to satisfy army vanity.

As much as I would like to stop for supper, I need to lose some weight, and getting into the new uniform is more important. I change uniforms at the tailor's shop and leave the second one with him. Finally, a uniform that fits and doesn't look like hell. Back to the office and another cup of coffee.

I lose all sense of time as I work in my windowless office. Finally, I take a break and stretch. It's nearing midnight. I lock up my office and head out. Tuttle's office is dark, but the door's open and I see the pulsing glow of his pipe. I enter. He's standing by the window, holding the blackout curtain aside, window open.

"Listen," Tuttle whispers.

The rumble of distant artillery.

We're too late.

Chapter Twenty
Lieutenant (junior grade) Arthur Beck

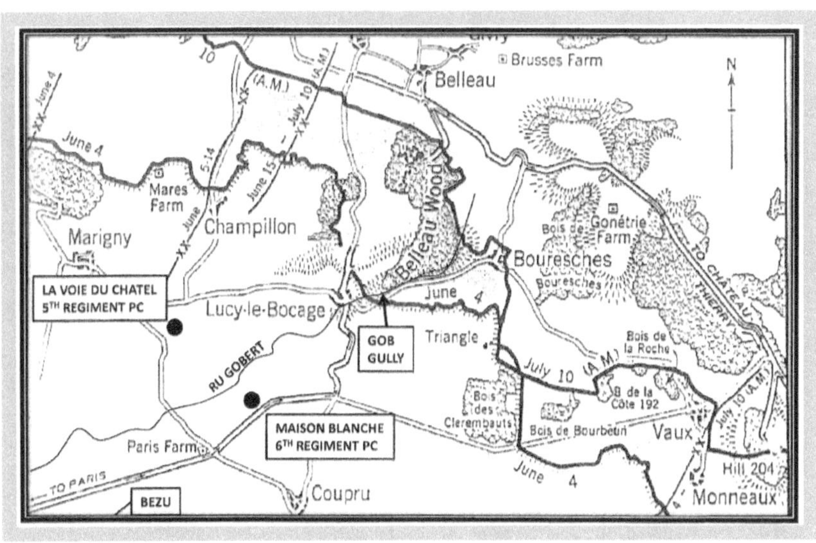

John F. Andrews

La Voie du Chatel and Vicinity
Sunday, June 2, 1918

Blasts from German artillery shells creep closer to the La Voie regimental aid station through the night. How can anyone can sleep with all the racket? I keep my uniform and boots on and go to the aid station several times to ask if I should take shelter in the cellar of the regimental PC across the road. They say no. Memories of sleepless childhood nights plague me—Dad's screams, the murmur of Mom's comforting words, the floor creaking as Dad paced, the cold tea in the bottom of the night's cups on the kitchen counter, and the bags under Mom's eyes the next morning. I abandon all hope of sleep as dawn breaks. My shaky hands fumble as I button my uniform coat and slip on the gas mask pouch, with no idea how to use the contraption. Asking will only expose me to more ridicule. I plop on my helmet—I hate the steel pot—awkward, heavy, no padding except for the leather webbing between my scalp and the steel.

So far, every push I've made to get to the surgical research unit has been met with a stronger shove in the opposite direction. My only option is to play along and keep my eyes out for an opportunity. No more whining.

These so-called surgeons seem like little more than glorified country GPs doing a little of this and a little of that. I am not among my peers. Their treatment of me is a sign of their professional jealousy, nothing more.

Well, that and my shaky hands. I can't control them. This is not me. Or is it? Maybe the psychiatrist was right when he said Dad's condition was genetic.

Colonel Neville's Fifth Regiment post of command—the PC—is in a large, century-old farmhouse on a rise with a commanding view. This is a farm compound, with a high stone wall surrounding the house and outbuildings. French barns are not like the one at my Aunt Minnie's farm in Wisconsin. These are lower stone-walled affairs. A road runs through the middle of the compound, the PC on one side and our aid station on the other. My cot is in a low building that was probably a goat shed.

"Sleep well, Hot Shot?" Lieutenant Commander Dessez asks as I enter the break room.

"No, sir."

It galls me to call him "sir." Any of them.

"It's a little like internship—sleep with one eye open."

"At Cook, we were only on call every other night, and nobody strafed us. Please call me Arthur, sir. I'm afraid that the men are getting too much amusement from 'Hot Shot.'"

"That train left the station before you got here. You're coming along on my aid station inspection this morning. Consider it part of your orientation. One point on customs and courtesies in the battle zone— don't salute anyone. That shouldn't be a problem for you, I suppose. If someone salutes you? Hit the deck."

"Why?"

"German snipers shoot anything that gets a salute. Hold your hands out."

I struggle to steady my hands while Dessez frowns. He leads the way to a small, stripped-down Ford Model T truck, the back end filled with boxes. He, a driver, and I cram into the front seat, and we bounce away from La Voie.

"First, we go north to Marigny," Dessez shouts. "Most of our regiment ended up around there. Before you ask, let me make it clear— things are not going well when a unit commander makes personal deliveries to the front. Right now, it's all hands on deck."

The drive to Marigny takes fifteen minutes, dodging potholes and foot traffic. "This battalion aid station takes care of our northern sector. Those ruts—" Dessez points to the right, "—are the road to Les Mares Farm. One battalion is up there, the 2/5. We locate the battalion aid stations as close to the front lines as safety allows so the litter-bearers don't peter out."

Marigny looks like the German artillery target that kept me awake last night. Two houses smolder through collapsed roofs. Stone walls are pockmarked, windows shattered. Men scurry as a shell hurtles in. I cringe when it explodes about three hundred yards away, my tremor rising with my pulse. Nobody told me that surgeons are stationed within artillery range.

The driver skirts the town and skids to a stop. We jump out, and Dessez plops a box into my arms. Now I'm a delivery man. Dessez carries two boxes as he works his way down a ravine to the aid station. I stumble twice on my way down the slope. We return to the truck for more boxes and then help the battalion surgeon organize the supplies.

"Looks like they hit you pretty hard last night, Les," Dessez says.

"Arty got too hot in town, so we moved here after dark," the man named Les says. "Good thing, too. One of those ruins back there was my station. I just hope they don't drop gas on us. That would complete my day."

"Oh, by the way," Dessez says, "Lieutenant Commander Lester Pratt, this is Lieutenant Junior Grade Arthur Beck, also known as Hot Shot. Les, you and George Crile are both from Ohio, right? Know him?"

"Of course. Good man. Why?"

"Hot Shot thought he had a spot in George's command."

"And here you are," Les says. "Welcome aboard, Lieutenant Shot. Your reputation preceded you." He laughs.

A shell streaks overhead. I duck as it hits Marigny.

Les and Dessez stand tall, as if they think they're bulletproof. Fools.

"What else do you need?" Dessez asks.

"Food, water, a safe building, our equipment, and a good night's sleep," Les says. "Other than that, we're jim-dandy."

We scramble out of the ravine and back into the truck. The driver takes the southeast road leading out of Marigny, then leaves the ruts and bumbles across a wheat field. "We'd have to double back to catch the road to Champillon, so here we go," Dessez says.

"Don't think the farmer'll chase us away, sirs," the driver shouts.

We bounce along for about a mile to Champillon, Marigny's smaller but equally damaged brother. We pull up to a stone farmhouse at the edge of the village. My nose becomes congested, and I wipe away a drip. I rub my eyes—they itch and water as though I'm allergic to something here. What now?

Dessez sneezes. "The Boche mix lacrimatory chemicals into their artillery barrages. Catch a whiff of this, and you'll flood your gas mask with snot and tears. Don't rub your eyes; that'll make it worse."

We go into the aid station and confer with the medical officers. The story sounds much the same, though this station seems better organized. After writing a list of needs, Dessez and I trot back to the Ford, unload supplies, and leave for our next stop.

I came here to do surgery, not deliver supplies or work in aid stations. I've seen dive bars that would be better suited for surgery than these wrecks.

"The aid stations are mixed up right now," Dessez says. "We set Champillon up for the 2/5, but it'll take care of the 1/6 since they're nearby. The next one is in the Sixth Marine zone, but we're still running it. Lieutenant Commander Wray Farwell, my counterpart in the Sixth Regiment, and I worked out a deal of sorts."

We creep along a dirt road, probably heading south, judging from the sun. My neck tingles as we pass a line of soldiers lying in shallow pits along the left side of the road, rifles in front of them as if they're about to start a battle. Is this the front line?

This much I know—without an operating room I'm as useless as one of these infantrymen would be without a rifle.

Chapter Twenty-One
Lieutenant (junior grade) Arthur Beck

The village of Lucy-le-Bocage is in better shape than Marigny. The aid station is in a stone house like the one in Champillon, though the walls are unblemished and the window glass intact. Its windows are taped to prevent them from becoming shrapnel, but not with the fancy patterns I saw in Paris. Green curtains block the inside view. Dessez leads the way through a doorway covered by green canvas tarps nailed to both sides of the wood frame. I could understand covering the door with one tarp, but this is odd.

The air smothers me with humidity and the odor of unwashed men, putrid wounds, alcohol, chlorine, and kerosene. My chest tightens with momentary claustrophobia in the low-ceilinged foyer of the small house. I need air. I breathe through my mouth, and the stench bothers me less after a few moments. I follow Dessez into what must have been the living room. French casualties lie on the floor; others sit with backs to the cream-colored plastered walls. They wear tattered, filthy uniforms, their faces covered by stubble, eyes downcast. One Frenchman with his right arm in a sling seems to stare at a faraway horizon, as though the walls are not here.

We wend our way through the crowd into the next room, where Lieutenant Orlando Petty, another fellow who must be a doctor, and six corpsmen work on the wounded. "Men, this well-dressed naval officer is Lieutenant Junior Grade Arthur Beck," Dessez says. "He's a surgeon, though I have yet to witness the proof thereof."

Petty gives me his usual hostile glare.

I'd like to hate him, but he's also the one who risked his life to save mine when we were strafed.

The other doctor says, "I'm Malcolm Pratt. Nice to meet you. Do I call you Arthur or Hot?"

This is getting ridiculous. No, it *is* ridiculous. But I'll play along. "Doctor Shot will do."

"Malcolm is Lester's younger brother," Dessez says. "Fully qualified surgeon." Dessez points to an olive drab blanket hanging from one wall. "The blankets over the windows block out gas and flying debris. We'll spray them with anti-gas solution when the time comes. The next room is our shock ward. Petty's our specialist in that fine art."

We enter the next room, where three shock tables stand empty. I've seen photos of these, though we have proper ones in Chicago. These are not true tables, but frames that hold the four handles of a stretcher at table height. Petty follows me into the room, saying, "This is low class compared to Cook County, but it's the best those of us living on the wrong side of the tracks can do. We fold three blankets on each stretcher. The bottom two hang down to form side-curtains that extend to the floor, leaving the foot and head ends open. We light a Primus camp stove underneath to heat the enclosed space. That radiates heat into the patient. The third blanket goes over our patient. We give him hot coffee or cocoa if he's conscious and doesn't have a head, chest, or abdominal wound. The whole point is to warm him up. The French came up with this system, and it seems to work."

"What'll you do if the Germans shell Lucy?" I ask, thinking of Marigny.

"Duck and pray," Petty says.

"Can't you use one of the cellars?"

"The ones here have only one entrance and narrow stairs that make stretcher handling difficult," Dessez says. "Everyone inside is trapped if it's blocked. We take our chances above ground and use the cellars as a last resort. That's why Les Pratt set up in the ravine."

We go outside, where a breath of fresh air delights me. I help carry the last of the supply boxes in, and then we head off. The driver takes it slow in the village as we pass soldiers. I guess some are army and some are Marines, but they all wear the same uniforms. Dessez tells the driver to stop on a low stone bridge at the edge of the village. He points at a shallow ravine that runs to the east, where it forms the south edge of a forest. "This is the Ru Gobert creek—everyone calls it Gob Gully. Creek's dry, thank God. See those men, down there?" He points at a group of corpsmen working the culvert below us. "That's our other aid station. We'll use it as a company dressing station for now. Remember where it is. You may need to know. In a hurry."

My pulse quickens. In a hurry? What the hell? Does this mean I'm going to work here? I sit on my hands, the tremor worsening.

An artillery shell whistles overhead, and I duck as it explodes a hundred yards away, showering us with dirt. "Glad that wasn't shrapnel." Dessez wipes off his helmet. "Better get out of here."

My gut clenches as I look toward the new crater, my rectum tight as the driver hits the gas.

Dessez orders the driver to turn west. "A little too close back there. You need to know where the stations are in case we move you to one of them."

"They look like glorified first-aid stations." I don't say what I really think. I am trying to get along.

"Our job is to triage, stabilize, and transport. Nothing fancy. Stop the bleeding, slap on a dressing, and get 'em out. I know you think your surgical skills will go to waste, but that's not my problem. When all hell breaks loose, I expect your expert hands to be steady."

My face warms. My hands shake. I cannot control them.

We drive against the flow of open-cab Liberty trucks filled with boxes, mule-drawn wagons stacked with crates, and animal-drawn cannons heading east. The driver turns on a southbound dirt road two or three miles west of Lucy. Traffic thins, but the rutted road slows us down.

I drum the fingers of my right hand against my knee as the country-side grows verdant and less trampled. My frustration is like a stew about to boil over. I'm a surgeon, not a Boy Scout trying to earn his first-aid merit badge. Why are they willing to work under these conditions?

After two miles, we enter a place called Bezu-le-Guery and park outside a small church. Men unload supply trucks, double-timing it between the church and a nearby school building. A tall, thin sergeant's shouts fill the air along with exhaust fumes and the odor of sweat.

Dessez points at one of several tents in the courtyard. "That tent's for gas cases. We get them unclothed right away, since the mustard gas sticks to cloth. You expose yourself if you touch it or breathe the fumes. Get a bunch of them in a room and you might as well gas the room. So we strip them out in the open and scrub them down over there." He points at an open shower set up next to a truck with a large tank in the bed. "After they towel off, we dress them in pajamas and admit them to the gas hospital. Mustard can take up to two or three days to show itself."

"Where's the gas hospital?" I ask.

"We hope to have one soon."

I know almost nothing about gas warfare. It's not a surgical matter, but the thought makes my gut feel hollow, as though it's one of many yawning gaps in my understanding of medical care in this war.

We walk into the church. Pews line the walls of the small nave. Four litter racks stand near the altar, where two teams of doctors and corpsmen work on French soldiers. The walking wounded sit in the pews and on the floor. Corpsmen hand out hot drinks as they circulate among patients. "I'm sure you know all this, so I'll only say it once. Casualties lose heat through inaction, evaporation, and open wounds. Most of the men we treat come in dehydrated. Heat and blood loss combined with dehydration equals shock. Warm drinks help. There's no other way to rehydrate these guys. No intravenous sets; no transfusions. Until the supplies are adequate, there'll be no hot coffee for the medical personnel—only the troops, so keep that in mind."

As we leave the church, Dessez points. "That's the triage tent. We converted the town schoolhouse into Field Hospital One. Don't mention that name to any French officers. They won't let us set up any hospitals around here. The less they know, the better. It has a shock resuscitation room, with six tables ready to go. The lightly gassed will go on the second-floor rooms until we figure out where to evacuate them."

Dessez asks a corporal where Major Richard Derby's office is. The corporal leads us to a second-floor teacher's office, saying that Derby should be back soon. Four desks crowd the room with a blackboard on one wall, a geometry lesson still on it. Derby is a major. Maybe I can make my argument for a transfer in case the subject comes up. It's obvious that Dessez has no intention of letting me go, but perhaps Derby will be more open to the idea. I go over what to say while we wait.

"Dick Derby is army, the assistant division surgeon," Dessez says. "He's an interesting man. His father-in-law is—"

Derby enters the room wearing a short leather coat with driving goggles loose around his neck. He's a shade under six feet, with handsome features, a trim mustache, dark brown hair, and distracted brown eyes. He looks up. "I was just out your way. The motorcycle sure is practical. You should get one. As long as you don't suffer from hemorrhoids."

"Thanks," Dessez says. "I'll think about it the next time I feel suicidal. This young fellow is Doctor Arthur Beck, surgeon extraordinaire from Cook County. I'll get it out of the way. He's going to demand a transfer to a place where he'll do real surgery. Somebody assigned him to Crile's unit. Someone else nixed that when we came up short."

Ambushed. The nerve!

Derby laughs. "If you pull that off, tell me how you convinced me so I can do the same. You didn't need to wear your best attire to make your presentation, you know. That uniform custom made? It's beautiful, aside from the dust."

Damn it. It's as though these people have planned all of this. Things are looking hopeless.

"Where do we stand?" Dessez asks.

"Don't know where the first real surgery will be done," Derby says. "My hope is Juilly, but my fear is Paris."

"That's absurd," Dessez snaps.

"You're preaching to the choir. Tuttle and his men in Paris are trying to set things up, but I'll tell you—this is a hell of a mess. Tuttle asked me what I needed, and I told him, without exaggerating, *every-*

thing." Derby takes off his helmet, pulls the goggles over his head, and looks out the window. "So, Dr. Shot, make the best of it. You're last in a long line of surgeons here who'd like to have Charlie Mayo's operating suite." Derby paces, favoring his left leg. "The evacuation distances worry the hell out of me. This place'll be full when we reach fifty. I hope Tuttle can scrounge some tents for us. The distance between the aid stations and here will cost lives. But that's only one of my worries."

"What else?"

Derby opens a desk drawer and pulls out the first map I've seen of the area. Derby rattles off a list of hospitals and locations that mean nothing to me.

" . . . So, the French won't give us the support they promised, but refuse to let us set up hospitals within any reasonable distance," Derby says. "I think we should set up our hospitals where we can and not bother to tell them. Asking the French for permission is like banging our heads against a wall."

"Think they'll come around?" Dessez asks.

"The French?" Derby scowls. "I have a bad feeling about that. There's a hospital in Juilly that we'll use as our evac hospital. Someone I'd like to meet someday sent army guards to protect our possession of it. I left a few of my people with them. I hope we can scare up some more. It could expand to maybe eight hundred if we can find the staff and a bunch of tents. The distance from some parts of the battlefield to Juilly is forty-four miles, with another thirty or more to Paris. If we don't get more ambulances, it'll be like the Civil War—mule-drawn wagons and field amputations."

"A man in serious condition is sunk," I say.

"He doesn't have to be in serious condition," Derby says. "Even minor wounds can fester and become gangrenous in the time it'll take to get them to a proper operating room. Know any Civil War veterans, Lieutenant?"

"My father."

"Combat vet?"

I nod as I stare at the blackboard, the room suddenly airless.

"I'm worried that we'll be no better than the surgeons were in his war."

Chapter Twenty-Two
Private Carl Larsen

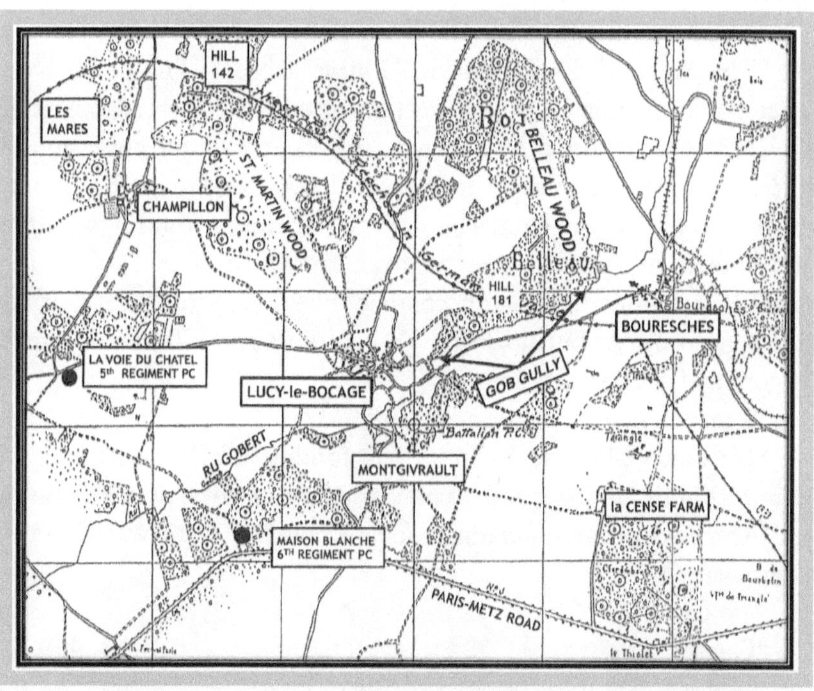

Maison Blanche Post of Command (PC) and Vicinity
Monday, June 3 1918

Colonel Catlin sent me to circulate among the units—to be his eyes and ears—while he organizes our PC. I work my way along the lines over the next two hours, watching Marines dig, bitch, and gaze across wheat fields at the unknown. French names befuddle Marine mouths, which has become a source of amusement for bored leathernecks. They rename everything they can't pronounce. Chief among the heretics are the privates. Their place names begin with *fucking* for the most part. Lucy Birdcage—Birdcage for short—and Gob Gully are two that stick. Champillon sounds more like *Champion*, but Bouresches is easy to say, even though most can't spell it.

The privates come from all over the nation and every walk of life— from Hiram to me, and the broad swath of the American mixing bowl in between. Hiram and I may be far apart in birth and background, yet we're not so far in spirit. I smile. Not far at all. I haven't run into him since we got here—wonder what he's doing?

One thing about a private talking with the privates—we trust each other. They know, from experience, that I will never attach a name to a comment. It's a matter of honor. And that's one cornerstone of the Marines.

Gotta get back to the PC.

Colonel Catlin, Lieutenant Colonel Lee, and Major Evans stand in front of a small map on an easel when I enter the PC staff room. Catlin says, "Carl, put on a fresh pot of coffee. This vile concoction stayed on the burner too long."

A big part of the coffee problem is that Sanitary chlorinates all our drinking water. That, and the fact that getting real coffee involves a certain amount of creativity.

I organize the percolator and set it on a Primus camp stove. The stove and coffeepot are at the end of a large staff room. A knot in my gut tightens as I think through my presentation. The colonel expects me to report on what I saw today. A private doing lieutenant's work might not sit well with the other officers.

"What did you see, Carl?" Colonel Catlin asks.

"Well, sirs, quite a bit. That map you have is more artistic than accurate, the roads in particular. The other terrain features are not exactly as shown, either."

"I reached the same conclusion," Catlin says. "Go on."

"The noise of the battle is growing closer, and the Heinies—er, the Germans—are lobbing more and more artillery by the hour. It's playing havoc on communications and supply. The signal corps boys gave me an earful. They have good phone lines from the regimental PCs back to Brigade. Everything from the regimental PCs to the front is unreliable. No sooner do they lay the wire than incoming artillery blows it up."

"What about the wireless sets?"

"Begging the colonel's pardon, but shouldn't someone from intelligence be briefing us?" Major Evans asks.

My balloon bursts.

"Privates hear things that lieutenants don't, and all our lieutenants are busy," Catlin says. "I enjoy Carl's ground-level view." Catlin looks at Evans, who shrugs. "I'm proud to lead a regiment that includes so many college men. We have the smartest privates in the AEF." He winks at me. "You graduated from Shattuck Academy, a military school, right?"

"Yes, sir."

"What colleges accepted you?"

"Carleton, University of Chicago, Columbia, Princeton, and Yale, sir."

Catlin turns to Evans and smiles. "I'll admit, Carl's young, but he's as bright as any of our new lieutenants. About the radios, Carl?"

I want to smile but stifle it. A colonel going to bat for a private. That's a rare event, but not with Colonel Catlin. Part of why I think the men would march into hell with him. I would.

"Worthless. You need a truck to haul them and their generators, sir. Signals told me that half the traffic on them is in German. We assume they can hear ours as well as we hear theirs. Runners carry most of the messages. We have a few pigeons in reserve, but they'll be useless if the Heinies lob gas."

"How do my lads look out there?"

"Well, sir, not very squared away. There isn't enough water to shave, much less bathe. The lack of deodorant is going to give away our positions soon. We can't get much water to the front lines. Men take turns running handfuls of canteens for refills over distances up to a mile. The Heinies dropped some gas on Lucy, so we can't use the well there until Sanitary tests it. The only things warm out there are the water, the weather, and the artillery—not the food. A few have dysentery, and it's not as though we have a laundry service or toilet paper. The only chow, other than field rations, is monkey meat."

Evans chuckles. "Monkey meat?"

"Yes, sir. It's canned meat that proves not all Frenchmen can cook. There's a lot of speculation about the species of origin. One private declared it simian, and it stuck. Honestly. I tasted some. Eating it would be a fellow's last act before dying from starvation. It tastes like a two-week-old corpse."

"How about morale?" Lee asks.

"Good, sir. The men are itching to get into action. The wait is driving them nuts."

"Now I know why they call you the Little Colonel," Evans says.

By Evans's expression, I can't tell if that's an insult or a compliment. I'll remember not to play poker with him. I've done my best. Hell, I'm just a nineteen-year-old private.

"Well done, son. Let's go for a drive. I need some air." Catlin puts on his helmet, snugs the chinstrap, and moves his gas mask pouch to the ready position in the center of his chest.

I check my gear and go outside to pull the car from a nearby shed. I gaze toward a buzzing noise in the sky. Heinie reconnaissance flight. They've forced us to hide our vehicles.

I drive the colonel to Montreuil. As we approach the town, nestled in a narrow, wooded valley, lines of Liberty trucks, camions, and animal-drawn wagons clog the road from the west. I pull to the side and park. The colonel gets out and walks forward. I kill the engine and follow. Mules clatter and bray as they struggle to pull wagons and artillery. The major in charge of supply transport shouts at four men struggling with a balky mule. I smile.

"Major, you've arrived in the nick of time," Catlin says.

"Yeah. My animals are played out. The men haven't slept a full night in three days, Colonel."

"My lads will be happy to have hot chow after you get the kitchens set up, but I'm particularly happy to see those machine guns. So far, we haven't needed them, but that'll change very soon."

The mule wrestlers scratch their pits and nether parts. So thoughtful of them to remember to bring a new crop of French cooties. One of the men bawls out a string of obscenities—Mister Worthington. He and his three would-be Ivy League friends wear dusty, sweat-stained uniforms. I can practically smell them from here. Worthington scowls and gives me the single-finger salute.

Catlin glares. "Major, I think that lad over there just gave me the finger."

The major shouts, "Worthington, you're going to clean shithouses for the duration." He wipes his brow. "Sorry, Colonel."

I glance up at Catlin, who gives me a conspiratorial wink. Lackeyhood has its advantages.

We head back to the Maison Blanche PC. I stay in the barn and tinker with the Caddy while the boss heads into the PC. The crackle of gunfire is creeping closer as the Frenchies shoot it out with the Heinies just beyond our front line, making me itch for a Springfield and a hundred rounds. It isn't a question of *whether* the Frenchies will break and run, but *when*. The faces of the *poilus* falling back through our lines tell the story better than any intelligence dispatch.

An hour later, I drive Colonel Catlin and Captain Tribot-Laspierre to La Voie for a meeting with Colonel Wendell "Buck" Neville, the CO of the Fifth Regiment. A Fokker triplane sporting black crosses on its wings passes high overhead. The lack of allied planes ticks me off. Where are they? They've gotten a lot of press, the fancy flying boys.

I walk over to the east side of the headquarters building while the bosses meet. Two elongated observation balloons sporting German crosses bob in the air far away. Everyone, including the officers, calls them *sausages*. Well, the privates called them *fuckers*, but that's now the first name of everyfuckingthing. At least when they refer to the Fokker triplanes, the name is not far from the truth—in every sense. The Frenchies fly a few patrols each day, but the dogfights I hoped to watch never materialized.

The Heinies begin to shell the area to the north. Hiram's unit is up that way, adding to my worries. A shell hits near the wall outside the farmhouse, shattering my reverie in a shower of dirt and stone fragments. I rush to take shelter with the others in the cellar as a barrage hammers overhead. The barrage ends at 1700 hours on the dot. We wait in the cellar for several minutes.

"Let's head up," Catlin says.

I follow the colonel to the observation post on the second floor of the PC while Colonel Neville and his staff return to work. The officers pull out binoculars. We have a clear line of sight to the north toward Les Mares Farm. Catlin pats me on the shoulder. "Carl, grab some glasses and watch. The 2/5 has the line on both sides of Les Mares. We moved a few of our machine gunners up there this morning. Lieutenant Colonel Wise's PC is at the farm. If the Boche don't fire up the artillery again, we'll have a box seat."

I have a feeling the Heinies were trying to hit our guys on the line with that barrage and shot long. Corpsmen scurry among the men in reserve. I see Hiram and another litter-bearer sprint while carrying a stretcher. Man, he's fast. And strong.

Scattered French *poilus* in their light blue uniforms retreat up a gently sloping, poppy-dotted wheat field toward the American line. There's a church steeple in the valley below. Men stop at times to turn and fire their rifles while others loose bursts from their light machine guns—French Chauchats. The Heinies pursuing them march in four precise skirmish lines a couple of hundred yards behind. These are like the skirmish lines the Frenchies drilled into us during our training last winter, called the line of sections attack formation. Two columns emerge out of the valley and follow the last wave of skirmishers.

"Speaking strictly as a military man, I have to admit those orderly Boche lines are a thing of beauty," Catlin says. "Look at how steady and precise they are. They move as one. This is an elite unit. I estimate more than a thousand, and who knows how many are behind in the valley below."

My heart surges as I scan across the precarious position of Wise's men. They're outnumbered. How can Catlin stand and watch this with so little worry? I put the binoculars down and realize the Heinies aren't quite as close to our line as they appeared through the lenses. Still, there are more of them than us. I'm wondering if I should warm up the Caddy in case we have to skedaddle.

"There is one problem they face, *les Boches*," Tribot-Laspierre says.

I like this guy, for what it's worth. Not a stuck-up prig like most of the Frenchie officers I've met along the way.

"Only one?" Catlin asks.

"*Oui.* The line of sections attack they are using only works when preceded by a rolling barrage. They must not have the artillery in place yet to do that. Without it, they are, how you say . . . ?"

"Like targets in a county fair shooting gallery," Catlin says.

A few of the *poilus* pause, as though they might reinforce a small outpost inside a stand of trees about a hundred yards or so in front of Wise's main line. Puffs of smoke appear in front of the outpost as the Marines there cover the French retreat.

The Heinie skirmish lines march like machines toward Les Mares. Their gray uniforms seem about to overrun the outpost when the front row drops. I've never seen that infantry maneuver. It looks like a planned action. Why did they all hit the deck at once? The simultaneous reports of several hundred Springfield rifles draw my gaze to the Marine line, where a wall of smoke rises in the air.

The Heinies pause as if rudely interrupted. Their machine guns rake the trees around the forward outpost as Marines burst out and sprint back to the main line. The Heinies re-form their lines and resume the march forward. I take a deep breath. So many. I want to run down and join the 2/5—to help fend off the horde about to overwhelm them.

The Heinies advance another fifty yards, and the front line does the same thing again. But this time, I have my binoculars focused on them. Splashes of crimson appear on the uniforms before they drop. The Marines, using their bolt-action Springfields, are taking down the Heinies as effectively as machine guns.

Some of the Heinies raise and aim their rifles. Delayed reports follow the puffs of smoke from their barrels, but Heinies continue to fall. The columns fan into new skirmish lines, and more die. Then our machine guns rattle, sending more Heinies to Valhalla or wherever the Kaiser's boys think they go.

"You see the problem of no rolling barrage," Tribot-Laspierre says.

"That is the finest marksmanship I've ever seen. My generals would never admit to this, but your men are better shots than ours."

"We pride ourselves on that point, Captain," Catlin says. "Thank you for the compliment. Seeing this makes me nervous about our own use of the line of sections tactic. The attacker is at a huge disadvantage unless he has an effective artillery screen."

"Our artillery does have that field registered, Colonel," an officer says. "I'll go down and let Colonel Neville know."

Shock waves from the nearby Twelfth Artillery rattle my chest. Seventy-five-millimeter shells rain down on the field like an iron squall, drowning out the rifle and machine gun noise. Only the smoke tells me that Colonel Wise's men are still peppering the charnel field. Soldiers caught in the open scatter in a disorganized retreat. Several minutes later, the Heinies re-form and move forward again.

What sort of officer orders an attack into a field like this? As much as I want to take it to the Heinies, I kind of feel for the poor ground pounders marching to their deaths.

The Heinies angle toward the farm buildings and are repulsed. Then they shift toward the Marine right. The thin line separating courage from stupidity strikes me as I watch the bloodshed.

"The thing that's more beautiful than the organization of those German lines is what we just did to them, don't you think, Carl?" Catlin asks.

"Yes, sir." I slip the binoculars back into the case. I sure as hell wouldn't want to be on the receiving end of what the Heinies got today. What'll happen when it's our turn?

Chapter Twenty-Three
Major Ab Johnson

Paris

The phone must have flattened my right ear for all the time wasted on it. I stand, rub my ear, and pull at the seat of my trousers. Three damned hours stuck on the phone—I'm ready to shoot some of the idiots I've had to deal with. I finally pried loose one of our new mobile surgical hospitals. It'll arrive in a few days, by which time we'll have an idea of where to set them up. I don't plan to tell the French about this. Getting through to the Second Division medical people is driving me nuts. Priority calls tie up the phone lines, and nobody considers my work "priority." When I manage to get through, the right person is never there.

A knock on my doorframe startles me. "Major, I have Lasnet on the line for you." Médecin Inspecteur General Lasnet's staff had refused to put me through before, so I ordered one of our clerks to call and wait on hold. Two can play at this game.

I speak French. "Ah, Colonel, thank you for taking my call."

"What do you want?" Lasnet's voice seethes with contempt.

"I'm calling again about the disposition of our medical units."

"The answer is still *non*. You speak French words; how do you not understand that one?"

"Well, I understand your hesitancy, with all the losses you've suffered . . ."

"Forty-five thousand beds!" Lasnet spits the words out.

Our intelligence man told me the French had lost closer to sixty thousand. "I have our Eighth Evacuation Hospital staff on the way to Meaux. They should arrive on the fifth if all goes well. I'll send some of them to Juilly—"

"Where we found your armed guards at a hospital I planned to use. Whose side of this war are you fighting on, *Major*?"

I've been wondering the same thing about Lasnet. "Juilly is too far back, though. We need to move our Field Hospitals 16 and 23 near decent roads and get them up and running. Jouarre and Luzancy are the logical spots, don't you agree?"

"I forbid that, as you know. If you think you can wear me down—"

"I would never dream of such a thing, Colonel." That is exactly what I'm doing, for the sake of the American sons getting wounded in the field. "But we need them closer than Juilly. What about Montreuil-aux-Lions?" I lick a trickle of blood that threatens to drop off my upper lip. The nasal packing limits my ability to intone—making it harder to speak my second native tongue—but the nose still bleeds from time to time, probably in concert with my blood pressure.

"Out of the question. Are you hearing impaired?"

"Perhaps we can find an out-of-the-way spot outside Meaux . . ." I say.

"As long as it doesn't interfere with my evacuation routes, I suppose."

"I'll see what I can do. Thank you, sir."

A print of Edvard Munch's painting *The Scream* hangs in my home office back in Butte. The French are living that painting. I mosey to Tuttle's office to find him mired in a stack of reports. I pace to get the blood flowing in my stiff legs while giving my progress report. "We have Evac 8 on the way. Ten trucks of supplies are coming from the south. I'm told that Second Division's supplies are trickling into Montreuil, but I can't tell what's arrived."

"Why's that?"

"I don't have a reliable contact person at Second Division. I speak to a different man each time—if I get anyone at all. They won't tell me anything of value over the phone for security reasons. Besides which, I think everything there is in a jumble."

"We need someone on the ground." Tuttle pauses. "That means one of us will have to stay at Second Division HQ." Tuttle points at me and raises an eyebrow. "Our boss, General Ireland, is in town. He and I are planning an inspection tour tomorrow morning. I think you should pack your essentials, go in my place, and stay there to be our eyes and ears."

I touch my nose, then put my hand down—I don't want to restart the bleeding. My throbbing face is an unpleasant reminder of the element that blind luck plays in my mortality, even in Paris. The reassurances I gave Helen about staying safe and out of harm's way are as phony as the war reporting Ira's censors are allowing in the newspapers. I have a bad feeling more lies are on the way.

Chapter Twenty-Four
Major Ab Johnson

Paris
Tuesday, June 4, 1918

This morning starts at the office before sunrise with a meeting with our boss of bosses, Surgeon General Ireland. Lieutenant Colonel Tuttle gives a report while Colonel Wadhams and I listen. Ireland glances at me from time to time, as though wanting to say something. The nose still throbs. At the end of the report, Tuttle leads us to the parking area.

"Major—get in a brawl?" General Ireland asks.

Here we go again.

"Yes, sir. Took on a group of naval officers at the New York Bar the other night—defending the honor of the army."

Ireland stares at me. Wadhams huffs. I keep a straight face as Ireland laughs and pats my shoulder. "I hope we didn't waste resources fixing the other guy."

"Guys."

We set off for Meaux, where we meet with Médecin Inspecteur General Lasnet, who reiterates the order that no hospital can be nearer than twenty-five miles from the front. I sense a little more respect from Lasnet than in my phone calls, probably due to Ireland's presence. My French intonation is also better in person than over the tinny Parisian phones. However, Lasnet acts as though General Ireland's single star isn't sufficient to move him on the issue of hospital locations. After the meeting, General Ireland says, "Major, you have a way with words. When we tried to work with Lasnet before, he was a pain in my backside. Now he's just a pain in the side."

"Sir, perhaps if you work on this from the back end . . ."

"It goes without saying," Ireland says. "You'll have to dance carefully with our host nation, but we can't let their panic prevent us from getting our job done. The Second Division assistant surgeon, Dick Derby, has some . . . interesting connections. Work with him. Don't consider this an order, Major, but I don't care how many French toes you step on."

I wonder what Derby's "interesting connections" are. We take a twelve-mile, kidney-bruising ride to Juilly. The pain the potholes will inflict on the wounded makes me shudder. The GMC ambulances Tuttle secured yesterday are lined up in the parking lot in front of the Juilly hospital. They roll in and leave as soon as the wounded are loaded. The GMCs are bigger than the Fords and have better suspensions. They'll be good for the trip to Paris, but not spry enough for the battle-field—one of many facts I've stuffed into my aching head over the past few days.

"Is there a security problem I need to know about?" Ireland points at the armed army guards around the hospital compound.

"Not as long as Lasnet's men stay away," I say.

Ireland chuckles. "Well done, Major."

Crews erect rows of tan canvas tents between the buildings. We go to the rear of the hospital. Bitter bile touches the back of my tongue at the sight of flies swarming a mountain of bloodstained dressings. I stare at the horizon to keep my stomach under control, glad my sense of smell is out of commission.

"Looks like the incinerator crew hasn't kept up with their work," Ireland says.

A private wearing a stained, disheveled uniform staggers from the back door, lugging a wooden box with blood oozing between the slats. He looks as though he hasn't slept in days as he struggles with his load.

"Are you part of the incinerator crew?" Ireland asks.

"No. I *am* the crew." The private looks up, and his face colors as he comes to a groggy semblance of attention. "Sorry, sirs. My hands are a little too full . . ."

"You need to incinerate those as soon as possible, son." Ireland points at the pile.

"I know. But they told me this takes priority." He moves closer and tips the box slightly. I break into a light-headed sweat at the sight of a hand and two lower legs, one greenish brown and marbled with gas bubbles. A brief image of seven-year-old Jack holding his prize trout at Rock Creek Lake flashes across my mind. Whose sons are no longer attached to these, and what suffering have they endured? I can't tell a Marine leg from an army arm. The rivalry, the disrespect I've felt for the Marines, is meaningless as the private dumps the contents of the box into the incinerator. I look up at the smoke fading into the azure French sky and feel my face grow hot with shame.

We enter the hospital through the back door. As we near the main stairs, a harried doctor approaches, dressed in white surgical scrubs stained with sweat and blood. He stops and stands at attention.

"When's the last time you slept?" Ireland asks.

The surgeon's face shows equal parts confusion and thought. "Maybe . . . yesterday? Not sure, sir."

"Please, Doctor, relax. How long are your shifts?"

"Twenty hours. Last night was a hot one. Artillery and gas, sir. We've been working all night."

"How many?"

"At last count? I think—195 wounded. Twenty didn't make it."

"And this is just the warm-up," Ireland says. "Three fresh surgical teams are on the way—when, Ab?"

Those are the navy teams. I hope Ireland doesn't blow his stack.

"As soon as they can get through the traffic jam between Paris and here," I say. "We've arranged for one team from Paris and two from a naval base hospital near the coast. Evac 8 is stuck at a railroad siding in Lorraine. It'll take another day or two before they're here."

"Ab and Tuttle have been working on the evacuation plan," Ireland says. "There's a rail siding near here. However, our French hosts refuse to give hospital train authorization between here and Paris. All transfers are by ambulance until further notice."

"God, that's a long ride," the surgeon mutters.

The tour moves to the surgical area, where we don clean scrubs and masks. The sight of two surgical teams up to their elbows in blood brings my nausea back. How do they get used to this? I swallow and struggle to not vomit as sweat trickles down my face. I've never seen surgery. There are three operating tables—two for surgery and the third to titrate ether, the only anesthetic available.

A private armed with a flyswatter circulates around the room nailing the bugs not caught by flypaper curling from the ceiling. I focus on the private and not the patients on the tables as the doctors talk. I wipe sweat from my face as the room seems to close in around me. Ireland finishes his conversation, and I stifle the urge to bolt in front of the general as we head toward the door.

After Juilly, we ride for an hour through lush countryside that reminds me of my boyhood home in Wisconsin, passing ambulances along the way. We inspect Field Hospital One at Bezu and then drive two and a half miles north to the division HQ in Montreuil-aux-Lions. The division surgeon and Major General Bundy, the Division CO, are gone. We find Assistant Division Surgeon Richard Derby talking with four officers in a staff room.

Derby shakes hands with Ireland and Wadhams. He turns to me. "Hope the other guy looks worse."

"Just ran with the bulls in Pamplona."

Derby coughs. "Uh, Major, the run's in July."

"Thanks. I'll remember that next time."

"You told me you brawled with the navy." Ireland frowns.

"Okay, I was just trying to have a cup of coffee with a friend when the building we were in blew up. Paris Gun got it."

"You know, that's a better story than the others," Ireland says. "So, Dick, tell me what's going on."

Derby shakes his head. "Damned French. Their trains have jammed up the rails so much that we can't get anything in."

"We'll just have to make do with what we have," General Ireland says. "I'm not a bit happy about this. We have help on the way. I hope it'll be in time. Maybe you can work some magic?"

Derby shrugs. "There's a limit . . ."

"On a brighter note, at least we have a battle cry," a colonel standing nearby says. "Seems as though a French major came up to one of our Marine captains, Lloyd Williams, Fifty-First Company of 2/5. The major gave him an order to retreat. Williams refused. The major took out a pencil and paper and wrote a direct order. You know what Williams said?" Heads shake. "*Retreat? Hell! We just got here!*"

"I like that," Ireland says.

"I wish a soldier had come up with that," the colonel says. "Once the press hears about it, it'll look like this show is all Marines." He pauses. "All right. Let's get back on track. We've had heavy German artillery bombardment across our sector. It missed our front for the most part, but the rear and reserve areas took it on the nose."

The colonel pauses, seeming to study my face, then continues. "Over two hundred casualties north of Marigny. Lucy's a smoldering wreck. There've been multiple probing actions across the line, all of which we've beaten back so far. French air support is a joke and there's no apparent plan to bring our flyers up here. We and the Third Division are all that stand between ten or twenty German divisions—the French either don't know or won't tell us—and Paris. We need at least two more divisions to echelon in depth. None are available. And where do our friends from medical stand?"

Ireland nods at me. I give a quick summary.

"By the way, I'm Preston Brown, division chief of staff," the colonel says.

"Oh, I'm sorry," General Ireland says. "This is Major Albert Johnson."

"You're the oldest major here, Major," Brown says. "Tee someone off?"

"Long story."

"Tell it to me sometime. I have a feeling you're going to get a nickname," Brown says.

"I answer to Ab, but I've been called many things in my newspaper work back in civilian life."

"I could come up with something about your nose, like *Snuffy*, but I don't think that befits a major in my army. You have any sons? What do they call you?"

"Two. *Pops*."

"Suits you. Best we have that out of the way now before some private dubs you *Gramps*. A Marine told me that the first name of everything around here starts with the letter *F*. I don't think you want that, either."

I shake my head. "I can live with Pops." The image of Jack and his brother fishing with me along the Clark Fork River flashes through my mind. How many of the boys out there will never fish again? Dead or missing their casting arms.

"Preston, I'm assigning Ab—*Pops*—to be the liaison between your division and Colonel Tuttle," Ireland says. "Tuttle'll handle Paris. I suspect Ab's ability to speak their tongue will get us further with the French than we would otherwise. Colonel Derby can work his special connections on Jouarre and Luzancy. Ignore Lasnet and get the job done."

"I just hope we can get this all together in time," I say.

"We've already failed by that criterion," Ireland says. "We're in trouble."

Chapter Twenty-Five
Medical Corpsman Lyle McCormack

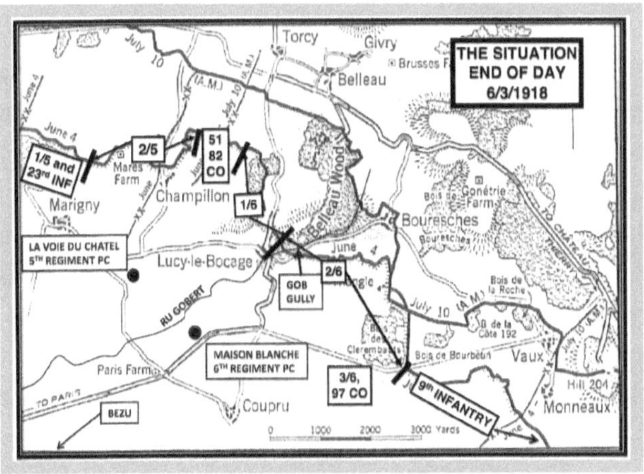

Fifth Regiment Aid Station, La Voie du Chatel

T he other corpsmen of the Sixth Regiment medical staff and I struggle to set up aid stations. The clock is ticking. No sooner was one order issued than another took its place. We're not alone. The privates grouse that as soon as they dig a hole *here*, someone orders them to dig another *there*. It's a pain in my ass—set up a station, then move it, then move it again. As far as my buddies and I are concerned, the men in charge of this don't know what they're doing.

Our team is working its tail off to set up an aid station at the Petit Montgivrault Farm, southeast of Lucy. A battalion PC across the road from us has changed hands twice in the past day. Dense woods protect us from the sun and German eyes. We set up the aid station in the largest of three barns, with a cellar we can use if the German artillery finds us. We shoveled out the shit, then swept it in a disgusting dust cloud. It reminds me of my chores on the Martin farm.

Navy Lieutenant Joel Boone, the Sixth Regiment assistant surgeon, catches my eye and motions me over.

"Sir?"

"They gassed Lucy. We're heading there to help. We'll do a practicum on the treatment of gas cases for Osborne and Dessez's new guy, Doctor Hot Shot Beck. Hot's a pretty funny first name. Know anything about him?"

"Sure. He'd just started teaching at Great Lakes during my last couple weeks there. His parents named him Arthur. Hot Shot's what folks called him in Chicago, behind his back."

"What's he like?"

"Well, sir . . ." I pause, look past Boone's left shoulder, and take a deep breath. Lieutenant Boone is about the same height as Arthur. "May I speak frankly, sir?"

"Why else would we be having this conversation?"

"All right, sir. On the good side, he knows his stuff. Friend of mine who worked at Cook County Hospital in Chicago said he's one of their best surgeons. Top of his class sort of thing. Two nicknames. Hot Shot, and . . ."

"And . . ."

"Meaning no offense, sir. Napoleon."

"Asshole with a stature problem."

I nod. "Not the worst, you know. But still . . ."

"Shorter than *me*?"

"Um." I look away. "'bout the same, I reckon."

"How'd he end up here?"

I tell him the story, leaving out the fact that I'd lived with a branch of Arthur's family.

"Get *Lizzy* while I scare up Osborne."

That name makes me smile as I head to the vehicle barn. The little Ford Model T truck is the regimental mascot. Dogs and such would never survive a gas attack. We call her *Lizzy*, short for *Elizabeth Ford*, in honor of Miss Elizabeth Pearce, the rich lady who purchased it and gave it to the Marines. Private Worthington hand-painted the name—*Elizaberth Ford*—on the side of the truck. Worthington, who is known now by the name "Worthless," is not a good speller. *Lizzy* started as an ambulance, but the back end sort of fell apart, and now she's what we call a "general-purpose" truck.

I crank *Lizzy* to life with two sputters and a cough. Lieutenants Boone and Osborne don their gas masks and settle into the front seat. I take my helmet off and slip my gas mask out of the chest pouch. They drill the routine into us until we can do it in our sleep. I fit the mouthpiece between my lips, pull the mask over my face, and cinch the head straps tight. Then I pinch the outer ends of the nose clip to widen it, fit the inner ends beside my nostrils, and release the nose clip so it blocks my nose. I take a breath to draw filtered air into my lungs, remove the mouthpiece, and blow air inside the mask to clear it—not necessary in the absence of gas, but it's protocol. I slip my helmet back on and cinch the chin strap. Boone gives a thumbs-up. Can't talk with the mouthpiece in place.

When we arrive at Lucy, the Fifth Regiment's version of *Lizzy* idles by a tent while corpsmen load gas victims into the back bed. The docs aren't wearing their masks—the gas must have blown away in the breeze. One gives us the "all clear," and we take our masks off and stow them. I put on rubber gloves, and this is the tricky part. My left little finger sort of flops around. It's a killer to get gloves on. I help the corpsmen load six blindfolded men into *Lizzy*'s back end, sitting them back-to-back along the center of the truck bed.

Boone sits in the middle while I get *Lizzy* in gear. Osborne wears the rosy-cheeked grin of a young man riding in a speedster with the top down on a fine Sunday drive. The men in the back end are not having such a fine day—all moaning, one yelping when we hit bumps. These

Fords have two-speed automatic transmissions, so at least I don't have a clutch and shifter to deal with.

I pull up to the regimental aid station in La Voie and shut off the engine while Osborne and Boone slide out. Arthur Beck and Orlando Petty walk over from a nearby building. Beck looks tight with anger while Petty talks, using his hands to emphasize some point as they approach.

"Look, I know you're frustrated by the lack of surgery here, but I frankly don't care," Petty says.

"All right," Arthur says. "Let's get on with it. What now? Ophthalmology clinic?"

"Gas clinic." Petty walks toward Boone. "Good morning, Joel."

My height estimate about Arthur and Boone was right. The two men are nearly identical in height and weight. Arthur wears his frustration like a suit of armor. But his shoulders slump, while Boone stands straight-backed, chest out, motioning the corpsmen to bring the patients to the gas tent.

"Mr. Beck, meet Lieutenant Joel Boone, the surgeon you should aspire to be," Petty says. "Joel, Hot Shot here thinks he's got the magic touch."

Osborne whistles, and I struggle to suppress a smile as Arthur's face colors.

"I'm a surgeon, damn it, not an ophthalmologist," Arthur says.

"The sooner you understand that you are neither and both, the better we'll get along," Boone says. "You're a naval medical officer. I frankly don't give a hoot if you like it or not. You're here, you wear the uniform, and I expect you to act like it. Now come on. We have Marines to take care of. Professor Petty'll give you and Osborne your first lesson in gas. Pay attention and stow the bellyaching." Boone starts toward the treatment tent. "By the way, nice uniform—custom?" He walks on without waiting for an answer.

Two corpsmen lead the blindfolded gas victims toward an open-sided canvas tent. The column shuffles along, each man with his right hand on the shoulder of the one in front. One corpsman leads the line, and another takes the rear position. They seat the men in the shade. Petty leads us into the tent. Boone says, "McCormack and I will demonstrate treatment while the professor teaches you about Yellow Cross."

I kept my gloves on since they're so hard to get on and off. The eye chair resembles a dental chair with an adjustable headrest and pedals to elevate and tilt the seat. A corpsman brings the first patient. I seat the private, adjust the chair, and ease off the blindfold. The man grips the chair arms and grunts while I work. I feel for the guy. Glad it's not me.

"Hot Shot—what do you know about gas?" Petty asks.

"There are several kinds, mustard and phosgene. And we wear these masks in case of an attack. Didn't get the impression they use it much. Not a part of my syllabus."

"When we need a bacteriology lecture, I'll call," Boone says. "In the meantime, McCormack, let's work on the first and show Dr. Shot how it's done."

I tip the chair backward and drape a towel around the man's neck. A corpsman holds a basin behind the private's head. I take position behind the patient while Boone fills a needleless syringe with a clear bicarbonate solution. The patient's face looks as though he's been stranded in a desert without a hat—angry red skin with blistering cheeks and eyelids swollen shut. I place my palms on the man's forehead and used my thumbs to pull his eyelids open. Tears stream from puffy red eyes, and the man's face contorts with agony.

I hate this part.

Boone dribbles the liquid from the syringe into the left and then the right eye. I give the patient credit—he doesn't scream. I dab the man's face dry with a clean towel, then apply a new blindfold.

"Yellow Cross," Petty says, "is commonly called mustard gas, but it has nothing to do with mustard. The odor is faintly reminiscent of that seasoning. The chemical name is dichloroethyl sulfide. The French and Brits call it Yperite. The Germans paint labels on their gas shells. Mustard has a double yellow cross, thus our name for it."

The other corpsmen and I seat two new patients while Petty talks. I'll assist Arthur. I'd rather help Osborne, but an assignment is an assignment. The injuries are similar to the first patient. The poor guy is miserable, no older than me. The thought of going through life with a white blindman's stick flashes through my mind as I loosen the blindfold. The fellow squirms in the chair, the muscles around his eyes spastic as light reveals angry red burns. We don't have enough morphine in our supplies to give these poor guys a dose before the eye irrigations. I wish we could.

"Yellow Cross isn't a gas," Petty continues. "It's an oily liquid that sprays out of the shell. The vapor is heavier than air, so it gravitates toward low areas like trenches, foxholes, cellars, and ravines. It persists for three to seven days and coats everything—dirt, plants, clothing, and equipment, thus the reason we wear gloves. As the gas evaporates off clothing, it will secondarily gas any enclosed area where victims are housed—*off-gassing*. We do the decontamination in open, well-ventilated areas whenever possible."

Osborne is halfway through his second patient by the time Arthur applies a fresh blindfold on our first. The dentist hums while he works, something that appears to irritate Arthur, making me want to smile. All the while, Arthur glances at my left hand and the useless little finger as it flops around at random.

"Yellow Cross is a lipid-soluble vesicant," Petty continues. "It enters cells by direct contact. Its acute manifestations are on moist surfaces, where it's converted to hydrochloric acid on contact with water. It does the same thing when it combines with the aqueous material inside cells, then eats its way from one cell to the next. Thus, the eyes, mucous membranes, moist areas, open wounds, and the respiratory tract are the first things injured."

"Doc, I don't mean to be an asshole, but am I ever going to see again?" the man in my chair asks in a pained voice.

"Probably. Most regain sight after a week or two. Some don't, so no promises. The sooner we wash out your eyes with this bicarbonate solution, the better."

Osborne finishes, and Arthur picks up his pace. Osborne hums whenever Petty isn't talking. I glance at Osborne, who winks with his right eye.

"That finger looks like a problem," Arthur says. "Get in the way when you do your work?"

"Sometimes, sir." My scalp tingles. I don't want to get into this.

"What happened?"

"Man thought I was misbehaving one time." I glance at Osborne, whose face becomes serious.

"Your dad?"

"Nah. Husband of a woman who took me in after my parents died." I don't want to explain this.

"Where'd you grow up?" Arthur asks.

"Wisconsin." We need to work, not talk.

"What town?"

"Beck, am I boring you?" Petty glares behind his glasses.

I take a deep breath. "Sorry, sir."

Petty continues. "Yellow Cross burns the respiratory epithelial tissues by the same mechanism, causing nasal, oral, pharyngeal, and bronchial inflammation. Heavy lower respiratory tract exposure can be fatal—by pulmonary edema or hemorrhage. Most of the time, though, it causes chemical bronchitis. Survival is determined by whether or not the patient develops an infection. Bacterial pneumonia is a deadly complication."

Osborne looks over at me with a slight grin as he hums. I give him a nod and continue to hold the eyes open while Arthur rinses them with the shaky hands that are now famous.

"The dermal effects are delayed," Petty continues. "At first, all you see is a mild inflammatory reaction that resembles sunburn. The damage continues over the next several days as the Yellow Cross worms its way from cell to cell. This causes blistering and damage similar to a thermal burn. The genitalia are a problematic area."

Osborne finishes with his last patient while Arthur continues.

I would never have understood a thing Lieutenant Petty said six months ago. But I pick up the medical stuff more easily than I would have imagined.

Arthur's mention of the finger brings back my time with the black-smith I worked with before moving to the Martin family farm. I shove those memories away. Concentrate on the job.

"We evacuate victims to a gas treatment unit, where we undress and shower them using alkaline soap. In this case, we thought we'd work the eyes first, then evacuate them to Bezu for the shower and a second eye wash. Gas troops clean exposed equipment with bicarbonate or alkaline soap. If a man can't evacuate, we recommend he strip, shake the residue out of his clothing, and soap himself down with canteen water, since most soaps are alkaline. Any questions?"

Boone lingers in the center of the tent while the corpsmen lead the last patients out. Osborne and I stand to the side. Despite the rank differences, Osborne acts like a mischievous older brother to me. When the corpsmen and patients are outside, Boone turns to Arthur. "Lieutenant, I don't need to be a psychologist to see you're unhappy here. What's got your goat?"

"I'm a surgeon, sir. A damned good one. I'm one of the surgeons doing the complex trauma and reconstruction work at Cook County. All I see here is derm clinic, eye clinic, and the stuff of internship. Any monkey can do what we just did."

"Nobody has ever called me a monkey," Boone says. "Look, doctor, a five-hour operation with a vascular repair *might* save a limb. In the last half hour, we prevented twelve cases of lifelong blindness. I'm a surgeon too, but I have a better understanding of the importance of *everything* I do, not just slicing and dicing. And don't ever play the short-man card around me. McCormack, Osborne, we have work to do." Boone leaves without looking back.

I crank the little Ford to life while Boone and Osborne settle into the seat. Both officers are silent during the drive to Montgivrault, but I can feel anger radiating off Boone as we bounce along the roadway.

I pull into the aid station barn and turn off the engine. Boone slides out and says, "Both of you, with me." He leads us to a small office he shares with Lieutenant Commander Farwell and closes the door. "Just what the hell was going on back there?"

"Could you be a bit more specific, sir?" A *what, me?* grin grows on Osborne's face.

Boone glares at Osborne for a moment, then grins. "You were under his skin like a bad case of scabies."

"Sir, remember, I'm from Chicago, just like him," Osborne says. "I did a rotation at Cook County. Never got to know him, but I saw His Highness in action. Great surgeon. Monumental asshole. A couple of my friends gave me an earful. Well, I let it drop about his nickname when I heard he was headed here. He doesn't like humming. We need to chop down the pedestal he stands on." Osborne smirks with rosy-cheeked innocence.

Boone shakes his head. "I'm not sure that'll help. Dessez is in despair. He needs a surgeon, not a first-class egotist. Petty tells me he thinks the guy was born with a silver spoon in his mouth."

My feet bounce, restless, and I glance at my gimpy finger. I meet Boone's eyes.

"And what was all that about your finger and Wisconsin? Enlighten me," Boone says.

My throat's dry and tight. Dagnabit, I hope my voice won't crack like a goofy thirteen-year-old. "Um, well, sir . . . well, I'll tell you a few things I know. If family is any indication, I think there's some hope for him. His family is tops in my book."

"You know him?" Osborne asks with an incredulous expression.

"Well, not him."

"But you know his family?" Boone asks.

"Yes, sir. His Aunt Minnie took me in." I draw a deep breath. Osborne's face turns serious.

"How was it they took you in?" Boone asks.

"Okay, so here's what happened. Mom died giving birth to my sister. Broke my old man's heart. Took me to a tavern, sat me down in a back booth. Got me a glass of water and a plate of pickled pig's knuckles. Said he'd be right back and walked out the door and my life."

"Ever find him?" Osborne asks.

"Nah." I remember gazing in the mirror behind the bar as the policeman led me out, afraid I was under arrest. "Years later, I heard he walked all the way to Beaver Dam, sat in a park, and put a bullet through his brain. Buried in the potter's field there, he is. I bounced from family to family. Most well-meaning, but they never lasted, you see. Then old Ziegelmann took me in. Bad one, he was—beat his first wife. Turns out, that first wife was the sister of Arthur's mother. After a few tries, she got a divorce. Big scandal. Ziegelmann's second wife let me in the house, long as I worked in his shop. I have the scars to prove it." I hold up my left hand with the deformed little finger.

"How'd that happen?" Boone asks.

"Didn't work fast enough one day. Put my hand on the anvil and smashed it. He figured that'd get me in line, and the loss of the finger wouldn't keep me from working in his shop. After their kid came along, they gave me the boot. Finally got taken in by the Martin family. Miss Minnie Martin is my angel. They sort of had a way of picking up strays."

"There were other orphans?"

"No. Dr. Beck's father was their first 'stray.' Took Fred Beck in after the Civil War. He'd been a prisoner at Andersonville and came out with soldier's heart—a bad case. Couldn't function at all for a few years. Later, he got better and married Miss Minnie's older sister, Anna. They moved to Chicago. By the time Miss Minnie took me in, Arthur was in medical school and too important to hang around the old farm. I know his sister and brothers real well, and they're all fine folks, they are. Don't get me wrong, he rubs me the wrong way too, but I gotta think there's some good in him, coming from that family. And none of that silver spoon stuff. Salt-of-the-earth family. I mean, I sort of hate to go to bat for him, but . . ."

"No. That's good to know," Boone says. "I hope we find the surgeon buried in that ego soon."

Chapter Twenty-Six
Major Ab Johnson

Fourth Brigade Headquarters, La Loge Farm

The staff car that brought me to Fourth Brigade headquarters at La Loge Farm drives away, leaving me under the shade of the towering oaks that surround the farm buildings. The downtrodden two-story stone house needs a fresh coat of whitewash, with ivy creeping up one side and a mossy roof. It's large enough for an extended family and farm workers. Weed and bramble overgrow grounds trampled by recent activity. Cars and motorcycles are parked in a nearby timber barn. The surrounding woods and abandoned appearance make it an ideal location for brigade HQ. My neck hairs tingle at the sound of artillery in the east.

I was on the phone all afternoon in a small office in Montreuil-aux-Lions, completing arrangements for a medical supply depot. Shipments of Red Cross supplies arrive today. A supply train with more will arrive in the next several days. I wasted an hour on the phone with three French rail control officers whose indifference made me yearn for a guillotine. They pretended they couldn't understand my French, and one hung up when I lost my temper and spoke both kinds of French to him.

I'm finding it harder and harder to be nice to these jerks.

Machine gun and rifle fire echo in the distance. I never imagined I would be in a place like this. At least Helen doesn't know—I'll have to keep it that way, for her sake. The reality of what Jack is heading into leaves my heart aching. Same with his good friend Bill, who is here now, somewhere nearby, with the Army Twenty-Third Infantry.

A sputtering buzz in the air high above makes me squint as I search the sky. Three Fokker triplanes fly over. A staff car drives up moments later. A vigorous brigadier general in his early fifties wearing a French Adrian helmet hops out. He has a commanding presence and a resolute, strong-jawed face. The other man in the back seat is a bit older, shorter, with a bushy white mustache on a kindly face. Major general, division commander. Bundy is his name, one man I could never get on the phone.

I walk over and don't come to attention, per protocol.

"You look like the oldest major in the army. What'd you screw up?" the brigadier asks. "Or did they bust you down for the brawl where you got that nose?"

"No brawl, sir. Johnson, Albert, sir. I also respond to Pops, courtesy of Colonel Brown."

"What, then?"

I take a risk, needing to deflect the age issue. "Bull riding."

The brigadier stares at me. "Sounds like bullshit to me. Speak French?"

"Like a native, sir."

"Maybe you'll be useful. I need someone who can bullshit the French. I'm Harbord, and this is our boss, General Bundy."

"Section?" Bundy asks.

"I'm your medical liaison from G-4-B, Generals. Colonel Wadhams ordered me to coordinate things between here and Paris."

Bundy stares at the sky. "Those goddamned planes up there. I've asked Billy Mitchell where ours are, and it sounds like they're safe in their hangars in Lorraine." Bundy's voice sounds older than he appears. "I'm still trying to get used to the newfangled things."

"I'd love to have some of our own," Harbord says. "That's the only way to shoot down those damned observation balloons. They have six of them up today—thorns in my side. I need to move troops, and now I can only do that at night. Let's get inside." General Harbord leads us into a large room that appears to have been the living room. Blackout curtains hang beside the open windows. A gentle breeze fails to erase the strong smell of cigarettes. A map easel stands next to a well-used metal desk with a green aluminum ashtray on top.

"So, Pops, how are you doing on the medical side?" Harbord asks.

"Three ambulance sections with twenty Fords apiece have arrived. We're establishing ambulance dressing stations for triage. Walking wounded to the regimental aid stations, the rest to the field hospitals."

General Harbord lights a cigarette. "Go on."

"We're doing our degassing at Bezu next to Field Hospital One. The Red Cross Military Hospital in Juilly is our evac hospital. Evac 8 will go there when they arrive in a few days."

"Base hospitals?"

"None," I say. "We'll use the Red Cross hospitals in Paris."

"Casualty handling capacity?"

"Poor. Our field hospital and the one in Juilly are too small. We can handle the current volume, but that's it."

"Why?" Harbord paces.

"Our battalion aid stations are over a half mile from the ambulance dressing stations across open fields. Litter-bearers can only carry so many. Ambulances can't drive in the open during the day without attracting artillery fire. At night, headlights make them a target, so they go without them. On these roads, the assistant driver has to walk in front and guide the driver."

"We've just come from French Corps headquarters," Harbord says. "They warned us that we're going to go on the offensive as soon as practical, and that means more casualties. You better get some grease on the skids. We don't have the specifics yet, but this'll be a big push."

Bundy nods his head while gazing at the map, seemingly content to let Harbord do all the talking.

"I'll do my best, but I only have what I have, sirs," I say.

"That's my problem too, Pops," Harbord says.

I take that as my signal to leave.

I go back outside the farmhouse. I've heard that Harbord is very bright. Bundy is a West Pointer. At least the Marines of the Fourth

Brigade will have professional army men leading them. But Tuttle's words from a few days before hang over me—neither man has combat experience.

My staff of one doesn't rate a motorcar, and a horse won't be practical. I walk to the barn to consider my options. An Indian motorcycle with a sidecar is parked next to the general's Cadillac. Hmmm.

Chapter Twenty-Seven
Major Ab Johnson

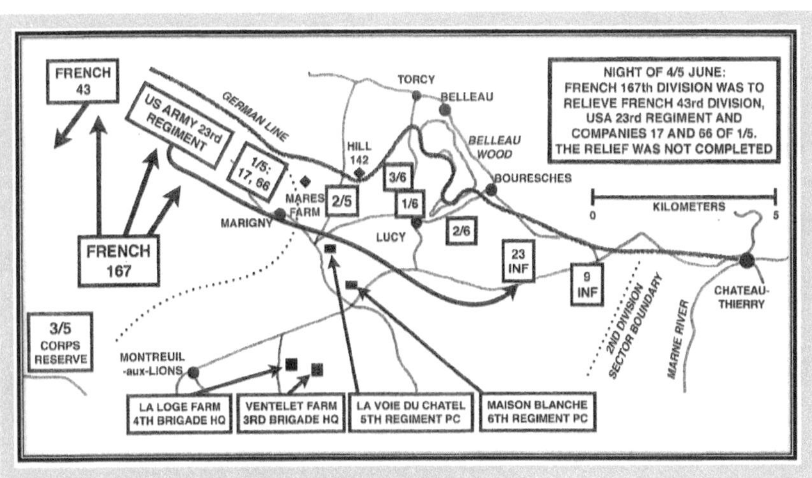

Fourth Brigade Headquarters, La Loge Farm
Wednesday, June 5, 1918

Road dust and frustration choke me as I attempt to become a gymnast at an age when I should know better. I'm trying to bend my legs and pull up with my arms to extricate myself from a motorcycle sidecar. The young guys make this look so easy. They're all thinner than me. I suppose if I start to do calisthenics with them it will help. But I hate push-ups. And sit-ups. And burpees. And running.

Knees crackle as I stretch and attempt to get circulation going to my feet before I embarrass myself by trying to walk into headquarters. So I act as though I intend to stand here like an idiot while my driver parks the Indian motorcycle in the shed behind brigade HQ.

The air is humid and redolent with the aroma of flowers in a neglected garden to my right. It's sunny with billowing clouds overhead in what would be a beautiful morning if not for everything we're doing here.

Colonel Brown and I discussed my transportation needs yesterday. He assigned a daredevil private as my driver and an Indian motorcycle with a sidecar to me. The Indian has a saddle-type seat, so sitting behind the driver is a no-go, at least for me. It took the two of us to squeeze and fold me into the sidecar. I'm going to practice getting in and out so I'm not so amusing to nearby privates. Maybe some deep knee bends will help. I hate them too.

Okay, my feet are no longer asleep, so I head into the building.

I'm here to give Major Derby a progress report. After that, I plan to find the personnel officer and look for replacement roster reports. Ira warned me about personnel being a mess. I do my best each day to try to find Jack's name on a roster without success.

Officers and enlisted men hustle by as I hobble down the hall. Tobacco smoke fills the air while a typewriter clatters and a phone rings. General Bundy, General Harbord, Colonel Brown, and several others stand next to the map in the staff room, speaking in hushed tones, Harbord pointing at a spot on the map. I head for an office several of us share, since none of us are tied to desks.

Derby motions me to a seat while holding the phone to his ear when I enter the cramped office. He hangs up. "I'd like to hear your report, but we better join the others and find out what's going on. This place went from busy to insane an hour ago."

"Why?" I ask.

"General Bundy came back from a meeting at French HQ. I don't have all the details yet, but I think we're about to descend into a nightmare."

Harbord is talking when we enter the staff room. "So 1/5 has to get into position by 0300 for the attack?"

Brown paces. "Yes. The French 167th will send a regiment to attack north while 1/5 hits Hill 142."

"There's one problem with that plan, General," a Marine major says. The man speaks with a light Southern accent. Youngish for a major, making me feel oldish. Built like he could handle my sidecar like it's nothing.

"Which you will solve, Major Smith," General Harbord says, sounding irritated by the interruption.

"Yes, General. But may I tell you the problem first?"

Harbord gives a curt nod. Bundy walks away from the map and stares out the window, as if he's seen and heard enough. Electric tension fills the room—voices clipped, postures rigid.

Smith takes two steps to stand by the map and points to a spot. "The French 167th isn't in place for that attack. Two companies of 1/5 are stuck holding that front. It's over a half mile to the spot the orders say they're supposed to step off. They can't move until the French get there, and that'll be sometime later tonight."

Colonel Brown frowns. "And sometime tonight will probably be after midnight, General. Major Turrill won't have enough time to organize his battalion before 0300 hours. Hell, he doesn't even know his battalion's going on the attack yet." Brown points at the map. "The French are ordering us to reposition every one of our units tonight for a major assault tomorrow. That's absurd."

"This would be a mess if we tried to do it in full daylight," Smith says. "But all the movements are at night with no lights."

Brown takes a deep breath. "It gets worse. Our entire front will go on the attack against an unknown number of Germans at an unknown time tomorrow using a plan and tactics the French haven't shared with me for security reasons."

One of the first things they taught in my officer's training program was the virtue of simplicity. This is anything but, and boys like Jack will be caught in the middle with orders that make me think of a mad marionettist playing three games of chess while on a unicycle.

"A tall order. How many of our units did you say are in position?" Bundy asks, still looking out the window.

Brown glares at Bundy's back. "As I just said, sir, none. The French are out of their minds."

"As always, Colonel, I appreciate your candor," Harbord says. "We have our orders, however. We say, 'Yes, sir,' and carry on."

A frown crosses Brown's face. "This is exactly the shit Pershing worried about with the French. We spent months working out doctrine at the Open Warfare School; we need to apply what we learned from their mistakes."

I stare at the map, neck tingling, gut tight. They're ordering thousands of troops to move without lights or maps and take up positions on unfamiliar terrain and go into battle after a sleepless night and no food. Did a German design this plan to ensure our defeat? I thought Marine officers were amateurs. That's nothing compared to the idiot who cooked this up. Any Marine corporal could come up with a better plan than this. I know I could, and I'm not in the infantry. Thinking as a supply officer, I can't imagine all the gear that will have to accompany these absurd movements.

I massage a knot in my neck. The lives of other fathers' sons depend on the officers in this room. Hell, Jack could be out there for all I know. What are Bundy and Harbord thinking?

Insane.

"Generals, if I may speak freely, sirs?" Colonel Brown's voice is strained. Harbord nods. "I think the French are more interested in saving face than anything else. The Boche whipped them before we arrived. Embarrassed General Duchene in particular. They were physically and psychologically defeated. Now, I admire aggressiveness and initiative, but we've just finally organized *our* defensive positions yesterday. The men are tired, hungry, thirsty, and might—*just might*—get hot chow after sundown tonight *if* they stay put."

"For what it's worth," Harbord says, "we asked him for another day or two. French command insists we attack tomorrow. They contend that another day will allow the Germans to organize *their* defenses, bring in more artillery, and be much more difficult to beat. I agree that they're reacting with wounded pride. When Paris is threatened, the

French seem to lose their ability to reason. The problem is this: They're in charge. We have our orders."

Brown crosses his arms in front of his chest. "Then we need to use American tactics—infiltrate under cover of dark and press the attack at first light. Moving at night is noisy—we need artillery to cover that. There is nothing stealthy about the movements of two thousand troops."

"I met with my counterpart at French Corps command," an artillery commander whose name I don't know says. "He ordered me to *not* raise the volume of our outgoing fire. They're convinced that the element of surprise will be lost with a thorough artillery preparation. I argued the point to deaf ears."

"Only way to surprise them is by nighttime infiltration," Brown says. "How the hell do we *surprise* them in full daylight across open fields when they have their damned observation balloons in the air?"

"French command refused to tell me when the rest of the attack will take place," Harbord says. "I can only hope they'll change their minds and let us infiltrate tomorrow night, like you suggest."

I pour myself a glass of tepid water and take a sip while I listen. My words to Jack haunt me. *Your officers are a pack of amateurs—you need the leadership skills West Point teaches.* Helen is right. I'm an idiot. I'm standing in a room where the generals are fools and the only men with a grasp of reality are Smith and Brown.

"What about air support?" I ask. Isn't it obvious someone ought to ask this? Hostile glares tell me it should not have been me asking.

"Holland?" Harbord nods to Smith. "Pops, this is Major Holland Smith. He's our intelligence man, even though he's a Marine."

Smith looks at Harbord with a blank expression. "There've been eighty-nine enemy flights over us today so far, and ten observation balloons. Our air support from French Squadron 252 is outgunned, outnumbered, and overextended. They sent up only one observation flight today."

"The report I got didn't say much," Brown says. "I think the men were bent over in the cockpit, kissing their asses goodbye. They barely made it back alive."

"I've sent a memorandum on that topic off to Chaumont, but I'm afraid there's nothing more I can do," Bundy says. "Our air squadrons are in Lorraine, and the French lost most of theirs in this sector in the past ten days."

I gaze at Major Smith, standing with a rigid back and a firm jaw. Smith is the only Marine in the room. How can they plan this without the input of the regimental commanders who will have to carry out these orders?

"A Marine intelligence officer and two men snuck along the gully between Hill 142 and Belleau Wood last night," Smith says. "He reported seeing a battalion-sized force enter Belleau Wood with cartloads of ammunition and machine guns. Trench mortars, too. I reported this to French intelligence this morning."

Brown sighs. "When I brought that up, their intelligence officer reacted as though I'd slapped him with a glove and challenged him to duel. He said that the Germans aren't even in Belleau Wood and that their lines are thin and weak. He says all we have to do is walk in and take possession of a vacant forest."

"Based on what information?" Harbord asks.

Brown shrugs. "He refused to share that with me. As far as I know, he's declared the area Boche-free, and on that basis, it would be an affront to French honor if the Boche don't comply with his opinion."

"That the same imbecile that brushed off our warning about the attack through the Chemin des Dames two weeks ago?" Smith asks.

"*Oui*," Brown says. "The same staffers attired in spotless, impeccably pressed uniforms."

"That's enough of that," Harbord says. "I remind you, we're under French command."

"Begging your pardons, sirs, but at what point will we bring Colonels Catlin and Neville into the planning process?" Major Smith asks.

The room is silent. Brown clears his throat while Harbord lights a cigarette.

"Wasn't time to summon them here," General Bundy says. "They'll do what all good Marines do—salute, say, 'Aye, aye, sir,' and carry out the army's orders."

"Damned Marines," the artillery officer mutters.

Smith's face remains impassive, but his eyes burn as though twin volcanoes might erupt. I take a deep breath. Stay calm. But then, those are the same sort of words I would have said two weeks ago. I scan the group—all eyes are on Smith. The clock ticks. That the fate of Jack's fellow Marines should be in these hands . . .

"Our written orders are explicit." General Bundy stands at attention, spine straight, shoulders rigid. "We attack tomorrow. I hope Colonel Brown's points about artillery and infiltration will somehow filter into French brains." Bundy pulls out a cigarette and lights it. "Dismissed."

Brown goes to the window and stares out, hands behind his back. Smith leaves without a sound. Bundy pulls on his cigarette. Harbord approaches us. "Can you offer anything encouraging, Dick?"

"I'll let Pops take the lead, sir."

"Sir," I say, "our ability to handle increased casualty flow will not support the sort of battle being planned. Field Hospital One is too small, and FH-15 just moved and isn't ready to accept casualties. Evac 8 is still days away. The surgeons in Juilly are exhausted, with a hospital that's bursting at the seams."

"Why are they so overwhelmed? Casualties are light so far."

"By French standards, they are, sir. But the Boche artillery fire was heavy the last two nights. We only have four teams of surgeons and one operating room working twenty-hour shifts. Their wards are full and will remain so until we get enough ambulances to move their patients to Paris."

"You're not prepared to handle the casualties of an all-out offensive," Harbord says.

"Sir," Major Derby says, "medical can't support an offensive at this time. In a week, maybe, but that's based on hope, not fact. I wish I could paint a rosier picture for you, sir, but I'd have to join the French army to do that."

"Can we expect any help from them, Pops?"

"No. We're on our own, sir." I glance toward the window, avoiding eye contact with the others in the room. How many more promises will be broken before this is over? The ones to Helen about staying far to the rear are now as false as those the French gave Pershing about medical coverage.

"I wish the French weren't in such a hurry to regain their honor," Bundy says. "But we'll have to make do with what we have. We're simply outranked and out-ordered here." Bundy sounds lost as he speaks the words.

I massage my neck. I think about that time with seven-year-old Jack, fishing for the first time—how proud he was after he netted his first trout. So many Jacks about to go into the biggest battle since the Marine Corps was formed in 1775. I told Jack, *The Marines keep swabbies in line while the army wins wars*. How can we win this war with fools in charge?

Chapter Twenty-Eight
Private Carl Larsen

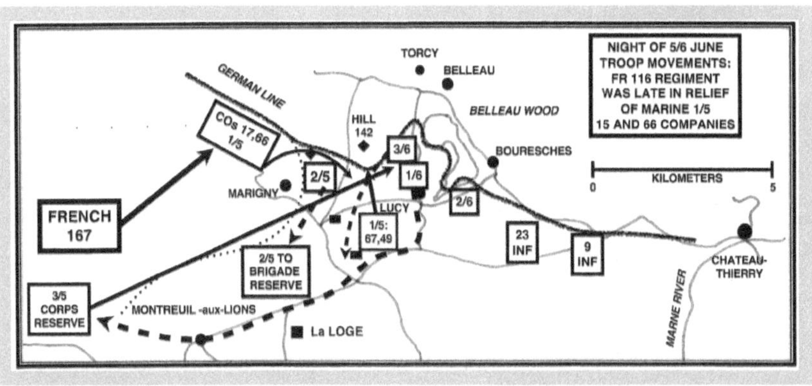

Fifth Regiment Post of Command, La Voie du Chatel

The rays of a retreating sun fade into night as I drive Colonel Catlin to Colonel Buck Neville's PC at La Voie. Night's the only time we can drive cars or trucks without attracting Heinie artillery. Air dominance has let the Germans register every intersection and parking lot within artillery range. They've lobbed a few toward various farms being used as PCs. I'm still rattled after a near miss earlier today. Colonel Neville looks up as the boss and I enter the room. Others stand around a small pencil-drawn map on a table, murmuring, holding steaming cups of coffee.

"I just about bought the farm today, Buck," Catlin says.

Neville raises an eyebrow. "How so?"

"I'd decided to move our PC up to a farmhouse near Lucy. A German shell hit the old one as we drove off."

"How's Evans?"

"Fine," Catlin says. "He was outside relieving himself at the time. I think he might have gotten a stain when he hit the deck, though. Rattled the Signals boys in the basement. Phones are down again."

Catlin's offhand manner amazes me. Is it courage? Combat experience? I won't be able to take a shit for a week.

My buddy Hank Lenert enters and hands an envelope to a lieutenant. Hank winks at me. The lieutenant opens the orders and hands them to Neville, who goes over to the map, muttering under his breath. Catlin and Lieutenant Colonel Logan Feland, Neville's second-in-command, move to Neville's side.

"Hell. Logan, look at this shit." Neville hands the note to Feland.

Feland reads the document and slaps the table. "Christ. Do they have any idea where our men are?"

The other officers in the room seem startled by the outburst. Feland turns to face Major Turrill, the CO of 1/5. "You're going to shit a brick." Feland clears his throat. "First Battalion, Fifth Marines, supported by the Eighth and Twenty-Third Machine Gun Companies and one company of engineers, will attack at 0345 hours to seize Hill 142."

"Goddamn it." Major Turrill looks at his watch. "Let me see that." Feland hands him the order. "They say we're to attack between two brooks that aren't on this damned map."

An intelligence officer says, "I've scouted that area. There aren't any *brooks*. They probably mean the dry ravines that run along the sides of 142. Maybe they had water in 1829 when they made the map the Frogs like to use."

"Have you or your men spent time in that area?" Catlin asks Turrill.

"No." Turrill's eyes are glued on the map. "Colonel, I can't get my whole battalion there in time to go over the top by 0345. The order says the 112th Regiment of the French 167th is attacking to the north with us on their right? Hell, the 167th isn't anywhere near there. Half of my men and the Eighth Machine Gunners are stuck on the line west of Les Mares Farm until 167 shows. This is ludicrous."

"Do any of you know where the other machine gun company and the engineers are?" Catlin asks.

The room is silent.

"We can't get word to them if we don't know where they are," Neville says. "Get Brigade on the horn and see if they know where these units are while I translate this mess into an operational order."

Major Turrill's eyes blaze. "Colonel, I know what I'm about to say may be out of line, but someone's got to say it. You and Colonel Catlin are the ranking officers in this division with combat experience. Don't you think you and he had better give our armchair generals a dose of reality?"

"You're right," Neville says. "That would be out of line. We have our orders, and we'll do our best to carry them out. Things are touchy enough between us and our army *friends*." Neville pauses and seems to struggle to control his anger. He writes a message on a slip of paper, folds it, and seals it in an envelope. "For what little it's worth, I agree with you, but we don't have time to argue."

"Buck, I better shove off and leave you to work," Catlin says. "I'm afraid of what awaits me at my shop. Good luck."

"I don't think that'll be enough," Neville says. "Say a prayer."

Chapter Twenty-Nine
Private Carl Larsen

Fifth Regiment PC, La Voie du Chatel
Thursday, June 6, 1918

The sun's up and so are the sausages as I run along the road from Maison Blanche to La Voie. I want to give them the middle finger when I hear the buzz of Heinie observation planes taking stock of us. I don't think a guy could fart without the Heinies knowing who, when, and where. Clear skies allow no secrets about where our guys are. The noise of a pitched battle near Hill 142 worries me. Did all of Turrill's guys get there in time for the show? I could have cut the tension with a knife at our PC. Nobody there has heard anything aside from the distant battle noise, so I'm running a message to Neville's PC since the phones are on the blink. Again. At least I got a ride partway.

It's a bitch to run in my woolen uniform and boots. I appreciate how good a runner Hiram is. The boxy gas mask pouch bounces in rhythm with my stride, strapped over my right shoulder. The worst is the damned tin pot jiggling over my noggin. There's no way to keep it from bouncing, and I don't have a free hand to carry the helmet.

I arrive at La Voie at a bit after 0700. I hand my message to a lieutenant and stick around in case there's a reply. Colonel Neville paces, reading the note. My buddy Hank Lenert rushes in with a report from Major Turrill. Looks like the only way to get messages back and forth will be runners—the Heinie artillery messed up the phone lines Signals laid yesterday. The distances, humidity, and need to run in full gear are going to wear the runners out if this keeps up.

"How did it look up there?" Neville asks Hank.

"Bad, sir. When the lieutenants blew their whistles for the attack, only two companies were there."

"Where was the rest of the battalion?"

Hank rocks from foot to foot, eyes averted. "Waiting for the Frogs to show. One company finally got there around 0530—they ran the whole way. Out of gas, most of them, when they arrived. The other didn't make it in until about 0600. The Eighth Machine Gunners got there, but no sign of the engineers or the other machine gun company. Colonel Feland and Major Turrill had some choice words for it all, which I will not repeat unless ordered, sir."

Neville drops his eyes to the message. "Turrill says: *Reached our objectives. We are throwing out strong points and are consolidating our positions.* Good. Word from medical is that they've received no casualties. Did you see many?"

"Not around the Battalion PC, sir. Can't say what's out in the fields. None of the corpsmen were at the PC, sir."

The phone rings, and the private manning it speaks up. "Colonel Neville? General Harbord on the horn for you, sir."

Neville puts the receiver to his ear. "Neville, sir." He listens. "Yes, sir. Word is that we've met our objectives, but our flanks are exposed. I'd like your permission to release a company from 3/5 to cover the right flank. Can you ask the French to make an appearance on the left?" He listens. "Really? Turrill reported that they hadn't shown up."

I glance at Hank, who shrugs.

"The French reached all their objectives?" Neville says. "I wonder how they did that without our noticing. No word on casualties, but I think they're light."

My jaw tightens. That isn't quite what Hank said. But I'm just a private. I know better than to contradict a colonel talking to a general.

"Yes, sir, it bodes well for the day," Neville says. "Any word on the next attack?"

I go to a sideboard and pour a glass of water. I'm parched and guess I'll be doing some running today. Hank joins me and gulps two glasses of the bleachy-tasting water. I don't mind getting a rest and pour myself another glass.

Twenty minutes later, another runner rushes in, stands at attention, and salutes. Neville takes the note from him. "Son, don't salute." Neville frowns. "A note from Turrill. The French artillery fired short and hit their own troops. They retreated and haven't been seen since. Our men need ammo and stretchers." Neville scribbles a message, folds the paper, and hands it to the runner. "Get this to Turrill."

Nothing for me yet, so I stick around and help the cooks make and distribute breakfast. I feel guilty—Turrill's guys haven't had a hot meal, no sizzling bacon and eggs, since we left Chaumont-en-Vexin. I snarf my share in honor of the guys who won't get any today—I trust any Marine would do the same. Hank has a plate too. Gonna be a long day.

Another message comes in from Turrill while we wipe our plates with bread.

Neville reads out loud. "Turrill includes a message from Captain Hamilton, the skipper of the Forty-Ninth Company: *Our position is not very good. We have been counterattacked several times but have held. Our casualties are very heavy. We need medical aid badly, cannot locate any hospital apprentices and need many. Ammunition of all kinds needed. All my officers are gone.*"

Chapter Thirty
Major Ab Johnson

Montreuil-aux-Lions

Battle noise to the north from Turrill's fight for Hill 142 fills the distant air. Uncertainty eats at me—feeling a bit useless to boot. I've tried to find rosters to see if Jack is here, and, if so, where. The main rosters are out of date. The only current ones are with the company first sergeants, and there's no way I can seek them all out, especially today. Lacking anything useful to contribute, I head to division HQ for a late lunch.

My driver pulls up in front of division HQ and helps me out of the sidecar. Jeez, I hate that—I know others are looking at an old man named Pops who can't get in or out of the sidecar without help. I stretch the sidecar kinks, then walk in with thoughts of the officers' mess. Loud voices and a peal of laughter draw me to the staff room. Generals Bundy, Harbord, and their staff stand around the map easel, bluing the air with cigars. I enter the room behind Colonel Brown, Major Smith, and Dick Derby. I use it as an excuse to pull out my pipe and prepare a fresh bowl.

Bundy faces Brown. "Ready?"

"Yes, sir." Brown points at the map. "The French achieved their objectives. Our boys took Hill 142." He turns to Derby. "Almost no casualties, right?"

"The aid stations report few casualties under their care, so far," Derby says in an unconvinced tone. "I have no information from the corpsmen in the field."

"The men are in good spirits and have fought off several counterattacks," Bundy says. "I've passed on the news to the French. Seems that Colonel Brown's casualty worries were unfounded. I'm still waiting to hear about the next phase of the offensive."

I add to the haze in the air as I stoke my pipe. The report sounds good. I hope it's true.

Hurried steps approach. A French colonel enters the room and places his briefcase on the table. He doesn't make eye contact as he pulls out a sheet of paper. "We didn't have enough time to translate this for you, so I will read. *The first part of the operation prescribed in paragraph two of the order having succeeded, the American Second Division will execute, this evening, the second part of the operation. The commanding general, American Second Division, will regulate the conduct of the operation. Signed Degoutte.*"

"This evening? Can you be more specific?" Brown asks.

"H-hour is 1700 hours," the colonel says. "The general wishes to maximize the element of surprise, so there will be no more artillery fire than usual. You will sweep through the Bois de Belleau and then proceed on to the ridges beyond Torcy, Belleau, and Bouresches. This will be easily done in light of the great success of your assault on Hill 142, no?"

"The reports from 142 sound good so far, but the day is not done," Smith says.

"Our intelligence about the Boche dispositions appears to have been right and yours wrong *again*. We have tutored you in proper battle tactics. Since your men are not experienced, the general dictates a line of sections attack."

"That requires a rolling artillery screen, Colonel," Smith says.

"Which won't be required since there are no Boches in the forest," the colonel says. "Major. Is your hearing impaired?"

The colonel glares at Major Smith, who returns the compliment in kind.

"The operation should be complete before sundown," the French colonel continues. "Our aviators will do an aerial assessment of your positions in the morning. Any questions?"

Bundy reads the order. "Operationalize this toot sweet." He hands the order to Brown.

Harbord walks to the map. "So Berry's 3/5 takes to the field in line of sections with Lucy on their right. In phase one, they'll sweep through Belleau Wood, then shift northeast and take the village of Belleau. Sibley's 3/6 clears the southern half of the woods and then proceeds to take Bouresches and the ridge behind it. Holcomb's 2/6 will attack from the south and support 3/6."

Brown scribbles on a notepad. "Who'll have field command?"

"Catlin," Harbord says. "Shift control of 3/5 over to him."

"An H-hour of 1700 hours doesn't give them enough time to get organized," Brown says.

"Colonel, perhaps you didn't understand me," the French colonel says. "How much time does it take to organize your Marines for a hike? A walk in the park? They will merely walk through the fields and wood to occupy an area where the Boches are not present. How hard is that?" The colonel grabs his briefcase and leaves.

The problem is, we know the Germans are in the woods. How many is uncertain. This will not be a walk in the park.

I stare out the window so the others won't see my face, which must be red. I glance at my watch—1315 hours. The army is used to taking hours, if not days, to create a complete battle plan with the accompanying orders and maps. It will be a miracle if they can do this all in time. And I thought Marine officers were bush league. This feels like sandlot football.

I don't know much about the specific tactics they're talking about, but I remember them saying that the line of sections attack requires a rolling barrage. If there are any Germans in the woods, our boys—my boys—will have a problem.

"Catlin won't let me down," Harbord says. "Dismissed."

The only Marine present, again, is Major Holland Smith, who the

French colonel chided into silence. I follow Smith out of the room. "Major, have a moment?"

Smith sighs. "Supply problem?"

"No. Let's get out of earshot. I'm about to erupt. Maybe I just need to talk with a Marine." I lead the way to my small office and close the door, motioning Smith to a seat as I creak into my own. "I'd like this discussion to be just between us."

"I can live with that."

"There is a lot you and I didn't say in there. How long do you think it'll take them to cut those orders?"

"Knowing them? Couple of hours."

"I haven't been with a combat unit before, but this doesn't seem like the way to plan an action of this scale."

"Please don't take this as an insult," Smith says. "It is merely a salient observation. Most of the men in that room have as much combat experience as you." Smith's face is tight with anger. "And this is not the way to do things. Hell, we know the Germans are in the woods. A battalion or more. We don't know their disposition or anything about the terrain. That French bastard doesn't know what he's talking about. The regimental commanders should have been part of the planning."

"My son's a Marine second lieutenant."

"Here?"

"Not sure."

Smith shoots me a knowing glance. "Okay, that explains why you don't seem like the kind of idiots I'm faced with from our hallowed army. What do you have in mind, Major?"

"Medical's the last to hear about things like this, or so Dessez complains. I'm going there next and plan to let him know what's about to happen. He and his men need to prepare."

"That's a violation of the chain of command . . ."

"How much trouble will I get in?" I cock my left eyebrow.

"Harbord won't like it. Bundy, if he notices, may hit the West Point roof. But it's not like there's a gag order hanging over us. Letting the regimental surgeons know is hardly a security breach, though that French buffoon may think so."

"Hell, what are they going to do, demote me and send me to France?"

Smith chuckles and gives me a conspiratorial grin. "That will make you the oldest captain in the army. And honored among Marines. Hell, Ab, you're a Marine father. Act like one."

It's as though a light comes on in my idiotic brain. He's right. I've been inching my way to that realization. My previous high opinion of my army is shattered as I realize they are sending my son's Marines, now my Marines, into a battle with a plan that would get an F at West Point.

"Let Dessez know," Smith says. "Make sure he talks to Neville. I'll get word to the right medical people in the Sixth. I'm afraid that Harbord will be so self-absorbed in writing the orders in proper war college format that he won't let Neville and Catlin know until the last moment. Hell," Smith exhales forcibly, "we're already past the last moment."

Chapter Thirty-One
Major Ab Johnson

My driver is tinkering with the Indian when I come out of HQ. "I better know how to run this thing. Give me a few pointers." He shows me how to start, shift, and run the motorcycle. Then he helps this old man squeeze into the damned sidecar, and we head to La Voie.

Noise from the Indian's engine drowns out everything else as I stew about what just happened. I know. I know, I'm not an infantry officer, just a fat pencil-pusher. But I know this is not the way to fight this battle. No wonder my French cousins have gotten so badly beat up. Now they want to make the same mistakes with my Marines. *My Marines.* There's a new one.

When we reach La Voie, the volume of battle noise to the north tells me that the fight for Hill 142 is not over. I dismiss my driver and recommend he find some chow. Then I head over to the medical station.

Lieutenant Commander Dessez is filling out a report at his field desk in the aid station. "Pops, I hear all the shooting, but we aren't seeing many casualties. I sent some men up to Turrill but haven't heard back."

"They're practically popping the champagne corks back at Division," I say. "They assume the next part'll be a cakewalk. The sixth sense of an old reporter tells me their jubilation is premature." I take a deep breath. "Look, what I'm going to say might get me in some hot water, but . . . well, shit, someone has to do it. There's going to be a big push with 3/5 at center stage." I tell him what I know. "Please tell Neville. They step off at 1700 hours. North half of Belleau Wood."

"Today?"

I nod, my throat too tight to answer.

Dessez scowls at his watch. Before I can say more, a breathless runner comes up and hands Dessez a note. His frown deepens while he reads. "From one of my corpsmen. He says to send everything we can—heavy casualties. We haven't seen them because they're still on the field. Shit." He looks toward the northeast. "Guys've laid out there for eight or nine hours. I'll have to set up more shock tables."

"What can I do?" I ask.

"Know how to drive that thing of yours?"

"I have a driver."

"Yeah, but you can ferry supplies in the sidecar. Up for a little adventure, Pops?"

"I got a quick and dirty lesson. Can't be that hard to drive." I rub my neck. I think I'm about to become an idiot again.

I'm a Marine father. Marines are in trouble. My mission is to make sure our medical personnel get the supplies they need by any means possible, right? This is work for an enlisted man, but shit, someone has to do it. I suppose that's my new motto. And my appointment calendar is free for the rest of the day.

I promised—*promised*—Helen I'd stay safe. But boys younger than Jack are lying in a field with shattered limbs and riddled bodies baking in the sun. What would Helen say if she knew Jack was among them?

"What can I take with me?"

"A surgeon. We only have two in Champillon. See if you can inspire some of your ambulance drivers to go. We'll load 'em with supplies." Dessez scowls. "You get started and I'll let Neville know."

Dad's words echo in my ears—*never volunteer*. I jog to the ambulance drivers playing cards and order them to fire up their vehicles. I shout at surprised navy corpsmen to load everything they can spare into the backs of the ambulances. I don't let anyone argue back or listen to gripes. We've got a mission, and we're going to accomplish it. My rank is handy at the moment.

I help load litters, dressings, and boxes of gear into the Fords. By the time I get back to my motorcycle, a surgeon sits in the sidecar, smoking a cigarette. We shake hands, and I forget the man's name in my rush, my mind racing about the decision I've just made, working out how to pull this off.

I lead a column, separating the four ambulances so a single shell can't take us all out. We leave the road and bounce through fields twice to avoid shell holes, arriving in Champillon fifteen minutes later.

A surgeon wearing a bloodstained apron sits on a stone wall behind the aid station, smoking a cigarette. Battle noise sounds right around the corner, rifle fire echoing in the woods, rattling machine gun bursts, and artillery explosions. I shut off the motorcycle as the ambulances back in, and men unload supplies. The doctor from the sidecar goes into the aid station, and I walk over to the man on the wall. "I'm Johnson, Medical Supply."

"Don't go out front," he says.

"Why?" I ask.

The surgeon pulls his apron to the side, pushes his hand into his coat pocket, and pokes a finger through a hole. "Sniper almost got me." He turns to me. "Lose your way, Major?"

"No, just my mind."

"Lot of that going around. Your gizmo there might come in real handy. They dumped ammo over there." The surgeon points. "The road between here and Turrill's PC is too dangerous for trucks. They need ammo and canteens first. After that, stretchers and medical supplies. Take those up and bring my patients back, and you'll be my personal hero. I better get back in. Thanks for coming." He pauses and asks, "How'd you get the shiners?"

"Busting broncos. French horses are ornery."

The surgeon grins and goes inside the aid station.

I pull a couple of cotton balls from my trouser pocket and stuff them in my ears while a private loads my sidecar. I rev the Indian and say a silent prayer, not that I think God can hear me over this racket.

Marines going in both directions crowd the two-rut lane to Turrill's

PC. Men returning with empty hands pick up and lug ammo cans and canteens. I get into the flow of traffic. One private elbows another, looking at me, saying something.

The sidecar threatens to break loose as I creep along the dirt road, navigating deep ruts around potholes, using my feet to push a couple of times. A passing corporal gives me a thumbs-up. The sulfurous tang of gunpowder fills the air. I wipe my brow, sweat stinging my eyes as I search for the headquarters group.

I finally find Turrill's post of command in the woods facing a broad downhill wheat field that ends in a tree line a few hundred yards away. Marines scurry around, crouching or hitting the deck when German artillery rounds scream in. My sphincter tightens. Two litter teams struggle uphill with their loads, bracketed by explosions. I duck at a shriek. An explosion showers me with debris. "What the hell type of shell is that?" I shout to a sergeant.

"Fucking whizz-bang, sir. German 77. Hate 'em. Flat trajectory sends 'em right at your face. Hit the deck when you hear one."

I scan the field and don't see the litter teams. Shit. They must be hit. I want to run out to help. A helmeted head pops up, and a litter-bearer stands, helping his mates heft their load. The stretcher bounces so much that I fear the Marine in it might fall out as the men carrying him run for their lives.

Turrill shouts, "Thanks. Aren't you a bit senior to be doing sergeant's work?"

The comment about sergeant's work stabs like an icepick. Two weeks ago, I would have asked Turrill if he had come up through the ranks.

"Shit, Major, someone's got to do it."

Turrill smiles. "What happened to your face?"

"Fight with the French general who wrote your orders." I smile. "You should see the other guy."

Turrill laughs. "If only."

"Where do you need these?" I point toward the supplies.

"Drop 'em over there." Turrill points. "Can you make a few more runs?"

I give a thumbs-up. Turrill runs to the north, where the only lieutenant in sight organizes a platoon. Two privates unload my sidecar and then help a wounded Marine into it, his arm in a sling and a splint on his ankle. It's too noisy to talk as we get moving. I pass a group of six Marines manhandling a wooden mule cart loaded with casualties on my way back to Champillon.

Two corpsmen take the Marine into the aid station while two others load the sidecar with canteens. The next two trips are ammo. Then two crates of grenades.

A bit before 1500 hours, I find Turrill. Things have quieted down for the moment, and I can hear him. "I have to head back to La Voie. I'm low on gas. Anything you want me to take back?"

"My love and appreciation for sending my men into the most poorly planned attack I've ever seen." He pauses and holds up his right index finger. "Nah—forget that. They'll just get mad. I know this one came straight from the generals."

"It looked like chaos to me."

"Yeah. I can't believe they made us do it this way. This would have been a rout if it weren't for Captain Hamilton. "

I look into Turrill's eyes and nod in agreement. This Marine father is ready to shoot that French colonel and the fool who ordered this.

Chapter Thirty-Two
Private Carl Larsen

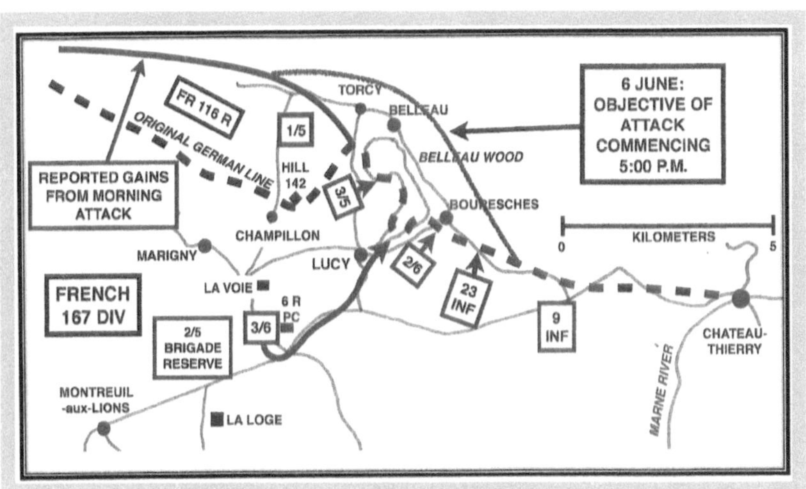

The afternoon heat after a sleepless night begs for a nap as I stifle a yawn. The only remedy is more coffee, but I was beyond my usual limit by 1000 hours this morning. I don't know about the others, but I'm running on fumes. My last chow was at La Voie this morning.

Colonel Catlin stands near a window in the staff room of the Maison Blanche PC. I brewed coffee and kept cups full all night as two-thirds of the Sixth Regiment traded positions with the Fifth. The racket of 3/6 moving to the woods behind Maison Blanche and 1/6 moving off the line along the same road kept everyone awake.

Captain Tribot-Laspierre and Lieutenant Colonel Harry Lee confer in hushed voices next to the map. Lee yawns and stretches while Tribot-Laspierre stifles his own.

"How long does it take those guys to cut an order?" Catlin says. "This isn't the War College where we had all day." He walks over to join the others at the map. "At least a little birdie gave us a heads-up about a big push through Belleau Wood. Sometime today. Feels like they expect us to wing it. The delays are driving me nuts."

A motorcycle pulls to a stop outside, and a lieutenant from brigade HQ enters the room moments later.

"Here are your orders, Colonel. Hot off the presses."

Catlin looks at his watch. "It's 1545, son. How long did it take them to punch out this order?"

The lieutenant's face reddens. "About two hours, sir."

Catlin towers over the lieutenant, glaring. "What were they doing, checking each other's grammar? My men have to line up in an *hour*? I don't hear artillery. What's the artillery plan?"

"Above my pay grade, sir. I assume the generals took care of it."

"I don't like the word *assume*, Lieutenant. Does Major Berry know about his battalion's role in this?"

"Another lieutenant is notifying Colonel Neville, sir. They'll let Berry know."

"I hope so. I don't have time to find him before they go over the top. Hell, Sibley and Holcomb's units'll have to run over a mile to get in position." Catlin reads the order after dismissing the lieutenant. "Carl, get Major Sibley in here toot sweet."

I go to the 3/6 camp, which is close to our PC, thank God. Marines are heading off, but I find Major Sibley and we go back to the PC. I follow the major into the staff room.

"I finally have something on paper," Catlin says. "Move your men up to Gob Gully, just beyond the culvert under the Lucy road."

"They're on the way, sir."

"How'd you hear?"

"I don't want to get anyone in trouble, sir."

Catlin faces Lee. "Harry, you stay here. If I'm going to run this show, I need to do it from Lucy. Tell Signals that their only priority is to keep the wire from here to Lucy live. Sibley, Laspierre, ride with me."

I run outside and pull the Caddy out of the barn. After the officers are aboard, I hit the gas and go faster than is safe on the road to Lucy, weaving around potholes, shell holes, and men. Four German sausages dance in the breeze to the east. The hair on my neck stands at attention. One of the Heinie bastards is probably calling in an artillery strike on us. I have to keep both hands on the wheel, which is a good thing, since I want to salute the Heinies with my middle finger.

Just past Lucy, I stop and let Sibley off. Then I goose the gas and jerk the wheel to the right, kicking up dust and gravel as we streak past Montgivrault. An artillery round hits fifty yards behind us. Then another to the west, and a third, closer. They're zeroing in, but I'm a moving target. I step on it, white-knuckling the steering wheel. Clods of dirt splatter the windshield like August grasshoppers. Something metallic smacks my helmet. This is crazy. My right foot threatens to bust through the floorboards.

The next tree line nears . . . so close.

Another explosion rocks the car to the left.

Every nerve in my body hums, muscles rigid.

Finally.

Inside the woods.

I relax my death grip that's threatening to break the steering wheel.

Air cooler, the artillery behind.

I ease up on the gas.

After a half mile, I skid to a stop at Major Holcomb's PC at La Cense Farm, the southernmost Marine unit. Catlin pats my shoulder as he gets out and runs to the PC. I idle the car under a tree and sprint to the PC. I could have stayed with the car, but I want to know what's happening.

Catlin holds a map, pointing with a pen. "Barry's 3/5 is on the left. They'll take the north and middle of Belleau Wood. Sibley and 3/6 take the southern end and press on to Bouresches. Holcomb, your battalion pushes forward on the south side to help take Bouresches and the ridge south and east of it."

Holcomb whistles. "Jesus, look at what 3/5 has to cross. What did Berry say when he heard about this?"

"I haven't talked to him." Catlin looks at his watch. "Neville is supposed to let him know." I glance at my watch—1620 hours. Catlin writes a note and hands it to me. "I need the fastest man in the regiment to get this through to Major Berry. We'll drive to Lucy, but after that you'll have to hoof it. Neville ought to have already relayed the order, and Berry ought to be organized by the time you get there. Too many 'oughts' to trust. Carl, you're my eyes. Watch the first part of their assault, then report back to me in Lucy. *Don't get involved.* Observe and report back to *me*."

A chauffeur, busboy, shoe polisher, and now a runner. When will I get to feel like a Marine? But I know, deep down, I am one. "Aye, aye, sir."

Our artillery begins to fire at Belleau Wood as we're driving back to Lucy. Light fire by anyone's standards—not the sort of heavy barrage I would have expected.

Heinie artillery responds, as usual.

The volume of arriving artillery picks up on the drive back to Lucy. The Heinie balloon observers would have to be blind not to see that something big is about to happen. Surprise, hell. What the generals couldn't understand is plain as day to at least one lowly private. I stash the staff car in a shed on the outskirts of Lucy. I run north along streets thronging with Marines hustling to new positions—NCOs shouting orders and a private cursing as he pulls an equipment wagon handle with three others.

My stomach tightens, and I pick up my pace after leaving Lucy. Two sausages float above us to the east. I'm on a road in plain sight, the hot sun beaming on me like a spotlight. I'm a rabbit in a carnival shooting gallery. The green wheat on both sides of the road flutters in waves from a soft breeze. I use one hand to steady the gas mask pouch bouncing against my chest.

I sprint.

The Heinies are shelling the field near my destination. Is anyone still alive there? Am I running to deliver a note to a dead man?

Something's odd about how our artillery is hitting the woods. I stop for a moment to get my wind, trying to make sense of the strange sight of artillery rounds exploding among the treetops. The dense tree crowns must be tripping the fuses. The shells are exploding a hundred feet above the ground. It's like the Heinies have an umbrella above them.

Dirt showers me when a shell blows a new hole in the field. Gotta get a move on.

I pass empty fighting holes the guys were calling their graves a few days ago. Part of me would like to crawl into one. I'm finally in a battle. But my orders are to be a spectator. I can't carry a gun and ammo—they'd slow me down too much.

Pour it on—the final uphill sprint toward 3/5.

Major Berry stands a hundred yards away, near the tree line of St. Martin Wood, gesticulating, pointing, and shouting words I can't make out. Heinie artillery pounds the area around Berry, disrupting his attempt to organize. Shrapnel zooms and whines by with high-pitched ricochets—how the hell will I make it through? And how is Berry still standing? Lieutenant Colonel Wise emerges from the woods to join him.

I push my legs harder, feeling naked as I sprint toward Berry. I was pouring coffee only an hour ago. Now this?

The scream of an arriving whizz-bang makes me hit the deck. Shrapnel streaks by—too close. I look up, get on my feet, and run. The only things between me and death are the air, my uniform, and blind luck.

Mostly luck.

Life and death now come down to nothing but random chance.

Quit thinking.

Run.

Berry and Wise are having an animated discussion. A man in an officer's uniform wearing a press corps armband stands talking with another officer. I recognize him—Floyd Gibbons. They let a reporter here?

When I reach them, I hand Berry the colonel's message. Berry reads it and hands it to Wise. "Goddamn it. You ever seen anything as absurd as this? My men aren't ready. Look at that fucking field we have to cross." Berry points toward Belleau Wood. "Four hundred yards before we hit the edge of the woods. I suppose that a line formation is what they expect. Truth is, there's no good method for what they're ordering us to do. Only bad ones."

Wise scowls and shakes his head. "Any intelligence on the woods?"

"No. I have a bad feeling about this." Berry scribbles a note, hands it to me, and points north. "Hustle up that way. The north end of my unit is the Forty-Fifth Company. Get this to their skipper. Tell him to get three platoons on the line and keep one in reserve if he can't read my scribble. Move!"

Chapter Thirty-Three
Private Carl Larsen

Crap is falling on my helmet as I dash to the north, ducking and dodging as if that will do any good. Dirt, broken tree debris, spent shrapnel—I can't tell. I'm pretty sure I'd be knocked out by now without the thing. Marines are scattered around, some behind trees, some lying in foxholes, looking at me like I'm a mad fool. And they're right.

I reach the Forty-Fifth Company at 1655 and find a lieutenant, no captain. "Sir, here's Major Berry's orders." I hand the lieutenant the slip of paper. "Line of sections—three platoons in the attack, one in reserve."

"You kidding? We're covering Turrill's flank. Skipper's at a meeting in Champillon."

A voice behind me speaks. A captain. "You men are now our left flank. Line up. Larsen, the Sixteenth is back in the woods, over there." He points to the southwest. "Tell 'em to line up to the south of us toot sweet. I'll be along as soon as I have these men organized."

I sprint within the seeming safety of the trees. That illusion dies with the zings of shrapnel ricocheting above my head. It takes me precious minutes to find two lieutenants leaning on each side of a tree to steady their binoculars, looking toward the east.

"Private, you have any idea what all that brouhaha is about?"

"Sirs, you with the Sixteenth?"

"Affirmative."

"Captain—what the hell, I forgot his name—your adjutant, that's the one. Told me to tell your captain to get to the edge of the woods and form up in line of sections. H-hour is 1700 hours."

One of the lieutenants looks at his watch. "Shit. That's ten minutes ago. What took you so long?"

"Had to go to the Forty-Fifth first."

"All right. We'll saddle up the men and head out." He pauses. "You know, privates don't give orders to lieutenants. It's supposed to be the other way around."

"Sir, I'm just passing them along."

"It's only because you have an honest face," says one lieutenant with a wry grin. The captain reaches us and the lieutenants get real serious.

Our artillery quits. The field between 3/5 and Belleau Wood is alive with incoming Heinie artillery. I watch two platoons of Sixteenth Company scurry to the line of departure along the eastern edge of the St. Martin Wood.

The lieutenants line up those remaining, shouting orders, pointing with directing canes to straighten their sections and dress the lines, all of which seems pointless.

I stand next to a tree, catching my breath.

Whistles sound.

Platoon leaders loft their directing canes and lead their Marines at marching pace into the field.

Flashes along the edge of Belleau Wood give me a momentary image of dancing fairy lights. But these aren't supernatural. They're Heinie machine guns, bullets as dense as Minnesota mosquitoes.

I hit the deck when bullets rip into the tree trunk beside me.

A string of machine gun rounds shred the troops. Marines fall.

Can't tell if they're dead or wounded.

Machine guns are a constant buzz amid the artillery explosions.

My ears ring, pulsing with my heart, lungs grasping for air as I crawl to a large tree. Okay, be the colonel's eyes and ears. I peer around the trunk. I'm on the west side of the battlefield, which resembles a shallow bowl with Marines in the middle.

The hilly forest of Belleau Wood forms high ground on the eastern side and wraps around to the north. The bowl slopes down from my position to a road that runs from Lucy to . . . well, I don't know where. The low point is the middle of the northern part of the field to my left. The ground then slopes uphill to the east, west, and south. Men there won't see Lucy, but the entire arc of Belleau Wood will see them. Out in the open, broad daylight, with no cover. This is going to end up just like the Heinies at Les Mares a few days ago.

I can hardly breathe while watching the lines of the Forty-Fifth and Sixteenth Companies march into the field, men falling, some running, others struggling to take cover on the ground in full view of the Heinies. Pink mist hangs over the field, and nobody is getting near Belleau Wood.

Another company battles to cross the middle of the field in front of me along the north-to-south rise. Machine guns cut them down, leaving my legs weak. A tear trickles down my right cheek.

Those are my friends out there.

Part of me feels like a coward, watching, wanting to rush in and help. But what good would that be? The colonel needs to know what's going on. He can't see this from where he stands, far to my right. I think I can see him, standing his full six-four, swinging his directing cane. If I can see him, so can the Heinies.

The idiot who planned this attack doesn't understand the terrain. Even a private can see that. What the hell are the generals thinking? The words of the poem "In Flanders Fields" call to me as I lie on my belly, transfixed. Poppies dot this wheat field, too. Heinie machine guns are the reaper's scythe, sweeping Marines from the field. My ass puckers as artillery shells blow gouts of soil and men—some whole, others in parts—into the air.

My heart feels like it wants to jump out of my ribs.

Cries for corpsmen fill the voids between the din of the guns and artillery, making me wish I knew first aid. I want to grab a Springfield and kill the goddamned Heinies. But I have my orders.

Corpsmen scurry among the wounded. Litter-bearers bound onto the field only to be cut down. A corpsman shot through the head hands something to the man he treats before toppling over. My legs seem rooted in the soil as I witness the slaughter.

I want to strangle the jackass who ordered this, to shoot the French bastard who told everyone the Heinies aren't even in the woods.

Not a single Marine stands in the field. I'm light-headed, breathing deep, heavy—heart hammering. The wheat courses in rivulets in the wake of machine gun rounds. The Marines of 3/5 are down or dead.

Wait.

Six Marines pop up and rush forward.

They hit the deck after ten yards.

Four others do the same on the left.

Sweat trickles under my arms, and a dribble crosses my forehead. The two small groups rush into Belleau Wood. It doesn't look as though there are any officers left.

A burst of machine gun rounds snap past, zinging among the trees behind me.

I lean forward and puke.

Gotta get back to the colonel. No other reports will be coming from this field.

Chapter Thirty-Four
Medical Corpsman Lyle McCormack

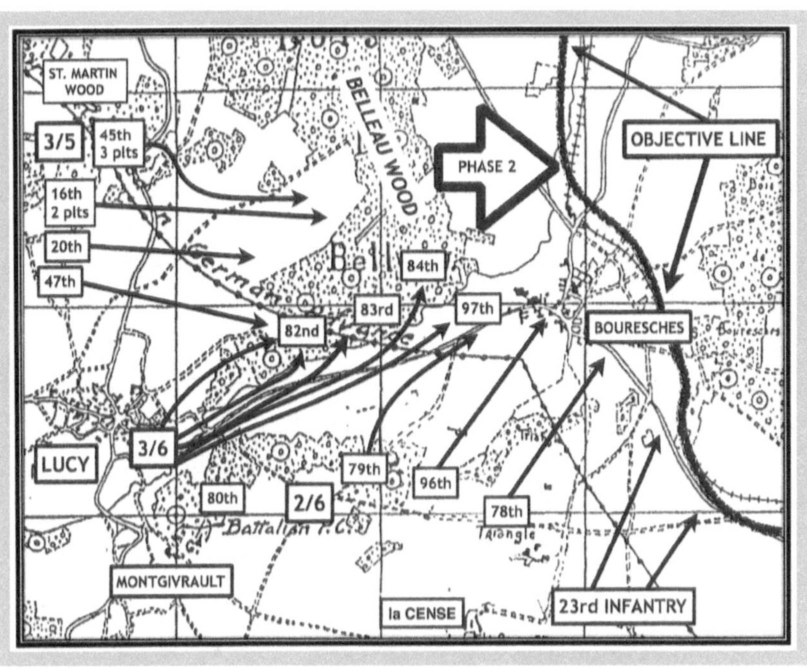

A Hun observation balloon bobs in the air as I sit on a bench under an elm on the east side of the Montgivrault aid station. A basket hangs below the gray sausage with the German cross. I sip from my canteen and dab a trickle of sweat threatening my left eye. I wipe my mouth with my sleeve. The battle's raging to our north. I have friends up there, like Welty.

Feeling pretty useless at the moment. Like everything is happening and I'm not a part of it. Footsteps come from behind.

"Mind if I join you?" Osborne settles onto the bench. "Things are tense." He cocks his right thumb back toward the aid station. "But we've triple-checked everything, and there isn't much else to do."

"Wonder if Gunny Stockham's outfit is part of the action. Kinda worries me, eh?" I point at the observation balloon. "Not much they'll miss."

"How'd you meet Gunny?"

"When we first went into the trenches, they had two corpsmen to a company. They assigned me to his, the Ninety-Sixth. Gunny takes the new guys under his wing. When he found out I was an orphan, like him, that did it."

The noise of a speeding car interrupts me. A staff car rushes along the road from La Cense Farm. I glance at the Hun observation balloon, then back, as the car bursts from the woods where the road crosses an open field. Artillery shells pepper the field, somehow missing the car. Pure luck. The car disappears in the next tree line. "Better get back," I say.

Lieutenant Joel Boone runs toward us. "I need two corpsmen to meet Ninety-Sixth Company at the front of those woods over there." Boone points at the Triangle Wood to the southeast, near where the lucky Cadillac came from.

"How soon?" Osborne asks.

"Fifteen."

"I'm game," I say.

"Me too," Osborne says.

"Osborne, you don't have to go," Boone says.

"I'll be more use out there. Now's as good a time as any for my baptism. Besides, Gunny Stockham told me I have an open invite."

Boone faces Osborne for a moment, then shrugs. "Don't be a damned hero. Follow McCormack's lead."

I scoot into the aid station and pull two medical shoulder bags off wall pegs. I sit next to Osborne and spill the contents of the bags out on the floor. "Don't know about you, sir, but I like to go through my bags with my checklist. Someone's supposed to pack and check 'em. But our lives might depend on 'em. Only takes a couple minutes." I pull out my list and read out loud as we load supplies back into our bags. Osborne reaches into a pocket and sticks two tourniquets into his. Most of the docs look down on these, but I think he's got a good idea. Then he grabs a handful of toothbrushes and stuffs them in one of his bags at the last moment. Danged dentists.

We jog through the Montgivrault Wood. Osborne doesn't have to do this. Hasn't he ever heard about never volunteering? The Ninety-Sixth needs two *corpsmen*, not a dentist. I stop and catch my breath when we reach the tree line. "Really, sir. Why are you doing this?"

Osborne's smile fades. "Ever feel like you're right where you're supposed to be? Doing what you're supposed to do?"

"Not really, sir."

Osborne's face turns serious. "Better get a move on."

"Wait till I'm halfway across, assuming I'm not dead." I point across the field. "We're heading toward that corner."

"What if you're dead?" Osborne raises his right eyebrow.

"Take a different route."

The image of a lone goose flying past a lakeshore crowded with bird blinds pops into my mind as I scramble across the open wheat field. I grip the two medical haversacks, but my gas mask pouch bounces with each step and my helmet flops from side to side. I feel as graceful as a gouty elephant.

Three Hun observation balloons float in the air with shadowy figures in the baskets who seem to stare directly at me. I let go of one medical bag, wipe a trickle of sweat before it blurs my vision, and glance to the left. A whizz-bang could head my way at any moment. I churn my legs harder.

I reach the edge of the woods and bend over, gasping for air. I will the Huns to not shell the field for a lone man as I watch Osborne run.

The smile on Osborne's face seems like that of a man who has found his place in the world. *Will I ever have that sense of belonging?*

When Osborne reaches me, I smile, still catching my breath. "Hope I can find you some teeth, sir."

"Almost every mouth here has a few."

"You remember to bring any toothpaste? Saw you sneak the brushes into your bag, eh?"

Osborne laughs. "Damn. Forgot. Look—over there. Those must be the gents we're supposed to join."

We jog inside the eastern edge of the woods and approach a confused jumble of several hundred sweaty Marines. Sergeants shout orders at privates with battle faces devoid of emotion. Clusters of officers stand apart, smoking, looking at maps. We finally find Captain Duncan's Ninety-Sixth Company huffing their way in. Two lieutenants bitch about the last-minute dash from their encampment at la Cense Farm, a mile to the south. Others check gear and catch their breath. The crowns of mature oaks and elms flutter overhead in a breeze that carries the stench of unwashed, sweaty men.

We face east toward the small hamlet of Bouresches nestled in the bottom of a broad north-south valley downhill from us. Belleau Wood lies behind my left shoulder, to the northwest. Bouresches is a good nine hundred yards away, across a poppy-dotted wheat field that curves downward on both sides. The right side slopes into a ravine that peters out south of the town. The left side ends along the Lucy-Bouresches Road that follows the south side of Gob Gully and Belleau Wood.

A shout catches my attention: Gunny Stockham, waving.

"There's the headquarters group, sir." I head over.

Stockham stands near Captain Duncan. The captain points out terrain features with a swagger stick as he talks. Gunny Stockham nods when we approach.

"Who's your friend, Lyle?" Duncan asks.

"This is Lieutenant Osborne, our dentist. Good as any doctor in a pinch, eh?"

"Duncan." The captain tamps tobacco into a straight-stemmed pipe and lights it. "Our objective is Bouresches." Lieutenant Cates is on my far left, shouting orders. Stockham pats my shoulder and hustles off to join his platoon while Cates uses an officer's cane to direct his men.

"Let's saddle up and move 'em out," Duncan yells as he walks into the sun-drenched wheat field.

We need a spot with cover for the company aid station. Toward my left, several one-pounder gun crews pull their pieces into a cluster of trees—the only logical place for an aid station in sight. Not ideal. Artillery positions are a standard target, but my only other option is the ravine on the south side of the field—too far from Cates's platoon. I wave a corpsman over. "Set up the aid station over there, in those trees." I turn to Osborne. "Long as that's okay with you, sir."

"Makes sense," Osborne says.

I wave a stretcher team to join us. "Reckon we'll need them soon."

The field is quiet. A battle rages to the northwest, on the other side of Belleau Wood.

It seems my life comes down to this moment, this place, and nothing else. How many friends have I seen for the last time? And what about us?

The sun warms my back as Osborne and I shadow Duncan's command group through the rippling green wheat. Sweat trickles underneath my helmet. I swallow and roll my neck and shoulders to loosen up.

Where the hell is our artillery cover?

The French pounded the importance of a rolling barrage into us. Always. Always. Always.

So where is it?

I glance to each side as lieutenants and platoon sergeants lead skirmish lines—orderly and straight, like we're on a parade deck. We're nothing more than range targets without a rolling barrage.

It'd better come soon.

My fists tighten as Osborne and I move forward, my breath faster. I wipe sweat from my eyebrows.

Others are looking around. Where's the screening barrage?

We're almost too far into the field for that now. A short round will hit us.

My chest feels empty. Neck tight.

Duncan shouts encouragement to the Marines, then plants his pipe in his mouth and points ahead with his swagger stick.

Bouresches and the southeastern corner of Belleau Wood erupt in a wall of machine gun fire. Marines fall. Duncan jogs to a nearby lieutenant, shouts and gestures with his stick, his words lost in the racket.

A Marine on our left goes down. Osborne dashes over. I follow, machine gun rounds ripping the air surrounding us. We dive down next to a private with a leg wound. I compress over the femoral artery while Osborne pulls one of his tourniquets out and wraps it around the leg. We put a dressing over the wound and wrap it.

The litter-bearers load the man on a stretcher and scoot back to the aid station. Hun artillery rains down like an April thunderstorm. The air smells of gunpowder and metallic blood mist. The noise is deafening. Machine gun rounds snap and zing around me. A scream to our right. I straighten my helmet, jump up, and sprint. Osborne follows.

A corporal lies on the ground holding his right flank, blood pooling below. Osborne rips open a medium wound pack and pulls the man's hands away from the wound. He puts a dressing on the entry wound. I wrap a wide bandage around the abdomen and secure the end with safety pins. I scan the field—more Marines down. No litter-bearers. "Sir, we'll have to carry him."

Osborne grabs the man's boots while I lift his shoulders. As we stagger back to the aid station, a puff of red spray hits my left cheek and Osborne staggers. I glance back—a rip in Osborne's left sleeve, blood dripping toward the elbow.

"I'm okay. Pick it up!" Osborne shouts. I pump my legs, hustling toward the aid station. When we set the corporal down, Osborne heads back onto the field before I can look at his wound. I follow. Osborne bends down and grabs a wounded man under the shoulders and pulls him back to the aid station. "Bring that other one," he yells, motioning with his head toward another Marine rolling on the ground. I don't bother to assess the man, just grab him under the shoulders and yank. The Marine screams as I pull.

The field erupts with Hun artillery.

A man to my left disappears in an explosion.

Osborne helps the other corpsman at the aid station with another of his tourniquets. His last one. I set my man down and look at Osborne, blood oozing from a fresh wound in his left thigh.

The dentist shrugs. He gives a forced smile.

My heart hammers my breastbone, lungs hungry for air, while I scan for the headquarters group. Captain Duncan seems to ignore the rounds snapping past and walks straight and tall. An artillery round hits fifty yards away and showers us with debris. A lieutenant to my left staggers and falls back, blood spraying out of his back—a corpsman runs to him. Stockham's Fourth Platoon is on the far left. Gaps in the line grow before my eyes. Stockham's lieutenant, Cates, shouts at his men and urges them on.

Men are down all over the field as Duncan marches forward, his senior sergeants beside him. Those nearer the ravine to my right have an easier go—so far. I hear a shout—Duncan motivating his Marines, pushing the advance against the tidal wave of German machine gun fire.

Then Duncan staggers backward, holding his middle, and falls.

The sergeants stop and crouch around their fallen captain. The first sergeant waves a hand toward us.

"Go." Osborne shouts.

I hightail it to Duncan. An artillery shell hits to my right and splatters me with body parts.

A dog tag gleams, floating through the air. It drops in front of me.

I pick it up.

The run takes a lifetime as rounds kick up dust on both sides and zip past my head like swarms of angry hornets.

Each breath, each footfall, could be my last.

I have a job to do in the meantime.

I kneel beside Duncan and rip open a wound pack.

Osborne kneels on the other side, face pained, gasping for air. Bleeding.

"Sir, what should I do with this?" I hold up the dog tag. Osborne takes the aluminum disc, slips it into his tunic breast pocket, and buttons the flap. When he does this, I notice a bloody gash on Osborne's left side. How is he still standing?

Duncan holds his bloody abdomen with both hands, choking out orders to his sergeants. I ease the captain's hands apart, and Osborne applies two large dressings to the mess. I grit my teeth—no time for an inspection and too much blood to make sense of the anatomy. No chance of survival.

I pull a long dressing roll from the pack and yell, "Sit him up. I'll wind this around." Another corpsman joins us. My hands are sticky with blood by the time we finish. We ease Duncan back down.

Osborne pulls a morphine syringe out of his bag, stabs the needle through Duncan's uniform near the shoulder, and injects the full dose.

"Aid station," Osborne shouts.

I take a quick look around—no litter bearers in sight.

The first sergeant pulls a woolen blanket from his pack, and we roll Duncan onto it. Osborne, the other corpsman, and the two sergeants grab the corners of the blanket.

"Osborne, let me—you're hit, sir," I say.

"Nah, I've got this," he shouts back. He's limping and tilts to one side, struggling to carry his load.

Bullets snap and buzz as though I'm in a sonic tunnel as we struggle uphill toward trees that now seem very distant.

Artillery rounds shred the field.

A whizz-bang screams by and explodes past the trees ahead.

We near the station.

We'll make it.

The world goes white.

Chapter Thirty-Five
Medical Corpsman Lyle McCormack

My head throbs as though I've been beaned by the blacksmith's mallet that ruined my little finger so many years ago. Pain pulses in every square inch of my body. I struggle to open my eyes. I was running one moment and now I'm in another moment, but which one? Where? My brain is stuffed with cotton.

The crackle of gunfire and thunder of artillery tell me I'm not in heaven. The other place? Fingers press on the right side of my neck—someone feeling for a pulse. I open my eyes. Duncan's sergeant seems to be on the edge of an emotion I don't want to witness. "How are the others?" I ask.

"Duncan's dead. So's your dentist, our first sergeant, and the corpsman. They stopped the shrapnel that should have killed us." The sergeant points toward the south. "That ravine's the only cover. Set up your aid station there."

Dagnabit. My ears ring. It's like I'm wearing earmuffs. I struggle to my feet, stagger, and the sergeant helps me back down. I flex my arms and legs—they work. Not bleeding much. I paw at my helmet, finding a new dent on the left.

"Gonna be okay?" the sergeant asks.

"Sure. Give me a sec. How long was I out?"

"Few minutes. Need me to stay?"

"No. I'll be okay." The sergeant gives me a pat on the shoulder and runs off. I fight a wave of nausea as I look around the field between us and Bouresches, searching for Stockham's platoon. I take a swig from my canteen, rise to my feet, and stagger back toward the fallen men. I concentrate on placing one foot before the next.

Osborne lies next to Duncan, his right hand still gripping the blanket. His chest and abdomen are shredded.

I take a knee.

The image of Osborne, his jokes, his playful humor, and the way that he kept everyone around him light-hearted replaces the death mask for a moment.

He should have stayed in Montgivrault. He didn't have to be here. He didn't need to die. Not here, not now. He talked about his destiny, his place in the world. And here it ends.

I'll mourn later.

I pry Osborne's death grip from the blanket under Duncan and slip the bloodstained medical bags off his shoulders. The dentist's head lolls to each side with the movement. I straighten Osborne's head, touch my friend's forehead, and run downhill.

The Hun machine gunners are having their way. A sniper in the church tower is particularly effective. A thin line of Marines—what remains of the Ninety-Sixth—march down the field, closing on Bouresches, Lieutenant Cates leading them.

Cates drops.

Another officer rushes from behind and leads on. I stagger in their direction. A knot fills my gut as I pick up the pace. The throb in my head spikes every time I plant a foot. I stumble, thrown off balance by the four medical bags. Stockham leads half of the remaining men. Four Marines rush past where Cates fell, heading for cover in the ravine the sergeant had pointed to.

I make my way toward Cates. But then he gets to his feet and follows his men in a drunken jog. I sprint toward the ravine. A stream of machine gun rounds buzz past, and my gait becomes a desperate lope, nose dripping, my mouth salivating with nausea about to erupt.

Bullets churn the lip of the ravine as I dive in headfirst, knocking my noggin when I land. Jeez, that hurts. I roll over on my back, gasping for air, head throbbing, vision clouded. As my breath slows, I sit up, crouch, and make my way to a small cluster of Marines thirty feet away. Survivors and discarded French gear litter the ravine. The French left everything but their skivvies in their retreat. More Marines jump into the ravine. Four of the men laugh, one pouring red liquid out of a canteen onto Lieutenant Cates's head.

"Goddamn it, Tom, don't waste that wine on my head, give me a drink," Cates says.

"Shit, Lieutenant, we thought you'd fucking bought it. That goose egg's gonna make it pretty hard to get your helmet back on."

Cates takes a swig and wipes his mouth on his sleeve. He lifts his helmet and traces the crease of a deep dent with one finger. "Used to curse this damned thing. I'll frame it if I make it through."

I touch the dent on mine.

"You with Duncan?" Cates frowns.

"Yeah. He's gone. First sergeant, too. So's my doctor—well, dentist."

"They sent a dentist? Here?"

"Yes, sir. Lieutenant Osborne."

"Shit, that's Stockham's buddy, right?"

"Yeah. Mine too. Great guy," I say.

"Here." Cates hands me the canteen. "You look like I feel."

I take a swig and hand the canteen to another Marine, who wets his whistle in grim communion.

Cates looks around and shouts, motioning at a group of Marines farther up the ravine to join us. "This is what's left of the company?" He pauses, holds out a hand to the man with the magic canteen, and takes another swig.

"We need to get to town. Follow me." Cates hands the canteen back and staggers forward along the ravine. He picks up an abandoned French rifle with a shattered stock, then digs around for ammo.

The battle rages around us, but our small band makes it into Bouresches unharmed. I'm the only corpsman. Cates blows his whistle. I follow his gaze. First Lieutenant Robertson heads our way with the remains of Fourth Platoon. Stockham brings up the rear of the ragged column.

Robertson counts heads. "Twenty-two."

"I think the Germans pulled out," Cates says.

"They'll be back." Robertson scans the buildings as he speaks. "Clean the town out and hold it. I'll go back and get reinforcements."

A surprised expression crosses Cates's face.

Huh?

With Duncan dead, Robertson is the company CO until replaced. He's in command. Why isn't he sending a runner back to Major Holcomb?

Robertson hustles back toward the ravine. Cates barks out orders, sending six Marines to form an outpost along the Lucy road to the west and another group to guard the southern approach. Cates leads the third group north. I take middle position in the small patrol. A rifle opens up above us as we round a corner. Four rapid shots. I hit the deck and hug the wall. Two men lie still in the street. That sniper in the church belfry. The rest may have left, but he's still here.

I crawl back around the corner. Cates motions the others to gather around. "Okay, two teams. You—" He points to a corporal. "—go back to that last corner and head around the left. I'll take the rest around the right." He touches his battered helmet. "And don't shoot me, okay? I'm tired of getting hit." He pokes a finger in his coat where another bullet entered near his left shoulder. A dab of blood covers his finger when he withdraws it. Then he pats a rip along his collar. "Doc can patch me up later. Move."

Cates leads our team along a side street. He motions the men to come to him and points toward a corner. He whispers to a private and then pats the man's helmet.

The private lies on the sidewalk and inches his way around the corner, leading with his rifle muzzle. He stops.

The noise from Belleau Wood crackles in the distance.

The private tightens his cheek weld and adjusts his feet.

I hold my breath, willing the private to steady his aim.

Breathe in—breathe out—throat open—squeeeeze.

I jump at the rifle report. The private works the bolt, eye glued to the sight, cheek to stock. "Hands in the air, sir," he says.

Cates peers around the corner, then motions for the others to follow. "Private, keep a bead on his noggin until we get up there."

We rush into the church and make our way up into the bell tower along narrow stairs. A frightened Hun holds shaking hands high. He's only a kid. The sniper lies dead, the back of his head missing. The space smells of sulfurous gunpowder and vomit. A splash of puke puddles on the floor next to the kid's boots. Bits of brain and black-haired scalp pepper a red stain on the plaster wall behind us. The kid vomits, ending in dry heaves.

A sergeant pushes the prisoner aside. He waves to the private down below and then raises his rifle. Three rapid shots ring in the belfry. The sergeant stares in the direction of his shots. "Got one, sir, headed for the north end of town."

"You and two others do overwatch here." Cates motions toward the prisoner. "Bring him along. When Robertson returns, have one of his men take this guy back. Lyle, take care of my men."

I clamber down the belfry stairs, peer out the church doors, take a breath, dash across the street, and work my way back to the two men who were killed by the sniper. I'm totally exposed as I pull their bodies out of the street and gather their rifles and ammo pouches.

One rifle will go to Cates. The other rifle? Corpsmen and medics are unarmed personnel. There are a few reasons for that. The most practical is that we have enough to carry. A rifle and ammo only add to a big load. Another is the idea that medical noncombatants should be treated differently, not targeted the same way as an infantryman. Hospitals won't be bombed, and ambulances are off limits. Those are the rules they taught us.

Well, the Huns aren't playing by those rules. I suppose I could be court-martialed, but my guys haven't cleared the buildings here, and there are so few of us that I'm keeping the other rifle. Besides, I'll have to be alive for them to court-martial me.

I open the bolt and check the ammo. Full magazine. Good to go.

I hustle back to our command group and hand a rifle to Cates along with two handfuls of ammo pouches. Hearing no objections, I join the others as we work our way through streets and buildings of the little village. I'll set up my aid station in one of the buildings; I just have to figure out which one is safe enough. A lot of them are wrecks.

The next half-hour is tense. I sidestep, back to buildings, peering around corners, imagining Hun eyes lurking in shadows, bayonets ready to skewer me, rifle sights drawing a bead on my head.

What I find are two wounded Marines.

Artillery shells scuttle in. Each chunk of debris that hits my helmet reminds me of Osborne.

The crackle of rifle fire waxes and wanes in every direction. My head throbs, and nausea gnaws at me as I work.

I help one wounded Marine to Gunny Stockham's outpost. The fellow was hit in the leg but can hobble with assistance. I paint the wound with iodine and wrap a dressing around it. The other casualty is in too much pain from a flank wound to be effective. I help him into a small stone-walled house behind Stockham's position.

This house is in better shape than many and will be my aid station. It also is not stripped as bare as the others. That makes me think the people here left in a hurry or didn't have a way to cart off their stuff. Makes me wonder about the stories of the folks who lived here.

I do a quick search, find a thick blanket, and throw it over the front window curtain rod. My patient has a through-and-through gunshot wound. The abdominal organs seem undamaged. I dab the entry and exit wounds with iodine, apply dressings, and wrap a large muslin bandage around to keep everything in place, followed by a shot of morphine.

Gunfire crackles to the east, followed by the deep rattle of a distant machine gun. I paint an iodine *M* on his forehead and fill out a wound card. After tying the wound card to one of his buttons, I say, "Stay here. Wrap this blanket around yourself. Don't drink. Understand?" The man nods. I search the house again. I need a hammer, nails, and more blankets.

Rifle fire erupts to the north.

I find a hammer and a few crude square nails in a kitchen drawer. On the way out of the kitchen, I trip on something, splashing water on the plank floor. I reach down and pick up a glazed ceramic bowl. It has a paw print and the name *Abby* on it. I set the bowl on the counter and move on.

The furniture is intact, clothing in closets, food in the kitchen. I say a thank-you to the residents for leaving us some chow. Upstairs, the beds are made. I pull blankets off what must be a girl's bed, tossing the teddy bear by the pillow on top of a dresser, wondering who is missing it. I was at the La Voie aid station when Carl Larsen brought two teenagers and their dog in. The girl was soaked with her mother's blood. The mother saved the girl by diving on top of her when a Hun plane strafed them. Their border collie was one I'd love to take home in another life. The boy, who is almost as tall as me, wore a French Chasseur beret. Abby. That's their dog's name.

Commander Dessez told me about them. This must be their home. Orphans like me. And Osborne. And Stockham. That's why I remember them. No time to dwell on that.

I haul the blankets downstairs. My gimpy little finger aches while I nail blankets over windows, reminding me of another hammer, another time in my life. An orphan. And like Osborne, I'm taking care of my family—these guys, half of whose names I don't know.

After I finish with the blankets, I find an oil lamp and fire it up. I glance around the sitting room. A photograph on the mantel over the fireplace shows two adults, smiling. The man is a Chasseur in uniform wearing his floppy beret, the woman slender and pretty. The two children stand next to them. Marcel and Geneviève—those were their names. Abby sits on the floor in front of them at a perfect dog form of attention. Seeing it chokes me up. For Osborne, for them, for my men— I must carry on no matter the cost.

I head out the front door, rifle at the ready.

If Lieutenant Robertson doesn't get through, it will be a handful of Marines and one scared-as-heck navy corpsman against the whole of the Kaiser's horde—likely my last day on earth. And the sun isn't even nearing the western trees. My watch says 1900. I've been through a lifetime in two hours.

Over the next hour, I work my way around the groups of Marines, checking for new wounds, going back and forth to look in on my wounded Marine. I keep my rifle safety off, a round in the chamber. I've never killed a man, but right now I'm not having any problem with the idea. The images of Osborne and Duncan sear my spirit and make me want to bayonet the Huns, but the only ones I find are corpses. Just as well. I leave 'em where they lie.

An artillery shell hurtles in, hitting a building on the next block. Something smacks my helmet. My vision narrows, then the stars clear and my head throbs more than before. I lean forward and vomit. How many times can this happen before I'm punch-drunk?

I explore the helmet with my fingers, find a new dent, then take a swig from my canteen to rinse my mouth. I used to hate my helmet. No more.

I round a corner on my way back to the dressing station. Lieutenant Robertson and a captain are leading a group of Marines. A truck speeds toward us. Hun machine guns rattle from the same direction. Ricochets zing and echo among the buildings. The men scramble out of the way as the truck squeals to a stop.

"Got a death wish?" shouts the captain.

"Heard you was low on ammo, sir," yells a sergeant major dismounting from the driver's seat. "Where you want this shit, sir?"

"You must be out of your fucking mind. Get it in here." The captain points at a building. "I can't believe you made it through."

"Captain, you bring any medical with you?" I ask.

"Yeah, they're around there somewhere."

I find the group and lead the four corpsmen to my dressing station. We snap on our flashlights and light a couple more oil lamps, and the room glows. We unload our medical bags to do an inventory.

"What the hell?" a corpsman mutters, holding up a handful of toothbrushes.

My eyes have seen too much for tears. I slump against a wall, holding my head in my hands. Danged Osborne.

Chapter Thirty-Six
Private Carl Larsen

Bullets fly by as thick as flies around a carcass as I sprint back toward Lucy. Trying to dodge them is useless, but I can't help myself. Machine gun rounds snap by, their hot breath brushing by my cheeks. Artillery rounds blast the field to my left. Ricochets dog me with their deadly song. I pump my arms, mouth wide, gulping air, neck hair tingling. This will be my last day alive if I keep running messages.

I try not to look at the field where 3/5 lies dying. But my eyes wander there the way the tongue finds a jagged tooth. I feel guilty watching as I run toward Lucy and not to them. A whizz-bang zooms past, shattering that delusion. I run faster, sweat running from underneath my helmet, the steel pot whacking my skull with each desperate stride.

A cluster of men stand near a copse of trees about a hundred yards away. I can't make out the faces, but the colonel is there, a head taller than the next man. Machine gunners line the ditch on both sides of Catlin, their Hotchkiss guns rattling. Gunpowder fog swirls around the headquarters group, giving it an almost mythical quality. The colonel shouts orders to two runners and points to places in the field with his directing cane as I get near. Captain Tribot-Laspierre stands next to Catlin, gesticulating and shouting. Bullets kick up the turf next to them.

My gut tightens—the colonel must know that the Heinies are zeroing in on him.

Tribot-Laspierre shouts, "*Mon* Colonel, you must take cover."

"Negative, Captain," Catlin shouts over the din. "My men need to see me. Some might lose their resolve if they don't. They see me— they carry on."

"But I think *les Boches* have figured that out. I don't see their commander."

"Sir, orders?" I ask between breaths. Sweat stings my eyes. A string of machine gun rounds pounds the earth ten feet to my right. I want to hit the deck, but as long as the colonel stands tall, I will.

"How's Berry?" Catlin shouts.

"Bad, sir. Didn't all get on the line in time. Two companies didn't know about the attack until after five, sir."

"I was assured they were informed." Catlin's voice is strained.

"His lieutenants went down in the first few minutes. Far's I can tell, the whole battalion is wounded or dead, sir. It was like what we did to the Heinies at Les Mares. Where's our arty, sir?" I swallow to loosen a knot in my throat.

Catlin frowns. "I wasn't consulted on that. They told me they wanted to surprise the Germans and not have artillery announce our attack."

Those bastards. The colonel didn't even have a say.

I close my eyes, not wanting to think the obvious. Like the colonel said at Les Mares, the artillery prep is a key element of this type of assault.

I gasp at the terrible sound of a bullet smacking flesh and bone.

Catlin collapses in a slow spin, red welling from the right side of his chest.

Oh shit.

I need to get the colonel to cover.

Tribot-Laspierre grabs the colonel under his left arm. I grab the back of Catlin's uniform tunic and cradle the right shoulder with my other hand. We drag him backward across the road and into a ditch.

"Get Medical!" Tribot-Laspierre shouts as two others join us.

Catlin lies on his back, seemingly unable to move his right side, gesturing for me to come near. "Get to Lucy," Catlin pants, voice weak. "Phone the PC. Tell Harry Lee he's in charge. See if there are any corpsmen left." The colonel seems to be in relatively little pain as he gasps out the orders.

I sprint the two hundred yards to Lucy, hoping Catlin's sniper won't waste a round on a lowly private. The weight of responsibility presses on me. I gotta get word to Lieutenant Colonel Lee right away. Delay will kill our guys.

Inside the village, I sprint past men rushing along the narrow streets —litter-bearers hauling empty stretchers and others hefting ammo crates off carts—all moving toward the fighting. Shouts and whistles fill the air between artillery blasts. I find the Lucy PC, stick my head in the door, and ask if they can send a message to Lee.

"Fucking phones are out," the signal corps man shouts.

"Ah, shit." What next?

I dash across the street to the battalion aid station. Lieutenant Commander Farwell and a couple of doctors work on a leg wound. I touch Farwell's shoulder. "Colonel's hit. He's behind the machine gunners north of town. We need help."

Farwell glances at the other doctors. "Finish up." He takes his bloody gloves off, snatches a medical bag. "Where's he hit?"

"Right chest. Looks bad, sir."

Farwell calls out to a corpsman. "Bring two litter-bearers."

I rush out the front door of the aid station and see a signal corps man revving up a motorcycle next to the PC. I run over. "Need a ride to Maison Blanche toot sweet."

"Hoof it, Private."

"I'm Catlin's runner. He's been hit. I have orders for Colonel Lee." My face tightens.

The other man shrugs. "Hop on."

When we arrive at Maison Blanche Farm, I order the motorcycle driver to stand by in case Lee needs a ride back.

I run inside and tell Lee and Major Evans what happened.

"Evans," Lee says, "hold the fort here. Tell Signals we need a live wire between here and Lucy, highest priority."

The signal corps man sits smoking on his idling Harley. Lee squeezes into the sidecar while I clamber behind the driver. I tap the driver twice on the shoulder. The motorcycle sprays gravel as it leaps forward. Cigarette ashes sting my face.

I hop off before the motorcycle fully stops and help Lee out of the sidecar when we pull up behind the Lucy PC. Lee tells the driver, "I need a working phone line to Maison Blanche. That is your only priority, understand?" The man nods and double-times it to the Lucy PC.

Lee and I run, crouching, along the road that heads north out of Lucy. Farwell and two corpsmen work furiously on Catlin. I'm amazed to see the colonel lying on the ground, giving orders to two runners. Farwell holds a bloody dressing near the colonel's right shoulder. As the runners depart, Catlin turns his gaze to Lee. "Harry, take over. Set up in Lucy . . . for God's sake . . . stick to cover. We don't need to lose . . . any more colonels. Let Neville know. Tell Harbord . . . about the situation. Berry's men are . . . wiped out." He seemed to choke on the last part.

A shell hits behind us—a thud followed by a pop.

"Gas!"

Chapter Thirty-Seven
Lieutenant (junior grade) Arthur Beck

Today's frustration is walking wounded triage. I look around the La Voie aid station and shake my head with a sigh. I'll forget how to do surgery if they keep this up. The battle rages while I look at minor injuries. I should be in an operating room working on the serious ones, far from the noise and action, far from a place where an artillery shell can land.

Not here.

The racket makes my nerves tingle. My tremor was better earlier but is now returning.

Lieutenant Commander Dessez runs in and motions me over. I finish jotting a note on a wound card and tell the corpsman working with me to send the man to Bezu.

"Colonel Catlin's hit," Dessez says. "Farwell went to take care of him. Take his place. The front's insane."

"Do what?" I ask.

"Farwell's in charge of surgery in the Lucy aid station. Go there. Petty's taking over while Farwell takes care of Catlin. Malcolm Pratt is there too."

"How am I going to get there?" I ask as I walk outside and look to the east. A brown haze lingers above the trees. The roar of the battle is volcanic. Eight German sausages float in the distance along with a few German observation planes circling above. My world gets smaller with each step, my heartbeat quickening.

"We're loading an ambulance with supplies. Ride up in that," Dessez says.

"Why was Farwell there? I thought 3/5 had Lucy."

"Combat lesson, Hot Shot. Do what's right."

In the distance, a motorcycle with a sidecar zigzags along the road from Champillon. Dessez wears a tight smile and then laughs as the motorcycle draws close and skids to a halt in front of us. The officer behind the handlebars wears goggles on a grimy, crooked-nosed face. Two corpsmen help a wounded lieutenant out of the sidecar.

"Welcome back, Pops," Dessez says. "Glad to see you're still in one piece."

"Where were you?" I ask.

"Between 142 and Champillon. Ferried supplies up and wounded back. Should figure out how to get a litter rack on the sidecar. These are a lot more practical than ambulances out there." Johnson pats the motorcycle handlebars.

"Up for another trip?" Dessez asks.

"If you mean, have I completely lost my mind?" Johnson shrugs. "I'll clear my calendar."

"Take Hot Shot to Lucy with a load of supplies."

"Gotta gas up. Get your gear, Arthur. Be back in a jiffy."

Dessez and I go into a nearby tent. I grab two medical bags and stuff boxes of morphine syringes into both. We finish and jog out of the tent to find the motorcycle maniac astride his mount. I cram myself into the bloody sidecar, then Dessez and a corpsman stuff Thomas leg splints in with me.

Johnson revs the engine once, kicks it into gear, and we speed off. I cling to the long steel splints to keep them from whacking my face, heart pounding as German artillery rounds shower us with dirt. Debris whacks my helmet and pelts my chest. The motorcycle bounces and weaves at breakneck speed. I spread my knees for support when we jerk to the side around a shell hole.

These idiots are going to get me killed.

Johnson slows down and pulls in behind a building in Lucy. The village is ragged, I assume from the shelling. My legs wobble after I pry myself out of the sidecar. "Major, been doing this long?" I ask.

"Just learned this morning. Kinda fun, eh? I'll get me one if I make it through this shit."

Corpsmen help one of the walking wounded into the sidecar. Johnson revs the engine and speeds off. I watch the motorcycle dodge around shell holes and shake my head. I take a deep breath and go through the blanketed back door.

Pandemonium engulfs me as I enter the sweltering aid station. Surgeons stand beside litters elevated on racks, with two corpsmen per table to assist. Orlando Petty works at a shock table, two corpsmen helping him with a wound. I walk over to Petty. "What do you need me to do?"

"Show me your hands."

Damn the bastard.

I hold out my hands.

I don't deserve this crap.

A sudden concussion squeezes my chest, and my ears ring. I look around as my heart hammers. The walls are intact. A shell must have hit next door. The roof rattles as though hit by golf-ball-sized hail. It takes a moment to realize the noise came from shrapnel and debris pummeling it.

My tremor is obvious. "I heard Colonel Catlin's shot." I put my hands down.

"Farwell went to take care of him," Petty says.

Four gas-masked men rush a litter into the station and set it on a shock table. Three yank their masks off, Commander Farwell among them. The two litter-bearers hustle out. Farwell pulls the gas mask off a face with bluish lips and ashen skin. I haven't met Colonel Catlin, but this must be him.

I don a pair of rubber gloves while Farwell cuts off Catlin's coat and pulls it away from a bloodstained dressing. I ask a corpsman to bring a stethoscope and slip the earpieces in. Farwell grabs another stethoscope and does the same. We have to be quick. If I were in Chicago, I'd take him straight to the operating room. Here? Shit.

"Let's sit him up," Farwell says. Two corpsmen hold Catlin upright.

"Colonel, take a few deep breaths," I say. Farwell and I listen to both sides. I yank the stethoscope out of my ears and slip it into my coat pocket. Something tells me I'll need it again. I place my left hand on Catlin's chest, percussing my right middle finger against the left. "Dull about halfway down. Hemopneumothorax. Don't think there's any tension."

"Agreed," Farwell says. "Let's redo the dressings while he's up. How you doing, Colonel?"

"Light-headed. Not much pain," Catlin says. "Yet. Can't move my right side."

Farwell and I dredge our gloves in alcohol, then clean and apply occlusive dressings on Catlin's wounds and roll a wide bandage around his chest to secure them.

Catlin looks at Farwell. "Verdict?"

"Exit wound's the same as the entry. Long rifle shot, probably. You have internal bleeding. I hope the pressure from the blood between the rib cage and the lung will staunch it."

"And if it doesn't?"

Farwell stands silent and blinks.

I've taken care of patients with penetrating chest trauma at Cook. Farwell is right. Some of them live. Most die. I look around the station. There's no way I can open him up, explore the chest, and stop the bleeding if it comes to that. We must get him out of here. Now.

"I see. Well, I'll remain . . . optimistic. When can we . . . get out of here?"

"We have an ambulance waiting, Colonel," Farwell says. "Let's go."

Catlin grins at me as I grab one handle of the stretcher. "Just . . . off the boat, Lieutenant?"

"Beck, Arthur, sir. Arrived two weeks ago. Haven't had a chance to get an army uniform."

"Do it—soon," Catlin says. "Those navy blues . . . will attract sniper fire as sure as a tall colonel will, son."

Two corpsmen hold the blankets covering the back door open, and we muscle Catlin into the stretcher rack of an idling ambulance.

"Thanks," Farwell says to me. "I'm riding with the colonel. Stay here to replace me. Good luck, kid."

I go back inside and team up with Petty to work on a lower leg gunshot wound. A corpsman cuts away the trouser leg while I dip my gloved hands in alcohol. The trick here is obvious—keep the gloves on and disinfect them between patients. Never touch the patient, only the disinfected instruments. The corpsmen do the contaminated side of the job. After we finish cleaning and dressing the leg wound, Petty says, "Hot Shot, give Malcolm Pratt a hand."

Malcolm Pratt is working on a through-and-through leg wound. We remove debris with clamps, paint the wound with iodine, lay a sterile dressing on the wound, and have the corpsmen apply the bandages.

When we finish, I glance around the room. An officer circulates among the wounded, handing out steaming mugs, talking, adjusting splints and dressings. "Who's he?" I ask Malcolm.

Malcolm looks up. "Chaplain Brady."

Litter-bearers carry in two stretchers. I order a corpsman to give the new cases shots of anti-tetanic serum. The corpsman gives them each an injection and then looks over their wound cards. He paints an M and a T on both men's foreheads with iodine. The M means the casualty has received morphine, the T for anti-tetanic serum. Malcolm says, "Jesus, they just keep coming. What the hell's going on out there?"

I look across the cramped, humid room. Litter-bearers and walking wounded move in and out. The doctors and corpsmen work with a constant hum of conversation punctuated by clamps clanging into disinfecting basins. My nerve endings tingle at the nearby artillery blasts. This is what we called meatball surgery at Cook. Like the emergency department, not the operating rooms. Not what I signed up for, but I did plenty of this in my internship.

Bellyaching isn't going to stop my patient's bleeding. I have a job to do.

Chapter Thirty-Eight
Private Carl Larsen

The Lucy aid station is a hothouse with more odors than my nose can process. Alcohol, sweat, blood, shit, fear. Part of me wants to run out, grab a rifle, and take it to the fucking Heinies. Another part wants to live. Lacking specific orders, I do the only thing I'm qualified to do here and brew coffee over a camp stove while the docs work on Colonel Catlin. The battle rages outside with continuous machine gun fire, intermittent rifle fire, and chest-pounding artillery blasts.

I'm as useful as a rock in a farm field while the docs work on my boss. I take a front stretcher handle when it's time to haul Colonel Catlin to the ambulance. As we load him, the Colonel touches my arm with his left hand. "You're a good man, Carl."

"What do you want me to do, sir?"

"Be a runner, Carl. Officers trust you. You're a natural . . . navigator. Keep your head down. Like to see you again."

"Aye, aye, sir. I'll see you later, after they fix you up."

We close the back of the ambulance and it speeds off—well, as fast as anyone can drive through the potholes in the damned road.

I go back inside, not sure I'm ready to run for my life yet. I help the corpsmen lift and carry stretchers while I think about my new orders.

Lieutenant Grant lies on the floor—I bring him a cup of coffee, wanting to look useful and find out what happened to him.

Two men heft the litter next to Grant's onto a trestle.

A wave of nausea rushes over me. Bile rises in my throat. I steady myself with one hand, light-headed, warm.

Shit.

Hiram.

I break into a sweat and gulp. Blood oozes around a bone jutting from Hiram Stoops's mangled right shin. I meet Hiram's gaze.

"Oh, jeez, Carl. Hurts so bad. Stay with me, please."

"Sure, Hiram." I grab Hiram's calloused hand and hold it. "You'll be all right." The words come out before I can catch myself. I blink away tears.

The weight of all the death and disaster of the day crashes down on me as if the ceiling has collapsed.

"I'm a goner, donchaknow."

"It's not that bad, Private," says a small navy doctor wearing fancy blues. "I don't think you're going to die from this."

I hold Hiram's hand, glancing between his face and the two corpsmen working on the leg. One cuts away the remnants of Hiram's puttee, leaving the boot on. The other slips a metal frame around the leg —an elongated U-shaped steel bar that runs between two padded semicircular rings. One ring fits in the groin, and the other curves around the outside of the hip. The short end of the U is about six inches below the heel of Hiram's boot. The corpsmen loop strips of cloth between the inside and outside bars to support the upper and lower leg in the frame while the little surgeon cleans the wound. One corpsman wraps a cloth strip around the ankle in a series of diamond loops and ties both ends to the frame beneath Hiram's boot.

The sight of bone sticking out is like a train wreck. I can't help but look while Hiram grips my right hand.

The other corpsman slips a six-inch wooden dowel between the wrapping strips beneath the boot and winds while his partner supports the leg below Hiram's knee. Hiram winces, sweat dripping off his face, gritting his teeth. The bone jutting out slips into the wound. The man doing the winding wedges the ends of the dowel between the two sides of the frame and secures them with short rope ties. I feel Hiram's hand relax. He looks better, no longer contorted in pain.

"What's that thing?" I ask the corpsman.

"Thomas splint. Bullet shattered your buddy's shinbone. The jagged bones'll shred the soft tissue without traction. When I twisted the stick around, it stretched the leg and pulled the bones apart. These babies are lifesavers."

"Think they'll be able to save his leg?"

The corpsman shrugs.

"If I can't run again, you might as well shoot me in the noggin," Hiram says. "That's the only thing I do good, donchaknow?"

"Hiram," I say, "I'd feel the same way. See how this plays out. Our docs are top-shelf. Besides, it'll give me a chance to keep up with you on our next run." I hold Hiram's gaze—he has that deer-eyed look again.

"I saw you talking with the colonel. Whatcha gonna do now?"

"I'm a runner."

Hiram's face sours. He points at his leg. "That's what happens to runners. And worse."

The spectacle of Hiram's leg and the carnage on the field leaves my chest empty. Hiram's right. How long will I last? Doom blankets me as I think about my new job.

Battle noise calls to me, but for the moment all I can do is hold Hiram's hand and curse whatever god or gods allowed this to happen. And the fucker who didn't order the artillery. If I ever meet that bastard . . .

Hiram nods off after another dose of morphine. I let go of my friend's hand and head outside. German artillery has hammered the thick-walled stone buildings of Lucy. Shrapnel balls and shell fragments lie like a jagged carpet on the streets. An acrid cloud of burning wood, manure, and sulfur hangs in a brown haze. Windows stand like the gaping eyes of a skull, the glass blasted away, the surrounding walls pockmarked. Several houses smolder through collapsed roofs. Others stand as though giving the Heinies the finger. The post of command occupies one of these. I find Lieutenant Colonel Lee inside the PC, writing notes for runners—the phones are down again.

Lee orders me to find out what happened to 3/5. I take a deep breath and ease it out through pursed lips—I barely survived my last run over there. I jog north and try to put myself in a different place while running along the Lucy-Torcy road. On warm summer days back home, I would ride my bicycle to the picnic area at Lake Harriet in Minneapolis. Then I'd run a double figure-eight course along the paths around Lake Calhoun, Lake of the Isles, and finally back to Harriet. Wide grassy parks surround the shores of the lakes. Sometimes I'd take off my Keds to feel the cool grass.

I hit the deck at a whistle overhead. It explodes fifty feet away. Debris showers me.

I pop up, sprint, and reach the edge of the St. Martin Wood. I now move in a crouch using tree trunks for cover and find the place where I met the lieutenants from Sixteenth Company two hours ago. I pass wounded stragglers and corpsmen along the way. I'm tempted to stop and help, but I have my orders. Not helping grates on me.

A corporal with his back against an oak trunk, smoking a cigarette, watches the others. I approach him when he looks up at me. "Where's Major Berry?"

He takes a slow drag and eases smoke through his nostrils with a face devoid of emotion. "Don't have the slightest fucking idea. He was out to my left. Check with the Forty-Fifth. Maybe somefuckingone up there'll know." He motions north with a tip of his head.

"How was it?"

"Totally fucked up. Fucker who cut our orders has it in for us. The fuckers slaughtered us. None of us got to the edge of the fucking woods."

"Thanks." And I mean that in more than one way. I scurry farther north, staying inside the tree line. Shells churn the field between Belleau Wood and us. The wounded lie unprotected in the midst of the artillery and machine gun fire. Poor bastards. I run faster.

I dive to the ground at a shriek. The shock wave sweeps over when it blasts the woods behind me. I glance back to see if any of the guys I just talked with were hit but can't tell.

When I reach Forty-Fifth Company, a dozen tattered, bloodied Marines sit against the tree trunks. A ragged soul crawls from the edge of the wheat field, hobbles in a crouch, and slumps behind a tree, gasping for air. Hank Lenert—uniform torn, his grimy face hard to recognize.

"Whatcha doin' here, Carl?"

"Colonel Catlin got his. Colonel Lee took over. Sent me to see what's going on. I'm a runner now."

"Might as well bend over and kiss it goodbye," Hank says. "What's going on is that the 3/5 is done for. Berry gave me a note. Can you take it?"

"Youbetcha." I take the paper from my friend and open it. *What is left of battalion is in woods close by. Do not know whether will be able to stand or not. Increase artillery range. Berry.* The time on it was 1810 hours. It had taken Hank forty-five minutes to crawl back.

"Berry's shot in the left arm. Hand looks like shit—bad pain. There's maybe twenty guys with him. All dinged up. He's waiting till dark. He'll have to pull back unless a lot more guys get to him."

I slip the note into my pocket, give Hank a pat on the shoulder, and run for it. I pass a dead man with a message bag over one shoulder—one of the runners whose name I don't know. I lift the strap over the man's head, slip it over my shoulder, and run with thoughts about the colonel and Hiram. Rage drives me.

Chapter Thirty-Nine
Major Ab Johnson

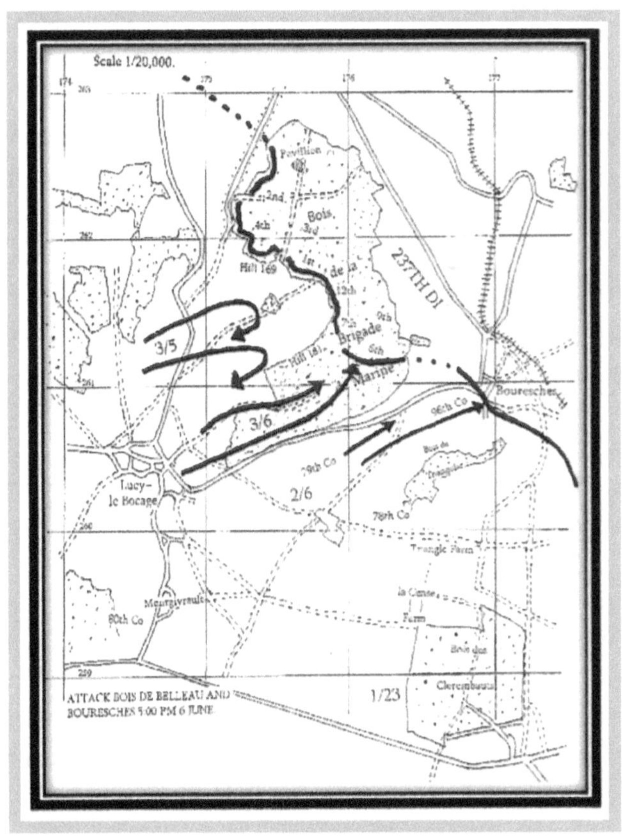

The motorcycle bounces along the road as I race from Lucy to La Voie. I hope I don't lose any teeth. The wounded private riding in the sidecar moans with each jolt. I'm too busy steering around the worst holes to groan with him. I'm feeling my age—back aching, ass saddlesore, and heart empty. I'll have failed my mission to Jack if he's anywhere around here. There are almost no lieutenants still standing, as far as I can see.

Two corpsmen run over when I pull into the regimental aid station. They help the private out and carry him to triage. I spill half my tobacco on the ground while fumbling with my pipe. I put the pouch into my coat pocket so I don't lose all of it. Commander Dessez jogs over.

"Mighty shaky, Pops," Dessez says.

"Nose is killing me."

"How're my men?"

"In what the generals term *good spirits*. By which I mean they aren't running away. The Boche artillery pounded the whole area all afternoon. I'm amazed that anything in Lucy is still standing."

"How's the supply situation?"

"They need more Thomas leg splints. The Germans have their machine guns aimed at leg height." I pause. "Oh, tell the corpsmen to quit marking the wounded by sticking a rifle into the ground next to them. Upended rifles are an aiming point. I'll give the Hun his due—no one is more diabolical."

"It's going to be a long night. You look bushed, Pops. I'm medically ordering you to take a break."

"Since you put it that way . . ." I gaze toward the east. "Aid station in Lucy needs ambulances when the shelling lets up. They're up to the gunnels in casualties." The pipe slips out of my hand. My lower back muscles seize as I reach down to pick it up. "I'll be at La Loge if you need me."

I use my right hand to lift my leg back over the seat of the Indian and head west to brigade headquarters while the sun plays "Taps" below the edge of the western tree line. After parking next to a staff car, I dust myself off and pull down the goggles to dangle around my neck. Several army staff officers in pristine uniforms stare at my face, then my collar pins, and amble away. I wipe a drip of blood from my upper lip.

I limp into the staff room. General Harbord looks up and cracks a grin. "Looks like you've been chasing old Pancho Villa through a Texas windstorm."

"Decided to make myself useful, sir. Helped Major Turrill till the afternoon. Spent the last three hours ferrying supplies and wounded between La Voie and Lucy."

"While I've been worrying myself nuts." Harbord gazes at the map hanging on the easel where Colonel Brown confers with a staff officer. "I plan and plan. When the clock strikes H-hour, I hear nothing but battle noise. A few reports, bits and pieces filter in. I've no idea what's going on out there."

I have a feeling I'm not going to the break room or a bed very soon. How can he not know what's going on? He's in charge.

"These damned Marine field commanders don't seem to think they need to report back to us." Harbord picks up a dispatch from his desk. "The few I've gotten so far are encouraging. This one came in from the Twelfth Field Artillery, at 1919 hours. *Attack went very well indeed, even beyond our most sanguine expectations. Marines have taken TORCY, BOURESCHES, including the railway station. Casualties have been very light. Messages come in to the effect that the artillery fire was most successful and delivered at exactly the right time.*" He puts down the dispatch. "The French tell us their 167th attained its objectives."

"When did they get there?" I rub my lower spine to ease the pain from knotted muscles. Whoever wrote that report needs a psychiatrist. Harbord needs a dose of reality, but I hate to be the one giving it to him.

"Late morning."

I wince—I've read less inventive fiction.

"I've heard nothing from Catlin," Harbord says. "Word came in that he was slightly wounded in the shoulder and that Lee went forward to assess the situation. And then a message reached us that Lee had taken over. But Lee's sent us nothing. They warned me when I took over a brigade of Marines. I'm thinking about relieving him."

I pull the pipe out of my coat pocket and tamp in tobacco with shaking hands, take a deep breath after getting the pipe going, and struggle to contain myself. My attempt to blow a smoke ring comes out a wheezy stream. "Well, General, I don't know where the artillery CO got his news, but it doesn't square with what I know. For one thing, the French 167th was neither seen nor heard from at Turrill's PC, and they should have been just to his left."

"French headquarters told me they were."

"Well, maybe in the opinion of their headquarters. Turrill told me that when the 167th advanced, their artillery fired short. They pulled back. Turrill's left flank hung in the breeze all day. I was there until about 1500 hours. The French didn't do a thing during the time I was up there."

"Probably attacked after you left." Harbord gives me a hard stare, as though force of will could make it so. "And Catlin?"

"Shot in the chest. He'll probably die."

Harbord frowns. "Shit." He pauses. "He's a good man. We went through the Army War College at Leavenworth together." Harbord strides to his desk and taps a cigarette free from the Chesterfield pack sitting on a stack of reports. I flick my lighter with a shaky hand when Harbord comes back. The room is still for a moment.

"We were told a machine gun nest held 3/5 up," Harbord says.

My jaw tenses at the words. I take the pipe out before I snap the stem. "That makes it sound like they hit a bump in the road, sir."

"That's the impression I got."

My back muscles knot again, and I almost yelp. Who is telling him this shit? I take a breath and ease it out. "General, I'd like permission to speak freely."

"Pops, we're nearly the same age. I need truth without varnish."

"I will say things you don't want to hear—or more to the point, didn't want to happen."

"That bad?"

"Worse." I stare at the map, not wanting to read his face right now. "I want to shoot the fool that told you that Belleau Wood was lightly held. *A* machine gun nest? Belleau Wood is one big machine gun nest. Light casualties? The men of 3/5 are all dead or wounded. The whole damned battalion *wiped out*. Nobody can go into the field to help the wounded, so the number of dead is unknown. The 3/6 and 2/6 fared a bit better, but they have heavy losses."

"And you didn't agree with the report about the French?"

"Sir, honestly, I stood in a spot on that hill where I would have seen the French if they were there. I'd have been translating between their CO and Turrill. Please believe me. They never showed up."

Harbord stands with a deepening scowl. Colonel Brown lights a cigarette. He's too much of a professional to say, "I told you so." The room is silent other than the tick of a clock on the sideboard. Harbord speaks. "I need more timely information. I blasted off a dispatch to Lee just before you arrived. I ordered him to send a report every fifteen minutes."

"Sir, if I may," I say, "he can't comply with that order and run his part of the show. Lee, like Catlin, took a very forward position to be in close contact with his troops. Communications are all by runner. The commanders can't be miles behind the action."

"We've been getting regular reports from Neville, though."

"Neville's far enough back that his phone lines are intact between here and there. But I was there. The reports getting to him are out of date by the time they arrive. Assume everything you get from Neville is old news."

"Should we use pigeons?" Brown asks in a cynical tone.

"A pigeon has more brains than to get anywhere near that goddamned place." I choke the words out.

"I was under the impression things were going swimmingly," Harbord says.

I think of Jack, swimming in Rock Creek Lake one summer when he was eight.

"The swimmer is drowning, sir."

Chapter Forty
Lieutenant (junior grade) Arthur Beck

Lucy-le-Bocage
Friday, June 7, 1918

Canvas tarps and woolen blankets smother the windows and doors to keep gas out. They trap heat, humidity, and odor within and give the station a timeless quality. I move from case to case, stopping bleeding, dressing wounds that need urgent surgery with no way to do it. It's 0315 according to my watch.

I pull my sweat-soaked uniform coat off, inspect it, and shake my head in dismay at the filth soiling it. I fold it and place it on the highest shelf I can reach—I'll get it dry-cleaned when I get back to civilization. My cuff links go into a pants pocket, and I roll up my shirtsleeves. Petty's shirtsleeves are rolled up, and Pratt's in an undershirt. Our exposed skin will suffer if mustard gas hits us. I dunk gloved hands into a pan of blood-tinted alcohol while watching Chaplain Brady administer last rites to a Marine.

Is it like this everywhere else in this war? How do any of them survive? This is so crude, so filthy.

Five men startle me as they come in through the back door with a rush of fresh air in their wake. "Ambulances outside," one shouts. "Load 'em toot sweet."

Petty supervises the evacuation. Four corpsmen and I take off our gloves and aprons and go out to unload supplies, water, litters, and splints from the ambulances. The muggy night air is a relief from the heat of the station. Litter-bearers slide stretcher cases in as soon as an ambulance is empty, stacking them three high in vertical racks. Walking wounded ride on a bench seat next to the litters and one in the front with the driver. There are no corpsmen. The men are on their own during transit.

The fresh outside air makes the oppressive heat of the aid station obvious when I go back inside. The mix of chlorine, alcohol, kerosene, the unbathed, and wounds is nauseating. The station seems as crowded as before the evacuation. I tie my bloody apron back on and am donning my gloves when a new artillery barrage rumbles behind us. I head toward the back door in fear that we just sent all those men to their deaths. Petty grabs my elbow. "Going out there won't help."

Petty and I go back to work on a gunshot wound, then clean and dress a hand laceration. About ten minutes later, two litter-bearers rush in through the back door. They set their burden on a shock table. "Sir, we need you stat," one of the men says. "Traumatic amputation."

Petty turns the laceration over to our chief pharmacist's mate to finish while I dash over. The amputation victim is a man we just sent out, a front seat ambulatory case. An Army Signal Corps major who left in one of the last ambulances twenty minutes ago. His arm was in a sling at the time. His right thigh is now a jagged stump of shredded muscle and bone. A Spanish windlass tourniquet tied near his groin is all that stands between life and hemorrhagic death. Where the hell did someone find that tourniquet? It's not standard issue.

The major's right carotid has a weak pulse—too shocky to give morphine. He's lost a lot of blood. How long does he have? How long will he stay unconscious? An image of the Civil War flashes through my mind—what did Dad witness? Mounds of severed gangrenous limbs? He would have heard men scream in agony while surgeons hacked off legs in seconds flat, only to have their pain rocket with the cautery iron. I need to be like one of those surgeons. Fast, definitive, no hesitation before the major wakes up, if he ever does. There are no anesthetics here, and morphine would kill him.

"Bring flashlights over," I say. Two corpsmen flick on lights while I dredge my hands in the alcohol basin. A third corpsman stands by the tourniquet. "Suture and hemostats." I turn to Petty. "I'll do the clamps. You handle the irrigation." A corpsman brings Petty a basin filled with Dakin's antiseptic solution and a syringe with a thin rubber hose attached. My tray includes a cluster of hemostats to clamp bleeding vessels.

"This thing's a goddamned mess," Petty mutters.

I snap the jaws of a towel clamp on a wad of gauze, soak it with Dakin's, and, ever so gently but quickly, dab the wound and tease the tissue to find the major vessels.

"I don't know where anyone got this particular tourniquet," I say. "It's the kind our corpsmen should carry." I look at the tourniquet corpsman. "When I tell you to, loosen the tourniquet. Plan to retighten it after about two seconds. I think that's the only way I'll find the major vessels."

I grab a hemostat, holding it near the area where the main branch of the femoral artery should be. "Okay, now."

I snap the clamp where arterial blood squirts. I don't see the artery, but I clamp a margin of tissue that should include both the artery and vein. Petty sprays the area with Dakin's.

My eyes never leave the wound as Petty hands me another clamp, concentrating on where the smaller branches of the femoral artery should be. I open the clamp. "Okay, same thing." Two warm pulses of blood hit my hand as I twist it to get a good angle, dig in, and squeeze the hemostat through a series of clicks.

Another hemostat. Petty washes away the fresh blood. We repeat the process until I have the main bleeders controlled in what now looks like a Christmas tree of clamps hanging from the stump.

"2-0 silk on a curved needle," I say.

"Sir, I'm not sterile. Suture's on the tray. You'll have to thread your own needles, sorry," the corpsman says.

"Not like home," Petty says.

"Don't distract me." I take a deep breath and stifle my desire to say more.

I thread 2-0 silk on a curved needle and put the needle in a needle clamp.

This is stitch and pray. Urgency presses from all sides. I glance at the major's face. Pale, still unconscious, but for how long? I jab the needle deep into the tissue, encircling the area around the hemostat on the femoral artery twice before yanking the suture off the needle and tying it. I leave the cut ends long for the surgeon who will inherit this case if the patient lives. I imagine what a university surgeon would say—*technique worthy of a gynecologist.*

No time to be pretty.

Next suture, same as the first. I repeat the process around each of my hemostats. When I'm finished, I say, "Loosen the tourniquet, but don't retighten it unless I tell you."

"Yes, sir, Lieutenant Beck."

Petty hands me a clean hemostat. "Bring the light over here." I point, and the other corpsman aims a flashlight. "Okay—now."

The wound oozes—no squirt. Good. I set the hemostat in my hand on the clean tray. "Be ready to retighten on my command." I slip my fingers into the handles of the hemostat on the superficial femoral artery. My eyes never leave the site as a dribble of sweat trickles down my right side. "Okay, that's good. Move the light here." I point at the clamp over one of the branch arteries. As I open it, blood spurts on my hand. I retighten the clamp, encircle the end with another loop of suture, then try it again. It holds.

We repeat the same steps with each clamp, reinforcing the suture in two more places. Leg movement and a groan tell me we've run out of time. Petty sprays the wound one more time as I scan it, the corpsman moving the flashlight in a circular search pattern. "Give him a half dose of morphine," I say. "Keep the tourniquet in place. Tighten it if he bleeds. Let's get a dressing on this."

I wrap the wound with sterile gauze and then a bandage while a corpsman holds the stump up. The major screams when the corpsman eases the leg down. He needs blood, but the closest transfusion might be in Juilly. Or Paris. Nobody mentioned that. He is not out of the woods.

"Show me your hands," Petty says.

I hold my hands out, fingers spread. Steady. "Go to hell . . . sir. We have work to do. Court-martial me when we're done if you want."

An explosion erupts next door. Rivulets of dust filter from the ceiling, and the roof rattles. I glance around the room—so many still wait. I take a deep breath of heavy air and dip steady hands in alcohol while the corpsmen lift another litter onto the rack. I inspect the fresh leg wound, then look up to see a lieutenant we had evacuated with the major. What is his name? Catlin talked with him. "Didn't I just get you out of here?"

"They shelled the road after we left town. Our driver was killed. I turned the ambulance around and drove it back."

"And you have a new wound." The man's name comes to me—Lieutenant Grant.

"How's the major?" Grant asks.

"Lost a lot of blood. He'd be dead if someone hadn't put a tourniquet on. We tied off the bleeders. Fancy stuff'll have to wait until we get him to the rear."

"His artery was pumping."

"He in your ambulance?"

"No. Hiram and I rode in the back of the last ambulance. Shells hit all around us. Almost tipped us over. Our driver was dead. I ran to the ambulance in front of us—on fire, men in the back dead, driver too. Only one not dead was the major—in the front seat, leg pumping blood onto the dashboard. I had a tourniquet in my med kit, put it on and then lugged him back to ours, cranked her up, and drove here."

"Where'd you get the tourniquet?"

"Doc Osborne gave me two. Told me they might be useful."

"And exactly perfect for that major. You did a hell of a job out there, Lieutenant. If he survives, it will be due to you."

"Hope I don't get Osborne in trouble. He's a good friend from college."

I frown. I didn't like Osborne, but he had courage I don't have. "He was killed in action at Bouresches."

Grant is silent as two corpsmen cut his trouser leg. A jagged piece of shrapnel protrudes from his thigh.

"This is going to hurt." I paint the gash with iodine and then tease the shard out with a clamp, noticing a fine tremor in my left hand. The corpsman and I finish up the wound dressing and bandage and move Grant back to the floor. How stoic I would be if someone just told me a close friend had been killed out there?

We toil on, but nearby artillery blasts distract me. I'm leaning over a patient when something explodes outside. My ears ring from the shock wave. It feels like the blast was only feet away. Dust trickles from the ceiling. Petty looks worried, blinking behind his round glasses.

The room explodes in a dust storm. My hearing is haywire. I reflexively lean over my patient. The ringing in my ears muffles a loud crack, clatter, and yelling. The ceiling collapses on the other side of the room. One of our corpsmen lies unmoving, a timber protruding from his chest. Another is pinned next to two litter patients.

"Dress this," I yell at the corpsman next to me. Petty and I rush toward the fallen timbers. Men bellow orders while others cry out in agony. A new odor enters the room.

"Fire!"

Chapter Forty-One
Lieutenant (junior grade) Arthur Beck

Corpsmen dash toward men trapped by the fallen ceiling. I feel like a small, weak boy, pushed aside by stronger, capable men lifting timbers, lath board, and rubble off the victims. Shouts of pain, orders, calls for help, and thundering artillery blasts overwhelm my understanding. Two corpsmen and a Marine heft the timber off a man, his chest crushed, dead.

Petty's face is suddenly inches from mine, hands shaking my shoulders, yelling, "Get all the supplies you can and go to the cellar."

I run toward the wound dressing room. The smell of smoke, deafening blasts, and debris raining in through the burning roof surround me as I pull my gas mask carrier strap over my head and don a helmet. Smoke stings my eyes. I pass Lieutenant Grant, wincing, limping, struggling to carry the back of Hiram's litter.

I scoop as many boxes of dressings as I can hold in my short arms and follow the others into the street. A shower of debris smacks my helmet.

Explosions roar, my hearing now far away.

Stumbling, regaining my footing, I follow two corpsmen. The town looks haunted—broken walls, buildings without roofs or windows, broken bricks, wood, and metal debris make footing dangerous as I stagger along.

Flashes followed by deafening explosions swarm around me. Men dash past in both directions. Louvered lanterns, the light pointing toward the ground, give spooky illumination. Faces of men I pass resemble ghouls in the light. I've died and descended into hell, haven't I?

The corpsmen lead me through a door and down a narrow stairway into a wine cellar lit by electric lanterns. Empty wine racks stand sentinel to a table, four chairs, and cobwebs hanging from the ceiling. I cough when I take a breath of the musty air. My brain is fuzz, my hearing blank. Is this another level in the inferno?

A scream from my right jerks my eyes to the wounded litter-bearer, Hiram, his face contorted in pain. Grant talks to Hiram as a corpsman injects a dose of morphine. I set my bundle on the table and bump shoulders with passing men who seem real enough as I rush up the stairs.

My mind clears when I get outside. If I'm in hell, so are all these others. We need clamps, basins, and alcohol.

Explosions pound my chest as I sprint back to the station amid flashes of light. Debris pummels me like a steel rain. The station shines like a lighthouse as flames dance in the roof timbers.

I push past someone into the building, rush to the room where I'd been working, and grab an empty basin. I blow out the dust and scoop handfuls of clamps, scissors, and scalpels into it. Bloody gloves and a bottle of alcohol go into another basin, then I hustle back before I burn to death in the aid station.

Macabre shadows move in the eerie light from a cold, bright star-shell flare swinging from a parachute high above.

I jog to the cellar door. The stairs feel narrower this time, with dim illumination trickling from below. One step sags and I lurch forward, clutching the basins. I stumble down two steps but catch myself before tumbling to the bottom, heart pounding, sweat blurring my eyes.

The cellar seems smaller, crowded, like an elevator with too many on board. The air is close, stifling—will we run out of oxygen and die? I'll be the dead canary in this mine. Petty stands at the center of the storm, conferring with the corpsmen, ordering them to check the men, pointing and directing them. How the hell does Petty stay calm when my skin crawls as though infested with lice? I take a deep breath and hope work will settle my nerves. I scratch an itch. Then another.

Lieutenant Grant's leg wound is bleeding again from his effort to evacuate others. I pull the old dressing off, inspect the wound, and secure a new dressing in place. Grant sits next to Hiram, who is grimacing. I order an additional dose of morphine for him, then move on.

A Marine corporal holds the hand of a sergeant with a penetrating chest wound—the sort that could only survive in a place like Cook County, not a wine cellar. I order a dose of morphine. Nothing more I can do.

The ground shakes with explosions merging into continuous thunder. Dust becomes fog in harsh lantern light. My lips tingle, head light, as though I'm only half here.

I'm hyperventilating.

Slow it down.

Corpsmen, Petty, and the other doctor work as I watch, rooted in place. Chaplain Brady gives last rites to the Marine with the chest wound, makes the sign of the cross, and pulls a woolen blanket over the man's head. He speaks to the corporal, patting him on the shoulder.

Brady sits down next to me. "Doctor, you going to be all right?"

"This place is a coffin."

Brady puts a hand on my shoulder. "Think of how your patients feel. Concentrate on them, their needs, their suffering, your job. That's how you get through. Do your job."

My hands shake, and I give up the pretense of trying to hide them. They tingle as I wipe sweat from my brow, now hot, air hungry, unable to think. The room spins, the edges of my vision growing dark.

"Here, lie down." Brady loosens my collar as he helps me down on the floor, putting a blanket under my head. "I'll see if Petty can take a moment."

I sit up, opening my shirt, sweat pouring now, my bowels about to let go. I glance at the stairway. Death above. Death below. My head seems like it's in a kettle drum during a Wagner finale. Sweat and a new feculent odor permeate the close, humid air. How long will my rectum hold out? Will I soil my pants if the next artillery round makes the cellar my grave?

Petty comes over, feels my pulse, and looks at my pupils with a flashlight.

"What's the verdict?" Brady shouts, his voice far away, Petty's face a blur.

"Beck, get a grip on yourself. Lie down. I don't have time to deal with you. Lie the hell down."

But I wrap my arms around my knees, tight to my chest, my mind too distant to register anything but fear. I can't form thoughts over the thunder reverberating in my ears, thumping my chest, pounding my soul.

I sit on the floor, rocking, hoping death will be quick, fearing it might not.

Chapter Forty-Two
Major Ab Johnson

Montreuil-aux-Lions
Friday, June 7, 1918

Something jostles my shoulder. I roll over. Then another shove. I'm groggy, not sure where I am. Artillery noise answers me. I slowly open my eyes to see a worried and weary Major Dick Derby. "Pops, we have a lot to do today."

"What time is it?"

"Oh-seven-hundred. Time's a-wasting. By the way, you look older in the morning."

"Thanks, dear." I groan and sit up, every hour of my forty-six years coming back to me. Whoever said that war is a young man's game was right. A filthy pile of jumbled clothes lies on the floor at the foot of my cot. I have one spare uniform in my bag. "How formal do you need me to be?"

"Wear the pile. *Salty* is the uniform of the day. Your face will help. Don't shave. Anyone asks about the nose today? You head-butted a Kraut."

I go to the bathroom and splash cold water on my face. I stare in the mirror at a mug that seems too old, grizzled, and bruised to be me. If

Helen could see me now, she'd save the Kaiser a bullet and kill me herself. My right eye twitches. After dressing, I meet Derby in the officers' mess. Several clean-shaven staff officers in pristine uniforms glare at me. West Pointers—they have their famous class rings on. I give Derby a report of my activities the day and night before. Derby seems more resistant to sleeplessness than me. Probably his medical training—and ten fewer years on this planet.

After chow, we venture to General Bundy's staff room. Bundy looks well rested, decked out in a tidy uniform. "Dick, I hope you have good news. The reports I've gotten have been confusing."

I'm sure he doesn't want to hear from me after my report yesterday.

Derby clears his throat. "Well, sir, I don't have accurate figures. The ambulance traffic from the aid stations to Bezu is continuous, as it is from Bezu to Juilly, and Juilly on to Paris. Those crews deserve medals—driving through barrages with no more sleep than the rest of us. We're working to secure more ambulances. The French tell us the railroads are clogged and still refuse to give us clearance for a hospital train. Juilly has processed more than nine hundred casualties over the past day or so. A direct hit destroyed the Lucy aid station. I haven't heard from any of the staff there, so I assume they're all dead. We're out of reserves. We've also lost Colonel Catlin—shot through the lung."

"How *is* Colonel Catlin? I heard he was slightly wounded," Bundy says.

I stand still, dumbfounded. He was in the room yesterday when I said Catlin could die from his wound. Wasn't Bundy listening to Derby just now? What's wrong with the man?

"Colonel Catlin is in Paris now," I say. "Shot through the lung, like Major Derby just said. Most die from a wound like that, sir."

"Why am I the last to know these things? How is Medical holding up?"

"We're not, sir" Derby says. "Fatigue will cause mistakes unless my people get rest. Our surgical teams are pulling twenty-hour shifts. But the wounded pour in continuously. Sir, the system is on the verge of collapse. The loss of our staff in Lucy, if they're dead, will be the straw that breaks our back. We have no reserves."

Bundy looks perplexed. "The reports I read sound more optimistic."

Derby yawns. "I worked at the aid station in Montgivrault last night. An artillery round hit, killing an ambulance orderly standing next to me. That poor fellow is dead from the shrapnel that would have killed me. The other man with us was wounded. My survival is nothing more than dumb luck. Inside, I assisted Major Farwell with a severely mangled arm. He had just returned after evacuating Colonel Catlin. Captain Boone, his second, worked like a man possessed. They lost one of their medical officers in the attack on Bouresches. I helped them for three hours."

"Oh, and by the way, sir," I say. "Farwell is a lieutenant commander, not a major, and Boone is a lieutenant. They're navy, sir."

"See what I mean, General? Fatigue is getting to us all."

After the meeting, I drive my motorcycle to La Voie. Derby nods off in the sidecar. After parking and rousing Derby, I go into the aid station, Derby staggering after me. We find Commander Dessez talking with Arthur Beck, who is lying in a cot in a tent ward, wearing a soiled undershirt. His tailored coat is nowhere in sight, his trousers torn and stained. He has the strange, faraway stare I've seen on some of the infantrymen.

Dessez walks over.

"What happened?" I ask.

Dessez speaks in a hushed voice. "Beck did a hell of a job—his surgical technique on a traumatic thigh amputation was superb—his speed remarkable, according to Petty." Dessez goes on to describe the events through the night. "Beck fell apart during an artillery barrage that destroyed their aid station and most of the town. I'm going to evacuate him to Bezu. Beck isn't the only incoherent one today. I'm amazed any of them held it together."

"How about the others?"

"One corpsman dead and another wounded. The rest are still going by sheer will."

I walk over to Arthur and pat his shoulder. He winces at the touch, never altering his gaze, unresponsive to my voice.

I dodge potholes and traffic on our ride to Bezu, and Derby nods off again. I shake him back to life when we arrive. Crews unload Ford ambulances while others slide blood-soaked litters holding groaning men into GMC ambulances for the long trip to Juilly. The litter-bearers stagger with their tragic loads, their eyes vacant like Beck's.

"What do you think will happen to Beck?" I ask.

Derby winces. "It's up to him. Some come out of it. Others never return. I don't think anyone has control over things like that. The term that comes to mind is *resilience*. We'll find out if he has that quality."

Derby rounds up a staff car and driver for the rest of the inspection trip after we finish at Bezu. We ride along in silence, and Derby drifts off again. My mind is racing with thoughts about Jack and all the Jacks I've seen, fighting, wounded, dead.

I look at every face we pass. One of them could be my son or his best friend, Bill Stevens, who's with the Twenty-Third Infantry. Maybe it's wrong to have a father in the same battlespace as his son. Or maybe someone like me, with my priorities and values, is exactly the person to clarify the human risk and costs to generals and staff officers who act as though they are playing chess.

Derby stirs with a yawn. "We'll look over a château in Luzancy. That might be a good location for a gas hospital. After that, the Catholic hospital in La Ferte-sous-Jouarre."

We spend the next three hours bouncing along the dirt roads and inspecting facilities and hashing out our plan. We both sleep most of the way to and from the supply depot. We drop off the staff car in Bezu and each ride our motorcycles to Montreuil like brother bikers. After we deposit our gear in an office, Derby's expression turns pensive. "Let me make a call or two," he says and leaves.

I shuffle stiff-legged to the coffee room, fill a mug, and stop at the staff room door. General Bundy stares at the main map. God, he spends a lot of time staring at it. A mixture of pity and anger fills me. Bundy is under the command of the French Sixth Army. The planning, if one can even call it that, since May 30 has been incompetent. General Duchene and his staff are to blame, in my opinion. Worse, they treat American lives as if they are disposable pawns. But Bundy and Harbord bear some responsibility as well. Many fathers' sons lost their lives in the past day due to Duchene's incompetence and American inexperience.

Of course, I wasn't in the meetings between Bundy and the French. So maybe Bundy did his best to push back the timetable, to explain that while everyone likes to think they can surmount any challenge and do the impossible, there *is* a limit. I don't know what Bundy has told General Pershing. I know Pershing has no love of the Marine Corps, but I do know he feared that our allies would throw American lives away like the kings of old did their serfs. And I feel like that just happened to the Marines.

I go back to the office. Derby speaks in French on the phone, thanking someone for being so understanding. "Well?" I ask.

"I moved the mountain. We better get cracking before someone changes their mind. Our valued allies are all too prone to that trait. We have clearance to use Jouarre. I'm going to imagine my French was so poor I also heard we could use Luzancy."

"How did you pull that one off?"

Derby winks.

I spend the rest of the day working with Tuttle by phone and Derby in person. Thoughts of Jack dwell just beneath the surface. Wounded men—boys—died during their long trips to Juilly and Paris. The French be damned—we need hospitals closer to the front. Evac 8 will arrive in Meaux on the evening of the eighth. Tuttle and I plan to split them into two groups. One will go to Juilly, the other to Luzancy to staff the new gas hospital.

By the time we finish working out the movement of units and supplies, the sun is not the only thing setting. Derby's inexhaustible drive flags, and I'm running on empty. I need food, then a cot.

Our clerk knocks on the doorframe. "Here are the latest casualty figures, sirs."

Derby's face tightens as he reads. He hands the report to me. Juilly has processed seventeen hundred patients over the past twenty-four hours—nearly two full battalions. Eleven hundred have been transferred to Paris by ambulance.

The number of dead is unknown.

Chapter Forty-Three
Major Ab Johnson

Fourth Brigade Headquarters, La Loge Farm
Saturday, June 8, 1918

The distant clatter of machine guns, echoing artillery, and thoughts about the dead and wounded rattle my sleep. I finally give up around 0600 and search for coffee. I take the steaming mug to my shared office. It's bigger than the one in Paris—I wonder if they gave that one to the next major to arrive.

I touch my nose. It's less tender than yesterday. Derby removed the packing yesterday, and there's been no bleeding. New smells assault me. The worst is the odor of rotting bodies—men lying in fields where retrieval and burial are not possible. I love words, but there are none sufficient to describe this stench.

Copies of two Paris newspapers lie on the right side of my desk. One sports a brown coffee ring after I lift my mug. I take a sip, set the mug aside, and drum my fingers on the headline article. The disconnect between reality and Floyd Gibbons's syndicated article galls me. I've devoted my career to getting stories right, and Front-Page Floyd has it all wrong. It brings back my friend Ira's comment about losing his journalistic soul. The magnitude of the losses leaves my heart empty. These are statistics to some—to me, each could have been Jack.

I'm taking this too personally. An officer in my role should be watching the numbers, doing inventories, and ordering supplies. But I can't divorce myself from the circumstances that surround me. I can't not be me.

Families will read Floyd's article and cheer, unaware of the truths that leave me desolate. The Marines lost thirty-one officers, mostly second lieutenants, and 1,056 men killed, missing, or wounded on the sixth of June. Most of the missing lie dead in the field west of Belleau Wood. These are lower than the medical figures from Juilly. The haphazard evacuation included casualties from late on the fifth to midday on the seventh, so the discrepancy makes sense. The hospital and aid station staffs were too swamped to write down the names of all the casualties.

Where the hell is Jack? That question lurks under every thought.

The tune from "Home on the Range" floats through my mind: *where never was heard a discouraging word . . .* and I add *. . . and deluded the generals all day.* If I ever had any faith in Bundy, it disappeared on the fifth. And as I listen to him in the briefings, it is also apparent that, unlike Harbord, his respect for the Marine Corps is less than robust. A commanding officer must respect and trust his men.

Harbord is well-intentioned—an intelligent man whose boundless optimism doesn't make up for his lack of prior combat experience. The man has been out of his depth. Harbord seemed to be so desperate for good news that he discounted the bad. Self-delusion is never good in a commanding general.

A general with combat experience would understand the euphemisms, the subtle undertones, the things left unstated for the official record. He would have cleared the decks when Captain George Hamilton reported *all my officers gone* in the fight for Hill 142. Colonel Neville, safe in his PC, had passed those words along with his assumption that Hamilton had panicked and exaggerated his plight. Hamilton had not. I understand why Neville had stayed put. But Neville's reports contained notes of optimism that wishful thinkers amplified with each step up the chain of command.

General Harbord has declared victory several times when nothing could have been further from the truth. A wise general would have waited for confirmation before passing the news on. But Harbord told Bundy, who announced victory to the French and AEF headquarters. From Pershing's headquarters, it went to the press, and from there it went around the globe. I stand and pace between my desk and the window. My right hand shakes too much to load my pipe.

Floyd's banner headline reads:

U.S. MARINES SMASH HUNS
GAIN GLORY IN BRISK FIGHT ON THE MARNE
CAPTURE MACHINE GUNS, KILL BOCHE,
TAKE PRISONERS

The headlines on the other newspaper are just as bad:

MARINES WIN HOT BATTLE
SWEEP ENEMY FROM HEIGHTS NEAR THIERRY

At least the byline on the second isn't Floyd's. I wad the papers and slam them into my wastebasket. I head to the mess hall to see if having something in my stomach will provide solace.

I start on a bowl of oatmeal when Major Derby settles into a chair across the table, nods at me, and digs into a plate of eggs and bacon.

After getting seconds, Derby comes up for air. "See the papers?"

"Yeah. Floyd's 'last dispatch' and all the rest."

"Was it his last?"

"No. But that's what they called it. I hear he's recovering from surgery in Paris. He's nuts, even by my standards. Floyd and his liaison officer went in with the first wave of 3/5. He was hit in the arm and the shoulder. A bullet blew out his left eye and exited the skull above. They tell me his eye hung by a thread. If he survives, he'll be the star of the press club, eye patch and all. I thought he had too much swagger before. Now he'll never have to pay for another drink."

"How'd he write it after that kind of injury? I don't get it," Derby says.

"How accurate was it?" I ask.

"It read like the press briefing before the battle."

"Remember, Dick, my day job is journalism. Let me tell you about a game war correspondents play. They write their story before the battle based on briefings and scuttlebutt. The challenge is to see how close you get to the real thing. The closer you are, the better. As the dust settles, you apply a light edit and rush your scoop to the telegraph operator you previously bribed in order to get it out ahead of your competitors."

"Really?"

"You can't believe how cutthroat this is. He who files first gets his byline on the front page, with a banner headline if it's a big scoop. Syndication spreads your story, and you're all over America—hell, the world. Second place drops you below the fold or to page three if you're unlucky. Third place gets you in section *C* beneath the announcements for the next meeting of the Odd Fellows. Gibbons is one of the best at the game."

"So someone filed his prewritten story?"

"Affirmative."

"Nobody bothered to check the facts?"

"Affirmative. This isn't the first time that a story went out ahead of the facts. The pressure to get the scoop is intense. And the *Chicago Tribune* loves to rattle a saber. Hell, their publisher, Bob McCormick, now Major McCormick, is over here commanding an artillery battery. To make matters worse, the powers that be back home forced General Pershing to tell the press they could identify the Marines in their dispatches, since they are part of the navy."

A throat clears with all the subtlety of a hand grenade, drawing my eyes toward the door. General Harbord walks in, followed by Captain Saunders from the division staff. We stand. Harbord motions us to sit down while Saunders gets coffee and food. I give Harbord a hand flourish, as if to say, *please take a seat, monsieur.*

"We were just talking about the press coverage, General," Derby says.

"Goddamn it. I've been tied up on the phone this morning, other officers *congratulating* me on the fine way my *heroic, plucky Marines* single-handedly won the war. I told the signal corps I'm in the latrine and not to disturb me if any more generals call."

Saunders brings trays of food and coffee for Harbord and himself, sits, and digs into eggs and bacon. While they eat, I repeat my story about the press corps and papers. After finishing his plate, Saunders lights his pipe, puffs, and says, "Goddamned Marine propaganda apparatus. What are the rest of us doing, slicing brie?"

"The papers make it sound like we won the battle, if not the war," I say.

"Not *we*, the goddamned *Marines*," Saunders spits.

Hmmm. Reminds me of me. The old me.

"The Marines didn't write the dispatches," I shoot back. "The only press officers on this side of the Atlantic are army." I concentrate on my plate. My rantings to Jack about joining the Marines hit me like a slap in the face. I take a deep breath, avoiding eye contact—I need to take a back seat for the moment rather than risk my credibility.

"Yeah, I know," Saunders says. "But Teddy Roosevelt was right, you know—Congress should roll them into the army and be done with it. This premature declaration of victory puts us in a bind. How do we now say, 'not so fast'? It's putting a lot of pressure on everyone from General Pershing down."

My eggs taste like crow at the memory of my last argument with Jack.

Harbord eats slowly, with a thoughtful expression. He dabs the corners of his mouth with a napkin, looks around the table, rises, and brings a coffeepot back. He tops off the cups as though we are guests in his home. Saunders's face reddens as Harbord settles in his chair.

"I agree—to a degree." Harbord pauses for a sip. "In the sense that the press coverage puts us in a bind. But we passed overly optimistic reports up the chain. I should have been more circumspect." He takes another sip. "I used to agree with the idea of the Marines being rolled into the army. Hell, I'd love to say my army trained and created the brigade I command. In fact, I'm proud as hell that I lead it. I feel a bit awkward, given my former position on the issue."

Derby lights a cigarette, staring at the ceiling as if collecting his thoughts.

"We are lucky these guys were available," I say. "Hell, our army couldn't put together four infantry brigades a year ago."

"Don't get me started on that, Pops." Harbord pulls out a cigarette. Saunders snaps open a silver lighter and fires it up as Harbord raises the Chesterfield to his mouth. "I wish the army had more units as good as this division. Look, the Ninth and Twenty-Third Infantry are great too —every bit as good as my Marines, I think. Except for one thing . . ." He takes a puff. "I've never seen any military organization that can shoot as well. Les Mares Farm was the finest display of combat marksmanship I've ever heard of. The army had better take a lesson from that."

"Still, General, don't you agree with Teddy that the Marines are redundant?" Saunders asks.

"I used to. Hell, what does America need two infantry organizations for? On the other hand, name me a battalion in my army that could have done what 2/5 did. Not just the accuracy, but the cool-headed discipline." Harbord pauses for a sip of coffee.

"We all know that large-scale war is the army's job," Saunders says.

God, that was me last year. Forgive me.

"The Marines are a bunch of swashbuckling romantics swinging from ropes in the yardarms of sailing ships, knives in their teeth and sabers flashing in days of yore," Saunders says. "They're peacocks in their dress blues—our version of the palace guard. I'll grant you, their band and color guards *are* impressive. And they had John Philip Sousa. Hell, we don't even have an army band. Mark my words, they should be limited to their ceremonial duties, guarding embassies, and keeping swabbies in line."

I struggle to mask my anger, both at Saunders and myself, as I hear my exact words from his mouth. Derby's expression quells my urge for a beat. I take a breath. Saunders is an idiot. I'm an idiot. Well, I'm trying to make that "is" a "was."

"Until I joined this brigade, I agreed with TR on all of the above," Derby says, emerging from his reverie. "But I'm with the general on this." He takes a sip of coffee and pours refills. "I'll tell you, TR is unequivocal on this point—well, hell, like everything. Never one to equivocate. I've been with him when he's talked about it over cigars and brandy. Based on what I've seen? I'll argue the point with him the next time I see him."

"You've spoken with Roosevelt?" Saunders faces Derby.

"My father-in-law." Derby shrugs.

Saunders's face becomes a beet.

Harbord raises his right eyebrow. "Well, I'll be damned."

So that's his *special connection*.

The clatter of plates, clinking silverware, and quiet conversation come back into the bubble that surrounds us as I ponder this new information. The son-in-law of any other president wouldn't careen around a battlefield in a motorcycle sidecar. But then, TR would do it on horseback if the War Department let him. So maybe it all makes sense.

"While we're talking about our Marines, General, I want to let you know that they've fought their hearts out, but they're done in," Derby says.

"I've tried to keep them fresh by shuffling units back and forth between the front-line and reserve positions," Harbord says.

"Pardon me for saying so, sir, but relieving one tired and hungry doughboy with another isn't working," Derby says. "Our reserves get no rest and little in the way of hot food while being shelled by the Boche. After yesterday, they're all dinged up."

"I'm trying to make do with what I have," Harbord says.

"We need air support so our men can move during daylight hours without the sausages calling in artillery every time someone farts in the wrong direction," Derby says. "I bet the Boche sleep at night while our boys stumble around from position to position."

"Speaking of which, where the hell are our dashing aviators?" I ask. "Preening themselves and adjusting their scarves in front of full-length mirrors?"

"Flying patrols a few hundred miles east of here, where we are supposed to be," Derby says.

Harbord flashes him a *how do you know that* look.

"My brother-in-law, Quentin Roosevelt, is a pilot with the Ninety-

Fifth Aero Squadron," Derby says. "He tells me they're chomping at the bit to get up here. But you don't move an air squadron on a dime. You need an airfield, and it isn't as though they have one of those sitting empty hereabouts. Even if they move the squadron to a French airfield, the crews, equipment, and supplies will take a week, maybe several, to get there. Quentin would fly here today if he could, but what good is he when he runs out of bullets or gas? He tells me they won't be here until the end of the month."

"Dick, you're more forthcoming than headquarters," Harbord says. "I've been trying to get a clear picture of that all week."

"It helps to know the right people. They aren't always at headquarters." Derby winks at me.

Chapter Forty-Four
Major Ab Johnson

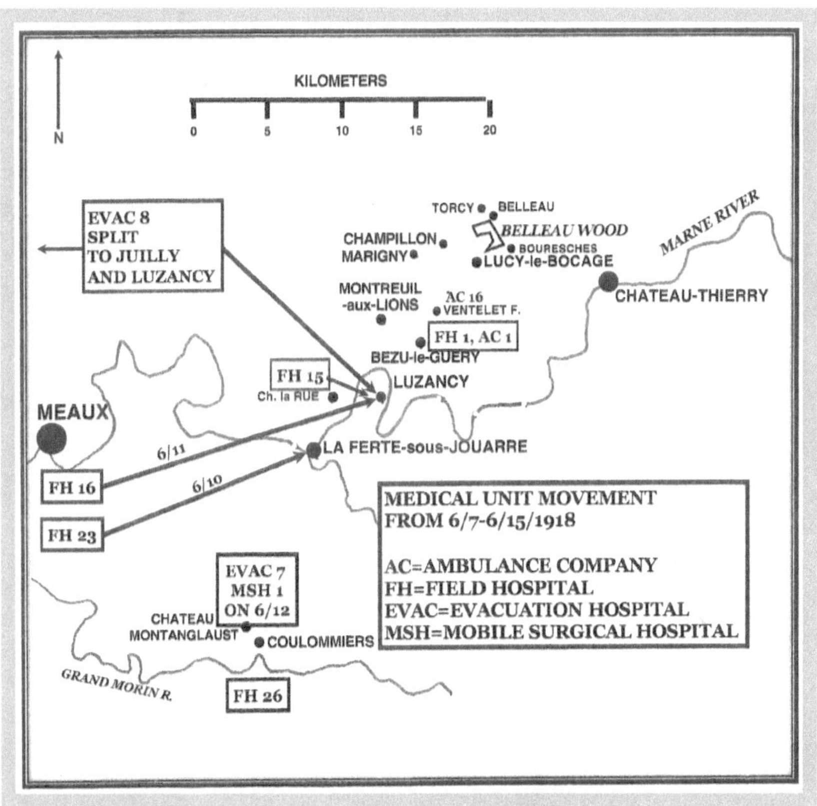

Monday, June 10, 1918

Thundering artillery reports from nearby batteries shake the cool, windless morning. I yawn. I spent the night helping move division HQ to Genevrois Farm after the Boche lobbed a few long-range shells near Montreuil. It was the first time I've seen fear in General Bundy's face. I rub my neck as I walk to the shed where I store my motorcycle. I lay a flashlight on a crate and slop gas into the fuel tank.

The last few days have been a blur as we struggled to get medical assets in place for the casualties flowing into the aid stations. I've circulated around the medical units, searching the faces of the lieutenants. So far, no Jack—my relief mixed with growing dread. The clock is ticking, its hands moving inexorably.

I hop on my motorcycle in the predawn darkness and head to La Voie to check in with Dessez. Desultory rifle fire crackles in the distance between the deep-throated *whoomph* of artillery pieces as I near La Voie. After checking in with the night crew and writing a new supply list, I spot Orlando Petty talking with Dessez. "How are things in Lucy?" I ask.

"Bad." Petty stifles a yawn. "Everyone's done in. No rest. The German artillery is zeroed in on Lucy. Not a lot of gas. Probably just waiting for the wind to change. Supplies have been getting up to us, though."

"How are the troops?"

"If there's a state beyond total exhaustion, they're there," Dessez says. "The fighting in the woods is brutal—hand-to-hand, boot-to-face. Most of those men go through Boone's station in Montgivrault. They pulled 3/6 out yesterday and are bathing the woods with artillery for an attack sometime today."

"You wouldn't be heading back toward Bezu, would you?" Petty asks.

"Why?"

"Check on Beck. Need to see if we can get him back before the next attack kicks off."

"Thought you didn't like him." I say.

"Well, I may have been a bit harsh. Of course, he *was* a horse's posterior."

I lead the way to the motorcycle and hand Petty an extra pair of goggles I lifted from a corporal in the motor pool when he wasn't looking. Petty hops into the sidecar while I rev the engine. My nose tolerates the bouncing better than yesterday. That's progress. But the odor of death is depressing.

After arriving in Bezu, I get Beck's location from a pharmacist's mate. Arthur is in bed in a cramped ward, a medical text in his lap. His color is better, and there is more life in his eyes as he looks out the window, seemingly lost in thought.

I clear my throat. Arthur looks over. Petty brings two chairs to the bedside. "How you doing?" I ask in a quiet voice.

Arthur holds his hands out in front and looks at them, then at Petty. They're steady. "Better. I slept the whole first day. Either that or I was catatonic. I don't remember which. The psychiatrist declared me sane, whatever that means."

"Think you can come back?" Petty asks.

"You *want* me? I mean, why would you, really? What good am I?"

"We need a surgeon. The question is whether you have it in you to come back."

"I'm afraid. I never felt so much fear as when we were down in that rat hole. I remember staring at the stairway. We'd have been trapped if a shell hit it. Or dead. When would they find us? I can't go into another cellar. I was drowning down there. It makes my chest tight just to think about it. I don't get how you guys do it—deal with the fear."

"I've never been so scared in my life," Petty says.

I take a breath. "The only people who don't feel fear in a battle are fools and lunatics. The rest of us either deal with it or cease to function. The thought of my son drives me—he's a Marine replacement lieutenant. What would I want the other men around Jack to do? I did what I hope they'll do for him." But what would I say if it were Jack in the bed instead of Arthur? Would I try to inspire him to go back into the battle?

Petty nods. "What drives me are my patients. Damn it, look at what those Marines go through. My fears are trivial compared to theirs. Their courage helps me get on with the job—for them." Petty's face colors as he says this, showing an ardor that I haven't seen in the professor before.

Arthur closes the book. "Back to my earlier question. Why would you want me? I'm the hot shot who isn't very hot, just shot."

"When we worked together in Lucy, your hands were rock-steady, quick, facile. Your decision-making was on target, and your work transformed from those pathetic earlier showings. I need *that* surgeon in my aid station. Okay, your reputation as a hot shot preceded you. Les Pratt and I have friends at Great Lakes. And Osborne was at Cook for a while. They warned us that you were an arrogant pain in the ass. They told us about your nickname at Cook."

Arthur stares at the end of his bed, face pale, as though lost in a memory that blots out the present. The sounds of the room come back to me—coughing, rustling sheets, a drapery cord snapping against a window frame.

"They also told us that we wouldn't get a better surgeon," Petty says.

Arthur startles and looks into my eyes, then at Petty. "I didn't know . . ."

"This is a team, not a one-man show. We needed your ego on the back shelf and your hands—and head—in the game. I finally saw that in Lucy. We need you." Petty stands and extends his right hand. Arthur takes it in his, and they shake.

"I better get back," Petty says. He releases Arthur's hand and faces me. "Can a swabbie bum a lift?"

Petty makes me jealous as he hops in the sidecar for the ride back to Lucy. Hell, he's only a couple years younger than me. None of the troops have been able to bathe with anything more than canteen water, and they've worn the same uniforms for twelve hot and horror-filled days. And there are no neat, tidy latrines, according to reports I've heard from the Marines. The worst part is how death and the dead linger in the air. We're inhaling them with each breath.

I head back to division HQ, thinking about Arthur. I've seen more and more men with the same sort of reaction. They're calling it shell shock. Some dismiss it as psychic or moral weakness, but it's more complicated than that. The true shell shock cases require evacuation to quiet areas far from the noise of battle. Many are never fit for frontline duty again. The ones like Arthur were exposed to more stress than their minds could handle. A shower, clean clothes, a few nights of shut-eye, and warm food revive them. They can go back to the fight. How it will affect them later and what unseen scars it will leave worries me. How would Jack react?

Bundy is talking with Harbord, Derby, and Brown when I enter the staff room. Derby motions me over, saying, "I hear the Fifth Regimental Aid Station was shelled today. None of the medical staff were hurt, but a roof collapse killed a number of their wounded."

"I had a pretty good taste of that last night," Bundy says.

My face tightens. Bundy will probably spin a tale to his great-grandchildren about the time he was caught in a huge barrage, exaggerating it the same way he amplified glad tidings from the front.

"Pops, making headway?" Harbord asks.

Thank you for changing the subject.

"Some," I say. "My next job is to set up the mobile degassing station at Ventelet Farm. We're opening the gas hospital in Luzancy tomorrow."

"Been pretty lucky about gas so far," Colonel Brown says. He points to the southern part of Belleau Wood on a map. "On other fronts, we now have Major Shearer running 3/5; they'll take over for 2/6 in Bouresches."

"Excuse me, sir, does 3/5 still exist?" Derby asks.

"The wonder of replacement troops," Bundy says.

My pulse surges, coursing through my face, my nose throbbing anew. Wonder? How can anyone treat the matter so lightly? Jack, are you out there now?

"And Shearer tells me that they're remarkably well squared away," Harbord says.

"I may be out of line," I say, "since I'm not an infantry officer, but didn't they lose almost all their lieutenants on the sixth? That means we have green officers leading green troops." My throat feels strained.

"Shearer has that in hand; defending Bouresches is a good way to season the new men and officers," Harbord says.

Brown frowns as he gazes at the map. "We hit the woods with artillery all night. Then 1/6 moved in at 0445 hours behind a rolling barrage. The word is that our losses are slight. Their CO reports that the woods are blown to mincemeat. We'll send 2/5 into the northern section tomorrow morning. It shouldn't be difficult, based on today's results." He pauses and studies the map. "Which is good, because all these men are beyond their limit. We need fresh troops."

"The French refuse to consider it," Harbord says. "It's insane to think a man can just will away fatigue."

"What are you going to do?" Derby asks.

"I'm out of options," Harbord says.

Chapter Forty-Five
Medical Corpsman Lyle McCormack

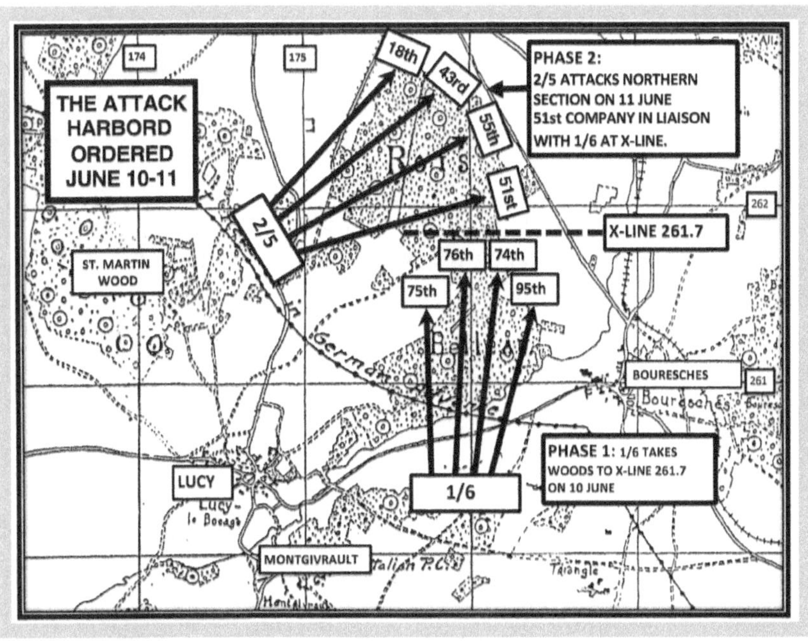

Tuesday, June 11, 1918

A steady breeze from the west blows away the worsening odor of those lying in the field in front of Belleau Wood. Good—let the Huns have it. My friend Frank Welty is out there—baking in the sun, rotting among them. Nobody has been able to retrieve the dead. Hun machine gunners along the edge of the woods shoot anyone going into the field during daylight. Going there at night with a lamp leads to the same result. The corpses and body parts have rotted to a point where getting them after dark is a mushy nightmare. The Kaiser's artillery scatters the remains in random bits and pieces.

Bouresches is still our moment of pride. Aside from it and Hill 142, the Huns have the upper hand so far. We hold what's left of Bouresches despite daily counterattacks. I can see the tactical importance of the town. Our machine gunners in Bouresches now cover the eastern side of Belleau Wood. They can even hit the village of Belleau, though the bullets probably lose most of their oomph by the time they arrive there.

They pulled me out of Bouresches to the Montgivrault aid station yesterday. I wanted to stay with my guys but was too tired to argue. Bouresches was a tough fight, but it was nothing compared to the stories I've heard about 3/5 and 3/6. The action in the woods hasn't quit since the sixth, and most of those guys haven't slept.

I sit with my back against the wall of the aid station, sipping warm chlorinated water from my canteen during a break, when the remains of 3/6 pass by in two ragged columns. Thin and hollow-eyed, they shuffle, each Marine following the one in front, faces showing no thought. One Marine I know gives me a nod in passing, face pale, uniform knees ripped, blood spattered over his torso—obviously not his. Others are in what officers describe as *good spirits*, which to me means *undefeated*.

They look like how I feel. Then a pang of guilt. The memory of rushing after Osborne into the fire, working with the dentist whose wounds didn't slow him down. I was untouched—physically—aside from my sore head and fuzzy brain. Why me? Why am I still not only alive but unwounded? Something isn't right. Not that I want a wound.

I have no tears left. Nothing but an empty pit. I take another sip of the tepid canteen water and spit it out. The smell of food draws me into the cellar below the aid station. After two bowls of warm stew, I find an empty cot. Scuttlebutt swirls around the room like smoke in a tavern. Worries about the fate of my friends keep me awake, restless.

I finally go to a table where guys are chewing the fat. One of the other corpsmen tells me about Frank Welty. My pulse pounds. "Yeah, I was in the field with him. How the hell I got out I'll never know. So Frank's taking care of five guys. Well, you know Frank. No job too big. Anyhoo, they're about a hundred yards short of Belleau Wood. He's hit by shrapnel twice and doesn't blink, just keeps working. Frank started on the fifth guy when a round smashed through his helmet. He handed his wound card booklet to the man next to him, saying, 'Make sure the chief gets this,' before keeling over. Can ya believe them beans?"

Frank's final act leaves me feeling empty, alone. The only one left in what I think of as my family is Gunny Stockham.

Thoughts about Frank's last minutes bring a surge—I pace, restless, unable to lie down. I have to do something.

As dusk gathers, word comes down that 2/5 needs corpsmen. I volunteer.

They send me to the Fifty-First Company, Captain Lloyd "Retreat? Hell!" Williams's unit. The Fifty-First just came off the line at Hill 142. I reach Williams's headquarters as night takes hold. Any light, even a cigarette, is a target. Nervous energy radiates in the hushed voices of Marines bitching that their *hot* food will end up in someone else's mess kit.

The words *hot* and *food* in the same sentence are an in-joke. By the time it gets to the lines, chow that was hot is lukewarm, grease hardening atop stew the cooks call *slum*. And like the lack of wounds, I feel guilty for the two bowls of slum I had at Montgivrault before joining the Fifty-First.

A flicker of light shines on the ground where several officers huddle under a hasty blanket tent held up by two privates. I crouch down next to the group, not sure where else to be. I glance in and see Williams.

"He what?" one lieutenant asks.

"Well, I'm not sure," Williams says. "Wise told us earlier that H-hour would be 0400, but now he tells me it's 0430 hours. Artillery prep starts at 0330. Didn't figure they'd need much after last night's fireworks."

"So are we going into the northern section of the wood like the boss planned?" a lieutenant asks.

"Not quite. Instead of coming at it from the north, we'll hit the northern section from the west and southwest sides." Williams points to the map. "Here's the problem—I know where 1/6 is *supposed* to be on this piece of shit map, but I don't know where they actually *are*. We're supposed to link up with them after we clear the northern section."

"How do we find them?"

"They'll be the ones not shooting at us," Williams says.

"Shit," another lieutenant says.

I stay near the headquarters unit—it's too dark to do anything else. H-hour approaches, and the barrage starts, too far to our left—north of where I thought it was supposed to be based on what I'd heard.

Captain Williams gathers his lieutenants beneath the blankets, going over the plan one last time. They roll up the blankets as the eastern sky lightens, and lieutenants order their Marines to form skirmish lines in hushed voices tinged with urgency. Mist carrying the reminder of death surrounds us as though we're about to march into one of those timeless battlefields. The men next to me adjust a strap here and a belt there, wordless. My now empty stomach tightens, my heart pounding. I shift from foot to foot, unable to stand still. Sweat trickles from my armpits. What have I gotten myself into now?

Skirmish lines materialize as dawn lightens. The first and second ranks disappear into the gloom to my front as they move forward. Morning fog hides Belleau Wood. The only thing missing is a bagpiper. I join the litter-bearers in the back line.

The sergeant standing on my right mutters, "The arty's got the wrong coordinates. That's supposed to be in front of us."

A lieutenant shouts, "Move!"

Mist swallows the men as we march forward. Dew-coated wheat swishes against my legs, soaking my leggings, chilling my skin. I keep pace, scanning from side to side. I stumble at the sudden shock of a bloated corpse two feet to my right. Then more. An arm. A headless torso blackened with rot. The sweet stench of decomposition becomes overwhelming. Would I recognize Frank?

I jog three steps, having fallen behind, looking at the horror surrounding me. There are too many corpses, too many shell holes, and too many body parts for where we're supposed to be. These are the dead of 3/5.

Dagnabit.

We're in the wrong place.

A shell blasts a gout of earth to my right. Then another to the front. I vibrate with the shock waves. I bend forward and vomit.

I wipe my mouth and double-time it to catch up.

The gray disk of a fog-shrouded sun rises in the low eastern sky. It gains strength and becomes yellow as we march. Our barrage rolls forward, too far to the north. Either they're hitting the wrong place, or we're off course. The edge of Belleau Wood emerges from the fading mist—two hundred yards ahead. My bowels almost let go when I trip on a lifeless leg.

Lights flicker along the edge of the woods, in front *and* to the right.

The air springs to life with the zips and snaps of machine gun rounds.

It doesn't make sense.

Fire pours in from the right, where they told Williams the 1/6 would be.

Where the heck are they?

Men stumble and fall. Others break and run toward the distant trees. Some hit the deck. I hustle forward. Each step could be my last. But if Frank could do it, I won't back down. No darned way.

But Frank's fate hangs over me.

I sprint and dive to the ground next to a private writhing in pain from a wounded leg. I dress the wound, jab in a shot of morphine, fill out the wound card, and wave two litter-bearers over. When they arrive, I move toward a gurgling scream to the left.

A lieutenant clutches his face, rocking from side to side on the ground. I give him a shot of morphine and say the same lies I used to hate a few days ago—"You'll be all right, sir; it's not as bad as you think; we'll get you patched up just fine." Fact is, he'll die. When the morphine kicks in, I move the man's hands to reveal a mangled face. A round must have hit him from the side, ripping through everything just above the upper teeth, the nose gone along with most of the upper jaw. The lower jaw swings loose, and the left eyeball dangles by its nerve.

Machine gun rounds sing the song of the devil above me as I fill out the wound card with thoughts of Frank's last moments. I give the man another dose of morphine. He'll be dead before they get him to the aid station. I check the man's damaged dog tag. The first name and serial number are unreadable—no time for niceties. I scribble on a wound card:

Date, hour, and station where tagged: *6/11/18, 0445 hr, Field*
Name: *Johnson, J*
Rank and Regt. or Corps: *2Lt. 51st Co, 5th Reg, USMC*
Diagnosis: *GSW face*
Treatment: *Bandaged, Evac*
Signature: *McCormack, HA2, USN*

I dart toward the deadly flickering woods and make it about ten feet before I find a body in two pieces, the midsection shredded by machine gun fire. I run on. My duty is the living—we'll mourn the dead later. I stumble over a bloated, blackened corpse. I check the dog tag with a sense of dread.

Not Frank.

Screaming to the right cuts me short. The woods are a hundred yards away. It might as well be a mile as I sprint toward the sound.

The middle of the man's right arm hangs by two shards of muscle, his face ashen. Blood loss and shock. Arterial blood spurts from the wound and soaks my right arm in sickening warmth.

I fumble a tourniquet out of my pack and tighten it into place. I wrap what's left of the arm in gauze and a bandage. Morphine on top of shock will kill the man. He'll have to live with the pain, but at least he might live. I complete a wound card, bullets coursing through the wheat around me.

If Frank could do it . . .

I mark the man's location with an upended rifle, bayonet in the ground. Then I remember what Boone told me about the Huns using them for targets. I pull the rifle out and move it about fifteen feet to the left—close enough a litter team might stumble upon him later, if any survive this mess.

I rise and trot forward in a crouch.

That's useless. The Huns set their machine guns to fire about a foot or a foot and a half above the ground. I run upright.

A dozen casualties later, I reach the edge of the wood. I slump down, back against a shattered tree trunk, gasping for air, looking left, then right, hands sticky and black with congealed blood and dirt. Wet with sweat.

Alive.

To my left, a body lies with neither legs nor sign of life. Probably from a grenade. After my breath slows, I move to the right. Twenty feet away, a sergeant, his back against a boulder, mutters softly, holding his belly. I kneel beside him. A machine gun beats a deadly staccato off to my right, where 1/6 is supposed to be. Did the Huns manage to sneak up on the whole battalion and slit their throats without firing a shot?

The Hun machine gun fires again, beating like a locomotive at medium speed.

Back to work.

Concentrate. Osborne never quit.

I stab a dose of morphine into the man's right arm and start the wound card. After the morphine kicks in, I ease the man's hands away. The abdominal wall is ripped open. The memory of Captain Duncan flashes through my mind. All that keeps the intestines in are the sergeant's hands. He'll never live. I pull out two large dressings and a bandage roll, trying to figure out how to get them around without sitting him forward.

A private crouches nearby, watching, face pale, a pool of vomit next to him, some hanging from his chin.

A greenie. But he has two hands.

I wave the private over. "Put both hands behind him. Lift him enough for me to get the bandage around when I tell you to."

We manage to wrap the sergeant's abdomen before the private retches again. The private scurries off as I complete the wound card. I give the sergeant another shot of morphine and move on.

One after another, I work my way among the casualties. Seems like everyone in the company is dead, dying, or wounded.

I take a breather at about 0800 and gulp from my canteen. Someone yells up ahead—"Corpsman!"

Dagnabit. I'm worn out.

Okay.

Artillery rounds blast the field to my right, rifles crackle behind me, machine guns stutter to the front. I'm the only guy here without a gun.

I run—the air pungent from gun smoke and rotting flesh, surrounded by shouts, curses, moans, and cries. I top a small rise.

Four Marines crouch around a wounded officer. I jog up.

The circle parts to reveal Captain Williams

Chapter Forty-Six
Lieutenant (junior grade) Arthur Beck

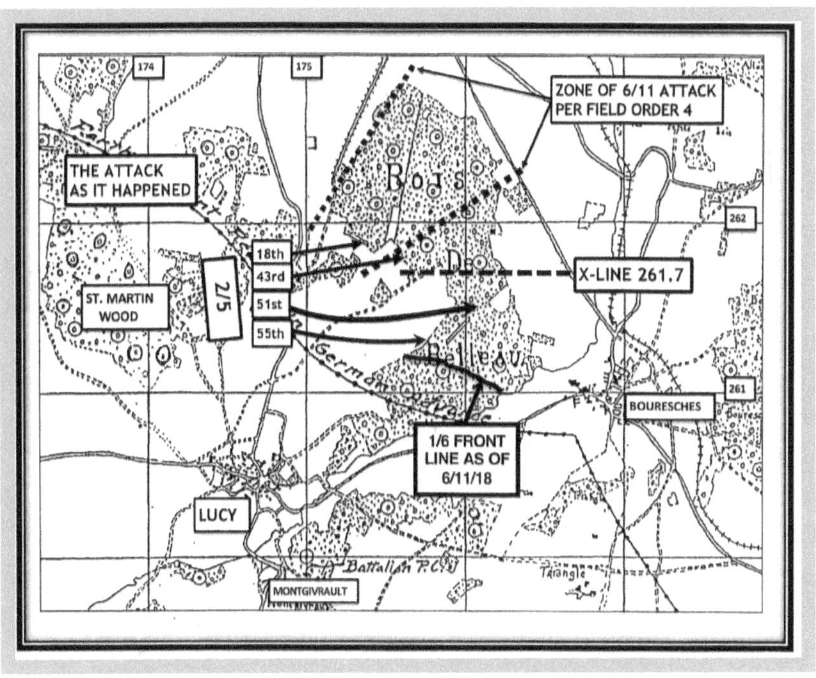

Lucy-le-Bocage

The back bench of the ambulance is killing my ass. They've declared me sane. I ponder the meaning of that word within the context of everything going on around me. I tried to distract myself while cooling my heels in the hospital. My injuries were, maybe are, mental. The men around me were physically wounded, making me feel like a shirker for the first time in my life. I wanted to get out of bed and take care of them. Memories of Dad's struggles plagued me.

At Cook County Hospital, I *was* a hot shot. In fact, I relished it—riding the fast track to tenure, lecturing at the American College of Surgeons, writing research articles. Boone and Petty hit that nail on the head. Weeden Osborne was on target too. In truth, I resented Osborne's accuracy. That a dentist could see through me so quickly was uncanny. Osborne's humor and courage are at once humbling and inspiring. The strafing ten days ago shook my self-confidence. The actions by Petty and Dessez that seemed abusive before now make sense. There is a difference between hazing and taking a gigantic ego off its pedestal.

The countryside rolls by, undamaged here, though some of the fields are beaten down where units have marched or camped. The noise of the Ford's engine blots out all else. Dust swirls in our wake, making me cough.

My hands are rock-solid steady. I'm not sure what to expect when I get back to Lucy. Will I hold it together? That night in the cellar revealed a terrified boy, a weakness the depth of which I've never plumbed. I choose to embrace the weak boy rather than pretend he isn't there. Know your weakness, own it, don't let it own you. It's part of me, but only one part. The whole is stronger than that single part.

This I know—I owe the others. Even Petty. Especially Petty. I couldn't imagine a forty-something endocrinologist doing meatball surgery in Lucy with me and doing it well. I am humbled that he has faith in me. Would the Arthur who got off the SS *Caserta* in St. Nazaire have given another doctor a chance like this? No.

I'm not that Doctor Shot anymore. Not sure who I am, but maybe I'll find out if I make it through.

I now wear an army uniform like everyone else. One set of my custom blues was lost in the fire, and the other is stuffed in a duffel somewhere, not to be used again until I'm on a ship home, maybe.

The Ford jerks to a stop when we reach the ambulance dressing station. I tighten the chinstrap on my helmet, jump out, and smile like Osborne would have. The place is busy with the wounded from this morning. My sense of urgency grows when I learn of a new offensive and find a signal corps sergeant who has room in his sidecar for a ride back to Lucy.

Gunfire rattles and pops in Belleau Wood as I approach a town that is sadder to behold every time I see it. It is more a series of rubble piles than the pretty village I first saw. We pull up behind a damaged building, and I hop out.

The aid station is above ground in a different stone house. Its smell, humidity, and heat assault me as I enter. The odd thing I see is that everyone is wearing their tunics instead of undershirts this time. It's hot, so there must be a story I need to hear. The uniform they issued me is a half size too big, so I get a little more ventilation than my custom blues.

Malcolm Pratt and Petty work on cases while a private with an orchard sprayer douses window and door blankets with anti-gas solution. The station chief and four corpsmen man the shock tables. I weave my way toward Petty, who works on a leg wound.

Petty glances up. "Glad you're back. The Germans are sending more gas." He stretches his neck. "Let's set up in the supply room. This place is getting too crowded."

"Should we wear anti-gas suits?"

"Only if you want to die of hyperthermia and dehydration. Keep your uniform coat on. Drink plenty of water. Cornelius Mack and Lester Pratt set up a gas station in Gob Gully."

Petty, two corpsmen, and I move into the supply room. "Feels like an elevator," I mutter. Boxes of supplies and spare gas masks fill one wall. The corpsmen set up a trestle table and place a litter atop it—a semiconscious Marine with a mangled arm and an iodine *M* painted on his forehead. I clamp and tie off bleeders while Petty assists—handy with instruments for an endocrinologist. I meet Petty's eyes when we're done, and he gives me a wink. The next case goes on the table—a bleeding scalp laceration.

Arriving artillery fire nears, like it did on the sixth, creeping under my skin. My hands remain steady as I suture the laceration with my normal speed.

After the scalp, a traumatic amputation occupies us, loosening and tightening a tourniquet while searching for the mangled remains of the femoral artery. After that, we toil with a gunshot wound to the head. The boy talks as though his mother is standing next to us while we work. No chance of survival, but neither Petty nor I is willing to let the kid's brains leak out through the open skull wound in front of his fellow Marines. At Cook, I would have criticized the surgical team for wasting its time. But here? Sometimes you have to do the hopeless as long as there isn't a viable one waiting. The wounded watch how we treat their buddies. We have to show we still have a shred of humanity—for the others, and for ourselves.

German wounded are coming in from the south side of Belleau Wood. The chief pharmacist's mate puts them in our room, since I speak fluent German. They sit with their backs to the supplies stacked along the outside wall. Four prisoners wait their turn when Petty and I finish with the head case.

Petty stretches and looks at his watch. "Let's take five. It doesn't sound like there's any gas outside right now."

The morning air is cooler than the aid station. The reek of human decomposition turns my stomach, more so after being away from it for a few days. We stand next to the front door of the building. I stretch aching muscles. Petty elbows me and points at four Marines lugging a heavily laden green blanket toward us. Petty shouts, "Run out of stretchers?"

"Yes, sir," a Marine says. "Captain needs an ambulance ASAP."

"Captain?" Petty asks.

"Williams, sir. He's wounded."

"Shit," Petty says. "Set him down. We better get a look at him before we send him back. Get a litter over here." Petty kneels next to Williams. "Much pain, Lloyd?"

"Not at the moment," Williams says. "The corpsman gave me morphine before I left."

"How long ago were you hit?"

"Two hours." Williams grimaces. "No litter-bearers left. Just blankets. My guys. Goddamn it. My guys were chopped apart in that damned field. I led them there. Those guys are my responsibility, Orlando. I want to wring the neck of the asshole that planned this attack."

"We'll evacuate you as soon as we can," Petty says.

"There's room on that ambulance." I point at an idling ambulance that just risked doing a supply run.

"Load someone else," Petty says. "We need to control his hemorrhage. I'll take responsibility. Get him inside."

I help the Marines and a corpsman roll Williams on a stretcher. I take one handle and help carry Williams into the aid station and onto the trestle in the supply room. He's bleeding from two gunshot wounds —one in the right shoulder and another in the right flank.

"What happened?" Petty asks.

"Couldn't see a thing in the fog. When it burned off, I found myself in the last place on earth I wanted to be. My orders were for the right side of my company to join with the left of 1/6. We were at least eight hundred yards south of where they should have been, but the Germans were still to my right. I kept veering to the right, but never found 1/6. I had one lieutenant and sixteen men left when we hit the woods."

"You work on the shoulder," I say. "I'll work on the other." I hold pressure where I think the bullet might be. "Belly isn't expanding."

The shelling nears. I compress the area around the bullet buried in Williams's side. I'd like to take it out, but that might make him bleed more, and we don't have anesthetics. Sweat plasters my shirt to my chest and dribbles down my legs.

An explosion blows me to the floor.

My ears shut off—no noise.

I lie on the floor, looking up at the sky through a gaping hole in the roof.

My brain's fuzzy. What?

Coughing. Choking. Blinking.

I rub my eyes and look over to see Petty, blinking.

Where's the roof . . . the outside wall?

Compressing the wound . . . can't remember the name . . .

Dust cakes Petty's face, his eyes darting, glasses askew.

Petty rights his spectacles and clambers up.

I try to get onto my feet. The world spins. I flop down.

Williams. That's who I was working on.

Shouts fill the room.

Wood smoke in my nostrils.

Williams lies on the floor, groaning. New bleeding. His chest. Still breathing. The two corpsmen lie still. Dead. I ease my way to my feet. Use a hand on the wall to brace myself against a wave of light-headedness. It passes—steady now. Petty struggles to lift Williams onto his shoulders in a fireman's carry. I help him heft the unconscious captain. We both keep our gloves on while I slip a gas mask pouch over Petty's head and then mine.

Petty staggers. I reach out to balance them.

Blood runs down Petty's back. I grab a spare dressing and shove it against a wound in the back of Williams's chest, shouting, "I'll hold while you carry. Go!"

A corpsman slips a helmet on Petty and tightens the chinstrap. Another plops one on my head. Petty staggers forward. I follow, supporting Williams's torso, taking part of the load while holding the dressing. We shuffle out of the aid station through a gaping hole where the door used to be. Two gas shells spew yellow-brown poison ten feet away. The double yellow crosses on the shell casings tell me all I need to know. The gas alarm clangs. No choice. Neither Petty nor I can put our gas masks on without abandoning Williams. Not an option.

Petty, Williams, and I are barefaced as everyone else dons their masks.

Petty double-times it, carrying Williams. The fifty yards to Gob Gully seem insurmountable. Gasping for air in our effort, pulling the deadly gas into our lungs, Petty more than me.

A building to my right explodes. Debris smacks my chest and helmet. Another shell hits in front. I'm using both hands to staunch bleeding as Williams's bare head lolls back and forth with each heavy step of Petty's boots.

Another shell hits, and something solid careens off my right hip. I stagger but keep pressure on Williams's chest. Jesus, that hurts—but I limp along. We reach the Gob Gully dressing station. One of the men motions for us to mask up. I help Petty ease Williams to the ground. I take my helmet off and pull out my gas mask while Petty struggles to find something to fix in Williams's wounds. I get my mask on, take three deep breaths of filtered air, spit the mouthpiece out, and shout for him to don his. Williams' face is bare; he's unconscious, mortally wounded. There's no hope, but Petty carries on.

Lester Pratt works on a man next to us. A corpsman dabs Pratt's mask in an odd way. It doesn't make sense. Then Lester looks up—bleeding from a wound near the right eye. The eyepiece of his mask dangles like a macabre eyeball.

I will Petty to get his mask on. He's taking deep breaths, gasping from the effort of carrying Williams here. Catching his breath amid the toxic cloud surrounding us.

Get the damned mask on!

Petty pulls Williams's gas mask out, looks at it, and tosses the mangled wreck away. The shrapnel that blew the hole in his chest must have driven part of the mask into the wound.

The shock wave of a nearby blast empties my chest and blows off my gas mask. I hold my breath and reposition my mask.

Petty crouches over Williams, yelling to his friend. "Breathe. Breathe, Goddamn it. Breathe!"

Petty glances at me, his face drawn in pain, eyes watering.

I point at my mask and try to gesticulate my panic for him.

A corpsman comes over with two basins, one with tools and the other with alcohol. The illusion of sterility. Dust and gas cloud the air. Okay, I'll give it a try. I grab a hemostat with my right hand and a wound pack with my left. I bend over Williams—pull the uniform back to reveal a gaping chest wound. I dunk the dressing in iodine and plaster it on the jagged hole. I help Petty fashion an occlusive dressing similar to the one I had placed on Colonel Catlin.

An artillery shell showers us with debris.

I lean forward to protect the wound.

Something hard whacks my helmet. I gaze at the contaminated wound in dismay.

We have to try . . .

We finish the occlusive dressing. Williams's breathing is ragged and shallow.

Petty finally dons his gas mask.

I use my hand on the dressing to create a one-way valve to let air escape from Williams's chest.

Petty uses both hands to compress a dressing as blood wells from a new upper abdominal wound—dark, nearly black blood—liver injury.

Shrapnel from the last blast.

Hopeless.

Williams is dying.

We work on. Petty won't quit. Williams was his friend—his responsibility.

The breathing is irregular, now short gasps.

Then it stops.

I feel for Williams's carotid pulse. Nothing. I look up. Petty meets my eyes, mask torn, one side hanging loose.

I shake my head. Petty nods, his exposed eye red, watering. He bows his head as though in prayer. I take a deep, slow breath.

Petty yells, "Let's get to the others."

I take my mouthpiece out and shout through the mask, "Get the hell out of here. I'll stay."

"We're up to our earlobes."

"Leave! Your mask is gone. You'll die."

"Get back to work." Petty turns to the next casualty.

Chapter Forty-Seven
Major Ab Johnson

La Loge Farm

The noise of the battle reminds me of the sixth as I ease my motorcycle to a stop in front of Fourth Brigade headquarters. I've named my Indian motorcycle *Helen* in honor of my wife, who has to be working with God to protect me. There can be no other reason why I still have a pulse. Two narrow misses this morning. One truck. One shell. Road dust coats me—teeth gritty, snot gray, coughing. I kick the stand underneath the motorcycle and hobble toward the door.

I enter the staff room to find General Harbord, Colonel Brown, and two staff officers in an animated discussion at the map. Cigar smoke blues the air. Harbord smiles. "Pops, good timing. Nothing but good news this morning, finally."

Oh no. Not again. But maybe it really is good news. I've gotten so used to them being wrong. One of these times they'll be right, I hope.

"The Germans moved on Bouresches early this morning," Colonel Brown says. "Our artillery obliterated them before they could organize." He takes a puff from his cigar. "Two-Five's assault went well—all objectives were gained by 0630."

"We've reeled in over three hundred prisoners, including three officers," Harbord says. "Intelligence is questioning them. I sent a note to General Bundy. The woods are ours! A press briefing is underway."

Brown, his back to Harbord, rolls his eyes at me.

What the hell does that mean? Does Brown know it's hogwash—again?

"We'll send another unit to relieve the boys as soon as they're done cleaning out the stragglers," Harbord continues.

Facts are what I need, but I don't think this is the place to find them.

I listen to the reports and read a few of the dispatches, wanting to get on the motorcycle and see for myself before I join the celebration. This is the second time they've declared victory. My reporter's inner voice shouts a warning. They may have done it again—this time without Floyd Gibbons's help.

I bid my farewells and rev up *Helen*. I ride to the Fifth Regimental Aid Station, where I find Dessez talking with one of the young surgeons whose name I don't remember.

"Able to wear a gas mask yet?" Dessez asks.

"Tried it on this morning," I say. "The nose clip only hurts when I turn my head." I touch my nose gingerly. "How's Lucy?"

"Same old shit. They're shelling the hell out of us. Hit the aid station—again. It caught fire, and they had to evacuate—again. We lost two corpsmen and several wounded, including a room full of prisoners. I need to get Malcolm Pratt up there. Word is that Malcolm's brother is wounded. We're so short, our dentist, Cornelius Mack, went up. Petty is gassed; we need to evac him."

I turn toward Malcolm. "I can take you."

"On that?" Malcolm asks.

"I really do know how to drive this thing. Is there anything else they need?"

"Gas masks. Their spares were destroyed," Dessez says.

"Lieutenant, I'll bring my motorcycle to the supply tent," I say. "Get what you need and we'll head out."

"Ever drive that wearing a gas mask?" Malcolm asks.

"Fear means you're still alive."

I take off my tin pot and put on my mask. The pincers of the nose clip do not feel good as I snug them tight with great care. I kick the

Indian into gear and head east after Malcolm is in the sidecar. Trucks and ambulances with rubberized fabric cab covers driven by gas-masked soldiers crowd the road. The mask keeps the road dust out as I navigate around new shell holes. When the traffic in front stalls, I look up and see three German observation planes and four sausages above Belleau Wood. I rev the throttle, turn into the field, and gun it. Grass whips the undercarriage of the sidecar as we bound past the traffic. My nose throbs with each jolt.

Dirt clots smack me after an explosion to my right. One whacks my mask, sending an ice pick of pain that blinds me. I slow until my vision clears.

Gun it.

Half blind.

Where the hell is the aid station? Lucy looks more like a quarry than a town. Buildings smolder, though there can't be much left to burn.

Medical teams scurry between the outdoor dressing station in Gob Gully and a building that must be the new aid station. I pull up next to an ambulance.

Malcolm hops out before we come to a complete stop. I follow him into the station. Wounded men sit with backs against the walls while the rest lie on litters, all masked up. The doctors wear masks except for Lieutenant Orlando Petty. His red eyes water as he works on a wounded limb with Arthur Beck, now dressed in an army uniform. Petty turns his head to the side with a coughing spasm that doubles him over. He spits on the ground—blood.

Malcolm Pratt tears open a box, grabs a gas mask, and taps Petty on the shoulder. He yells something to Petty, who steps back while taking off his apron and gloves. Malcolm helps Petty pull the mask on.

Arthur holds his hands in front of him and then motions Petty to leave. I guess I'm his ride. Malcolm argues with Lester, who bleeds from a wound below one eye, both eyes weeping, red. Malcolm helps his brother into a gas mask, and the two go to my motorcycle. Petty sits in the sidecar. I lean forward to a stand to let Lester sit behind me. I gun it and weave away from Lucy, wondering where I left my sanity. But then, where else would I want to be?

All the while I look at the Marines we pass, looking for Jack among those not wearing gas masks. We've lost so many lieutenants that I have to think he might be here, somewhere. I hope not in this gas.

I can't get the tune "Home on the Range" out of my head—the one with my extra line for the generals. The celebration at headquarters—another victory of hope before fact. I don't have the time or patience to set the fools straight.

Petty's cough worsens.

I speed with growing desperation. Petty needs help. Bezu feels so far —damn it.

"Hold tight," I shout, and open the throttle. We zip through a field. Each minute gives the gas more time to corrode these surgeons' skin, eyes, and lungs.

I drive straight to the degassing tent and wave corpsmen from the gas team over.

Corpsmen hustle Petty and Lester away.

Will I ever see either of them again?

Chapter Forty-Eight
Major Ab Johnson

Wednesday, June 12, 1918

After a restless night with little sleep, I stop by the intelligence office at division headquarters. I manage to get the Paris editions of several American daily newspapers from a lieutenant who always wears a clean uniform with sharp creases.

Today's *New York Times* runs a banner headline announcing: "Brilliant Victory in Wood."

If only it were true.

In reality, the Germans still hold the northern half of Belleau Wood.

Reading the fantasies of the uninformed and being unable to do a thing about it drives me nuts. I'll write a book. If I survive.

None of that allays my rage about what Jack will be walking into, or my anger about what other fathers' sons are going through.

Losses among second lieutenants horrify me. The desperate need for replacements means that the Marines will have to accelerate their already short training cycles. Those in the pipeline will be fed into the breach on arrival. Jack . . .

Derby and I risk our careers as we beg, cajole, and finally order the movement of a mobile degassing unit closer to Lucy, at Ventelet Farm.

Colonel Wadhams won't mind us using his name. Despite the optimistic mood at Division, I visit hospitals teeming with casualties and staff pulling twenty-hour shifts. I haven't been able to find out about Orlando Petty or Lester Pratt. All I know is that Petty's at the new gas hospital in Luzancy and Lester Pratt is in a Paris hospital.

Helen and I bounce to a stop outside La Loge Farm. Another motorcycle heads into the parking lot, an officer in the sidecar. When the man takes off his goggles, I recognize my old friend, Ira Cunningham. Ira's age shows as he unfolds himself out of the sidecar. I hope I didn't look that pathetic before I took over driving mine. Ira stretches his back with a loud groan.

"Look what the cat dragged in," I say. "I thought you were going to Chaumont."

"Was there a short time. Now I'm Colonel Nolan's intelligence fireman, being sent hither and yon. This is hither, right?"

"More like yawning hell. What are you here for?"

"Intelligence."

"That'll be a refreshing change," I say. "Let me know if you find any. How long are you here?"

"My orders are vague."

I pull out my pipe and tamp in a plug of tobacco. I'd laid off it for a few days after all the gas exposure. "Come." I lead the way to my office and close the door, clicking the lock. "I'm ready to scream. The generals are driving me batty."

"Like most of the army."

"Right," I say. "Look, I take back everything I said about Marine officers. They have more combat experience than ninety-five percent of our army brethren. Our army treats them like they're asylum inmates. Sure, they have their limitations too. The one responsible for the latest fiasco is a lieutenant colonel named Wise. I listened to his latest briefing. He sounded drunk."

"Shit."

"Yeah. Thing is, it's not alcohol. He was so worn out he could barely stand. His unit's been on the line since the first—done in doesn't even begin to describe it. He's leading another attack today, but it seems like a fool's errand. It's so frustrating to watch, especially since I'm supposed to only talk when asked."

"Any word on Jack?"

"The personnel department is so fouled up they're of no help. The only thing I can do is ask around and keep my eyes open. Hell of an army we're in."

"Yeah, hell of an army."

"Glad to have you here, old pal. Maybe I'll recover some of my sanity," I say. "I can only hope that rubs off on a few others around here."

Chapter Forty-Nine
Lieutenant (junior grade) Arthur Beck

Lucy-le-Bocage

A Gordian knot screams in my neck from leaning over wounds for hours. Petty—damn him—breathed in so much gas. Is he still alive? I owe him. Of all people, he believed in me despite my shortcomings. Believes, not believed. I'll be optimistic. How do you pay that back? I didn't have a chance to say anything, to express my gratitude. Not even a simple *thanks* before he finally evacuated in Pops's sidecar.

Malcolm and I stay in Lucy Birdcage, as all of us call it, after evacuating Petty and Lester. We've done what we can to degas, shaking out our uniforms to get the mustard off, spraying each other with bicarbonate solution. All the while, Malcolm has fretted about his brother.

We're working on a patient with a deep shrapnel wound in the right buttock. Masks are off for the moment, inside the "new" aid station.

The patient will lose too much blood in transit unless we do something. The man is unconscious from shock, but how long before he dies if we can't control the hemorrhage? My eyes sweep the wound. We tried packing and binding it, but there's one artery that refuses to quit bleeding. We can't send him out like this.

The German shelling waxes and wanes. They're shooting occasional gas again, though not at the moment. I used to admire the chemical and pharmaceutical industries of my cousins' fatherland—my fatherland too. No more.

"How long have we been at this?" I ask.

"This butt or this day?" Malcolm looks up with red eyes.

"Both, I guess. I don't remember. Did we sleep last night?"

"I don't know—is it day or night?"

I grab a hemostat off a tray next to the table while a corpsman holds the edges of the wound apart. Malcolm shines a flashlight as we search.

Where is that thing?

I think I see it.

"That's the devil that's been giving us trouble." I snap a hemostat. The bleeding stops. I loop a suture around the hemostat and tie off the area around the artery.

Malcolm keeps the beam on the spot when I release the hemostat and dab the wound with a gauze pad. Watching. Watching.

Malcolm irrigates with Dakin's solution to get a little disinfectant on the surface. Good enough. I pack the wound with sterile gauze and apply a dressing. We wrap the bandage tight to compress the wound. The corpsman fills out the wound card while I dredge my gloves in a basin of alcohol.

The door tarp snaps open and the chief pharmacist's mate yells, "Dressing station's hit—we need help."

"Again?" I mutter.

We keep our gloves on as we don our gas masks and helmets and rush to Gob Gully. I hit the dirt when I hear the whistle of an approaching artillery shell. After a turf shower, I sprint. Shock waves thunder from the shelling, shaking my teeth and rattling my brain. A brownish-yellow gas haze lingers in Gob Gully. Senior dentist Lieutenant Commander Cornelius Mack took over the station when Lester and Petty evacuated. Gas-masked Marines crowd the station in the deadly mist. Mack's gas mask is torn, the mouthpiece still in his lips but one eyepiece dangling. I motion for him to get out of the gas, but Mack shakes his head and returns to work. I clamber down the rocky incline. Mack coughs. "You and Malcolm take care of that guy over there."

Malcolm and I join two corpsmen struggling to control bleeding from a hip wound. The man is too unstable to move. The oily gas will coat inside the wound and cause more damage, akin to pouring acid into the wound. I grab a hemostat in each hand while Malcolm holds the wound edges apart. I snap the two hemostats on bleeders and grab two more. The hemorrhage continues. The noise of the battle is distant as I search for the other bleeders.

Malcolm makes a grunting noise, one finger pointing. I squint and finally see it. I snap a hemostat in place. That does it. We'll have to finish the job outside the ravine. Malcolm and I help roll the Marine on a stretcher.

I look over at Mack, now working on a leg wound. We have to get him out. Two corpsmen bring a new patient. Malcolm shouts through his mask to give a hand. I take the assistant role, holding the edges of a gaping flank wound as Malcolm works.

The artillery barrage picks up, steeping the gully in more gas. We can't bring the casualties into the battalion aid station now—gas evaporating off the uniforms will make it as toxic as the gully. We can't work above the gully without exposing everyone to shrapnel. We need a protected area, but where? And how would we get there with the explosive storm raging above ground?

We're stuck in the gully, bathed in oily gas.

I lose track of time. Carry on. Work. Do what Petty would do.

A tap on my shoulder catches my attention. A corpsman motions and points to a line of corpsmen and litter-bearers carrying and helping the wounded toward one of the skeletal, roofless buildings—a new outdoor aid station. The artillery barrage has petered out, but I've been too busy to notice over my ringing ears.

Malcolm and I move to the new station. A bell rings—the signal that we can take off our gas masks. The lull in the shelling is letting ambulance crews cart off those ready for transport. The numbers in the station finally come under control. I make my way over to Cornelius Mack. "Sir, Malcolm and I can take this now. You need to degas."

"No," Mack says. "There are only two of you. Look, the damage is done. I can still work." He turns to our chief pharmacist's mate, who is assisting him. "Have 'em bring the next one." He takes a breath and coughs, tears running down the reddened skin of his face. "The sooner you get back to work, the sooner we can all get out of here. I'm not leaving until the last Marine is evaced."

Damn it. He's going to kill himself. But we are shorthanded. He has a point.

A half hour later, things finally settle down. I'm desperate to get Mack and the chief out, regardless of Mack's opinion. Malcolm is holding his own, so I run to the battalion PC on the next block. I stay at the door and shout, "We have a couple dozen gas casualties on the west side. I need two trucks to evacuate them to the degassing station. That includes our chief pharmacist's mate and three doctors. Tell them to send up more gas masks and three more docs." The signal corps man gives me a thumbs-up.

The outdoor aid station is full, but most of the Marines are ready for transport. The acute cases are as stable as they're going to get. Tears streak Mack's cheeks, his nose an angry faucet—he doubles over in a coughing spasm. I pace, hands behind my back. What's taking them so long?

Chapter Fifty
Lieutenant (junior grade) Arthur Beck

Someone yells that trucks and a medical relief team have arrived. I grab Mack's sleeve and pull him to an open-bed Liberty truck. He argues, and I order him to go. He points to his rank insignia during a coughing spell. I tell him he's medically unfit to continue. He quits arguing. I help load other patients. Malcolm and I hop on the tailgate, and the truck leaves.

I'm exhausted. I didn't get much gas in my lungs, which I think is a miracle, given the time it took Petty and me to get Williams out of the aid station.

"We should have stayed back," Malcolm says.

"The crew that came in on these trucks is on shift now," I say. "I feel fine, too, but we need to wash up and get clean stuff on. I'm sure our uniforms are saturated."

"They're still shorthanded."

He's right. I sigh. There's nothing I'd like better than a shower and cot, but the crew that replaced us is too thin. "We'll think of something. Besides, Malcolm, you stink. We both need a shower."

The ride to the degassing station at Ventelet Farm takes fifteen minutes. It's a few hundred yards southeast of La Loge, a smaller version of La Voie with stone farm buildings. We hop off the truck as soon as it stops and help unload others.

What I see looks like Jules Verne wrote the scene.

Gas troops wear suits made of rubberized fabric and thick rubber gloves, their gas masks tucked in chest pouches. They guide us to a waiting area while others spray the trucks with degassing solution. A corpsman orders everyone to form a line. A doctor and corpsman walk along the line, separating the severe, moderate, and mild cases into groups. We're in the mild group.

The gas officer shouts, "Don't eat, drink, or even swallow! Spit if you have to. The gas in your mouth will poison you. Sit on the benches. No exertion."

Mack and our chief pharmacist's mate sit with the severe group, many coughing, some wearing blindfolds. Mack's face is crimson, nose and eyes watering, coughing. This isn't supposed to happen to dentists. But what happened to Osborne wasn't supposed to, either.

I offer to help; a sergeant tells me to stay put—that I'm the patient now, not the doctor. Malcolm asks if the sergeant knows where Lester went.

"Sir, you all look the same to me," the sergeant says. "Luzancy is your best bet."

A tanker truck idles at one end of a fifty-foot canvas tent. Next to it is a cargo truck loaded with crates.

The clatter of rifle actions and shouting draws my eye. A gas sergeant paces in front of infantry troops. "Unload your rifles. Pistols, too. Actions open. Rifles into the crate on the right. Pistols in the other. Your other shit goes in the third. The only things you keep with you are helmets and boots. Everything else goes in the crates."

"How 'bout my watch?" a man near me asks.

"Keep your valuables—watches, compasses, girlie pictures."

"Get our collar pins off," I tell Malcolm. "When they give us a choice of pajamas or uniforms, snag a uniform. I have an idea."

A gas NCO—a corporal—leads us to two wooden boxes filled with powdered lime, one on the ground and the other at waist height. I know the drill. When it's my turn, I take off my rubber gloves, run my hands through the lime, and do the same with my boots. We take off our uniform coats and toss them in another bin.

The gas NCO leads us into the tent, where we take off our helmets and dip them in a tank of limewater. Malcolm slips his rank and medical pins into the upturned helmet, and I do the same.

A staff sergeant in his thirties speaks in the loud singsong of a South Carolina drill instructor. "Now, *men* and *sirs*, I'll take you *through* this *step by step*. Reeemain standing and keep off the running board behind you. You will stand on that when you are *done* with your shower. Now place your helmet *in* the numbered cubbyhole behind you. All valuables go in the helmet." He waits.

"Reeemove your shirts and put them in the shirt receptacle." The staff sergeant points at a large wooden barrel. "Now, shoes, boots, puttees, and socks off and set them in front of you." He waits. "Reeemove your skivvies and place them in that receptacle." He points at another barrel. "Do *not* sit down."

I stand in self-conscious nakedness—the runt of my litter, though starvation has lightened everyone's load.

"Note the number behind you," the staff sergeant chants. "Now *proceed* to the shower room and stand under the shower head with your number." We take our positions in silence. "You will *note* a spray bottle on the floorboard at your feet. Spray yourself with soap, starting with your head and ending with your feet. *Do not* neglect your privates." I soap up. "I will run the water for fifteen seconds. After that, scrub yourself and lather the soap, starting with your head all the way down to your tootsies." Tepid water sprays from the shower head. I scrub. The soap stings my eyes. After two minutes, the staff sergeant shouts, "I will now start the water. You have thirty seconds to rinse off. Don't dawdle. This ain't the fucking Ritz."

I rub and rinse as water rushes over me.

"Now stay where you are, sirs and peons. My private will give you *each* a towel. Dry yourself off, head to ankle, in that order. Then, in reverse order of entry, you will return to your previous position in the main tent. As you exit, wipe your feet and place the towel in the towel barrel. Then walk on the running board back to your position. The gas officer will spray your eyes, nose, mouth, and throat. You will then be issued new clothing. When you have your clothing kit, you may dress."

The gas officer spritzes bicarbonate solution in our eyes and then uses an atomizer to spray the inside of each nostril and then the mouth. They go from man to man like an assembly line. I pick up a size small officer's clothing kit and follow the running board back to my spot and dress. Malcolm and I exit the tent, pinning on our medical and rank pins, donning our helmets with a few drips on my wet scalp.

The gas crew directs us to open-bed trucks for transport to the gas hospital in Luzancy.

"Follow me," I say. "Do as I do. We're now gas officers heading to an inspection." I grab two fresh gas mask satchels from a crate. We both slip them over our heads and walk like we're on a mission.

"We go on that truck and we'll be in the gas hospital for two days— guaranteed," I say. "How the hell are they going to staff Lucy Birdcage?"

"If we don't arrive at Luzancy, though, won't they arrest us?"

"They'll have to find us."

Chapter Fifty-One
Private Carl Larsen

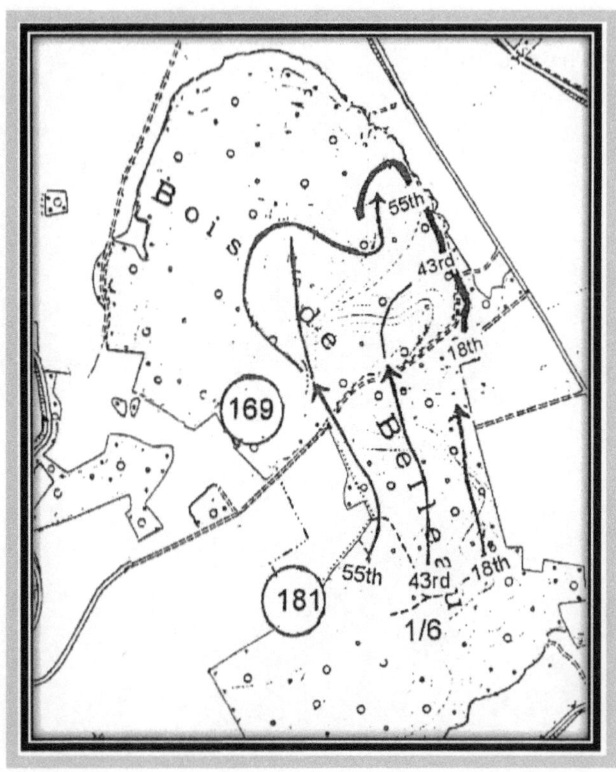

Belleau Wood

The helmet whacks my noggin as I sprint, holding the messenger bag and gas mask pouch. I'm running across the field between Lucy and Hellwood. Fifty yards to go. I dodge around a blackened leg—my breath catches in my throat. Damn. I trip on something and teeter on the edge of a shell hole. I've got to watch my footing, not the dead. But how do I not look at them?

This is the southern part of the field where so many have died. We hold the southern half of the wood now. The Heinies still own the north half. They can't see this part of the field except from the air. I carry a message to Lieutenant Colonel Wise, who commands what's left of 2/5, in the northernmost line in Belleau Wood. I turn north and slow to an easy jog along the western tree line.

Human decomposition, dysentery, and the sulfurous smell of gunpowder meld with the musty odors of the residual mustard and phosgene Doctor Heinie prescribed in large doses. I follow a well-used path into Hellwood. In front of me, the hilly jumble of boulders strewn with shattered timber resembles the aftermath of a tornado. The winding path through the woods snakes up a hill, then down through a ravine, up another hill, and down through a gully.

In Hellwood, which is what everyone calls it now—except the privates, who add an F-word to the front of it—I can't see more than about twenty feet in any direction. The trees still standing are skeletons, most stripped of leaves. Body parts and shreds of clothing hang from them like satanic decorations. It's tough to move faster than a drunken sailor. I go past exhausted men from 1/6 and make my way to the 2/5 headquarters in the narrower waist of the woods. Artillery fire picks up far to our north when I arrive.

Marines mill around, eating, cleaning rifles—which is one of the favorite things for Marines to do when they aren't being ordered to do something else. Makes me want a rifle of my own. I hand the message to a haggard lieutenant. Wise stands, writing a note, his uniform sagging, torn, filthy. I always thought his eyes were a little like a basset hound's. They're red and seem to melt with fatigue.

I sit on a nearby rock and sip warm canteen water while two lieutenants grumble about the artillery barrage being too far north. Wise hands the note to Hank Lenert and sends him back to Neville's PC. We runners take turns like in a relay race. Helps keep the legs fresh. Wise paces, looking to the north, a grimace on his face. Most of the men wear resigned looks as they do their pre-battle rituals and check their gear. Some stare at a horizon seen only by them.

At half past five, one captain, the remaining lieutenants, and a handful of platoon sergeants lead their Marines forward.

They make it less than fifty yards.

Heinie machine guns open up, rifles fire, grenades explode.

Colonel Catlin would have called this a "front-row seat." I wonder how he's doing. Haven't heard a word in days.

I want to get in the fight, but Wise orders me to stay with the headquarters unit. Marine battle screams fill the air between machine gun bursts. Two Marines charge forward. Blood spurts from one's back. He wavers, then crumples. His buddy, bleeding, crawls behind a rock and lays down fire with his rifle. I want to grab a rifle from one of the fallen. There are plenty strewn on the battlefield in front of me.

Wise paces, shouting orders, then scurries to the right. I shadow him as he moves back and forth along the line to see the battlefield. To stand on a high point would invite a sniper's shot like the one that felled Catlin. Wise staggers back and forth, like a runner who's gone beyond the limit.

"Find Milner. He's up that way, I think." Wise points. "Get a situation report."

I pull my compass out, take a bearing, and set off in the direction of Wise's pointed finger. I dodge around rocks and ruined tree trunks and hop over bodies. Most of the fire is to my left. Part of me wants to stop and give first aid, but I'd probably do more harm than good. Roiling masses of black flies feast on bloated corpses with green-and-black marbled skin. The artillery has blasted the dead into a gruesome anatomy lab. I pass two enormous rats gorging themselves on the face of a Marine with a gaping hole where his chest should have been. The sight tears at the remaining shards of my humanity. I struggle to concentrate on my job. I can't afford tunnel vision.

A small group of Marines rush a machine gun. The gun cuts them down two yards from their goal—all dead, as far as I can tell. A lone Marine charges in from my right. Before the gunners can traverse their weapon, he leaps into the pit—bayoneting one while he smashes the other in the face with his boot. I rush forward. The Marine corporal looks at me, the front of his uniform soaked with blood. He points toward the right.

I run alongside him, scanning the area, looking for threats, new energy tingling in my limbs. I hop over a dead Marine, stop, turn back, and crouch down beside the man. Dribbles of my sweat make spots on the back of the man's helmet. I roll the Marine over.

Bitter bile hits the back of my tongue. Saliva fills my mouth. I puke twice.

The kid's no older than me, still warm, dead from a gaping upper abdominal wound. I gulp back another wave of nausea. After a deep breath, I fumble with the buckle of the dead man's cartridge belt, my blood-soaked hands slipping as I secure it around my waist. I pick up his rifle, the bayonet dark with blood. I dash to my right, scanning side to side, desperate to find the corporal.

A yell pierces the air. The corporal grips his rifle in both hands, parrying a blow from a huge Heinie a half a head taller. I run toward the two, gripping my rifle in both hands, eyes on the fight. The corporal kicks the Heinie's left knee. The giant howls in pain, but the corporal loses his balance, dropping his rifle as he falls. The Heinie staggers toward the corporal, his back to me, and lifts the Mauser above his head for a butt-first blow. I take aim at the man's back and pull the trigger.

Click.

I pull the Springfield back for a bayonet strike.

No time to risk another misfire.

The Heinie's Mauser begins its killing arc toward the Marine.

The giant's back looms in front of me. I focus on my target, taking a deep breath.

I plant my left foot behind the hulk, then let out a Viking shout and thrust the rifle forward with all my might.

The rifle shudders.

The bayonet grinds into the man's back.

I stand transfixed in the moment. Dead weight pulls the rifle. I grunt and shove the body away from the corporal, who rolls twice to his left, grabs his rifle, and stands, panting. "Thanks."

The Heinie lies facedown in the grass. I yank. My rifle doesn't budge. I snort and pull. A gob of spittle flies from my mouth.

"Shoot," the other guy says.

"He's dead."

"Shoot and pull. Recoil'll free it."

I yank as I squeeze the trigger.

Click.

I cycle the bolt. A round pops out—a misfire. I pull the trigger—nothing. Cycle the bolt—no round in the chamber. Shit. I feed in a stripper clip from one of the ammo pouches and cycle the bolt again, then squeeze the trigger.

Warm, wet spray covers my face. The bayonet comes loose. I hold the rifle forward, blood dripping from the bayonet, and cycle the bolt.

I should have checked the magazine when I picked up the rifle. Rookie mistake. Too much time polishing boots.

An odd smell. What is it?

Aftershave cologne? On the Heinie? Who'da thunk.

"Know where Milner is?" I ask.

"No fucking clue."

"I'm under orders to find him."

"I outrank that order. Come on, Marine."

Chapter Fifty-Two
Private Carl Larsen

The corporal double-times it toward the noise of battle, which filters back to me as if I'm coming out of a trance. I follow. Rifle and machine gun fire surround us, our heads on swivels, seeking prey. Seeking Heinies.

The surrounding trees are more intact than in the southern end of Hellwood. Artillery has damaged some, but others still stand. The underbrush is thick in places, the grass beaten down.

The corporal stops and slumps behind a boulder, panting. I drop beside him. My uniform sticks to my chest. My hands are black with blood and dirt. The corporal looks at me and motions toward the right. "Maxim."

He clicks his tongue. I follow the man's gaze.

Three Marines hunker down behind a boulder thirty feet away. Their sergeant draws an attack plan in the air with his right index finger. He points at himself and draws his finger in a circle to the right. I give him a thumbs-up.

The sergeant speaks to the two Marines with him, then looks at us. He holds up three fingers for a countdown. On *three*, the corporal and I sprint in a broad leftward circle. I pour it on, dodging rocks, brush, and shattered wood.

Yells erupt from the opposite direction. As I near the nest, the gun crew is aiming toward the noise. They look down, fumbling for weapons. I leap over the side of the emplacement with a Marine battle yell that doesn't seem as though it comes from my own mouth. I drive the bayonet into the ammunition man's side. The corporal smashes the gunner's helmet with the butt of his rifle twice.

I yank my bayonet out, leaving my enemy writhing on the ground, screaming. His filthy, ageless face is tight with agony. His eyes lock on mine. A rifle shot startles me. Life leaks through a new red mass spreading where the man's heart was beating moments ago. All three of the Heinies are goners.

"You Catlin's orderly?" the corporal asks.

"Was. Larsen."

"Good work. Come on."

The corporal and sergeant lead our fire team forward. Three others join us at a trot. The corporal dives behind a boulder and points to his left. A machine gun chops the air, three gray Heinie helmets bobbing inches above the rim of the nest. Shooting at a group of Marines. The sergeant lays out a plan. "Go on my mark." The noise makes it almost impossible to hear him. The corporal looks at me, then the sergeant, and nods.

The sergeant shouts, "Go!"

The corporal and I jump up and sprint. I scan the area around us as we dodge obstacles. The Maxim crew fires a long burst at the Marines attacking them from the front. A scream. One Marine hit. The others on his team come into sight from the opposite direction. Our two teams converge on the nest at the same time. My bayonet silences the gunner.

With a yell, I give the bastard three extra thrusts for the Marine he shot.

The other two lie dead. Then I see it—the chain between the machine gun and the gunner's leg. I use my bayonet to bob back the dead man's head. What the hell? Shit, he's just a kid. Can't be more than sixteen.

Shouts from the right catch my ear. I look around for the corporal, who points and sprints toward the sound.

A Marine lies in a small clearing, writhing, blood staining his left thigh. Another Marine rushes toward him. A shot rings out. The rescuer falls. We hunker down behind a rock formation. I take off my helmet and slither to the right.

The shot sounded like it came from above us—in a tree?

Where is he?

Above. I scan the trees, searching for a sniper.

I lead with the front sight of my Springfield and ease my way around the boulder, peering into the trees, seeking my target. Each inch seems like a lifetime. Those Marines are lures to draw others to their death. Sweat and blood glue my uniform to my shoulders and hips. I blink away a dribble of sweat threatening my left eye. The moaning of the two men urges me on, but I can't rush or he'll see my movement.

I move an inch.

Watch.

Another inch.

There.

A boot planted on a tree branch. I ease the front sight up ever so slowly, a slight tremble in my arms. I slow my breathing, trying to remember how many shots I have left.

Three? A good rifleman would know. I make sure my safety's off.

I snug the stock to my cheek, eyes searching for the target's center. I can just make out the top of the helmet and bring my front sight in line with a dark area of leaves where the torso must be. I tighten my cheek weld.

I slip the pad of my right index finger on the trigger . . . slow breath in . . . out . . . throat open . . . take up the trigger slack.

The Springfield smacks my shoulder. My right ear rings. I cycle the bolt in a fluid motion and hope my ammo count is right. My eye never leaves the target. Nothing moves.

The branches tremble. A body tumbles in a flurry of leaves and bounces off a lower limb with a loud crack before sprawling on the ground.

"Go!" A shout from the left.

I run toward the sniper, Springfield to my cheek, front sight never leaving the man's chest. I'll put another round into him if he moves. He's still breathing. His rifle lies next to him.

The damned Heinie lies on the ground, his lungs tearing the air, blood spreading across the left side of his chest. Pink froth foams from lips on a face that looks like it has never felt a razor. I look into eyes as blue as mine. He could have graduated from high school with me last year. I glance at the wounded Marines for a moment. The others with me are tending to them. I break my cheek weld and lower the bayonet onto the Heinie's chest.

He'd used the wounded for bait. Fuck him. The bayonet shatters a rib as I jam it into the chest. The boy's screams mixed with my Viking yell, each staring into the other's pupils.

Then the eyes go lifeless.

My muzzle indents the Heinie's chest, the bayonet going all the way through to the ground. I plant my right foot next to the rifle, jerk it free, and jog over to the others. My heart pounds cadence against my breast-bone. I glance around. The illusion of glory lies in ruins around me. The Heinie was just doing his job, like me. He'd have done the same to me if I were lying there. I've heard the stories from others. This is kill or be killed. Before this, I thought I'd be frightened, or maybe exhilarated. None of those words fit. This is more like an electric current humming through me, hyper-alert, sense of smell heightened, assaulted by more odors and sounds than my brain can analyze, muscles wired.

The corporal pats me on the shoulder. Litter-bearers and a corpsman scamper toward the wounded men, so recently used as bait. Our team forms a perimeter as the corpsman shouts orders to the litter-bearers while pulling a tourniquet tight on the bleeding leg. I top off my magazine and hunt for more snipers in the trees. The sergeant leads us to the right after the litter-bearers haul the wounded away. I take my compass out—we're going northeast.

The uniforms of the men with me are wet with gore, filth, and sweat. Their hard, grimy, blood-spattered faces are primeval. Blood and rage glue my hands to my rifle. We double-time it, eyes scanning for the next foe.

Voices in front bring us to a halt. The sergeant ducks behind a fallen tree, motioning us to join him. Scattered rifle fire echoes in the woods along with shouts, screams, and distant cannon fire. I crouch near upended roots and inch my way around. Marines surround about sixty disarmed Heinies next to a partially destroyed octagonal stone building.

A Marine lieutenant appears relaxed as he talks with a Heinie captain, both smoking. The Heinie reaches into a pocket and hands the Marine something. We make our way toward the group. The officers stare at us as though we're ghosts. As we near, the Heinie captain says, "*Mein Gott*, your troops are most reckless fellows."

The Marine lieutenant nods. "I'll have two of my men lead you and your company to our Battalion PC, Captain."

"Lieutenant Milner, sir?" I ask.

"Yeah."

"Colonel Wise sent me to find out how things are going."

Milner stares at the guys with me. "Seems like we're doing pretty well. But we don't have the whole place under control yet. Tell him to send more men up."

"All right. I'll head back and let him know." I pat the corporal, whose name I still don't know, and run off.

Lieutenant Colonel Wise looks at me with weary eyes when I get back. "Carl, I assume there's a reason your report took four hours to reach me."

"Yes, sir."

"Doesn't look like I have to ask why. Find Milner?"

"He said to tell you to send more men up."

"Wonder where he thinks I'm going to find them." Wise scribbles a note and hands it to me. "Get this to Neville."

I pick up the rifle.

"Leave the rifle. I may need it."

Chapter Fifty-Three
Major Ab Johnson

La Loge Farm
Thursday, June 13, 1918

My actions on the sixth have earned me an unexpected reputation—that of a lunatic. I suppose that's a step up from an idiot. They're right, of course. I'm too old and should be wise enough to know better. The only thing more common here than lunacy is courage. I don't think the latter applies to me—just doing my job.

Still no sign of Jack. I check when I can and keep my eyes open. No word. I haven't seen Bill Stevens either.

I manage to get a shower, then talk with several neatly attired staff officers over breakfast. They're out of touch with the battlefield. Their bravado is typical of those in the rear echelons. One thing I noticed in my first tour of army service is that bravado is proportional to the distance between the man and the battlefield. Those in the shit say little if anything outside their unit.

My biggest concern now is the condition of the Marines themselves —sleep- and food-deprived, filthy, infested with lice, many with dysentery. *Done in* is the phrase I hear time and again. Harbord has asked for a relief force to come in and give his men a rest, but someone seems to stand between him and AEF command.

I go to the intelligence office and find Ira Cunningham, alone, reading a report. Ira looks up over his reading glasses. "How you doing, you old buzzard?"

"Ready to explode," I say.

"What about?"

"Where do I start? Hear about the gas attack?"

"Of course. Sounded like your new degassing station worked well."

"In the nick of time. What do you know about the relief issue? We've been requesting it since the tenth, and it seems like Chaumont is stonewalling us. French doctrine is no more than five days in continuous contact with the enemy without relief, and they're supposed to be running this show. Our boys have been in the shit for two weeks solid."

"I'm pretty sure I know which feather merchant is responsible. Remember Lieutenant Colonel Walt Gordon? Pershing sent him here to look into that last week. One of my backchannels told me he reported that your boys are fit, raring to go, and in no need of relief."

"I remember him. But how could he know? He never left headquarters."

"Magic of creative staff work and statistics. Like I said—feather merchant." Ira winks. "Hell, they're Marines and he's army. Who cares?"

"Don't rub it in. Any chance we can get something through that backchannel of yours?"

"Not good enough to overrule a colonel."

My neck tenses. What'll it take to get Ira to move on this? My jaw muscles tighten.

A worried expression crosses Ira's face. "I'll see if I can feed it up the intelligence stovepipe, but don't get your hopes up. Seems like there's more than that. What else is sticking in your craw?"

"It's odd. Somehow, I've become something of a confidante of General Harbord's."

"Must be your honest face."

I laugh. "I guess I've used my old techniques—the ones for cultivating *sources*."

Ira raises his left eyebrow. "Really?"

"Seems like he needs someone to talk to. In confidence. And . . . maybe I'm thinking about after the war—if I survive. An article? Maybe a book. Won't hurt to know the general's mind."

"Impressions?"

There are a number I need to keep under my hat, even with a friend. "He's one of the brightest people I've ever met. Incredibly hard working. Systematic, methodical. No meaningful combat experience before this. Not biased against the Marines like I was. Not a West Pointer—which at this moment seems to be a big plus. He's learning fast."

"Fast enough?"

I take a sharp breath in. "No." I ease the breath out. "Mistakes he's making in June, he probably won't make in July."

"It's still June."

"Aye, there's the rub, to quote *Hamlet*."

"Bundy?"

"He seems cowed by the French above him. He must have done something right to make major general. I think it sticks in his craw to be commanding a division with Marines. Like most of his army contemporaries, he looks down his nose at the Marine Corps. The one holding this division together seems to be Colonel Brown. He ran the army open warfare school before coming to the division. He had the right ideas about how to do the attack on the sixth, but Bundy was hogtied by the French battle plan—and there, I blame General Duchene. If folks back home knew? They'd fire Bundy and send a guillotine over on the next ship for Duchene." I stand and grab my helmet. "Up for a ride?"

Ira groans. "In your sidecar?"

"Best one in the division, I promise. Know how to use your gas mask?"

We leave division HQ on *Helen* for the field hospital at Bezu and talk with several Marines in the enlisted ward. Our best source turns out to be a corporal with Fifty-First Company named Pickering, who tells us about the fight and the dreadful condition of the Marines in the woods. It's a frank conversation—the sort an army staff officer like Lieutenant Colonel Gordon wouldn't have with a lowly corporal. Pickering is a very intelligent and perceptive young man from a well-to-do family. It seems odd that his education and connections hadn't led to a commission. Which makes me think of Jack and Bill—both college graduates, one commissioned and the other enlisted.

After that, we head to Lucy. Intermittent artillery shells reverberate in the distance. A steady breeze from the west ensures that gas will not be a problem today. I check in with the aid station staff and introduce Ira. Beck and Malcolm Pratt look fatigued but are holding steady. Both have irritated-looking eyes. They ask about Lester Pratt and Orlando Petty. I've lost track of Petty and Pratt.

I go outside and look toward the southwestern arm of Belleau Wood, nearest Lucy. Desultory shots echo in the northern section.

"Time to take a hike and see the place." I know the southernmost portion is safe and lead the way south to Gob Gully, picking my way toward the shattered forest. Residual gas lingers in low spots. I move up higher in the depression, mingling with the flow of Marines heading to and from the woods. Ira stumbles and curses behind me.

"Smells like a train loaded with dynamite blew up in the stockyard," Ira says.

After two hundred yards, I mount a rise and enter the wood. The descriptions I've heard are accurate. "Shit. Looks like a hurricane blew through," I say. Piles of fallen wood and boulders as big as boxcars obstruct the view in every direction. After walking thirty feet, I can't tell north from south, unable to see more than fifteen or twenty feet in any direction. Fragments of branches and trunks threaten to spear me if I turn the wrong way. I'll be impaled if I have to dive for cover. Battle detritus lies scattered everywhere, shreds of uniforms, packs, boots, broken guns, shrapnel, mess kits.

"Add latrine to my last description," Ira says. "Shit, what's that?" He points toward something hanging from a tree branch twenty feet away.

"Leg." I choke back the urge to vomit and hear Ira do the same.

We wind our way through the remnants of the three battalions. The area is pocked with shell holes and foxholes occupied by Marines. Some clean rifles or sharpen bayonets while others smoke. I stop to talk with a cluster of veterans and then to a group of replacements. The veterans sit apart from the greenies. I make my way over to two men standing apart from the rest. A buck sergeant is talking with a first sergeant about the same size as Joel Boone and Arthur Beck. His weathered face looks as old as me. The phrase "old salt" comes to mind.

"Got a moment?"

"Got lots of moments, sirs," the buck sergeant says.

"I'm Johnson. This is Cunningham, from G-2. We're assessing the condition of your men."

"'Bout time someone did. Name's Stecker."

"Daly," the older man says.

I take a deep breath. First Sergeant Daly is a living legend. Two Medals of Honor.

"How are the men holding up?" I ask.

"Well, sir, we're in good fighting spirits," Stecker says.

"I can see that," I say. "But we're not here to include your names in a report. I'd prefer to skip the hogwash you have to feed to army officers taking notes and tell us the unvarnished truth, off the record. Is this unit in any shape to go into battle?"

"Wrong question, sir," Daly says. "Been in battle since we got here. The right question is—how long can this unit continue to fight and remain effective?"

I give him a *go on* roll of my right hand.

"Major, a Marine never quits," Stecker says. "But there's a point when he's done in. My men hit that days ago. The replacements are as full of spirit as they are scared shitless. This unit needs a breather—showers, fresh uniforms, take a shit in peace, and get a few good nights of rack time. Hot chow would do a world of good." Stecker pauses and looks at his men.

"I have all these replacements to deal with." Daly looks straight in my eyes. "Hell, we had months of training before we went into the trenches in Verdun. The greenies are barely out of boot camp. No gas training. Haven't had a chance to set 'em straight. Don't know their names. New lieutenant doesn't know mine. Major, between you and me, he scares the shit out of me. Most of my privates have been in the Corps longer than him, fresh out of college and all."

The last comment stabs my heart. I struggle to keep my face

composed as I fish a cigarette pack from my coat pocket and offer one to Daly and another to Stecker. I slip one between my lips and strike the wheel on my lighter. I light Daly's first. Ira lights one of his own. We puff as we look around at the men.

"Heard about your battle cry," I say, glancing at Daly.

Daly winces. "Gibbons made that up. I didn't call my men sons of bitches. I might have said something like 'For Christ's sake, men, come on. Do you want to live forever?' But Major, it was in the heat of battle."

"Besides, Gibbons was nowhere near there," Stecker says.

"Great battle cry, regardless," I say.

We puff on our smokes, out of words, as I look over the Marines around me.

"Didn't smoke till I got here, sir." Sergeant Stecker eases smoke out his nostrils. "Used to think the fuckers stank. Helps cover the stench."

"Here." I hand him the pack.

Ira hands his pack to Daly.

I finish the cigarette and field strip the remains. "Thanks." Ira and I spend another hour poking around, mostly to make sure the lieutenant Daly talked about is not Jack Johnson.

Ira and I arrive at General Harbord's headquarters after 1500 hours. Harbord and Brown stand by the map in the staff room, talking, Harbord pointing. Harbord motions me over. "Pops, Major, you look like you've been on the dusty trail again. Where've you been this time?"

"Ab and I talked about the relief matter," Ira says. "Went to do something Lieutenant Colonel Gordon forgot to do."

"When Walt Gordon was here, he didn't say anything about reviewing the need for relief," Harbord says. "Well, you know how much pressure we're under to keep a stiff upper lip, as the Brits say. If I'd known, I'd have been blunter on that. Now—"

"Do you have any couriers going to Chaumont soon?" Ira asks.

"End of the day."

"I'll type up a memorandum and send it to my boss. Not my job, but my orders are vague enough that he probably won't fire me."

"I hope he can help," Harbord says. "Bundy doesn't seem to be pushing it. The French only take him seriously when he declares victory. I'm rotating the units to give the men some rest. But I'm replacing the exhausted with the tired, and in so doing, depriving both of sleep and chow."

"In the meantime?" I ask.

"Another sleepless night. Everyone is moving tonight except 1/6."

"Shit." I take in a sharp breath. I shouldn't have said that.

Chapter Fifty-Four
Medical Corpsman Lyle McCormack

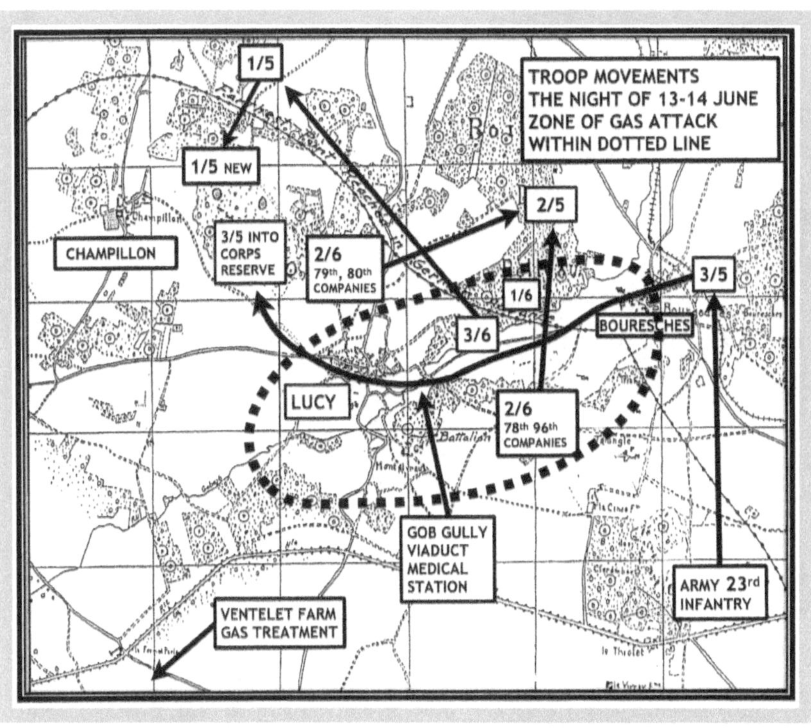

Belleau Wood

Patching up the survivors of Captain Williams's company went well into the evening of the twelfth. The dead lie where they fell in a field still owned by Hun machine gunners. I think about the guys I took care of yesterday. The private with the leg wound made it out. Lieutenant Johnson, the one with the destroyed face, is still out there. I hated leaving him, but I took care of thirty more guys in the time it would have taken me to get him back—if we even made it. Like lieutenants, there are few of us original corpsmen left.

Arthur ordered me back to the regimental aid station after we brought Captain Williams in. Lieutenant Boone sent me to bed after I polished off three bowls of stew. I wrote up copies of the wound cards of those I figured were dead, like the lieutenant, and handed them to Boone before I hit the sack. Today, Boone has kept me busy at Montgivrault but hasn't let me go back into the woods—the boss seems to understand that a man can only take so much. He's an exceptional leader.

Boone sends me to Gunny Stockham's platoon after supper—another bowl of stew, but at least it's hot. The Ninety-Sixth is in the woods east of Montgivrault. About half of the trees stand intact, giving us some shade from the blistering sun. The air's muggy but smells almost clean here. That's a relief. Marines sleep in foxholes while others talk, smoke, and clean rifles. I find Stockham in a foxhole, smoking, chatting with a corporal and Second Lieutenant Cates. Stockham looks up as I come near. "Look what the dog dragged in."

"Haven't seen a dog in a couple weeks," I say. "Last one was a border collie named Abby. She was with two kids from Bouresches—orphaned between here and there, by the way. But that was before all this started, eh?"

I look into Stockham's eyes. A silent message passes between us. We've been there too, orphaned, and hope the kids and their dog land in a good place. But are there any good places for orphans in a country ravaged and bankrupted by war?

"Dogs are too smart to come anywhere near this hellhole." Stockham inhales a lungful of smoke. "If we had any brains, we wouldn't be here, either. Some idiot reported that Bouresches was over-run. Ordered us to rush in to retake it. Turns out it was just a panicked greenie lieutenant. Thing is, those bastards—" He points at the German balloon observers floating in the eastern sky. "—watched us the whole time. They know we're here. Can't figure why they haven't dropped arty on us. Always do. Makes me think they're cooking up something special. I don't want to stick around to find out what. Keep your helmet on. I got room in this hole. Stay close."

Cates sits on the rim of the next foxhole. "Place isn't safe. With them watching, we'll have to wait until dark to move out." Cates removes his helmet and gas mask box, then dribbles canteen water over his head with a satisfied sigh.

I fidget, checking and rechecking my gear in the fading evening light. Rumors swirl about a move into Hellwood, but no orders come. I work my way among restless Marines, checking their wound packs while they grouse about the Heinie sausages staring at us.

At full dark, I want to get a move on. Where are the orders?

The woods are black now. The murmur of quiet conversations surrounds me along with the occasional clatter of gear as Marines shift around in their foxholes.

A star shell pops above us and floats in the night sky. Ours or theirs? It casts everything in creepy shadows. We still don't have orders to move, and everyone's getting antsy.

Don't they know we've got to get out of here?

Grinding noise from the west catches my ear. Word of food sweeps over the company like a wave, and a welcome aroma calls my name.

The mess staff from Montgivrault rolls in with their kitchen carts filled with hot stew. Men jump out of their foxholes, mess kits in hand, moths to a flame. My stomach growls as I join the line—at the end, since I had some stew earlier. Louvered lamps light the carts as the cookies dish out hot chow.

Stockham and I sit on a log in the light of a star shell bobbing high above. First Lieutenant Robertson, the company commander since Captain Duncan's death, ambles over with their new first sergeant and a corporal. "We move out at 0100 hours. The arty'll pop off some star shells to give us light. It should be okay to use lanterns until we're within about a hundred yards of 2/5."

"What's the path like?" Stockham asks as Lieutenant Cates sits down next to me. Cates doesn't have his gas mask pouch in place. He must have left it in his foxhole when he went for chow. I want to say something, but figure Cates knows what he's doing.

"Bad during full light," Robertson's corporal says. "Twists and turns. Your men can shoulder their rifles. We'll be in 1/6's sector. Tell 'em not to hit the deck if we take fire. The fallen wood is so jagged that you might as well dive on a bayonet. Have each man keep a hand on the pack strap of the one in front. I'll be in the lead."

"Think our replacements'll hold together, Gunny?" Robertson asks.

"Haven't done much night navigation, sir," Stockham says. "I've spent a lot of time the past few days hammering the fundamentals into them. Still, sir, I wish I could work with them a few more weeks. There's a lot of things that aren't automatic yet."

A chugging sound to the east.

Dagnabit.

Arriving shells.

Big ones screaming in.

The ground erupts. Shrapnel zips and zings, ricocheting among the trees.

I drop my mess kit.

We scramble for our foxholes amid shouts and explosions. In the faint light, I see a cloud arise. Hot stew showers me—a shell must have hit one of the carts.

I fumble with my gas mask pouch while I hoof it to our foxhole. The greenies behind me pile into the nearest foxhole. The chaotic scramble is like a crazy version of musical chairs. My heart pounds as a nearby tree erupts. The shriek of hot wind and shrapnel blows by my head. The world is a fractured jumble of Marines running among dropped lanterns and mess kits, harsh white star-shell light, shadows, tree trunks, and foxholes.

A musky odor penetrates my nose. Dagnabit, mustard gas.

Where's my foxhole?

Get the danged mask on!

Shrapnel howls.

The gas alarm clangs.

I drop my helmet and crouch down next to it and get my gas mask.

Something whacks me in the back.

I'm face down on the ground. I sit back up.

Dagnabit!

Mask in front of face. Mouthpiece in. Inhale. Pull mask over and tighten straps. Mouth out of mouthpiece. Blow out. Adjust goggles. My helmet is four feet ahead of me. I crawl and plop it on. My vision is foggy through the goggles. Where is the danged hole? Someone double-times past me. Stockham. I get up and hustle after him. Gunny dives into a foxhole. I tumble in next to him. A guy already in the hole grunts as we pile on top of him.

I reach into my medical pouch and fumble with my rubber gloves. Danged little finger. Shouts from the unmasked bore into my heart—probably greenies. I pop my head above the rim of the hole. Haunted light illuminates a chaotic scene with men scrambling, diving into the holes, clutching at the gas masks hanging from their chests, voices lost in the barrage and muffled by mouthpieces.

Stockham hops out and runs among the men, guiding the new guys to foxholes farther back, helping them don their masks.

Heck.

I get up and dart twenty feet to my left to help a man clutching for his mask. Shrapnel whistles through the air so close I feel its breath.

Shouting draws my eyes—Lieutenant Cates fumbles around his chest, his gas mask pouch missing. Cates yells, "Hall! Hall!"

Each man carries his own mask—we've got no spares. You don't offer your mask to another man unless you want to die a miserable death.

How could Cates, of all people, lose his mask? Cates scurries to a foxhole and drops in. Stockham runs toward ours, giving a thumbs-up. I drop into the hole, next to Stockham. The greenie we crushed when we first jumped in has left. Must have found his foxhole. I poke my head above the rim to look toward Cates's foxhole. What the heck? A Hun gas mask below an American helmet rises above the foxhole. A hand comes up and adjusts the mask, then gives me a thumbs-up gesture.

Corporal Hall must have taken the Hun mask for a souvenir. Now Cates wears it.

I'd laugh if anything here was funny. I hope nobody shoots him by mistake.

High-explosive rounds keep us in place while they drench us with gas. It smelled like mustard before I got my mask on.

Voices cry out in pain. Shock waves pound my body as though I'm on the bottom of a football pile-up with everyone kicking. I hug the ground, surrounded by the continual roar of explosions.

My air cuts out. Can't breathe.

I pull a breath—nothing—paw at the mask, the mouthpiece, the hose.

The respirator box strapped to my chest is pressed between the ground and me. That's it—my body's blocking the inspiratory tube on the filter box. I inch the box to the left.

Air flow. Slow, deep breaths. The panic fades.

The shelling continues. High explosives that shoot the air from my lungs, shrapnel zinging and careening like hail, and the gas. We knew it. We needed to move. Where were the danged orders? We shouldn't have waited for them.

A young voice screams for a corpsman, louder than a masked man can muster.

Then another.

Dang it.

I face Stockham, who pounds a fist into the dirt and scrambles out of the hole.

I follow.

Chapter Fifty-Five
Medical Corpsman Lyle McCormack

Corpsmen and litter-bearers are up. Shrapnel howls, and ricochets zoom through the trees. Dim light flickers from the kitchen cart lamps dropped in the confusion. Haze hangs in the air—dust and gas— made worse by filth on the yellow lenses of my gas mask.

Stockham motions me over, holding the beam of a flashlight on a Marine writhing on the ground with shrapnel wounds. I pull morphine out of my pack and jab the needle into the man's arm. I place a dressing and bandage on the largest wound. No wound card—no time and too dark. Stockham moves away, and I turn on my flashlight while I dress two more wounds. It's not like the flashlight will give away our position. Stockham works on a Marine five feet away, probably hit by the same blast as the man I'm finishing with. I scoot over and give the man a dose of morphine and look over the wounds.

"We've got to evac these boys," Stockham shouts in a voice muffled by his mask.

To run through the metal storm surrounding us is suicide. But we already made that choice when we left the foxhole. We can't leave these guys out in the open or in a gas-filled hole. I give Stockham a thumbs- up.

There are no litter-bearers in sight. They must be dead or already carrying men to the aid stations.

I hate fireman's carries.

Stockham helps me heft one on my back. Stockham shoulders the other like he's been doing it his whole life. We double-time it toward Montgivrault.

An explosion. A flash of pain.

Facedown in the dirt, as though God's own hand slapped me.

The man I was carrying smothers me.

My ears are haywire.

I roll the wounded man off and gasp for air. I snap on my flashlight. My man is unconscious—pulse good, though, and no new wounds. I crab-walk my way over to Stockham, who seems okay. The man he was carrying bleeds from several new wounds. Worse, his gas mask hangs in tatters beneath his helmet. The private's terrified eyes bore into me as I take care of his wounds. Immediate evacuation is his only hope.

Stockham yanks the private's helmet and shredded mask off. Then he pulls his own helmet and gas mask off.

What's he doing?

Stockham slips the carrying pouch over his head. "Open your mouth!" Stockham roars.

The private shakes his head. "No, Gunny."

"That's an order!" Stockham puts his mouthpiece in the private's mouth and positions the mask over the private's face in a practiced motion. "Clear it!" Stockham shouts over the din. He loops the pouch strap over the man's head and plops the helmet in place, tightening all the straps. Stockham puts his helmet back on and shouts, "Move!"

I shoulder my man as Stockham does the same.

Why the hell did Stockham do that?

Would—could—I do the same?

I don't have a death wish.

But then, why am I carrying a wounded Marine through this barrage?

Carry on.

My heart sinks when I see the Montgivrault aid station up ahead.

Flames lick the roof timbers, lighting it up like a beacon. A gas-masked man approaches. Reflections on his goggles make him look like a phantom. A muffled voice says, "Are you insane? Where's your mask, Gunny?" The man's a major—Holcomb?

Snot drips from Stockham's nose, tears streaming from puffy eyes. "His ripped, sir. I put mine on him," Stockham rasps.

"The station's kaput. Head to Lucy. Don't come back. Go!"

The shelling lightens between Montgivrault and Lucy. The highest concentration seems to be on our old position. Stockham coughs as we stagger forward. My breath rasps through the filters as I lug my load. The man stirs.

Stockham's cough sounds wet, urgent.

Up ahead, flickering lamps light the Lucy aid station. They seem so far away. I adjust my load. A coughing spasm stops Stockham. I stand beside him. "Go!" Stockham stumbles on.

The Lucy gas station is nestled in the Gob Gully culvert. Two corpsmen help us ease our casualties down and take charge. The muffled voice of a diminutive doctor, who must be Arthur, says, "Our spare masks were destroyed. Get the fuck out of here, Gunny!"

"Too many down back there. Give us each two litters." A coughing spasm stops Stockham.

"You're crazy."

"Give us the litters, doc."

Gunnery sergeants have a tone of voice that shuts the door on debate.

I look at him, eyes watering, face contorted, and will him to stay here, to evacuate to a degassing area, to give himself a chance to survive. Like Osborne, I love this great Marine.

Please.

Gunny muscles two litters onto his shoulders and staggers back toward our unit.

And I know he loves his Marines.

I heft collapsed litters over each shoulder and follow. My muscles scream as metal litter hinges dig in with each footstep. I stumble on something soft, regain my balance, and rush to catch up. A coughing spasm halts Stockham. I gasp for air through the resistance of the filter. Mist swirls in the star-shell light.

"Move," Stockham rasps.

The shelling picks up as we near Ninety-Sixth Company. We flick on our flashlights to find the wounded. Gas fog lurks above the ground while we work our way from casualty to casualty. We meet up with two other corpsmen and work together.

Stockham's cough worsens. I aim my flashlight at him. His face is red, melting in tears, snot, and bloody froth around his mouth. Stockham staggers to the next casualty, his cough continuous now. I move over to help, but Stockham shoves me away.

I scoot between foxholes and tap on a few Marines to carry litters with us. They help roll three wounded onto the stretchers. I aim my flashlight toward the sound of a disheartening wet wheeze. Gunny Stockham lies on the ground, gasping. I lug a litter over to him and motion three Marines to help me roll Stockham onto the litter. He's too weak to fight us, which tells me how bad he is. His eyes are swollen shut, bloody froth bubbling from his lips and nostrils.

I take my mouthpiece out and shout, "You guys get the other litters. We're all going to Lucy. Go!"

We need four to carry Stockham. I struggle to keep my grip on the right front litter handle, using one hand and then the next, fearing I'll drop my friend. Wet coughing pushes me to double-time it, pulling the others along.

A shell burst knocks us over in a shower of dirt. I check the others. Three minor lacerations. Masks intact. Stockham looks worse. "Move!"

My left forearm muscles burn, fingers cramped with pain. I change my grip, legs churning, willing the others on.

I search for the dim lamps of the aid station.

Where the dickens are they?

Light. A flicker.

Shadows moving.

Lucy.

As we near, I make out the sides of an ambulance. I take my mouthpiece out and shout to an approaching doctor. "Gas case. Gunny Stockham. He's in bad shape."

"Let's get a look at him."

"Nothing you can do here. He needs the gas hospital stat," I say.

"You sure?"

The doctor's flashlight plays on Stockham's bloated red face.

We load him into the ambulance as the doctor orders the drivers to get to Luzancy as fast as possible.

But I know it's too late. I order the three who helped me carry Stockham here to go to the degassing station. We're all contaminated as heck. I grab two collapsed litters. The men here are not wearing their gas masks at the moment. I take a few breaths without mine. It's so much easier to breathe without it. My heart is broken. Stockham sacrificed himself for men he may or may not have known. All he needed to know, and all I need to know, is that they're Marines.

"Where are you going?" the station chief asks.

"Back to my guys."

"Keep your fucking mask on."

"Aye, aye, sir."

Debris and spent shrapnel smack me as I hustle back to my unit. Litter frames dig into my shoulders. The image of Stockham's face seems to hover next to me. Figures emerge from the gas haze, backlit by the burning Montgivrault aid station. Major Holcomb leads what is left of the two companies west on the Lucy-Bouresches road.

I hand the litters to two privates and use my flashlight to check Marines as they trudge by. Light from the burning aid station flickers among men who seem like masked apparitions. I hear coughing over the noise of the shelling. I work my way to the back of the line. Gas effects will be worse there. The other corpsmen and I separate men with torn uniforms and masks, ordering them to head to Lucy. They'll be no good in a fight. "Anyone left back there?" I ask the last man in the line.

"Nobody alive."

The ragged column departs Montgivrault, our shadows before us. How many of my friends lie dead or wounded around the aid station? Is Lieutenant Boone still alive?

I gasp for air, pulling hard through the filter box, hoping it will hold. They never told us how long the filters are good for. My chest heaves, empty.

Gunny.

Part of my spirit is back there.

I'm the only orphan standing. The time I introduced Osborne to Stockham seems like a lifetime ago. I remember those two orphaned French kids, only a few years younger than me, burying their dead mother in Lucy.

I feel so alone. As though I lost the last member of my family.

The column turns right and staggers through Gob Gully, about a hundred yards east of Lucy, and then follows a path about twenty feet from the tree line, along the western edge of Hellwood. I grab the pack strap of the man in front of me to keep him from falling. We take a winding course around smoking gas shells. A shell screams in and we hit the dirt. Debris smacks me. When it settles, I hustle toward the front of the column to be with what's left of Major Holcomb's headquarters unit.

The path heads into Hellwood, and now we snake our way between boulders, fallen trees, and shell holes. Twenty minutes later, louvered lanterns spill weak light onto a collection of Marines with bare faces ahead of us. Lieutenant Colonel Wise waves a flashlight along our column. "This it?"

"Most of my men were gassed." Holcomb strips off his mask.

"Some relief force." Wise shakes his head.

I want to shoot Wise. Doesn't he know what we just went through?

Instead, I walk away, strip off my uniform, and shake it to get the oily mustard gas residue off. I gaze at the ruined trees in the lantern light, thinking about Stockham—the hand of friendship he offered us orphans, the courage of his sacrifice. Stockham is sure to die. Part of me understands, but if it comes down to it, would *I* do the same?

I sit next to Lieutenant Cates.

"Here, use this." Cates hands me a bar of soap. He's naked, covered with soapsuds.

"Thanks, Lieutenant." I soap up with canteen water, just as Stockham and I taught the greenies—the soap neutralizes the mustard. "Glad you found that mask, sir."

"How's Gunny?"

"Bad. Don't think he'll make it."

"Shit. He's my best man."

"And my last friend."

"McCormack, you're surrounded by friends."

Chapter Fifty-Six
Major Ab Johnson

La Loge Farm
Friday, June 14, 1918

General Harbord shouts into the phone. "This is a mess. The gas officers are out doing an assessment." He listens. "Should have their report back in a few hours, sir." A pause. "I'm sure it was hell back there too, sir." He slams down the receiver, muttering an obscenity.

He turns to me. "I need some air." His face is haggard, red with anger.

"Mind if my friend from intelligence tags along, sir?" I ask.

"I could use some intelligent company." Harbord slips his gas mask pouch into the alert position, puts on his helmet, and walks out of the room. We climb into the general's staff car, and Harbord orders his driver to take us to Colonel Neville's headquarters in La Voie.

"One of the worst things about command is the not knowing," Harbord says. "Not knowing what's happening up front. Not knowing what's happening to your men. Or even worse, knowing bad things *are* happening and having to wait for hours to hear the details. Phone lines go down, runners are killed, messages are lost. By the time the message for an emergency artillery strike arrives, conditions may have changed.

All your men may be dead. Or perhaps they won a hard-fought victory only to have their own artillery obliterate them. You heard about the panicked lieutenant in Bouresches." He holds his right thumb and forefinger up with a quarter-inch gap. "We came this close to wiping out 3/5 —again—because of that idiot. The men out there aren't the only ones who don't sleep at night."

The driver turns left onto the road to La Voie.

"It was easier when the commanding general sat atop his horse on a hill overlooking the battlefield," I say. "When artillery used cannonballs, soldiers had muskets and swords, and nothing traveled faster than a horse."

"If only we had secure wireless sets," Harbord says. "Honestly, Pops, if we make it through this war, it will be smart to invest in a company making those."

"We're working on it, sir, but I'm not sure we'll have much soon," Ira says. "And we're way behind everyone else on codes and ciphers. Hell, the whole concept of intelligence needs to change. When the highest-ranking officer with an understanding of the value of intelligence is a colonel . . ."

"Tell me about it. Your boss, Nolan, is the only colonel to head a full G-Section in the AEF," Harbord says. "I've encouraged Pershing to promote him."

The car pulls in front of the Fifth Regiment PC in La Voie. Ira wanders off toward the medical building when I enter the PC. Colonel Buck Neville leans over a map in the staff room.

"Status report, Buck?" Harbord says.

"Things are not good, sir," Neville says. "My men are exhausted . . . well, you know the story. Raw nerve is all that keeps them going."

"And the fact that they're Marines," I say.

"I've been requesting relief since the tenth, but we painted too rosy a picture of our morale to Walt Gordon," Harbord says. "The earliest relief might—*might*—be on the twenty-fifth."

What he doesn't say, but I know, is that Major General Bundy makes comments that tell me he still has it in for the Marine Corps. I'm pretty sure that if the Fourth Brigade was army, they'd have gotten a break. Of course, I can't prove that, so I keep my trap shut. Majors don't take on major generals in this army without ironclad proof. The matter grinds on me as I listen.

"Jesus." Neville stretches his back. "When 2/6 arrived to relieve 2/5, Wise refused to leave. Not enough men to hold the zone."

Neville goes to a desk. He opens a drawer, grabs something, and returns to General Harbord. "Here, we think it's about time you put these on." Neville hands Harbord two Marine Corps collar pins.

Harbord looks down at the pins.

Neville smiles. "Well, General?"

"Give me a hand." Harbord stands at attention.

I take one pin and Neville the other. We remove Harbord's army collar pins and replace them with the Eagle, Globe, and Anchor. Neville stands at attention and salutes. I join him. Harbord returns it with a determined glint in his eyes and smiles as his hand comes down.

"Thank you. I'm honored, Buck." He takes a deep breath. The pins seem to have done more to lift Harbord's spirits than anything I could have imagined.

"Buck, you have any more of those?" Harbord says.

Neville goes to his desk and returns.

"As the honorary Marine commanding the best damned brigade in the war, I would be honored, Colonel Neville, if you will help me perform my first act in that role." Harbord steps next to me. "Let's make a Marine father official too."

They secure the pins on me, and it's my turn to salute. The old me would have objected. The new me feels a warm flush of pride, though I'm humbled that these men think I deserve these pins I know Marines hold sacred.

"Let's get back to La Loge," Harbord says. "We have a battle to win."

I follow Harbord out the door. Commander Dessez and Ira stand by the road, talking. I approach. Ira's face is like a ghost.

"What?" I ask.

"Pops, come on over to my office. I have something to show you," Dessez says.

I poke a fresh plug of tobacco into my pipe and stop to light it. I jog to catch up with Dessez and follow him into the aid station. Dessez sits down behind his field desk and picks up a book of wound cards. Ira stands at the back of the room. Dessez looks up with an expression that sends a knife through me. "What's wrong?" I ask, not wanting to hear the answer.

"Take a load off." Dessez points to a campaign chair next to the desk.

"What?"

"Well . . ."

"What." My mouth is dry, throat tight, pulse quickening.

"The first letter of the first name is *J*, but the rest of the name and the serial number were unreadable." Dessez hands me a wound card. My hand shakes as I read. *Johnson, J, 2nd Lt.* My chest is empty. Airless. My life boils down to a single card breaking my heart.

I hand the card back and stare at the floor, my vision blurred.

The only sound is the pulse in my ears, as though only part of me is in the room.

Jack.

Dead.

A hand reaches out—Dessez—bringing me back into the world. "Where is he?"

"The corpsman said he was still alive when he left him, but he was in the middle of the field with a mortal wound. Fifty-First Company. You know what happened to them."

"Did he make it to the aid station in Lucy?" Ira asks, his voice weak, distant.

"Still in the field."

"But how do you have the wound card?" Ira asks.

"That particular corpsman wrote out a copy of the card on each man he thought wouldn't make it," Dessez says. "Not standard procedure. You ever meet a corpsman named McCormack? Lyle McCormack?"

"No." I'm stunned. Unable to think.

"You sure he died?" Ira asks.

"We've evacuated all the living," Dessez says. "We haven't been able to retrieve the dead from that area. The Germans shoot anyone who enters that field."

"Yeah, I understand," I say. "I wouldn't want to lose any of our boys that way." My vision clouds. My head seems bloodless, light, far away—unable to comprehend what I'm hearing. I take a deep breath.

"We don't know if it's your son," Dessez says. "Might not be."

"Or it is, and he died alone, out there . . . still there."

"Can I do anything?"

Jack. Oh God, Jack.

"Don't write my wife, please. Not until we know for sure." I turn to Ira, who wipes his eyes with a handkerchief. "Keep it under your hat, old friend."

"I'll let Lieutenant Cooke know," Dessez says. "Notification would go through him. He's about the only officer left in that company."

"I need air. Thanks for telling me this yourself." I get up and stagger out of the tent. Ira follows.

Ira and I walk through La Voie in silence. When we approach the last tree in the lane, Ira stops and envelops me in his arms. We stand, me sobbing, filled with memories of walks in Butte with the kids, hikes in the mountains, camping trips, fishing. Ira lets go with a soft pat on my back. I wipe my eyes and start walking toward La Loge.

It feels as though I'm walking through a tunnel, the sounds, sights, and smells around me blocked out. My mind sifts through two decades of voices and images. I try to grasp them, as though I might lose each in the next moment as another memory drifts before me. How will I tell Helen?

"I can't believe it," Ira says. "I remember the times we had when the kids were, well, kids. Out at your place, Jack and Trudy playing in the sandbox. Best friends." The last words die in Ira's throat. "Thing is, Ab —might not be Jack."

"I suppose." But at the moment, all I see is a death mask of Jack's shattered face with a gaping hole. A gaping hole in my heart.

I touch my new right collar pin and hold my finger on it. Jack, please forgive me.

"No, I mean, how many Johnsons are in the service?" Ira says. "And how many have a first initial of *J*? Jack's not the only one. I don't think we should rush to conclusions."

"Yeah, but how many of them are Marine second lieutenants? Replacement officers? The pool gets much smaller."

"Still, I bet there's more than one."

"Frustrating thing is, I don't know." I stop to stare toward the east, where the distant crack of rifles and stutter of machine guns echo. "I need to go out there—find out. You with me?"

"Ab, think about it. His body's in the northern part of the field. The Boche shoot anything that moves there. And what if we find the body? Is that the last memory you want? To see him like that? You heard Dessez—he was shot in the face. You might not recognize him."

"I'd know."

"And when a sniper shoots you, Helen loses two in that damned field," Ira says. "What the hell do I tell her then, if they don't shoot my old bald head?"

"I suppose you're right."

"What would Jack tell you to do?"

"Stay alive. Carry on. Take care of his Marines. Our Marines."

Chapter Fifty-Seven
Major Ab Johnson

Jack is dead. Like the other lieutenants, NCOs, and privates, he was little more than a pawn, a statistic to the generals and politicians. Catlin's wound had a greater impact on the generals than a dozen lieutenants, or a thousand Marine privates. My jaw tenses and anger rushes from my heart. Jack's now a statistic to the staff officers wearing perfectly starched shirts, scurrying from room to room in headquarters buildings throughout France. Just another cipher on the page of a report in triplicate. A Marine, and we all know they don't count for much. Don't we?

And here we are, Ira and me, amid them, but not part of them. Not real staff officers—no careerist desire to become colonels or generals. Just answering a call, hoping for peace and a return to an editor's desk.

I touch my Marine collar pin. I'm the biggest idiot in the world.

The saddest idiot in the world.

The idiot who sent his son to war without a blessing or a prayer.

We're about halfway to La Loge when Ira stops. "I hear the impeccable Lieutenant Colonel Gordon's here, doing what staff officers with perfectly pressed uniforms do. I have an idea of how you can honor all the J. Johnsons in the Corps. Let's create a little theater." Ira lays out his plan while we walk.

He's trying to distract me. To cheer me up. And I'm pretty sure he isn't going to give me a gun, though I feel like using one on Gordon.

After arriving back at Fourth Brigade headquarters, Ira and I stay in the staff room while news filters in. Harbord, Brown, and Smith are in the room with us. In typical staff officer fashion, Lieutenant Colonel Walt Gordon is at division HQ, nowhere near the front.

I steel myself and compose my face to hide the emotions boiling underneath as I listen to the gas officer's report. "The Germans used high-explosive and shrapnel shells to fix the troops in position while drenching them with Yellow Cross. The area involved is over one mile long and about half that wide, centered along Gob Gully. Between six and seven thousand gas shells. They're still dropping it in, though it has slacked off. Sir, we have about twenty-five hundred men in that zone."

"Casualties?" Harbord asks.

"Incomplete, sir. Best guess is between seven and nine hundred—so far."

The room is silent.

"General, any word from your source regarding relief?" Colonel Brown asks.

"Pops?" Harbord asks.

"What?" The question, and the name, startle me. I take a deep breath, trying to clear my head. "I should let my man from intelligence answer that."

Ira clears his throat. "Gordon is singing your praises and telling everyone at headquarters that there is no need for relief."

"And they're sending the good news to the French. Here's what our French commander says." Harbord picks up a dispatch and reads: "*The commanding general, American Second Division, will make all necessary dispositions for the liberal echelonment in depth of the Marine brigade, in such manner as to permit resting the battalions by reliefs within that brigade.*" Harbord crumples the paper and pitches it across the room.

I want to crumple the bastard who wrote it. I clasp my shaking hands behind my back. My new Eagle, Globe, and Anchor pins whisper to me. "To say that requires complete ignorance. How many men does he think we have? What he's ordering is physically impossible unless we shrink our front to a couple hundred yards." I look over at Ira, who nods.

Harbord dismisses the gas officer and the others, including Ira, and then motions for me to shut the door. I take a seat while Harbord settles into the chair behind his desk. "Regardless of what our army brethren say about our Marines, Pershing told me this is the finest brigade in the AEF. It probably stuck in his craw to utter those words, but there you have it. And I've been proud to lead these men. But it breaks my heart to see how they look now. Any other unit would've folded under the conditions they've fought in for these past two weeks. Gordon must be demented."

"I . . ." I want to tell Harbord about Lieutenant Johnson, but the words stick in my throat. I blink back tears and take a deep breath. Ira's plan crosses my mind. "My friend Ira told me Gordon's at division HQ. Feel up for a ride, sir?" I struggle to keep my face neutral. The Montana part of me wants to find a rifle and simply shoot Gordon. But words are my sharpest weapon. "Let's stop at the degassing station before we meet our *esteemed* Lieutenant Colonel Gordon. We owe our Marines a visit."

I round up Ira, and we ride with Harbord in the back seat of the general's Cadillac to the new gas treatment station at Ventelet Farm. The top is down, and I gaze at the sky while thinking. Manipulating a general's emotions is dangerous, but I want Harbord in the right mood for the meeting. It's the least I can do for the parents of the boys being processed there. Jack's men. My Marines.

We first speak with the gas officer, who has a drawn face. "How many?" he says. "Hell, they're still bringing them in by the truckload, sirs. Four hundred twenty before noon. Current tally is over six hundred." The gas officer points at a truck loaded with men. "I've never seen this many patients in a week, much less a day. We don't know if we're coming or going. Hell, we ran out of pajamas an hour ago. The men have nothing but blankets to cover their naked hides for the trip to the gas hospital in Luzancy."

"How long will they be out of commission?" I ask. I know, but I want to make sure Harbord doesn't suffer any of the usual optimistic delusions.

"Well, there are some who aren't even gassed," the gas officer says.

"But they're out of gas, if you know what I mean, sir. Medically, those men—and I'd say there are a hundred or two—need at least forty-eight hours of observation for delayed gas effects. They're too played out to go back on the line to do anything more than die. You'll get the mild cases back in a week or two. The moderates? Some'll be ready in two to four weeks. Others won't be back. Don't expect to see the severe cases again."

"What are the proportions of each?" Ira asks.

"Can't tell for forty-eight hours. Expect a ten percent death rate."

"So," Ira says, "we know there are twenty-five hundred men in that area. That means about two hundred and fifty will die. A whole company."

"Of course, only time will tell, Major."

"Thank you, Doctor," Harbord says. "We'll let you get back to your work." Rage radiates off Harbord like heat on a Death Valley road.

Harbord seems lost in thought as we ride along the road to Luzancy. We pass a truckload of naked men, standing against the side rails with blankets over their shoulders. The men stare at us, then several salute. Then others. Harbord's face is about to break. "Stop the car." Harbord slides out, motioning us to follow. He gazes at the truck, all of the men saluting. "Ten-hut!" barks Harbord.

I stand at attention, swallow hard, and salute Jack's fellow Marines. Tears cloud my eyes.

How many rear-echelon staff officers would have stopped the truck, ordered the men out, and taken names for saluting out of uniform in a battle zone? The Walt Gordons of the world would. I gird myself for the lunacy awaiting us at our next stop. I'm ready to say things that will lead to my court-martial.

Chapter Fifty-Eight
Major Ab Johnson

Anger throbs in my chest. I take a deep breath. All I see now is red. When we reach division headquarters, Harbord is out of the car and up the steps before us. I think we have him in the right mood. Ira and I follow Harbord into the staff room, where Colonel Brown is talking with Walt Gordon, who looks up when Harbord strides in. Gordon's smile melts.

"Heard they tossed a little gas your way," Gordon starts.

Harbord takes a deep breath. "They soaked over twenty-five hundred of my men with mustard. We just came from the degassing station, where they've seen over six hundred, with many more on the way."

"I got the impression it wasn't that bad, according to the reports I've seen," Gordon says. "You might want to check your statistics, General."

"If you bothered to look, you'd have known." Harbord's face colors. "Speaking of which, were you assessing the condition of my brigade relative to relief the last time we talked?" Harbord's voice is tense.

"Yes, as part of my liaison duty."

"You never asked me if my men needed relief."

"I prefer to reach my own conclusions—based on facts rather than opinions."

"My opinion doesn't matter?" Harbord's face is red.

"I prefer the facts, as I see them. Everyone knows that's the fundamental of good staff work, Jim. Statistical analysis is critical to good strategic planning. You know that from the War College."

"Facts? Did you ask Colonel Brown or any of the others?"

"No, for the same reason. You all remarked about your men's good spirits. I remember comments like 'morale excellent' and 'conduct magnificent.' *You* told me that though they were tired, they hadn't and wouldn't give an inch. After that and a thorough data review, I concluded that while relief is desirable, it's not essential." Gordon's hands are clasped in front of him. His left eye twitches.

"And you based that conclusion on the facts—" Ira says.

Gordon frowns at Ira. "As I observed them—"

"Here at headquarters—" Harbord says.

"And I went up to visit Colonel Neville—"

"Who practically never leaves his PC. How many Marines did you talk with?" I ask.

"Colonel Neville only. The judgment of enlisted Marines is hardly to be trusted. This is a staff-level issue. And I looked at the roster numbers—"

"Are you aware that we've gotten a number of replacements?" Harbord asks.

"Thank God for that. Your casualty rate is . . . unusually high . . . " Gordon's voice sounds accusatory.

The right corner of the general's mouth tightens.

"How much training have those replacements had, Walt?" Harbord frowns.

"That's not my department." Gordon smiles. "I was under the impression Marines are spawned, not trained."

"Indeed. Not your department." Harbord takes a breath that reminds me of a pitcher winding up. "Well, a lot of those replacements were thrown into the line upon arrival. They didn't know who their platoon leader was, nor did the platoon sergeants or the lieutenants know them. Many arrived in Europe less than a month ago. We're in such a goddamned rush to get men on the line that we're sending replacements with inadequate training into this buzz saw." Harbord's hands clench at his sides.

"I can hardly help it if the Marine Corps doesn't adequately train its men . . ."

"These are American boys you're talking about," I say.

My next words will be professional suicide, but, shit, someone has to do it. For all the Jacks still alive out there. "You made your assessment based on some facts, but not all of them. You didn't ask the right questions, and even if you had, you wouldn't have understood the answers. In my book, Lieutenant Colonel Gordon, you're an idiot."

Gordon's face contorts. "That is impertinent, *Major*. Watch yourself." He stares at my collars, then at General Harbord's.

I want to knock his jaw to England.

Deep breath.

"What are you going to do, demote me and send me to France?" My voice is strained. I'm struggling to not shout. "Hell. We're a roomful of army officers making decisions about Marines—an outfit we've traditionally looked at as though they're a different species."

My neck muscles are ropes. "And in a way—they are. You don't assess Marines by talking to army staff officers wearing pristine uniforms back at headquarters and looking at sheets of numbers. You go to the goddamned front lines. The hospitals. Their encampments. You talk to the sergeants *and* the privates. Don't ask about their spirits or motivation. Ask about their food, how much sleep they're getting, do they have cooties, are they getting enough water. You *look* at them, judge their condition with your damned *eyes*."

Gordon pulls out a pen and a small notebook. "Your name, *Major*."

"Johnson, Albert, USAR." I stand at attention.

"In addition to the other charges, you are out of uniform with those Marine collar pins, *Major*." Gordon writes a note, a smirk on his face. "You too, General."

I aim my eyes into Gordon's. "Now shut up and listen, *Colonel*."

"No major in this army tells me to shut up. I'll have your—"

"It's about time someone does." I pace. "Here are a few cultural *facts* you need to know, *Colonel*. Your career may depend on your ability to listen to me." Two can play the threat game. If they do court-martial me, my trump card is the shit I can bring down through my friends in the press, who'd love the story. "These Marines know there are many in our fine army who *want* them to fail. I'm betting you're one of them. *Spawned?* That was the word you used. Well, they know what you think. Marines will *never* admit weakness to an *army* officer. They may be too done in to stand, but they'll never ask for relief since that could be construed as weakness. That determination halted a German advance that multiple French divisions couldn't stop. But we have lost so *many* Marines. The ones remaining are so depleted that they're fast becoming ineffective. There are few, if any, units in any army that wouldn't have collapsed long before this point."

Harbord puts a hand on my arm as if to say *that's enough*. He glares at Gordon, then speaks in a quiet voice, seething with danger. "I have asked for relief since the tenth. You told Pershing we didn't need it?"

"Yes—"

"Based on some facts. Spare me the echo. Well, now here's the mess you've saddled me with. The *little bit of gas* you talked about has cost me two out of my six battalions *today*. I've lost two battalion commanders. Before the gas, I was down to about fifty percent experienced effectives. Now? I'm not sure I have any left."

"I have to weigh the—"

"To quote a major who is now up for promotion, *shut up*. I'm ordering you to spend an hour helping at the Ventelet degassing station and then tour the gas hospital in Luzancy. They're nearby. If you have any guts, don a gas suit and go up to the woods. And don't talk with the officers. Talk with the troops who've had the shit kicked out of them for the past two weeks. Then report to me. If you don't obey my orders to the letter, I'll have to jot down *your* name in *my* notepad." He smiles. "Colonel Brown, would you kindly find my pad?"

"General, may I remind you, you're not in my chain of command," Gordon says.

"Walt, if you value your career," Brown says, "and I suspect that's one of the few things you *do* value, you'll obey General Harbord's direct order. General, you're still a friend of Pershing?"

"I should have played that card in this relief issue," Harbord sighs. "Get him on the phone. I've had it."

"Yes, sir. Our next stop has to be French Corps headquarters. We need to have a tête-à-tête with them," Brown says. "I'll make sure we're expected. I'll personally put in that call for you, General."

"Pops, I want you along for the Frog circus," Harbord says. "We could use someone who's been out on the front lines and speaks French —both versions. And Walt, to the degassing station. That's a direct order. Disobey, and I'll make sure Second Lieutenant Gordon gets his command. We're short on platoon leaders."

Words that stab my heart.

Chapter Fifty-Nine
Major Ab Johnson

La Loge Farm
Tuesday, June 18, 1918

Dressing Gordon down doesn't make me feel any better. Asses like him spend careers perfecting the art of what I call "interior warfare" rather than the real thing. I'm sure he's an expert. My Marine collar pins and reaction to the news about Jack may have gotten the best of me. I told Major Smith about it later. He grinned and told me he'd love to have the opportunity to do the same thing, though he has a career to worry about. He said, "Someday." I hope I live to see it.

I head to the officers' mess at HQ to see how blackballed I am. I need coffee, food, distraction. My thoughts never leave Jack. How will I tell Helen? Ira recommended I wait until I have confirmation, and I know, in my mind, that he's right. My heart is split and broken. I don't want a telegram man handing her a yellow slip with the news. I want to be the one, to be there, face to face with the woman I love more than my own life.

What were Jack's last thoughts? His mother? I hope. Our last argument? My harsh words? I pray not but fear so. At the most crucial moment in my son's life, I failed him. I didn't keep the faith. I was an idiot. How can I ever face Helen again?

The days are better than my restless nights—work demands my attention. But a pall of despair clouds my thoughts and sharpens the razor's edge of my emotions. I struggle to focus and asked Derby to double-check my work out of fear of making a mistake. I see the concerned looks in others' faces. Dessez and Derby talk with me frequently, but I haven't told Harbord. He has enough on his mind.

I barely held it together when Harbord, Brown, and I met with the French about the need for relief. The French commanders refused at first, but relented when it became clear Harbord had decided to do it with or without their blessing. The threat of Pershing becoming involved seemed to move them.

Battleship-gray clouds hang low, keeping German observation planes on the ground, so I can be outside without worries. I squeeze tobacco into my pipe, sitting on a bench outside the building, with nothing to do for the moment. I rub my eyes, scratchy from constant chemical irritation and lack of sleep. My nose is still tender but doesn't throb any longer. My sense of smell is better, which is bad.

Ira Cunningham walks out of headquarters, stops and lights a cigarette, then ambles over. "Didn't they ever tell you to look busy, especially when you aren't doing anything?"

I can read Ira's moods as well as he reads mine. He's pale, drawn, and slumps down next to me. It may be Jack, but I suspect there's more. "What's got you looking so grim?"

"Well, Jack, of course. Trudy's Bill is missing. I heard five days ago. I went back to Paris tied up in knots about whether to tell Trudy, or what to tell her."

"I hadn't heard." I've been too preoccupied with my own grief to notice, not that anyone would have told me before this. Bill was Jack's roommate in college. He, Jack, Alice Simmons, and Trudy were a foursome through college. I had hoped Jack and Alice would get something going, but they just remained friends. "What did you decide?"

"I told Alice three days ago and asked her advice."

"I hope she told you to not hold it inside."

"Yeah. So I broke the news and my daughter's heart yesterday evening. I couldn't stay there. Alice is looking after Trudy."

"How's Alice?"

"A wounded heart. Staying strong for Trudy. Fighting her own battles. She's got a mountain of courage she does not understand. Like our guys."

"How's Trudy?" I ask.

"Devastated. At least she has Alice for support." Ira puffs on his cigarette. "I've found there are several Marine lieutenants named J. Johnson. One James, two Josephs, and one John, in addition to our Jack. At least two are with the replacement battalions here, though where is hard to pin down even for an intelligence sleuth like me. You find anything more?"

"Nah. This whole place is still a mess. The only accurate accounting of personnel names is in the muster books that the first sergeants keep. Or in Washington, but I have no connections there. Look, I think we're fooling ourselves to think it was anyone else. A fiction I dearly want to believe, but fiction nonetheless."

To hope Jack's alive means another father will experience my grief. There is nothing fair in this. And now, Bill.

"Heard your demand for relief was effective."

I smile. "Yeah, next day, in fact. Harbord finally convinced higher authority to bring in the Army Seventh Infantry. They were sitting on their hands on the far south side of this front in reserve. Some of our army brethren hereabouts thought the Seventh would show the Marines how it's done and finish the battle."

"Did they?"

"Listen." I point toward the east, where rifles crackle, machine guns chatter, and artillery thumps. "A fiasco. We thought maybe it was just the Marine officers who weren't trained in map and compass. Well, turns out our fine army didn't do any better."

"Shit. I mean, Jack knew that by the time he was twelve," Ira says.

"Yeah. They're putting the Marines in again soon. At least Harbord isn't doing it all in one night. He's learning." I relight my pipe. "We better walk. Sit too long here, someone'll find something for us to do. Let's go inspect our men."

"Which unit?"

"Doesn't matter. I don't intend to inspect anything, but we better look busy about it."

"Any repercussion from Gordon?" Ira asks.

I spit on the ground. "Fuck him and the horse he rode in on. Nah. If there were, I'd be commanding a latrine platoon by now."

"You're not on the court-martial docket in Chaumont. I checked."

We cross a trampled wheat field overgrown with weeds and poppies. The trees along the western edge have full green crowns fluttering in a westerly breeze. The noise of the battle seems distant. "Some of our Marines are in reserve here. Let's inspect them."

"Better see who their lieutenants are, don't you think?" Ira says. "Doesn't look like you're getting enough rest—those bags under your eyes."

"During the day? I stay busy. It's at night. Can't get my mind off Jack. The memories flood in. When I'm alone? Tears. There are times I'm all choked up. Driving me crazy."

Ira pats my back.

Cool shade surrounds us as we enter a wooded encampment. The lush treetops hide green canvas tents from aerial view. We watch a sergeant drill Marines. He looks familiar—I search my memory.

The sergeant croaks a guttural cadence while Marines drill, Springfields at right-shoulder arms, boots falling in unison. "Luufft, luufft, luufft, raaght, luufft . . ."

"The greenies of May are the old hands now. Surgeons, too," I say. I chuckle and point at my nose. "Remember when I got this? That navy surgeon?"

"How could I forget?"

"Hot Shot Beck. Disaster at first. Now he's as solid as they come. He volunteered to stay in Lucy to help the surgeons with the Seventh Infantry."

The sergeant calls, "'Bout face, fuhward harch!" Boots still in unison —except one. The sergeant yells, "Johnson! Get the fuck in step. Think you're in the fucking army?"

My heart misses a beat. No. Not Jack. The small private keeps his eyes forward and corrects his stride. Then it comes to me—Sergeant

Stecker. Ira and I met him in Belleau Wood. Stecker halts the half platoon and dismisses them. I motion Ira to follow as I approach Stecker.

"Sergeant Stecker, got a sec?"

"Yes, sir."

"How do your new men look?"

"Mostly squared away, other than Johnson there. Little goofy. Half of 'em's scared shitless and trying not to show it. The rest should be and seem too cocky. Till they talk with the old hands. Least I know their names, sir." He peers at my collars. "Are you some sort of secret agent, sir?"

"Why?"

"I swear you were wearing army collar pins the last time we met, sir."

I point at Ira. "He's the one with intelligence." I tell him how the pins ended up on me.

"Well, sir, I've heard talk about someone called Pops. It is my privilege to now know who you are."

"Speaking of Johnsons, you run into any lieutenants by that name?" Ira asks.

"Two, but they're in other companies, so I don't know 'em."

"Remember which companies?" I ask. A trickle of hope rises. No, I can't do that to myself.

Stecker squints and looks away. "Nah, sorry, sir."

"Thanks." I face Ira. "Let's have a look around, see if we see any familiar faces."

We search the encampment for the next half hour but don't find Jack. All the while I hold on to a thread of hope that seems as thin and delicate as a strand of unraveling lace.

Chapter Sixty
Lieutenant (junior grade) Arthur Beck

Luzancy
Saturday, June 22, 1918

We needed continuity in the aid station, so I stayed to help orient the army surgeons with the Seventh Infantry when they took over in Lucy Birdcage. My fellow navy surgeons who weren't hospitalized were beyond exhaustion. I owe them. I had my rest while they tried to figure out if I'm crazy.

Crazy is a fluid concept. I take no position on my sanity.

So I did something Dad warned me about—I volunteered to stay.

Good thing I don't have another psych eval coming up.

The Seventh Infantry came in full of bravado, some trash-talking the Marines. They made several futile attacks, the only accomplishment of which was experience for their army surgeons and medics. After the last attack ran out of steam on the afternoon of the twenty-first, Dessez ordered me back to Bezu, where I surrendered to a cot and descended into a delicious slumber with a full stomach, scrubbed skin, and clean sheets.

I touch my fine leather suitcase. The one I brought. The other was "lost." No matter. They're from a different world, a different person I no longer know or respect. I pull out my one remaining custom navy uniform. What a peacock I must have seemed when Osborne and Petty first saw me. What a perfect ass.

I get in my ill-fitting army uniform and leave my tent, toss the navy one in a burn barrel, and hitch a ride to Luzancy. I hear Petty is a patient there.

The gas hospital occupies a large three-story mansion with a cobblestone parking lot. Draperies flutter through banks of open windows. I make my way in and ask an attendant for Petty's location.

The large, airy respiratory ward must have been a banquet room before the war. It has a high painted plaster ceiling with gilded crown molding and two crystal chandeliers. Dark rectangles on the wallpaper mark the spots of removed picture frames—family portraits? Thin curtains billow in a breath of wind. Twenty beds in four ranks, each about four feet apart, fill the room. Wet, heart-rending coughing draws my eyes to a man wearing a black rubber oxygen mask. Dressings shroud his face. Orlando Petty is in the next bed, textbook in his lap, an oxygen cannula in his nose. A large green tank stands behind his bed. Others in the room cough, several with blindfolds and facial dressings. I pull up a wooden chair and plop down, causing Petty to look up.

"Sorry, I was trying to block out that Gunny's noise." Petty nods toward the man in the next bed.

"Gunny? Don't they separate the officers and enlisted?"

"I refused. I want to be with the men I treat."

"How are you?"

"Not good. Bronchitis. Can't tell if it's chemical or bacterial. My phlegm is bloody. They put me on oxygen two days ago."

"Much pain?" I ask.

"Hurts like hell to cough."

The gunnery sergeant—a rank exclusive to the Marine Corps—in the next bed goes into a severe coughing spell. A hospital assistant comes to tend to him. The corpsman lifts the oxygen mask, wipes bloody sputum off with a towel, and repositions the mask amid murmured words of reassurance.

"Brought him in on the morning of the fourteenth," Petty says. "Been going downhill since. It's hell to listen to him. I couldn't sleep last night. Wanted to try to help, but there's nothing I can do except think, *there but for the grace of God*. I could be him tomorrow if I get pneumonia." He points. "That fellow in the corner has it. I think he'll go soon."

I gaze around the room. Everything I've been through trifles in comparison to the suffering surrounding me. I was a complete ass when I took care of the gas victims at La Voie. I swallow hard at the memory of Osborne humming and McCormack helping.

"We got off on the wrong foot," I say. "I'm sorry."

"You were a piece of work when you arrived." Petty laughs, triggering a coughing spasm. He puts a towel over his mouth. A long minute later he holds it out in front of him and looks at dark, clotted blood, panting. "We all have things to be sorry for. Each time I sleep, I have the same nightmare about Williams—the explosion, the fire, carrying a friend I couldn't save." He sighs. "He'd be alive today but for my decision. You were right when you said to put him in the ambulance."

"You didn't know. You did the right thing. He would have probably hemorrhaged to death on the way to the field hospital."

"I know that *intellectually*, Arthur," Petty says. "My *heart* refuses forgiveness."

The man in the next bed begins coughing again, interrupting my train of thought. The cough settles into rapid, ragged breathing. An attendant talks with someone at the door. I look over at Lyle McCormack. Lyle comes over and pulls up a seat next to the other man without noticing us.

"Lyle . . ."

Lyle looks over. "Doc. I . . . I mean, sirs. I didn't . . ."

"You're here to see this poor soul?" Petty asks.

"Yeah. I've been desperate to get here," Lyle says. "Couldn't get away sooner."

"I know what you mean. Who is he?" I ask.

"Our Gunny, Fred Stockham."

"Jesus," I say.

"I didn't know," Petty says, his face flushed.

Lyle moves close to Stockham and speaks near his ear. He holds

Stockham's hand while he speaks. He turns and asks, "Think he'll make it?"

Petty and I exchange glances. Then Petty says, "No. He's very near the end, Lyle. I've been with him since he came in. I didn't know his name, just his rank."

Lyle wears an expression I've seen on too many faces—looking through the walls to a place miles away. "He took his gas mask off and put it on one of our wounded Marines. He felt responsible. We went back to help the others—that's when he collapsed."

"I remember when you brought them in," I say. "He and you took the litters." I stare at Stockham, remembering the night. His willing sacrifice, his decision to go back when reason said he shouldn't. His eyes and nose weeping onto an already blistering face when Lyle carried him back on the stretcher. Lyle's words: *Nothing you can do here.*

Lyle turns to Stockham, still holding his hand. "Hey, Gunny. The guy you carried to Lucy? Docs tell me he'll make it. You saved him."

We sit, listening to the sounds of coughing, wheezing, raspy breath, and the tick of a wall clock. I turn to Lyle. "The family says hi."

Lyle looks up, confusion clouding his face.

"Aunt Minnie," I say. "She and my sister wrote and told me to keep an eye out for a kid with a gimpy little finger named Lyle. Why didn't you say anything?"

"Well, you being an officer and all . . ."

"Yeah. And a perfect ass. I don't blame you."

Lyle holds Stockham's hand until the Gunny stops breathing. Lyle wipes his eyes.

I turn to Petty. "You gave me the courage to carry on. The courage to have the honor of serving this Marine." I nod toward Stockham. "Thank you."

"I have faith in you," Petty says.

"I won't let you down."

The chaplain joins us and says a prayer. At *amen*, my vision clouds. I wipe a tear and glance at the others. Lyle's face contorts in pain, tears rolling down his cheeks. Petty's face is grim, eyes downcast. Is this what's in store for him? I pull out a handkerchief and dab my eyes.

I think about the Doctor Hot Shot Beck who arrived three weeks ago with disgust. Then a feeling of pride swells in my breast, not for myself, but for those next to me. I straighten my back, hand my handkerchief to Lyle, and put an arm around his shoulder. We stand for several minutes, my mind far away, envisioning Dad on the battlefield, in the prison camp, screaming at night.

Forgive me.

Lyle and I go to the clean storage and gather washcloths and towels. Lyle removes Stockham's dressings. We clean the remains of his face, then the rest of his body while Petty looks on. Conversation in the room stills while we work, and it seems as though the artillery noise fades. I unfold a clean sheet to shroud Stockham. Two orderlies help us load him gently onto a cart. I turn to Petty. "I hope you get better. You're our best."

I take the foot end of the cart and help Lyle roll Gunnery Sergeant Fred Stockham to the morgue. How many more selfless heroes have to die to end this stupid war?

Chapter Sixty-One
Major Ab Johnson

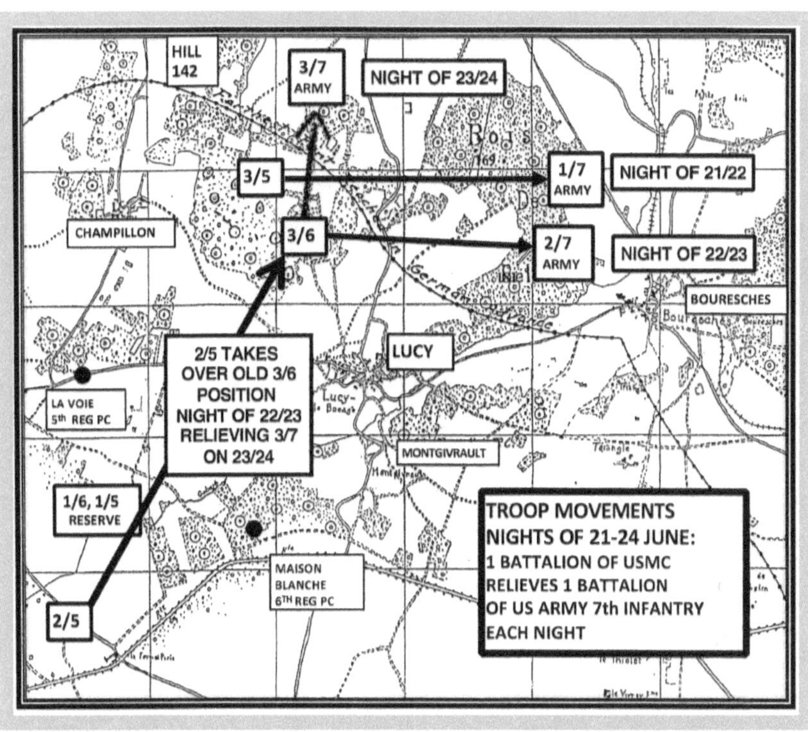

La Loge Farm
Monday, June 24, 1918

Sadness fills my heart, thinking of Jack. Bill is still missing in action. In this war that can mean several things, including dead. A black veil has hung over me since hearing of the death of *Johnson, J., 2nd Lt.* But I have the still living men and boys to think about, so I slog on, moving medical assets around as need and opportunity arise.

My Marines—I like the sound of that—got a break. The battle-weary rested, cleaned up, and got hot food while the Army Seventh filled in. The Seventh had little success cracking the Boche hold over the northern section of Belleau Wood. Harbord ordered the Marines back into the fray but did the replacement over three nights instead of moving everyone at once.

After another restless night, I get up, down a cup of java, and decide to get a look at things. There's a knife edge of light along the eastern horizon as I head out on *Helen.*

I can finally use my headlight now, and the bumps don't bother my nose. Battle noise from 3/5's latest assault on the northern section of Belleau Wood grows louder as I approach La Voie. I check in with Dessez and get a list of items they need to restock. I stop by the aid stations at Champillon and then Lucy. I speak with some of the less severely wounded Marine privates from 3/5 and get the impression that their latest assault accomplished little more than to generate casualties.

Dawn breaks as I head to Bezu. I pull to the side of the road to watch a burial detail at the edge of the small hamlet. These are the ones who had made it to Bezu only to die in the hospital. They aren't the bloated corpses that still litter the field and woods where it remains too dangerous to risk their removal. Jack. How will the burial details treat him? What will they say about his corpse?

I don't recognize any of the burial party. The army, in its finite wisdom, had originally ordered the litter-bearers, corpsmen, and their army brethren to bury the dead. The job poisoned their morale. Derby and I finally convinced my superiors to use non-medical troops for the depressing chore. I watch the detail for fifteen minutes, only half seeing them, the other part of me in the Flint Creek Range of Montana fishing with Jack.

After Bezu, I head back to La Loge, where I find General Bundy talking with Harbord and his staff. Colonels Neville and Lee are there along with the Marine battalion commanders, for a change. I wonder what occasion leads the senior staff to include Marines in their discussions.

Wearing Marine Corps pins has had an effect on both Harbord and me that I wouldn't have predicted.

Harbord motions me in. I stand to the side and listen while Major Shearer, the CO of 3/5, gives his report. A French lieutenant colonel from corps headquarters in a pristine uniform stands across from Shearer, smoking a cigarette in an ivory holder. His uniform and pose are like a community theater caricature of a French aristocrat, nose high enough in the air to make me want to trim the man's nose hairs.

With a hatchet.

"I lost one officer and about 110 men yesterday," Shearer says. "We had a hell of a time evacuating the wounded. Sixteenth Company was so depleted that I asked 3/6 to send two platoons to bolster them as they withdrew to their old line. Someone—who wasn't there—reported a four- to five-hundred-yard advance. I want to find the bastard."

Shearer pauses and lights a cigarette. "The enemy has more machine guns and crews in there than we can handle. Each gun position is covered by at least two others. The way we attacked them is the only one I know of. Infantry alone can't dislodge them."

"What's the condition of your men?" Harbord asks.

"We have parties running back to Lucy to get water; they have to hand-carry it. Rations are scarce. The men and officers are very tired, but they retain their spirit."

"With their spirit holding, is there any reason not to press the attack?" the French officer asks. "My general is quite explicit; the woods *must* be taken at *all* costs."

"I suppose we could try again." Uncertainty lingers in Bundy's voice.

My neck muscles tighten at the words. Get a spine, Bundy.

"Begging the general's pardon, and out of no disrespect for my *esteemed* French colleague," Shearer says, turning an angry glare on the French officer, "that idea stinks. What about today or tomorrow will be any different from our previous attempts to do the same thing using the same tactics?"

The French officer's face reddens, his eyes like daggers boring into Shearer. "I must insist."

"Then grab a company of your *poilus* and come back to the line with me," Shearer says. "*You* lead the attack. By the way, Marine officers lead from the front. I'll have my last remaining lieutenant loan you his directing cane and whistle."

"General," the Frenchman says, turning to Bundy, "do you tolerate such . . . *impertinence* from your subordinates?"

General Harbord holds up a hand. "I agree with Major Shearer. In word *and* spirit." He glares at the Frenchman, who holds his gaze for a few beats, then looks away, blowing a stream of smoke into Shearer's face.

The look in Shearer's eyes suggests the Frenchman should take a quick exit after the meeting if he plans to keep his uniform in an unbloodied state.

"We've tried and tried," Harbord says. "The Germans have done a brilliant job. When this is all over, we need to study how they did it. Unless someone above me in the chain of command wants to *personally* lead the next assault, I'm going to order Shearer's men back a few hundred yards. I'll order the artillery to bathe every square inch from 3/5's current position to the town of Belleau in high explosives and shrapnel tomorrow from 0300 to 1700 hours in the afternoon. At 1700, we will lay in a *rolling barrage*—" He stares into the Frenchman's eyes. "—behind which 3/5 will attack. Major Shearer, I'll order 2/5 and 3/6 to support you from the sides."

"I'll have to confirm such an expenditure of artillery with the general," the French officer says.

"Tell him it's nonnegotiable," Harbord says. "Let him lead the charge if he disagrees."

I smile. Harbord finally understands.

Chapter Sixty-Two
Private Carl Larsen

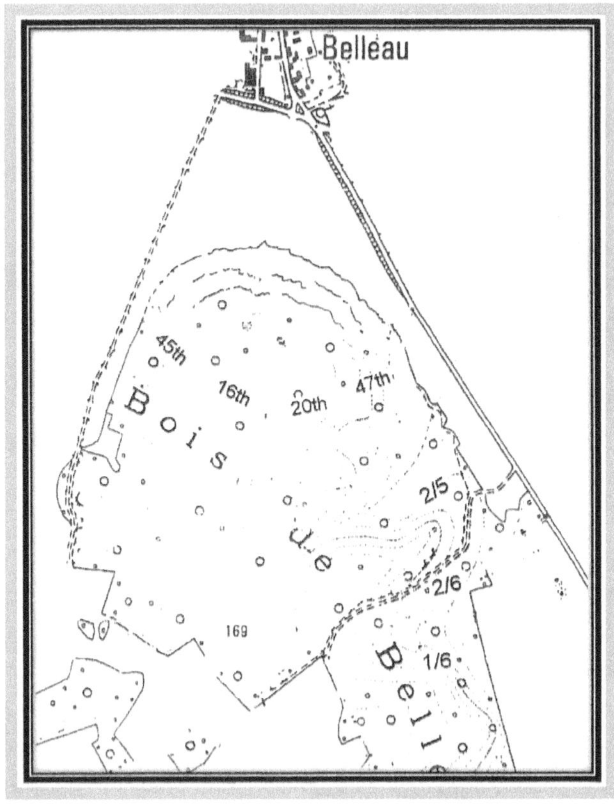

Belleau Wood
Tuesday, June 25, 1918

It's funny how you can sleep through an artillery barrage. Ours pounded the northern woods while I had a dreamless slumber. Hank Lenert and I are assigned to run messages for Captain Case's Forty-Seventh Company as the men of 3/5 prepare to finally boot the Heinies out of the woods. I peer around the edge of a rock across the rugged terrain that separates us from the Heinies. A lieutenant about twenty feet back stands, looking up and down the line. I glance over at Hank and roll my eyes. "I hope this isn't the same old shit." Hank shrugs. We were run ragged in the earlier attack. Hank and I are now among the elite runners based on nothing more than the fact that each of us still has a pulse.

"Doing any better?" Hank asks. "You've been a little scarce since you went in with 2/5 on the twelfth."

"I got my wish that day, or what I thought was my wish. Took it to the Heinies—hand to hand, bayonet to flesh, all that. Bloodlust—all that rage and frustration bursting like an artillery round. Not a thought in my head, totally in the moment, aware of everything, searching for the next Kraut to kill."

"What changed?"

"Guys I killed? Could have been me if I'd been born in Germany."

"Regrets?" Hank asks.

"Not really. Just, well, I don't feel—I don't know what. Glory. There was no glory in it. Just my job. To kill guys like us."

"They kill us too," Hank says. "Over and over. Hardly any old lieutenants left."

"Whatcha think of the new one?" I ask.

"Johnson?" Hank scratches his chin. "I like him. Moves like a mountain man."

"Yeah, that's what I notice. Catlike. Quiet. Soft feet. Stillness when he's not on the move." Lieutenant Johnson is my height, lanky, with blue eyes on a face that seems familiar in a way I can't quite place.

Captain Case signals the attack with a hand wave. Marines move forward in silence. I'm glad that the lieutenants have finally learned that their whistles are the signal for the Heinies to open fire. Hank and I stay with the headquarters unit as Heinie machine guns open up. I'm amazed there are any left after the artillery barrage. Fewer, though. And I hope the gunners are seeing double and have aching heads.

I watch Johnson's platoon. The lieutenant waves two privates forward, his hand low to his right hip, as though sneaking up on a bear —low, stealthy. Then he jerks his hand forward and the three rush a Heinie gun pit while bullets streak around them. They leap over the top and disappear. A minute later, they pop out, blood dripping from bayonets, the lieutenant now carrying a Heinie Mauser. Another machine gun lays fire on them, somehow missing. Two more Marines join as Johnson and his men charge from the pit, staccato machine gun bursts and crackling rifle fire swallowing up shouts. Makes me smile. Never seen a green lieutenant seem so at home. A born hunter.

A Marine charges a machine gun with a rebel yell, raising his rifle. A line of bloody geysers erupt from his back as a nearby machine gunner cuts him down. One of the other runners rushes forward, dips down, and picks up the man's rifle. This guy's nuts. He runs, shouting, straight at the gun and leaps into the pit, bayonet first. A surge flows through my limbs. I drum my fingers on my message bag and look over at the captain. "Skipper, he could use some backup." My legs are springs set to let go.

"Sit, Carl. I need you for messages."

Bodies from previous attacks litter the field in front of us along with scattered arms, legs, a head unrecognizable with greenish-black rot. Mess kits, helmets, rifles, and gear lie scattered among the dead—enough to equip a battalion, most broken.

Lieutenant Johnson and his squad lead a line of prisoners. He shouts, "Got me a few Boche. What do we do with 'em, sir?"

"Assign a couple privates who need a break to take them to the aid station. Make them carry stretchers back to Lucy. Our guys have their hands full. Tell them they'll get a hot cup of real coffee when they get there."

"Will they?"

"Hell if I know."

A sergeant approaches with six disarmed Marines, smiles growing on haggard faces as they approach. The sergeant shouts, "Got some of ours back. Taken prisoner yesterday." I can barely hear the words over the battle noise.

"Welcome back, boys. Shouldn't have any trouble finding yourselves new rifles," Captain Case says.

A half hour later, Case motions Hank and me over. Case and his team hunker down on the near side of a rise, peering at a group of unarmed Heinies crouching in a shell hole. It looks like they want to surrender. One walks forward with his hands up. A Heinie machine gun to the east chops him down. The gunner hunches over his Maxim machine gun, helmet shrouding his eyes. Another Heinie moves forward with the same result. Five of them rush over the lip of the hole. The gunner nails three. The rest sit in the shell hole out of the machine gunner's sight and share cigarettes. I can't see their faces well enough to read their reactions to what just happened.

Case glances around and gives a *come-on* arm motion to someone behind us. Lieutenant Johnson and his ragtag squad take a knee next to us.

"Orders, sir?"

"See those bastards over there?" Case points at the machine gun pit. Johnson squints, eyes darting, searching, then winks.

"Do your magic," Case says.

Johnson motions his squad to follow. His team steals from rock to rock like backwoodsmen. The Heinie's eyes are cloaked under his low helmet as he fires disciplined bursts at the men trying to surrender. His ammo man watches in the same direction. Two cats eyeing the same squirrels. Johnson's men sneak around behind the machine gun nest, then fan out in a forty-five-degree arc. Johnson holds a fist up, glancing from man to man. The lieutenant counts down on his fingers, then all five pop up, sprint, and yell as they crest the pit, bayonets plunging. They roll the blood-covered Heinies out, yank the machine gun toward another Heinie nest now shooting at them, and lay down fire.

"New guy looks good, eh?" Case says.

"Lieutenant Johnson, sir?" I ask.

"Yeah. Told me his old man taught him to hunt, somewhere in Montana. We need to get the wounded out of here. Hank, go tell medical to get teams up." Case scribbles a message on the page of a small notebook, rips the sheet out, and hands it to me. "Get this to Shearer."

It takes me twenty minutes to get to the 3/5 Battalion PC. Major Shearer looks pleased as he reads the note and scribbles a new message. Marines supervise Heinie prisoners carrying litters in the direction of Lucy. They're accompanied by the walking wounded from both sides in a long stream from the meat grinder behind us.

"I need this to go to Neville," Major Shearer says. "Scoot over to Lucy and see if they have a working phone. If not, get a ride to La Voie."

I run through the ruined woods and across the grotesque wheat field. The danger here is mostly from Heinie artillery, which is quiet today. Recovery teams are starting to pick up the dead from battles since the sixth, except in the northernmost part of the field. I pass now-familiar corpses, some of which I've used for landmarks at night. Their condition makes them seem less human. That helps me not think about Frank Welty, who is one of them.

When I arrive in Lucy, I hand the message to a harried signal corps lieutenant and leave. I stop into the aid station to find some cocoa. They keep the pot on and now have enough to share with lowly runners. The place is hopping. Doc Beck speaks fluent-sounding German as he takes care of a Heinie sergeant. He started rough, but I'd trust Beck with my life.

Chapter Sixty-Three
Private Carl Larsen

Belleau Wood
Wednesday, June 26, 1918

A nudge wakes me. I blink twice. Still night. Major Shearer says, "You and another runner head up to Yowell and get me a progress report. They're up to the left somewhere." I look at my watch in the trickle of light from Shearer's blanketed PC—0330. The woods ahead are pitch-black.

I pat Hank on the back to wake him and explain our orders. I pull out my brass radium-faced compass. It doesn't have a direction labeled *left*. I take a bearing on the direction Shearer pointed.

We start a cautious hike in what I think might be the correct direction. But *left* becomes a wide arc as we work our way around face-smacking brush, toe-stubbing rocks, and body parts that—well, everyone tries to avoid. It's impossible to be stealthy in the inky night without a light to see all the gear rattling beneath our feet. We try, though. I pull out my compass again and continue on a northwest course, where *to the left somewhere* might be.

We stumble and grope as our route becomes more uncertain with each step. We come across a squad from Captain Case's Forty-Seventh Company.

"Which way is the Sixteenth?" I ask them. Three point in an arc that spans about 180 degrees. I set a course based on hope.

"Where ya think we really are?" Hank asks five minutes later in his Texas drawl.

"I thought you were in charge," I say. Yeah, I know, Shearer asked me first.

"Hard 'nuff when it's light out."

Trees are shattered giants listing at impossible angles among piles of rocks and bramble in the lightening dawn. It looks the same from south to north, east to west. One thing that's eerie—there's no shooting. No shelling. The place is spooky quiet. Nothing to cover the rattle of a mess kit when my right foot hits it.

I can't tell which level of hell we're walking through. We pick our way between obstacles, trying not to curse too loudly at the pokes, trips, and near falls.

"Any notion, Carl?"

"Youbetcha. We're somewhere in France," I say.

Hank chuckles and stops. "Fuck it. I'm ordering this column to halt and take five. Should've hit the Sixteenth by now. Reckon ya took too many lefts."

"Aye, aye, sir." I sit. "You outrank me?"

"The only things I outrank are you and pond scum."

I pull out the compass. It doesn't help as we sit on a fallen tree trunk.

"Shit." Hank points.

I follow the direction of Hank's finger. The muzzle of a machine gun stares into my eyes. Ten feet, if that. I hadn't noticed it moments before. Dawn is tricky that way. My face flushes like when a teacher caught me passing a note in class. Only this is worse. The gunner must not have seen us. Yet.

We slowly lie down. Nothing happens. I look at Hank and shrug. Maybe the gunner is asleep. Or dead. I edge my head up. The gunner stares into my eyes, takes his left hand off the breech, and motions us over. He has us dead to rights.

I try not to piss my pants as I stand up, hands in the air, and walk toward the machine gun emplacement. Three other Heinies aim rifles on us. "Been nice knowing you, Hank," I mutter.

Sweat dribbles from my armpits, and my rectum tightens. I don't want to be one of the guys who shits his pants when they shoot him.

Two Heinies hold us at bayonet point while another pats us down, opening our message bags, dumping out the two chunks of bread I hadn't told Hank about. Three chocolate bars fall out of Hank's bag. He looks over and shrugs. An officer walks up and scowls at us. I snap to attention. It can't hurt.

"Who are you?" the officer demands in accented English.

"Um . . . Ah'm Private Lenert, sir." Hank's Texan accent seems to rise with his emotions.

"Larsen, Private Carl, USMC, sir."

"What unit are you with?" The officer asks. His voice sounds tired, almost bored.

"Mind if that man gets his bayonet out of my ribs, sir?" Hank asks. The officer says something, and the two pull their Mausers back a few inches.

"Thanks," Hank says. "Well, sir, Carl here's with the Fifth Marines, and Ah'm with the Sixth, see?"

"Carl—good name. Is Larsen Danish?"

"No, sir, Swedish."

"Ah, the Vikings were fierce warriors." The Heinie officer almost smiles. "Do you know how far from your lines you have strayed?"

"Honestly, sir," Hank says, "so dark last night, musta got turned around."

The sound of artillery in the background and the crackle of gunfire brings my mind back to the battle as I entertain thoughts of my impending firing squad. More Heinies surround us. I'm feeling like a bare-ass chimp in the monkey house at a zoo. Must be a whole company of them. We really stepped in it. The ones aiming their bayonets at us set their rifle butts on the ground. One lights a cigarette. Their tattered uniforms are filthy, faces as gaunt as us Marines. Some look like they might still have some fight in them, but most shuffle, with the lost eyes of men beyond the limit. A look I know well. The machine gun dominated my vision so much that I hadn't noticed the others. The Heinie officer is a short, slender man with a ramrod spine, sharp features, and gray eyes, about thirty by the look of his smudged face, a *hauptmann*—a captain—by the insignia.

"Your Sixteenth Company, commanded by Captain Yowell, has been giving my men trouble," the captain says. "Captain Case's Forty-Seventh, also. Who are you with? And why are you unarmed?"

"I'm a runner, sir," I say. "I'm with 3/5, Major Shearer."

"That is the battalion in this attack. Are there plans to reinforce them?"

"Yessiree," Hank answers before I can form a reply. "Ah'm Colonel Lee's runner, see. He's sending the Sixth Regiment up. Whole kit 'n caboodle. Been moving in all night. They's gonna to come charging up the gut a little after dawn." He pauses to squint toward the eastern horizon. "Which would be any moment now, I reckon."

I keep my face still as I listen to Hank's yarn.

"Is this true, Viking?" the captain asks.

"Yes, sir." Why not? Hank's lying, but . . . in for a penny . . .

"So, the entire Sixth Regiment attacks—soon?"

"Yes, sir. Any minute now, dontchathink, Hank?" I say.

Hank tilts his head as though listening to something distant and nods.

The captain walks off and talks with four lieutenants beyond earshot. One seems to disagree but cowers under the captain's glare.

The captain comes back and stands before us. "We have injured men in need of medical attention. Your artillery is making their evacuation impossible. Your aid station . . . is it still located in Lucy-le-Bocage?"

"Yes, sir," I say. How does he know so much? Their intel is a hell of a lot better than ours.

"Do you have any doctors who speak Deutsche?"

"Sure, sir," I say. "Doc Beck. *Sprechens* it as though he's the Kaiser's own doctor." One of the few Heinie words I know.

"His first name wouldn't be Arthur, would it?"

"Don't know, sir. Only first name I'd heard was *Hot Shot*, but I think that's a nickname."

"Interesting," the captain says.

Chapter Sixty-Four
Private Carl Larsen

Gotta remember not to play poker with Hank. The captain and his lieutenants jabber in German. A lieutenant snaps his heels—how can his boots be in good enough condition to do that?—and walks off. The captain turns to us. "My men and I wish to surrender. We are all tired of this. I do not wish death on any more of the men I am responsible for. Will you lead us back to your headquarters?"

"We'll be happy to, sir," Hank says. "Though I think you might want to put your guns down. It'll look better that way."

"Of course." The captain barks out an order. Soldiers open bolts, empty magazines, and stack rifles. "I am Hauptmann Ochs. I am your prisoner now. I must formally surrender to an officer, not a private. If it meets your approval, we will drop off my wounded at the aid station in Lucy with *Herr Doktor* Beck."

"Alrighty, sir." Hank starts walking.

"Private Lenert?" Ochs holds a compass and points about a hundred degrees to the left. "Lucy is that way."

"Oh," Hank says. "Say, uh, thanks, sir. Still a mite turned around, see?" We head off in the new direction. Ochs and his lieutenants lead their men while I walk beside him. I look back at a long line of gray uniforms and Heinie helmets. Litter-bearers carry eight men on stretchers, followed by the walking wounded, trudging along in the dispirited shuffle of surrender.

Ochs says something to his lieutenant. They pull Lugers from their holsters. He checks one and hands it to me. "I hear these are . . . how do you chaps say? Sought after. You and Private Lenert should be armed. Your . . . bonus . . . for not shooting my men is that you get to keep the Lugers, as long as your officers don't confiscate them for themselves."

"I've never used one of these." I examine at the pistol.

"It is simple." Ochs shows me how it operates while we walk. "I have left the chamber empty. That way it can't go off by accident. My men will not be in need of shooting today, but you had better hold it when we go through your lines. As Private Lenert says—it looks better that way."

"I see what you mean, sir. Thank you, sir." Respect never hurts. Besides, for a Heinie, this Ochs fellow seems decent. Reminds me of how little difference there is between us enemies.

"We will unload the others and keep them as gifts for your officers when we surrender."

Our line snakes its way through the jagged wood, Hank and me in the lead. I don't hear machine guns. Not much for rifle fire. The smell of death worsens near our line. A baffled gunnery sergeant shouts at us to identify ourselves. Hank tells him not to shoot, that we're taking prisoners back on Major Shearer's orders. I hope Shearer isn't nearby to hear Hank's version of reality. The surroundings become familiar as we wind our way among tree trunks, boulders, and the dead.

We lead the train of prisoners toward Lucy. Hank sidles up next to me, Luger loosely in his hand, index finger nowhere near the trigger. "Here's my plan, see. After Lucy, we march the rest back to brigade HQ. Turn 'em over to the general hisself, what say?"

"Hot coffee and chow?" I ask. I could use both.

"My thought."

I tell Hank to hold his Luger like a Marine when we march into Lucy, one on each side of the officers. Marines and corpsmen gawk at us. I ask a corpsman if Lieutenant Beck is on duty when we reach the aid station. The man ducks inside. A minute later, an exhausted Beck emerges, wearing a bloodied apron.

"Carl, what've you brought me?" Beck asks.

"Lieutenant, Hank and I caught these old boys by surprise, and they're our prisoners now. They've got some wounded and need a doctor who can *sprechen* Deutsche. I'm betting you're our man."

Beck gives me a resigned look. He faces Ochs. The two snap to attention and salute. Smiles gather on both faces, and Ochs pats Beck on his shoulder. They talk in German like old buds. I look at Hank, who seems to share my confusion. Ochs shouts out an order. The lieutenants go back and lead the wounded forward. Beck pulls out a pack of Chesterfields, takes one and tosses the pack to Ochs, who takes one and hands cigarettes to his officers. Beck holds up his lighter, and the men lean in, Ochs first.

"Carl, we're going to keep some of these prisoners to use as litter-bearers. Ours are done in. Hauptmann Ochs has agreed to detach ten of the stronger men for this duty, if that's acceptable to you and your partner."

"Aye, aye, sir." What else can I say?

After the wounded are brought into the aid station, Arthur *sprechens* more Deutsch with the officers and says, "All right, Carl, you can take your captives back. Where are you taking them?"

"Hank and I thought we'd take them to brigade HQ."

"Good idea. Hot food there." He turns. "Hans, I'll take good care of your men. I'm sorry about the circumstances."

"Pass my regards to the family, Arthur," Ochs says.

"They'll be relieved to know you're alive and well." Arthur pats him on the back.

Hank and I resume our positions on each side of the officers and lead on. As we pass the Maison Blanche PC, big trouble appears.

Two army corporals stop us. "We'll take these prisoners off your hands."

I gotta think like Hank. "Well, you see," I say, "Major Shearer gave us strict orders to take these Dutchmen back to Brigade. Captain Ochs here is a big fish, and the major ordered Private Lenert and me to personally make sure he surrenders to nobody below a bird colonel back at HQ."

The corporal studies my face. I stare back, pupil to pupil, the same as when I bluffed a classmate holding a full straight. I had a pair of deuces.

"All right, I suppose. Stay off the road."

We walk on. After we're out of earshot, Ochs says, "You must play poker."

"Now and then, sir. Why?"

"Your face didn't belie the falsehood you told that chap back there."

"Oh, yeah. I don't suppose you do that in your army, but a private's gotta get a little creative sometimes."

"I don't imagine the Hollanders enjoy your term *Dutchmen*, when you refer to us."

"Well, then, it's a good thing there are none of them around here today." I smile. I like this guy.

We march the column alongside the road and turn right at the lane to La Loge Farm, leaving baffled looks in our wake. I tell Hank to present our prisoners, since he was the author of the bullshit that had made this possible. I don't care about credit, long as I get chow and nobody confiscates my Luger.

Hank marches up to the headquarters building as several staff officers gawk. A major with a crooked nose climbs off a motorcycle, pulls his goggles down, and walks over. I don't know his real name, but the officers called him "Pops." Hank stands at attention. "Major, sir. I'm Private Lenert, USMC. What should we do with these prisoners we've just captured?"

The major seems amused. "Thank you, Private. Well done."

"Captain Ochs here says he has to surrender proper-like to at least a bird who's a colonel," Hank says.

I stifle a laugh.

The major shows no surprise. "Wait here a minute. I'll see if there are any birds in this coop." Hank looks at me with a crooked grin after Major Pops enters the building. A minute later, the major emerges, followed by Colonel Brown, General Harbord, and General Bundy. Jackpot.

Ochs shouts an order. His column snaps to attention. He and his officers salute. "General Bundy, I am Hauptmann Ochs of the First Battalion, 347th Infantry. I formally surrender to you."

"Are these the men who captured you?" General Harbord points at Hank and me.

"*Ja.*"

"Hauptmann, how many men do you have here?"

"Seventy-eight men, four officers present. We left eight wounded at the Lucy aid station with *Doktor* Beck, along with ten to serve as litter-bearers."

"How did they capture so many?" General Harbord asks.

"You train your privates well in the art of subterfuge." A wry grin cracks Ochs's rigid face. "I would not play poker against either of them if I were you, sir."

"Well, they're Marines, after all," Major Pops says.

"Pops," Harbord says, "show these two Marines to the officers' mess. Our fine young staff officers need to see some real Marines for a change. I'll see who's around to do the formalities."

"Major." Ochs reaches into a pocket and pulls out an Iron Cross medal. "Do you know *Herr Doktor* Arthur Beck?"

"As a matter of fact, I do," Major Pops says.

"Please convey this to him with my thanks for taking special care of my men. He is an honorable man. I meant to give this to him in Lucy."

Chapter Sixty-Five
Major Ab Johnson

La Loge Farm

Private Lenert stands at an uncertain form of attention while Carl's back remains straight after presenting their prisoners. Harbord and Bundy head into headquarters, and a detachment of soldiers leads the prisoners away. "Wait here, but for chrissakes, take a load off," I say to the two. "I'll be back in about five minutes, and we'll get you boys some hot chow. Hide those Lugers if you know what's good for you." I go into the building with a note burning a hole in my pocket. The Carl and Hank comedy show had interrupted my real mission.

I chuckle and shake my head as I enter the staff room. The two generals and Colonel Brown are in a light mood. Harbord fires up a cigarette. "Pops, ever see such a thing?"

"No. I'll treat our young privates to lunch and get the rest of the story. This is one for my book." I pull the slip of paper from my coat pocket. "I really came to deliver this message personally. Colonel Neville wanted to come, but he's a little busy."

"And probably didn't want to ride in your damned sidecar," Brown says.

"Yeah, probably." I clear my throat. "This message is from Major Shearer, and I quote: *Belleau Wood now US Marine Corps entirely.*"

"Think this one's credible?" Brown asks.

I stroke my right index finger over the note, rub the finger against my thumb, and hold my hand up. "Ink's dry. This time, I think it's true, though I wouldn't send it to Chaumont or the French until you get independent confirmation."

Harbord smiles and slaps my back. "That's what I've been waiting for. Thanks for bringing it, Pops." We shake hands. Harbord's smile fades. "Casualty figures?"

"Yes, sir. The 3/5 lost 250 men," I say.

"They didn't start at full strength, did they?"

"No. They started with about 750. Neville estimates the German losses at about 450, along with 300 captured—not including those our creative privates brought us."

Harbord says to Brown, "Consolidate and get 3/5 the hell out of there. They deserve a hot meal and a rest."

"Oh, speaking of that, I have a lunch date with a couple of privates. If you'll excuse me, sir?" I start to leave.

"Pops." Harbord's voice calls from behind. The word brings a flash of Jack to me. He motions me to join him over by the window.

"Sir?"

"Why didn't you tell me?" Harbord asks.

"What, General?"

"You've been wearing a shroud these past two weeks. I've been trying to figure it out. Then I learned that a Second Lieutenant Johnson died in Fritz Wise's blunder."

"I didn't say anything . . . well, I'm not sure, it could be another Johnson. The company was nearly wiped out, and nobody knew much about the lieutenant. He'd joined them that day, and the records were a mess . . ."

"Second Lieutenant *James* Johnson, USMC. Not sure where he's from, but I'll personally write to his family when we get his paperwork."

I steady myself against the window frame, knees weak, staring out at the trampled, weedy lawn. The world becomes a blur as tears flood my eyes. A hand under my left arm steadies me. Harbord leads me to a chair. Colonel Brown sits on my right, offering a cup of coffee.

Harbord pulls up a chair. "Pops, I can't begin to imagine what you've been going through." He hands me a cigarette.

"I—" I'm unable to form thoughts into words.

"When did you hear? I mean about the other J. Johnson?" Harbord asks.

"Right after Neville and I pinned you and you put the Eagle, Globe, and Anchor on me." It seems so long ago. I blot my eyes with my handkerchief and then take a drag on the cigarette. Better than usual. Must be a select blend. "What unit is Jack with?"

"Forty-Seventh Company. His CO told me he was like having Daniel Boone on his team. You taught him well," Harbord says.

I smile. "Had a game when he was a kid—Bridger's Boys. I taught my sons standard hunting skills—stalking, stillness, and stealth. The most famous mountain man in our neighborhood was a fellow named Jim Bridger."

"Forty-Seven is mopping up in the north end of the wood," Harbord says. "I'm ordering you to do an inspection. I'll be offended if you write a report."

I finish my coffee. "Thank you. I have a couple of privates I promised to take to chow first."

Relief floods me as I go outside to find Carl and Hank. I wipe a tear from the corner of my right eye as I lead them into the officers' mess. Several army staffers frown as I take the privates through the line. The two need showers and new sets of everything. Carl recounts the events of the past night while Hank attacks his plate. The story of Arthur's meeting with Hauptmann Ochs along with the medal stir my curiosity. I'll spend some time with my diary tonight. This one is precious.

All the while I'm thinking of Jack. Alive. Jack.

As we eat, Carl keeps glancing at me as though there's a question he wants to ask. By this point, though, the whole affair has more unasked questions and unspoken answers than I can process. After he finishes gorging himself, Carl says, "Hank and I need to head to the woods. Don't want the major to think we're AWOL."

"I can give you a ride as long as you guide me to Shearer's PC."

"Why the hell would you want to . . ." Carl begins.

"Just heard my son is there. Jack. Lieutenant with Forty-Seventh."

"Shit," Carl says. "I mean, sir. I thought there was something familiar about you. I saw him. Hell of a Marine. Sure, I'll take you there."

Hank climbs into the sidecar, and Carl scoots behind me when I kick *Helen*'s engine to life.

The silence is so strange, other than the noise of my motorcycle and the engines of trucks and ambulances. The Boche commander probably realizes that many of the men marching in the rear areas are his, now prisoners. Marines on foot, animal-drawn ammo carts, and supply trucks clog the roads—prisoners coming back and supplies going forward. And ambulances. Many ambulances.

I park behind the Lucy aid station. Hank heads off while Carl stays with me. I have one thing to do before I head up to see Jack—though all I want to do is dash through the field and find my son. Arthur Beck and Malcolm Pratt talk with two other doctors and their chief pharmacist's mate inside the station. I join the group. "Well, I guess it's official—the woods are finally ours."

"The wounded haven't slowed down much, though," Arthur says. "It's taken a while to get through the casualties from the last day, but at least they're all out, those still alive."

"We just came on duty, so it's Arthur's chance to get some sack time," Malcolm Pratt says.

I reach into my pocket and hand the Iron Cross to Arthur. "A souvenir and gift of thanks from Hauptmann Ochs." Arthur's face colors. "I'm curious, how do you know him?"

"My third cousin," Arthur says. "Our family is on both sides of this war."

"You're not alone," I say, thinking about friends back in Omro, Wisconsin, where I grew up. A lot of German immigrants in that area. "Any others?"

"His brothers. One's dead, the other in hospital. Conrad and Heinrich."

"Just found out my son, Jack, is alive. Up in the woods."

"What the hell are you talking to us for?" Arthur says. "And thanks."

A motorcycle with a faulty muffler pulls up as I lift the blanket covering the door aside. Dick Derby hops out of his sidecar and says, "Word's out. Jack's okay. Why the hell didn't you tell me?"

"Just heard."

"Friends need to know these things, Pops. Don't be a clam."

"I'm heading up to see him—" I say.

"Hate to rain on your parade, but we're under orders to report to Paris toot sweet. Big scandal. We're center stage."

"But—"

My chest is empty—as though the blood rushing through my heart a moment before has disappeared. Paris? Goddamn it. After all this time . . . Jack is a half mile away, and they want to pull me away for some administrative bullshit?

Chapter Sixty-Six
Major Ab Johnson

Lucy-le-Bocage and Belleau Wood

Derby and I stare at each other.

"Court-martial me if you want, but I'm going up there." I nod toward the woods. "I'm this close . . ."

Derby's eyes bore into mine.

After a long moment, Derby pats my shoulder. "Find him, my friend."

I kick my motorcycle to life. Carl rides in the sidecar. I head up the Lucy-Torcy road—a byway that has seen almost no motorized traffic for the past month. I dodge around holes in the damaged road on our way north. I leave *Helen* when we reach the northern section of Belleau Wood. Carl leads me along a well-worn path toward the northeastern section. I pass walking wounded, looking into each man's eyes, afraid to miss Jack. Would I recognize my own son? I look into the eyes of a private who has the thousand-yard stare so common for those coming out of combat. Poorly shaven face filthy with dirt and gore. Helmets jangling at crooked angles, uniforms tattered. Marines in victory. I stop and stare at each passing litter, hoping Jack is not being carried out.

Sweat trickles down my back and infiltrates my armpits; I wipe a dribble away from my right eyebrow.

The walk seems interminable. The horror is worse than I had imagined. It's all I can do to keep my stomach from erupting from the reek of death. Corpses and bits of humans litter the smoldering wreckage of the forest. Flies feast on the dead and piles of human excrement. Broken rifles, dented helmets, and tattered gear litter the forest floor. I see a battered mess kit filled with dirt—probably used to dig a foxhole. Marines wander amid the carnage, gathering equipment, others loading the dead into carts, hauling them away across the field where the other *Johnson, J.* died. The most amazing thing is the quiet—no shooting, no artillery. Just the voices of men whose ears must still ring from weeks of racket. Carl walks ahead, silent.

A command group stands on a small rise, a major pointing with his directing cane, lieutenants and sergeants nodding heads, talking. Carl says, "There you are, sir," and leaves.

Jack.

I stumble and nearly fall, then pick up my pace, heart swelling, the blood coursing through my limbs, spirit lightening. Major Shearer nods as I approach.

"Pops?" Shearer and Jack say at the same time.

Shearer looks at Jack. Jack's expression is one of shock and confusion.

Then Shearer and Jack laugh.

I rush to Jack, tears welling, heart pounding, and envelop him in a bear hug.

"I take it you know each other," Shearer says.

I release Jack and pat his shoulder. "Yep. And before I say anything else, I owe Jack and all of you an apology. Hell, I owe the USMC an apology, and I belatedly offer it now."

"Um, Pops," Jack says, "what's that on your collar?"

"Well, someone thought I was acting more like a Marine than a fat old army major, and pinned his accusation on me," I say.

"Jack, your father's a bit of a legend here," Shearer says. "I think I understand you both better now. Lieutenant Johnson, I need you back here in one hour. You may want to see the contraption that your old man drives. I have no idea why he's still alive."

Jack leads along the maze of trails through and out of the wood.

"Before anything else, Jack. I love you, son. And I'm so proud of you and your Marines."

"Pops, I always knew that. I didn't take it as an insult. Just another challenge. Like your land nav problems when I was a kid. Same thing. You may have been angry, but mine was only short-lived."

"It's been hanging over me."

"Sorry it was," Jack says. "I thought you'd be safely eating escargot in Tours or Paris. You let Mom know where you are?"

"Kinda left that out of my letters."

I give him a short version of the long story as we walk, ignoring the ruin surrounding me. "When I heard that Second Lieutenant J. Johnson was killed with Fifty-First Company, my world collapsed."

After sharing memories for twenty minutes, I lead Jack to the motorcycle. Jack's spirits seem a bit better, though the fatigue of battle and loss clearly hang over him. When we round a corner and the motor-cycle comes into view, Jack says, "What would Mom think?"

"I named the bike *Helen*. Think that'll help?"

"No." Jack laughs.

"I'll let you drive it sometime when you're off." I give Jack another hug. "Better get back. I'll be around La Loge when you manage to get out of Hellwood. I'll try to figure out what to write to your mother. Love you, son."

"Love you too, Pops."

Chapter Sixty-Seven
Major Ab Johnson

Thursday, July 4, 1918

There's no parade, no punch or lemonade, no pretty girls, and especially no Fourth of July fireworks. The only pyrotechnics in our possession are the Very pistols used to signal to the artillery. The first sergeants confiscated them for fear a drunken private might signal for a barrage. The privates managed to secure a good supply of hooch. My old Paris friend, Henri Barton, sent me a case of wine, but that's another story.

After the briefings, meetings, and drills, I eat lunch with Jack and Arthur. We three adjourn to a bench outside the mess tent. For the first time since May, I have nothing to do. Jack pulls out a novel while I listen to the murmur of nearby conversations and Arthur fires up his pipe.

"Who went to the big show?" I ask, lighting my pipe.

"Farwell and several others," Arthur says. "Pratt and I briefed the army guys taking over for us. We still have supplies in the Birdcage, and they'll probably use our station until they can boot my cousins out of Torcy and Belleau."

"Plans this afternoon?" I ask.

"Nah. Happy to say I don't have a damned thing to do except smoke."

We sit through two pipefuls of silence before I raise a subject I've been mulling over for the last two hours. "I was thinking of going up to the Birdcage. The Twenty-Sixth Division graves teams are there. Kind of feel like I should . . . I don't know. Pay homage."

"I suppose. I kind of hate to watch, though," Arthur says.

Carl Larsen approaches, engaged in an animated conversation with a corpsman. Arthur motions them over. The corpsman gives me an uncertain look. Carl smiles.

"Who's your friend, Carl?" I ask. "I don't think we've met."

Carl starts to answer when Arthur says, "Turns out Lyle McCormack here worked on my aunt's farm in Watertown, Wisconsin, back when I was too preoccupied with my own importance to visit. By the way, Lyle, I have a couple of letters for you to look over when you have time. Aunt Minnie says to write."

"Seems like a lifetime ago, eh?" Lyle looks away, blinking.

I look at Carl. "Still have the Luger?"

"Shhhh. *They* don't know. I kept it outta sight."

"Mum's the word," I whisper.

"Lieutenant Beck," Carl says, "I was meaning to ask. You hear anything about my colonel—Catlin?"

Arthur shakes his head.

"My friend Ira saw him recently, in a Paris hospital," I say. "He's short of breath—won't be back here. But they think he'll make it."

"Hear anything about a private named Stoops?" Carl asks.

"Ira told me Hiram will never run again, but still has his leg," I say.

"We're heading up to the Birdcage. Want to come?" Arthur asks.

Carl's face turns sour. Then he shrugs. "Nothing else to do."

I abuse my rank to get a staff car, and Carl drives, passing supply trucks. It's odd to see them in full daylight. A burial crew works in a cemetery on the outskirts of Lucy, but we drive by. Carl parks behind the aid station. The place looks and smells the same, but calm has replaced the frenzy of the past four weeks. "I'm going to pop in and say hi," I say.

I go in the back door and find Lieutenant Commander Dessez,

Lieutenant Boone, and Chaplain Brady briefing three army surgeons. Ira walks in while we discuss the processing of the dead.

"God, Ab, Jack's outside. What're you doing?"

"A little tail-end business I forgot to take care of earlier," I say. "How are things in Paris?"

"Trudy's brokenhearted. Bill's still missing. I'm here to find out what happened to him."

"I'm sorry to hear that."

"Glad Jack's okay," Ira says.

"For now." I choke as I say the words.

"Two of you buried the hatchet?"

"Yep."

We go out the front, which has an actual door now. I stop and gaze to the east across the pockmarked wheat field toward Belleau Wood. "It's like looking across the River Styx." Parties of soldiers wearing gas suits, gloves, and surgical face masks scoop remains onto green woolen blankets and load them into wheeled carts. The carts bounce and buck through the field to Lucy's newest graveyard.

Marines have a commitment: *Never leave a man behind*. Here, the dead were always in front of their comrades' eyes, even if we couldn't retrieve them until now. The dead have infinite patience. How many fathers of the sons in that field clutched at the sliver of hope found in the word *missing*? False hope made this field what it now is, where so many of the missing became carbon-based memories mingled within the vapor of high explosives and mustard gas. French commanders hoped the woods were empty. American commanders hoped the French were right. The dead hoped for the best and said, 'Aye, aye, sir,' as they marched to their deaths. It's hard to imagine what their families back home would think or do if they knew the brutal truth.

A tan, open-sided tent with a large red cross provides shade for the mortuary staff working at two rows of tables. They wear surgical masks and rubber gloves that come halfway up their forearms. Those not in undershirts have rolled their sleeves up. The gravediggers are either bare-chested or wear strap undershirts, bareheaded, sweat glistening in the hot sun. They're digging a long trench rather than individual graves.

The only noise comes from the flapping of the tent in the breeze, and the shovels.

"Get us some gloves, please," I say. "I have a job to do."

I give Ira a pat on the back. "Go. Look for Bill. The others and I will stay here."

Arthur, Lyle, and I find fresh surgical masks and wipe a thick finger-load of Mentholatum along our upper lips to cover the bile-raising stench hanging in the air. I take off my coat and shirt, don a surgical apron over my undershirt, and slip on rubber gloves. The three of us take our places alongside the graves registration men to help search the pockets of the dead while Carl and Jack grab shovels. Ira goes to the Lucy PC. Arthur, Lyle, and I tuck personal possessions into small cotton bags that will be returned to grieving families. We call out the identity of those whose aluminum dog tags are still readable. One corporal enters the information in his logbook, and another labels a grave marker.

We work in silence—a quiet murmur here, a softly spoken name there, the clicks of shovels hitting rocks.

There are not enough trees in France and not enough Frenchmen left to nail together all the coffins this war demands.

After searching and identifying each corpse, we wrap him in the blanket his remains came to us in, tying both ends with rope. There are many *unknowns*. There are parts and pieces we cannot match. Is Trudy's Bill among them? I know that's why Ira is elsewhere, dreading what, or who, we might find. After setting each bundle in the burial trench, a soldier hammers a marker into the soil above the head of the body.

We work through the afternoon. Additional soldiers and Marines come to help. I look up from my work and smile, watching my son. Jack's shovel work seems to motivate the other diggers. Jack is alive, but this place is brutal proof of life's fragility.

At around 1600 hours, I stop, reading the tag hanging from the body on the table before me. Blood rushes from my head. I look skyward from the mangled corpse, shot in the head. I take a dry gulp and glance at the corporal in charge of the logbook. Arthur told me about this corpsman a few days ago when we talked about stories I might use if I write a book.

"Sir? You all right?" the corporal asks.

I take a breath of mentholated air. "Welty, Frank. PM-2. USN." I remember someone telling me the story about his death on the sixth.

Lyle and Carl walk over and stand at my side. We empty Frank's pockets in silence, then wrap the blanket and Arthur ties the ends. We carry Frank to the trench and ease him into the next spot in line. I move aside as the other three stand in silence, Arthur in the middle, his hands on Carl's and Lyle's shoulders. After several minutes, we go back to work.

At 1700 hours, the men in the field stop. The rest of the dead will wait their turn. Carl jogs to the aid station for water. The rest of us relax, stretching sore backs.

The condition of the men who never made it to the aid stations is beyond anything my imagination could have conjured six weeks ago. I've become a surrogate for their own fathers. I glance at Jack and say a silent prayer. I look over to Arthur, thinking back to the silly Napoleonic character reporting for duty with a Teutonic click of the heels, like something from Gilbert and Sullivan. I smile—Jack and I have drilled Arthur in his salute and the customs and courtesies of the service over the past few days. I think we have the start of a good friendship with Hot Shot Beck, as he is no longer known.

Carl emerges from the back of the aid station carrying several canteens. Lieutenant Commander Dessez, Lieutenant Boone, Malcolm Pratt, and Chaplain Brady follow. I pour water over my head to cool down. Carl gathers our uniform shirts and coats, handing them out as he moves from man to man. Ira walks up from the PC and stands next to me.

"No luck so far," Ira whispers in my ear.

"Chaplain Brady, I'm sorry you've been so busy," I say.

"Thank you for helping with my flock, Major. All of you."

"It was my honor," I say.

"Lieutenant Beck," Dessez says. "Pops tells me he and a greenie lieutenant have been working on your naval education."

Arthur gives him a sharp nod. "Aye, aye, sir."

The men who collected the dead from the field gather at the grave, swelling the number to about two dozen while Brady talks with Carl and me. Brady opens a small book and leads us in a prayer for the dead.

I'm too old for this, but perhaps, just perhaps, a few moments of lost youth have graced me with their fleeting presence. More important, I found Jack alive, at least for the moment. And war or not, moments are all we ever get. I glance at Arthur, who had volunteered for an assignment that had vanished and, like me, learned something far more important—faith. Not the religious kind—I've already got that—but faith in our comrades. My Marines.

"Ten-hut!" I come to attention.

Arthur leads us in a silent salute.

Afterword

I am honored that you chose to read this novel. Thank you! I made every effort to portray the historical events in this novel with as much accuracy as possible. I take full responsibility for any factual errors. Some are deliberate for the sake of the story, with scenes or actions within scenes that are entirely fictional. Here is my opportunity to tell you what is true and confess my speculative and fictional sins.

Ab Johnson, Arthur Beck, Lyle McCormack, Carl Larsen, Jack Johnson, Ira Cunningham, Alice Simmons, Ben Grant, Hiram Stoops, Walt Gordon, Capt. Saunders, and Private Worthington and his crew are figments of my imagination. Nearly all the other characters are based on real people, though their conversations, actions, and thoughts are fictionalized.

Fiction allows the author's imagination to fill gaps that inevitably occur in the historical record. Major Richard Derby probably didn't pull any Roosevelt family connections to make things happen, but he could have. The idea of Ab Johnson's motorcycle was inspired by Derby, who barreled around the battlefield in a motorcycle sidecar. The character of Lt. Colonel Walt Gordon was based on an Army staff officer who I chose to not name. It was impossible for this Marine father to read his analysis regarding the relief of the Fourth Brigade and not feel my blood boil a century after the fact. Some readers may find their favorite story about the Battle of Belleau Wood missing in this novel. I hope they will forgive me. There are too many stories of individual sacrifice and heroism to include in this novel.

Ab Johnson was not based on any real person and is not autobiographical, even though I am a Marine father twice over. It is unlikely that a US Army major would do some of the things he did in the novel. His actions are ones I'd like to think a Marine father in his position might imagine doing. I'm not aware of anyone using a motorcycle to ferry supplies and wounded during the battle for Hill 142. The scene where he and Major Smith conspire to inform the regimental commanders of the pending battle on June 6th was fictional.

I changed Henry Lenert's story by adding Carl to it. Lenert was alone when the better part of a German company surrendered to him. He knew where his lines were and didn't stop in Lucy on his way to the brigade HQ. I made up his speech idioms, and the part about the Lugers (which were coveted battlefield souvenirs). I thought it looked better that way.

Maps were included to help readers understand the geography. The troop movements and dispositions during the Battle of Belleau Wood were complex and best shown in maps. Please forgive me if I was off by a hundred yards here or a quarter mile there. I'm a physician, not a cartographer.

The motorcycle on the cover is probably not an Indian. My cover artists and I couldn't find any open-source photos of Indians with sidecars. I chose the Indian since that was the motorcycle Derby used. The soldier pictured has a messenger pouch, which Ab Johnson may have needed to stow papers as he worked his way around the supply side of the battle.

Afterword

Grammarians who use *The Chicago Manual of Style* might take exception with my decision to capitalize the words "Marine" and "Marines". I did this deliberately to fall in line with the way Marines and Marine publications treat the words. Grammarians can throw copies of *Chicago* at me, but Marines have guns. Semper Fi!

I didn't portray General Bundy in a very good light. The Marines under his command didn't seem to have a high opinion of him. It appears he didn't have a high opinion of them, which only got worse after the difficulties the Seventh Infantry had in its relief of the Marines. He was in a very difficult position as an American general under French command. I suspect that instances like this led to the current policy that American troops only go into battle under American command. General Pershing fought for this but was overruled by higher command in this battle.

The Battle of Belleau Wood played an important role in the history of the inter-service rivalry between the US Army and US Marine Corps. Marines were used for ship boardings and small infantry actions within the context of naval operations prior to 1900. The Navy owned the seas, and the Army owned the land. Army opinion was that the Marines fought skirmishes while the Army won wars. Army leaders objected the idea of two infantry organizations in the American military all the way past the end of the Korean War. Teddy Roosevelt had advocated rolling the USMC into the US Army. The fact that the press extolled the daring do and ferocity of the Marines in the Battle of Belleau Wood only served to fan the fires of US Army resentment.

Historians debate the importance of the Battle of Belleau Wood. The battle didn't win the war. However, it stopped a critical break-through by the German Army that appeared to threaten Paris, and thus the outcome of the war. The Germans outran their logistics and may have reached their limits by the time they reached the Château-Thierry sector. The French and Americans didn't know that at the time. The perceived threat to Paris drove the French to desperation. The Fourth

Brigade of Marines met the tip of the German spear by pure chance. The Second Division, the US Third Division and the French 167th combined to stop the last big German advance during the war. After this battle, along with actions by the French and British farther north, Germany moved in only one direction: Backward.

This novel focuses on the Marines and Navy Medical. That is not to denigrate the heroic actions of the US Army during the battle. The Second Division's Army Third Brigade fought valiantly alongside the Marines. The US Army's Third Division fought a vicious battle in and around Château-Thierry while the Battle of Belleau Wood raged. The story of "The Rock of the Marne" Third Army Division is for a different novelist to fictionalize.

The importance of the battle to the USMC is the subject of less debate. Prior to the battle, the USMC was a small organization that didn't fight big battles. Some historians call the Battle of Belleau Wood "The birthplace of the modern Marine Corps". Others debate the point. I consider it to be a crucible—in essence, the fulcrum upon which USMC history turned.

The matter of what happened to battlefield commanders like Lt. Col. Wise is an interesting question. He was an experienced commander. He knew how to read a map and communicate. Yet, during the actions between June 11-15, he misinterpreted communications, maps, and directions. The maps he and the other battalion commanders had were inadequate and June 10th was the first time he had been in the woods. He, like his men, was starved, sleep deprived, subjected to an unknown amount of toxin exposure, and was pummeled by repeated shock waves from artillery shelling. I speculate that Wise suffered from a combination of what we now call acute combat stress syndrome along with an element of traumatic brain injury.

The effects on the short- and long-term brain function of humans subjected to artillery barrages is a subject that has received little formal study for understandable reasons. Much of the recent work on blast-related brain injury relates to singular or repeated events but not the effects of sustained bombardment over many hours. Wise and his men were on the receiving end of intense bombardment on multiple occasions. He was blown out of his foxhole by a nearby explosion on one occasion. It is dreadful to think of what these explosive forces did to the delicate connections within the brains of the troops on both sides.

The long-term complications of gas injuries are clear, however. Dr. Orlando Petty tried to rejoin the Navy after the war but was denied because of physical limitations due to the gas exposure that led to his Medal of Honor. After the war he suffered from "ill health" until his suicide in 1932. He was a brilliant endocrinologist who played a significant role in diabetes care at the time when insulin first came into use.

The exact wounds and circumstances that led to Captain Lloyd Williams's death were not clear to me. I was therefore left to speculate and tried to fill in the blanks as well as I could. I hope the Williams and Petty families will forgive any inaccuracy on my part. Likewise, Gunny Stockham's exact actions and wounds aside from the gas exposure were unclear to me. He was probably not in the Luzancy gas hospital when he died. I chose to portray his death the way I did to show the impact of his loss on men who knew him.

My descriptions of the fictionalized real people in this novel are as accurate as I was able to make them with limited resources. Black and white photographs of the people involved helped. Details like height, weight, build, and eye color were invented where I could not find accurate information about those attributes. The only service records available to me were furnished by André Sobocinski, the historian of the Navy Bureau of Medicine. If I have offended any of their descendants, I hope they understand I didn't intend to do so. Whether they cussed or smoked is unknown to me. I toned down the salty language significantly, and hope Marines will forgive me for f-ing doing that.

I am hard on the French Army in this novel. I wrote from the perspective of the Americans who fought in Belleau Wood. Available memoirs don't have many positives to say about the commanding general of the French Sixth Army. The movement of the Second Division at the end of May was probably even more chaotic than I portrayed it. The scene where General Pershing arrives to find his division on the move without his knowledge is not recorded in his memoir of the war. I found it in a biography about Navy Lt. Joel Boone, who had no reason to not tell the truth. Many accounts document that the French command kept battle plans secret from their American allies until the last moment for "security reasons". This bedeviled American commanders throughout the war. The French "intelligence" about Belleau Wood was as deficient as I portrayed it.

Marines were treated with distain by some French officers and returned the lack of respect on the spot. The incident with Captain Lloyd Williams is a legendary example. The Marines respected the hardship French troops had suffered and their courage and skill as soldiers. Various Marine memoirs reflect a great deal of compassion for the French civilians displaced by the war, the subject of my novel *Dogs Don't Cry*.

One historical inaccuracy I uncovered is the spelling of Lieutenant Junior Grade Weeden Osborne's first name. He spelled it Weeden. If you're interested, visit my website biography about him for the details.

Please consider reading my other Novels of the Great War. They involve many of the same characters and show events from differing perspectives. These include *An American Nurse in Paris* and *Dogs Don't Cry*. You will find background information and photographs that relate to the events portrayed in this novel, the real people involved, and World War I medical care in my website, https://johnfrederickandrews.com. There is a link on the website to sign up for my newsletter.

Acknowledgments

My thanks to you, my reader. I hope you found the story rewarding and enjoyable, to the degree anyone can "enjoy" a novel in a war setting. If so, please give the novel a "star" rating where your purchased it. A few kind words in a review also help other readers choose this novel. Independently published novels depend on this sort of feedback.

I offer my thanks to the many people who helped me craft this novel. My first reader, Susan Piechowski, MD, tolerated my long hours of research (including two WWI battlefield tours), writing, and revision of this and my other novels. She reviewed and proofread each revision. Thank you, Sue.

My critique group, Wordpardners, played an outsized role in helping me craft this story. They include Marilee Aufdenkamp, Rex Griffin, Scott Hibbard, Margaret Rodenberg, and Mike Torreano.

Thanks to my "beta" readers including Henry "Buz" Page, Paul Zimmerman, Gloria Zimmerman, Richard Anderson, Joe Kullman, Spencer Millimen, Patti Draude, Ray Rigel, Tom Mack, DDS, Chuck de Maille, Rob Fraser, Lieutenant Colonel Matthew Andrews, USMC, and Staff Sergeant Michael Andrews, USMC (Ret.). I hope anyone I left out will forgive me.

Jenny Quinlan from Historical Editorial provided great advice with a developmental edit, a copyedit, as well as feedback and encouragement over the years. Her colleague, Aaron Redfern, did the final copyedits. I thank them for correcting my always-deficient grammar and recommend them without reservation.

Generative artificial intelligence played no role in the creation of this novel. The early versions of this novel were written before generative AI was commercially available. The manuscript was written using Microsoft Word for Mac. Later versions of this software may have had an AI interface, but the only features used in this novel were spell- and grammar-check. Every keystroke was made by the author.

More Visual did the excellent cover art. I took the back cover photo near Les Mares Farm.

This novel could not have been written without heavy reliance on historical source material, and the advice of several experts on the history of the Battle of Belleau Wood. I was fortunate to be able to correspond with the late George B. Clark. He was a remarkable historian and prolific author whose books and monographs formed the foundation of my understanding of the battle. He reviewed the third revision of this novel for historical accuracy. My work with him focused on the military aspects of the battle.

I made the map at the front of the novel and those at the beginning of Chapters 12, 18, 27, 28, 32, and 44. The maps at the beginning of Chapters 22, 34, 45, 46, 54, and 61 include overlays I created and superimposed on a base map used with permission from the late George Clark in his monograph *The History of the Third Battalion 5th Marines, 1917-1918*. Pike, NH: The Brass Hat, 1996. This appears to be an open-source military map. The map at the start of Chapter 39 was used with Clark's permission from page 101 of *The United States Army Second Division Northwest of Chateau Thierry in World War by John W. Thomason, Jr.* McFarland, 2006, edited by Mr. Clark. The maps at the start of Chapters 20 and 25 are my modifications of maps used with Mr. Clark's permission from his *Devil Dogs: Fighting Marines of World War I*. Novato, CA: Presidio Press, 1999, page 75. The maps at the start of Chapters 51 and 62 are from the same source, pages 163 and 195 respectively, in their original form.

Colonel William Anderson, USMC (Ret.) and Colonel William White, USMC (Ret.) reviewed full manuscripts of early revisions for historical accuracy. Colonel Anderson also provided a sounding board for some of the medical history and many other details. Thank you, Bill! I corresponded with Lieutenant Colonel Peter F. Owen, USMC (Ret.) about the accuracy and plausibility of my fictional account of the gas attack on the 96th Company in Chapter 54. André Sobocinski, the historian with the US Navy Bureau of Medicine and Surgery, provided thoughts as well as many documents and photos from Navy BUMED archives. These helped in my accounts of the US Navy medical men in this novel and the biographies on my website.

I took two WWI battlefield tours with Military Historical Tours, the first led by Colonel William White and Lieutenant Colonel Gary Andrejak, USAF (Ret.), and the second led by James White and historian, Staff Sergeant Steven Girard, USA (Ret.). Historian Gilles Lagin led our tours of Belleau Wood and provided a great depth of understanding about the battle and the people who fought it. The opportunity to have my boots on the ground with these historians was critical to an understanding of the terrain.

Discussion Questions

This novel was not written as a "book club novel". That said, I can imagine a room with a few Marines, a Navy corpsman, and a couple of Marine Corps parents sipping Famous Grouse (no white wine, please) or coffee while chewing the fat. Or, perhaps, a book club that may have read one of my other Novels of the Great War and wanted to see the other side of the story. If that's the case—thank you, and I'll take a glass of pinot gris, please. I will be happy to participate in book club discussions about any of my novels.

The Novels of the Great War series explore broad, universal, themes. These include friendship, love, the love of parents for their children, and the effects of war on the people involved. The characters in all these novels are affected by war in different ways. Acute battle stress and post-traumatic stress syndrome affect several characters. Other themes explored include the core values of the USMC: Honor, Courage, Commitment. The critical importance of kindness and compassion are key features in every character.

Here are a few themes and points to consider, whether in a group, over a Famous Grouse, a white wine, or a cup of Joe:

Discussion Questions

1.   Had you ever heard of the Battle of Belleau Wood before?

2.   Discuss the importance of the Battle of Belleau Wood in the context of other military actions taken in 1918.

3.   In what ways did the Battle of Belleau Wood change the US Marine Corps?

4.   Were you aware of the inter-service rivalry between the US Army and US Marine Corps?
   a.   If so, please discuss how this battle affected the rivalry.
   b.   Could this rivalry have played any role in the decision to not give the marines relief earlier in the battle?

5.   Who is the character you relate to the most?

6.   Who is the most sympathetic character?

7.   Did Ab Johnson become a credible representative for Marine families?

8.   Did you know about the Paris Gun and its role in long-distance artillery attacks on Paris during the war?

9.   Many people are aware that chemical warfare was used in World War One. Did you learn and understand more about it after reading the novel?

10.   For military and historian readers: what do you think about the battle planning, strategy and tactics used at Belleau Wood?

11.   How do you think the lack of air support affected the battle?

12.   Discuss your reaction to the battle and its casualties.

13. Discuss how you think the American public might have reacted had they know what you now know about the battle, its conduct and leadership, and the casualties.

14. For medical readers: did you find the medical scenes to be credible? Did you gain any new insights for how medical care was delivered on and near the front lines in this war?

15. What in the novel angered you the most?

16. What in the novel broke your heart?

17. What in the novel made you proud?

18. Do you understand any more about Marines than you did before you started the novel?

19. Do you understand any more about Navy Medical than you did before you started the novel?

20. Discuss courage.

21. Discuss the role of honor in the novel.

22. Discuss how the concept of commitment plays a role in the novel.

23. What moment of kindness struck you the most.

24. Discuss your favorite moment of compassion.

Bibliography

Akers, Herbert, H. *History of the Third Battalion, Sixth Regiment, U.S. Marines.* Hilldale, MI: Akers, MacRitchie, and Hurlburt, 1919.

American Armies and Battlefields in Europe. American Battle Monuments Commission; Washington D. C. United States Government Printing office, 1938.

Anderson, William T. *Gunnery Sergeant Fred W. Stockham: Contempt of Personal Danger. Leatherneck,* June 2008; 91,6.

Anderson, William T. *The Bravest Deeds of Men, A Field Guide for the Battle of Belleau Wood.* History Division, United States Marine Corps, 2018.

Asprey, Robert B. *At Belleau Wood.* New York: G.P. Putnam, 1965.

Axelrod, Alan. *Miracle at Belleau Wood: The Birth of the Modern U.S. Marine Corps.* Guilford, CT. The Lyons Press, 2007.

Camp, Dick. *The Devil Dogs at Belleau Wood: U.S. Marines in World War I.* Gloucester, MA Zenith Press, 2008.

Catlin, Albertus W. *With the Help of God and a Few Marines.* New York: Doubleday, 1919.

Clark, George B. *Devil Dogs: Fighting Marines of World War I.* Novato, CA: Presidio Press, 1999.

_____. *The History of the Third Battalion 5th Marines, 1917-1918.*Pike, NH: The Brass Hat, 1996.

_____. *The Second Infantry Division in World War I: A History of the American Expeditionary Force Regulars, 1917-1919.*Jefferson, NC: McFarland, 2007.

_____, ed. *His Time in Hell: A Texas Marine in France: The World War I Memoir of Warren R Jackson.* Novato, CA: Presidio Press, 2001.

_____, ed. *The Devil Dogs Chronicle: Voices of the 4th Marine Brigade in World War I.* Lawrence: University Press of Kansas, 2013.

_____, ed. *The United States Army Second Division Northwest of Chateau Thierry in World War*

I, by John W. Thomason, Jr. McFarland, 2006.

Cochrane, Rexmond C. Gas Warfare at Belleau Wood, June 1918. *Gas Warfare in World War I, Study Number 1, U.S. Army Chemical Corps Historical Studies.* U.S. Army Chemical Center, Maryland, 1957.

Crozier, Emmett. *American Reporters on the Western Front, 1914-18.* New York: Oxford University Press, 1959.

Crumley, Beth. *"Elizaberth Ford"-A Model T Truck in France.* Marine Corps Association and Foundation Blog; January 31, 2012.

Davidson, Henry P. *The American Red Cross in the Great War.* New York: Macmillan, 1919.

Derby, Richard. *Wade in, Sanitary! The Story of a Division Surgeon in France.* New York: G.P. Putnam, 1919.

Bibliography

Dock, Lavinia L, Clara D. Noyes, Fannie F Clement, Elizabeth G. Fox, Anna R. Van Meter. *History of American Red Cross Nursing.* New York: Macmillan, 1922.

Gibbons, Floyd. *And They Thought We Wouldn't Fight.* New York: George H. Doran, 1918.

Harbord, James G. *Leaves From a War Diary.* New York: Dodd Mead, 1925.

Harbord, James G. The American Expeditionary Forces; Its Organization and Accomplishments. Transcript of a lecture presented to the Army War College, February, 1929.

Heller, Charles E. *Chemical Warfare in World War I: The American Experience, 1917-1918.* Leavenworth Papers, No. 10. Washington D.C.: U.S. Government Printing Office, 1984.

Ireland, M.W., ed. *The Medical Department of the United States Army in the World War. 14 Vols.* Washington, D.C.: Government Printing Office, 1923-1927.

Johnson, Katherine Burger. *Called to Serve: American Nurses Go To War, 1914-1918.* Master's Thesis submitted to Department of History, University of Louisville, August, 1993.

Lee, Burton James. Experiences in Surgery with the Second Division of the American Expeditionary Force. *General Bulletin, The Society of the New York Hospital*: Volume 1, Number 12, July 1, 1919.

Mackin, Elton E. *Suddenly We Didn't Want to Die.* Edited by George B. Clark. Novato, CA: Presidio Press, 1993.

McClellan, Edwin N. *The United States Marine Corps in the World War.* Washington D.C.: U.S. Government Printing Office, 1920.

Miller, J. Michael. *The 4th Marine Brigade at Belleau Wood and Soissons.* University Press of Kansas, 2020.

Neumann, Brian Fisher. *Pershing's Right Hand: General James G. Harbord and the American Expeditionary Forces in the First World War.* Ph.D. Dissertation submitted to the Office of Graduate Studies of Texas A&M University. August 2006.

Owen, Peter F. *To the Limit of Endurance: A Battalion of Marines in the Great War.* College Station, TX: Texas A&M Press, 2007.

Pershing, John J. *My Experiences in the World War. 2 Vols.* New York: F.A. Stokes and Co.,1931.

Simmons, Edwin Howard, and Joseph H. Alexander. *Through the Wheat: The U.S. Marines in World War I.* Annapolis, MD: Naval Institute Press, 2008.

Stallings, Laurence. *The Doughboys.* New York: Harper, 1963.

Sobocinski, Andre Baden. "A Navy Surgeon "Over There": The Reflections of Dr. Joel Boone, Regimental Surgeon in the Great War." Office of Medical History, BUMED, 2013.

Strott, George G. *Navy Medics with the Marines, 1917-1919: The Medical Department of the United States Navy with the Army and Marine Corps in France in World War I.* Reprint, Nashville, TN: The Battery Press, 2005 (Original publication: Washington D.C.: U.S. Navy, 1947.)

United States Army in the World War, 1917-1919, Military Operations of the American Expeditionary Forces, Volume 4. Washington, D.C.: U.S. Government Printing Office, 1948.

Bibliography

Wise, Frederic M. and Meigs O. Frost. *A Marine Tells it To You.* New York: J.H. Sears, 1929.

About the Author

John F. Andrews began writing fiction in 2012. His novels leverage his fascination with history along with his knowledge and experience as a physician and a Marine Corps father. The latter has given him an intimate understanding of what it is like to be a service family member. It led to an intense interest in the history of the United States Marine Corps and the US Navy medical personnel who provide the medical care for Marines.

Andrews was born in Chicago and raised in Wisconsin and Minnesota. After earning a BA in psychology, he completed medical school at the University of Minnesota. He trained in internal medicine at Beaumont Hospital in Royal Oak, Michigan, and then completed a pulmonary medicine fellowship at the University of Chicago. He earned board certifications in Internal, Pulmonary, Critical Care, and Sleep Medicine. After a successful practice in Green Bay, Wisconsin, he and his wife, Sue, moved to Manhattan, Montana. He joined his local volunteer fire department and trained as an EMT and basic wildland firefighter, became its medical officer, and served on the department for seven years. John and Sue moved to Arvada, Colorado, in 2024 where they enjoy family and the magnificent Rocky Mountains.

Also by John F. Andrews

An American Nurse in Paris

Medical journalist Alice Simmons has one last chance to stay alive in this story of courage, humility, determination, compassion, and hope during the last year of World War One.

Alice's quest to become a war correspondent careens headlong into a wall of sexism and deceit after her arrival in Paris in 1918. The suave officer in charge of the American Army press office refuses to let Alice leave Paris while her male counterparts scramble to the Front during the German spring offensive. One evening, his misogyny escalates to a drunken assault. Alice manages to fight back, but then her attacker begins a campaign of false accusations to cover his crime.

A nursing position in an American Red Cross military hospital is Alice's only hope to remain in France. It turns into the best scoop of her career. Wounded marines and soldiers from the Battle of Belleau Wood flood her ward. A tragic death amid the human wreckage of war unlocks Alice's compassion and her capacity to love, both long-buried after a childhood tragedy. Her patients' courage inspires Alice's fight to restore her honor and open her heart.

Dogs Don't Cry

June, 1918 . . .

A dog's devotion, courage, and intelligence stands between two French teens and despair. Love and determination sustain the threesome as they flee the tidal wave of war. A story of hardship, peril, resilience, and hope.

Abby is the Durand family dog, a companion for fifteen-year-old Marcel and his sister, Geneviève. Marcel is plagued by doubts about his courage as he approaches military age. Geneviève has severe pneumonia and is convinced she will soon die. Evacuation is ordered as the German army barrels toward their home village. The doctor tending to Geneviève warns their mother that the rigors of evacuation will kill the young girl on the eve of her thirteenth birthday. Their mother waits until the last moment to leave their home in search of shelter.

A disastrous escape leaves them orphaned and alone.

Marcel and Geneviève must find a distant relative, Cousin Henri, who lives near Paris. However, they have never met him, are not sure of his last name, and don't know his address. Abby is the key—Henri is her former owner, though she begs to differ on the "owner" concept. If anyone can find him, she can. The teens confront their worst fears while seeking refuge amid the chaos of war, armed only with their faith in Abby.